Vineland confirms the truth about Thomas Pynchon.

"*Vineland* is, quite simply, one of those books that will make the world—*our* world, our daily chemical-preservative, plastic-wrapped bread—a little more tolerable, a little more human. . . . The voice—absolutely unmistakable and absolutely inimitable—has not changed since *V.* and *The Crying of Lot 49.* . . . It is—OK, I'll *say* it—*the* American voice of the late twentieth century."
—*The Los Angeles Times Book Review*

"The nervy, anarchist energy is still like that of no one else."
—*Boston Sunday Globe*

"Thomas Pynchon is in fact our great author of popular lore, the man who realizes its potential and seriousness."
—*Atlanta Journal & Constitution*

"There is no mistaking Pynchon's prominence in the intellectual mainstream."

—*Newsday*

"Pynchon remains our premier connoisseur of uncertainty, wicked tropes, anticlimax, the seductively dangled loose end."
—*Chicago Tribune*

"This novel is as funny, as smart, as lyrical, and as subversive as any American fiction of the past decade, but the most remarkable thing about it is the purity of its desire to get through to us."
—*The New Yorker*

"Vintage stuff—funny, fantastically inventive, packed with improbable erudition"

—*The Times Literary Supplement*

PENGUIN BOOKS

VINELAND

Thomas Pynchon is the author of *V.*; *The Crying of Lot 49*; *Gravity's Rainbow*; and *Slow Learner*, a collection of short stories; as well as *Vineland*.

VINELAND

Thomas Pynchon

PENGUIN BOOKS

PENGUIN BOOKS
Published by the Penguin Group
Viking Penguin, a division of Penguin Books USA Inc.,
375 Hudson Street, New York, New York 10014, U.S.A.
Penguin Books Ltd, 27 Wrights Lane,
London W8 5TZ, England
Penguin Books Australia Ltd, Ringwood,
Victoria, Australia
Penguin Books Canada Ltd, 2801 John Street,
Markham, Ontario, Canada L3R 1B4
Penguin Books (N.Z.) Ltd, 182–190 Wairau Road,
Auckland 10, New Zealand

Penguin Books Ltd, Registered Offices:
Harmondsworth, Middlesex, England

First published in the United States of America by
Little, Brown and Company, 1990
Published in Penguin Books 1991

1   3   5   7   9   10   8   6   4   2

The characters and events in this book are fictitious. Any similarity
to real persons, living or dead, is coincidental and not
intended by the author.

LIBRARY OF CONGRESS CATALOGING IN PUBLICATION DATA
Pynchon, Thomas.
Vineland/Thomas Pynchon.
p.   cm.
"First published in the United States of America by Little, Brown
& Company, 1990"—T.p. verso.
ISBN 0 14 01.4511 7
I. Title.
PS3566.Y55V56   1991
813'.54—dc20   90–44384

Printed in the United States of America

For my mother and father

Every dog has his day,
and a good dog
  just might have two days.

  — Johnny Copeland

VINELAND

LATER than usual one summer morning in 1984, Zoyd Wheeler drifted awake in sunlight through a creeping fig that hung in the window, with a squadron of blue jays stomping around on the roof. In his dream these had been carrier pigeons from someplace far across the ocean, landing and taking off again one by one, each bearing a message for him, but none of whom, light pulsing in their wings, he could ever quite get to in time. He understood it to be another deep nudge from forces unseen, almost surely connected with the letter that had come along with his latest mental-disability check, reminding him that unless he did something publicly crazy before a date now less than a week away, he would no longer qualify for benefits. He groaned out of bed. Somewhere down the hill hammers and saws were busy and country music was playing out of somebody's truck radio. Zoyd was out of smokes.

On the table in the kitchen, next to the Count Chocula box, which turned out to be empty, he found a note from Prairie. "Dad, they changed my shift again, so I rode in with Thapsia. You got a call from Channel 86, they said urgent, I said, you try waking him up sometime. Love anyway, Prairie."

"Froot Loops again I guess," he muttered at the note. With enough Nestle's Quik on top, they weren't all that bad, and various ashtrays yielded half a dozen smokable butts. After taking as much time as he could in the bathroom, he finally got around to locating the phone and calling the local TV station to recite to them this year's press release. But — "You'd better check again, Mr. Wheeler. Word we have is that you've been rescheduled."

"Check with who, I'm the one's doin' it, ain't I?"

"We're all supposed to be at the Cucumber Lounge."

"Well I won't, I'll be up at the Log Jam in Del Norte." What was the matter with these people? Zoyd had been planning this for weeks.

3

Desmond was out on the porch, hanging around his dish, which was always empty because of the blue jays who came screaming down out of the redwoods and carried off the food in it piece by piece. After a while this dog-food diet had begun to give the birds an attitude, some being known to chase cars and pickups for miles down the road and bite anybody who didn't like it. As Zoyd came out, Desmond gave him an inquiring look. "Just dig yourself," shaking his head at the chocolate crumbs on the dog's face, "I know she fed you, Desmond, and I know *what* she fed you too." Desmond followed him as far as the firewood, tail going back and forth to show no hard feelings, and watched Zoyd backing all the way down to the lane before he turned and got on with his day.

Zoyd headed down to Vineland Mall and rolled around the lot there for a while, smoking up half a joint he'd found in his pocket, before parking the rig and going into More Is Less, a discount store for larger-size women, where he bought a party dress in a number of colors that would look good on television, paying with a check both he and the saleslady shared a premonition would end up taped to this very cash register after failing to clear, and proceeded to the men's room of the Breez-Thru gas station, where he shifted into the dress and with a small hairbrush tried to rat what was on his head and face into a snarl he hoped would register as insane-looking enough for the mental-health folks. Back at the pump he put in five dollars' worth of gas, went in the back seat, got a quart of oil out of the case he kept there, found his spout, punched it in the can, put most of the oil in his engine, except for a little he saved to mix in the can with some gas, and poured this into the tank of an elegant little imported-looking chain saw, about the size of a Mini-Mac, which he then stashed in a canvas beach bag. Prairie's friend Slide came wandering out of the office to have a look.

"Uh-oh, is it that time again already?"

"This year it snuck up on me, hate to think I'm gettin' too old for this."

"Know the feeling," Slide nodded.

"You're fifteen, Slide."

"And seen it all. Whose front window you doin' it to this year?"

"Nobody's. I'm givin' that all up, window jumping's in my past, this year I'm gonna just take this little chain saw into the Log Jam and see what develops from there."

"Um, maybe not, Mr. Wheeler, you been up there lately?"

"Oh I know there's some heavy-duty hombres, badasses, spend all day narrowly escaping death by tree, not too much patience with anything out of the ordinary, but I've got the element of surprise. Don't I?"

"You'll see," weary Slide advised.

He sure would, but only after spending more time out on 101 than his already fragile sense of humor could take, owing to a convoy of out-of-state Winnebagos on some leisurely tour of the redwoods, in among whom, on the two-lane stretches, he was obliged to gear down and put up with a lot of attention, not all friendly. "Gimme a break," he yelled over the engine noise, "it's, uh, a Calvin Klein original!"

"Calvin doesn't cut nothin' bigger than a 14," a girl younger than his daughter screamed at him out her window, "and you ought to be locked up."

It was well into lunchtime when he got to the Log Jam, and he was disappointed to find nobody at all from the media, just a collection of upscale machinery parked in the lot, itself newly blacktopped. These were to be the first of several rude updates. Trying to think cheerful thoughts — like assuming the television crews were only late — Zoyd collected the bag with the saw in it, checked his hair one more time, and went storming into the Log Jam, where right away he noticed that everything, from the cooking to the clientele, smelled different.

Uh-oh. Wasn't there supposed to be some loggers' bar around here someplace? Everybody knew it was high times for the stiffs in the woods — though not for those in the mills, with the Japanese buying up unprocessed logs as fast as the forests could be clear-cut — but even so, the scene in here was peculiar. Dangerous men with coarsened attitudes, especially toward death, were perched around lightly on designer barstools, sipping kiwi mimosas. The jukebox once famous for hundreds of freeway exits up and down the coast for its gigantic country-and-western collection, including

half a dozen covers of "So Lonesome I Could Cry," was reformatted to light classical and New Age music that gently peeped
at the edges of audibility, slowing, lulling this roomful of choppers
and choker setters who now all looked like models in Father's Day
ads. One of the larger of these, being among the first to notice
Zoyd, had chosen to deal with the situation. He wore sunglasses
with stylish frames, a Turnbull & Asser shirt in some pastel plaid,
three-figure-price-tag jeans by Mme. Gris, and après-logging shoes
of a subdued, but incontestably blue, suede.

"Well good afternoon pretty lady and how fine you're looking,
I'm sure in another setting and mood we'd all like to know you
as a person with your many fine points and so on like that, but
from your fashion message I can tell that you are a sensitive type
person who'll appreciate the problem we have here in terms of
orientational vibes, if you follow —"

The already confused Zoyd, whose survival instincts may not
have been working all the way up to spec, decided to produce the
chain saw from his bag. "Buster," he called plaintively to the owner
behind the bar, "where's the media?" The implement attracted
immediate attention from everyone in the room, not all of it technical curiosity. It was a tailor-made lady's chain saw, "tough
enough for timber," as the commercials said, "but petite enough
for a purse." The guide bar, handle grips, and housing were faced
in genuine mother-of-pearl, and spelled out in rhinestones on the
bar, surrounded by sawteeth ready to buzz, was the name of the
young woman he'd borrowed it from, which onlookers took to
be Zoyd's drag name, CHERYL.

"Easy there cowgirl, now things're just fine," the logger stepping back as Zoyd, he hoped demurely, yanked at a silk cord
on a dainty starter pulley, and the lady's pearl-handled chain saw
spun into action.

"Listen to that li'l honey purr."

"Zoyd, what th' heck you doin' this all the way up here for,"
Buster deciding it was time to intervene, "no channel's gonna send
no crew this far out of town, why are you not down in Eureka or
Arcata someplace?"

The logger stared. "This person is known to you?"

"Played together in the old Six Rivers Conference," Buster all smiles, "those were the days, huh Zoyd?"

"Can't hear you," hollered Zoyd, trying to maintain a quickly fading image of dangerousness. He throttled the nacreous pretty saw reluctantly back first to a ladylike bass line and then to silence. Into the echo, "See you did some redecorating."

"If you would've come around last month, you 'n' 'at little saw, could've helped us gut the place."

"Sorry, Buster, guess I did come to the wrong bar, I sure can't saw any of this stuff, not with the money you must've put in . . . only reason I'm up here is is 'at the gentrification of South Spooner, Two Street, and other more familiar hellraisin' locales has upped the ante way outa my bracket, these are all folks now who like to sue, and for big bucks, with hotshot PI lawyers up from the City, I so much as blot my nose on one of their designer napkins I'm in deep shit anymore."

"Well, we're no longer as low-rent as people remember us here either Zoyd, in fact since George Lucas and all his crew came and went there's been a real change of consciousness."

"Yep, I noticed . . . say, you want to draw me a, just a lady's-size beer there . . . you know I still haven't even got around to that picture?"

They were talking about *Return of the Jedi* (1983), parts of which had been filmed in the area and in Buster's view changed life there forever. He put his massive elbows on about the only thing in here that hadn't been replaced, the original bar, carved back at the turn of the century from one giant redwood log. "But underneath, we're still just country fellas."

"From the looks of your parking lot, the country must be Germany."

"You and me Zoyd, we're like Bigfoot. Times go on, we never change, now, you're no bar fighter, I can see the thirst for new experiences, but a man's better off sticking to a specialty, your own basically being transfenestration."

"Mm yes, I could tell," commented another logger, his voice almost inaudible, sidling in and laying a hand on Zoyd's leg.

"Besides which," continued Buster, imperturbable, though his eyes were now fixed on the hand on the leg, "it's become your MO, diving through windows, you start in with other stuff at this late date, forcing the state to replace what's in your computer file with something else, this is not gunno endear you to them, 'Aha, rebellious ain't he?' they'll say, and soon you'll find those checks are gettin' slower, even lost, in the mail and say there Lemay! my good man and good sport, let's have a look at the palm of that hand up here on the bar a minute? 'Cz I'm gonna read your fortune for you, how about that," guiding by strange jovial magnetism a logger's hand that would just as happily have been a fist up off of the leg of by now mentally paralyzed Zoyd, or as the (it seemed) smitten Lemay kept calling him, Cheryl. "You will have a long life," Buster looking Lemay in the face, not the hand, "because of your common sense and grasp on reality. Five bucks."

"Huh?"

"Well — maybe just buy us a round, then. Zoyd here does look a little strange right now, but he's out on governmental business."

"I knew it!" cried Lemay. "Undercover agent!"

"Nut case," confided Zoyd.

"Oh. Well . . . that sounds like interesting work too. . . ."

Just then the phone rang, and it was for Zoyd. His partner, Van Meter, was calling from the Cucumber Lounge, a notorious Vineland County roadhouse, in high agitation. "Got six mobile TV units waiting, network up from the City, plus paramedics and a snack truck, all wonderin' where you are."

"Here. You just called me, remember?"

"Aha. Good point. But you were supposed to be jumping through the front window at the Cuke today."

"No! I called everybody and told 'm it was up here. What happened?"

"Somebody said it got rescheduled."

"Shit. I knew someday this act would get bigger than me."

"Better come on back," said Van Meter.

Zoyd hung up, put the saw back in the bag, finished his beer, and made his exit, blowing broad show-biz kisses and reminding everybody to watch the evening news.

*

The Cucumber Lounge property extended back from the disreputable neon roadhouse itself into a few acres of virgin redwood grove. Dwarfed and overshadowed by the towering dim red trees were two dozen motel cabins, with woodstoves, porches, barbecues, waterbeds, and cable TV. During the brief North Coast summers they were for tourists and travelers, but through the rainy remainder of the year, occupants tended to be local, and paying by the week. The woodstoves were good for boiling, frying, even some baking, and some of the cabins had butane burners as well, so that along with woodsmoke and the austere fragrance of the trees, there was an all-day neighborhood smell of cooking in the air.

The lot Zoyd tried to find a parking space in had never been paved, and the local weather had been writing gullies across it for years. Today it was enjoying a visit from the media, plus a task force of cop vehicles, state and county, flashing their lights and playing the "Jeopardy" theme on their sirens. Mobile units, lights, cable, crews everywhere, even a couple of Bay Area stations. Zoyd began to feel nervous. "Maybe I should've found something cheap at Buster's to saw on anyway," he muttered. He finally had to pull around back and park in one of Van Meter's spaces. His old bass player and troublemaking companion had been living here for years, in what he still described as a commune, with an astounding number of current and ex-old ladies, ex-old ladies' boyfriends, children of parent combinations present and absent, plus miscellaneous folks in out of the night. Zoyd had watched television shows about Japan, showing places such as Tokyo where people got into incredibly crowded situations but, because over the course of history they'd all learned to act civil, everybody got along fine despite the congestion. So when Van Meter, a lifetime searcher for meaning, moved into this Cucumber Lounge bungalow, Zoyd had hoped for some Japanese-style serenity as a side effect, but no such luck. Instead of a quiescent solution to all the overpop, the "commune" chose an energetic one — bickering. Unrelenting and high-decibel, it was bickering raised to the level of ceremony, bickering that soon generated its own house newsletter, the *Blind-Side Gazette,* bickering that could be heard even out on the freeway by the drivers of hurtling eighteen-wheelers, some of whom thought it was radio malfunction, others unquiet ghosts.

Here came Van Meter now, around the corner of the Cuke, wearing his trademark face, Wounded Righteousness. "Are you ready? We'll be losin' the light, fog's gonna come in any minute, what were you doin' all the hell the way up to the Log Jam?"

"No, Van Meter — why is everybody here instead?"

They went in the back way, Van Meter furrowing and unfurrowing his forehead. "Guess I can tell you now you're here, is there's this old buddy of yours, just showed up?"

Zoyd went sweaty and had one of those gotta-shit throbs of fear. Was it ESP, was he only reacting to something in his friend's voice? Somehow he knew who it would be. Here when he needed all his concentration for getting through another window, instead he had to worry about this visitor from out of the olden days. Sure enough, it turned out to be Zoyd's longtime pursuer, DEA field agent Hector Zuñiga, back once again, the erratic federal comet who brought, each visit in to Zoyd's orbit, new forms of bad luck and baleful influence. This time, though, it had been a while, long enough that Zoyd had begun to hope the man might've found other meat and be gone for good. Dream on, Zoyd. Hector stood over by the toilets pretending to play a Zaxxon machine, but in reality waiting to be reintroduced, this honor apparently falling to the manager of the Cuke, Ralph Wayvone, Jr., a remittance man from San Francisco, where his father was a figure of some substance, having grown successful in business areas where transactions are overwhelmingly in the form of cash. Today Ralph Jr. was all dolled up in a Cerruti suit, white shirt with cuff links, touch-them-you-die double-soled shoes from someplace offshore, the works. Like everybody else around here, he looked unusually anxious.

"Say Ralph, lighten up, it's me's gotta do all the work."

"Ahhh . . . my sister's wedding next weekend, the band just canceled, I'm the social coordinator, supposed to find a replacement, right? You know of anybody?"

"Yeah, maybe . . . you better not fuck up this one Ralph, you know what'll happen."

"Always kidding, huh. Here, let me show you the window you'll be using. Can I have them get you a drink or anything? Oh by the way Zoyd, here's an old friend of yours, come all this way to wish you luck."

"Uh-huh." He and Hector exchanged the briefest of thumb-grips.

"Love your outfit, Wheeler."

Zoyd reached, bomb-squad careful, to pat Hector's stomach. "Look like you been 'moving the mustache' there a little, old amigo."

"Bigger, not softer, *ése*. And speaking of lunch, how about tomorrow at Vineland Lanes?"

"Can't do it, tryin' to make the rent and I'm already late."

"It's im-por-tan'," Hector making a little melody out of it. "Think of it this way. If I can prove to you, that I'm as bad of a desperado as I ever was, will you allow me to spring for your lunch?"

"As bad as . . ." As what? Why did Zoyd keep going, time after time, for these oily Hectorial setups? The best it had ever turned out for him was uncomfortable. "Hector, we're too old for this."

"After all the smiles, and all the tears —"

"All right, stop, it's a deal — you be bad, I come to lunch, but please, I have to jump through this window right now? is it OK, can I have just a few seconds —"

Production staff murmured into walkie-talkies, technicians could be seen through the fateful window, waving light meters and checking sound levels outside as Zoyd, breathing steady, silently repeated a mantra that Van Meter, claiming it'd cost him $100, had toward the end of his yoga phase last year hustled Zoyd into buying for a twenty that Zoyd hadn't really enjoyed discretionary use of. At last all was set. Van Meter flashed Mr. Spock's Vulcan hand salute. "Ready when you are, Z Dubya!"

Zoyd eyeballed himself in the mirror behind the bar, gave his hair a shake, turned, poised, then screaming ran empty-minded at the window and went crashing through. He knew the instant he hit that something was funny. There was hardly any impact, and it all felt and sounded different, no spring or resonance, no volume, only a sort of fine, dulled splintering.

After obligingly charging at each of the news cameras while making insane faces, and after the police had finished their paperwork, Zoyd caught sight of Hector squatting in front of the destroyed window, among the glittering debris, holding a bright jagged polygon of plate glass. "Time for the bad," he called, grinning in a nasty way long familiar to Zoyd. "Are you ready?" Like a snake he lunged his head forward and took a giant bite out of the glass. *Holyshit,* Zoyd frozen, *he's lost it* — no, actually now, instead Hector was chewing away, crunching and slobbering, with the same evil grin, going "Mmm-mm!" and "*¡Qué rico, qué sabroso!*" Van Meter went running after a departing paramedic truck hollering "Corpsman!" but Zoyd had tumbled, he was no media innocent, he read *TV Guide* and had just remembered an article about stunt windows made of clear sheet candy, which would break but not cut. That's why this one had felt so funny — young Wayvone had taken out the normal window and put in one of these sugar types. "Euchred again, Hector, thanks."

But Hector had already vanished into a large gray sedan with government plates. News-crew stragglers were picking up a few last location shots of the Cuke and its famous rotating sign, which Ralph Jr. was happy to light up early, a huge green neon cucumber with blinking warts, cocked at an angle that approached, within a degree or two, a certain vulgarity. Did Zoyd have to show up next day at the bowling alley? Technically, no. But in the federale's eyes there'd been a glint that Zoyd could still see, behind the one-way auto glass, even as the nightly fog rolled up over the great berm and on toward 101 and Hector was driven away into it. Zoyd could feel another hustle on the way. Hector had been trying over and over for years to develop him as a resource, and so far — technically — Zoyd had hung on to his virginity. But the li'l fucker would not quit. He kept coming back, each time with a new and more demented plan, and Zoyd knew that one day, just to have some peace, he'd say forget it, and go over. Question was, would it be this time, or one of the next few times? Should he wait for another spin? It was like being on "Wheel of Fortune," only here there were no genial vibes from any Pat Sajak to find comfort in, no tanned and beautiful Vanna White at the corner of his vision to cheer on the Wheel, to wish him well, to flip over one by one letters of a message he knew he didn't want to read anyway.

ZOYD made it home in time to view himself on the Tube, though he had to wait till Prairie finished watching the 4:30 Movie, Pia Zadora in *The Clara Bow Story*. She fingered the material of the lurid print dress. "Crazy about this, Dad. Fresh, rilly. Can I have it when you're done? Use it to cover my futon."

"Hey, do you ever date logger types, fallers, choker setters, that sort of fellow?"

"Zoy-oyd. . . ."

"Don't get offended, is it's only that a couple of these guys slipped me their phone number, see? along with bills in different denominations?"

"What for?"

He did a take, squinted closely at his daughter. Was this a trick question here? "Let's see, 1984, that'd make you . . . fourteen?"

"Nice going, like to try for the car?"

"Nothin' personal, jeez." Zoyd had been removing the large and colorful dress. The girl shied away in mock alarm, covering her mouth and making her eyes round. He was wearing ancient surfer baggies underneath, and a dilapidated Hussong's T-shirt. "Here you go, it's all yours, mind if I check myself out on the news?"

They sat together on the floor in front of the Tube, with a chair-high bag of Chee-tos and a sixpack of grapefruit soda from the health-food store, watching baseball highlights, commercials, and weather — no rain again — till it was time for the kissoff story. "Well," chuckled news anchor Skip Tromblay, "an annual Vineland event was repeated today, as local laughing-academy out-patient Zoyd Wheeler performed his now familiar yearly leap through another area plate-glass window. This time the lucky establishment was the infamous Cucumber Lounge, seen here in its usual location, just off Highway 101. Alerted by a mystery caller,

TV 86 Hot Shot News crews were there to record Wheeler's deed, which last year was almost featured on 'Good Morning America.' "

"Lookin' good, Dad." On the Tube, Zoyd came blasting out the window, along with the dubbed-in sounds now of real glass breaking. Police cruisers and fire equipment contributed cheery chrome elements. Zoyd watched himself hit the hardpan, roll, come up, and charge the camera, screaming and baring his teeth. Footage of the pro forma booking and release wasn't included, but in Tubal form he was pleased to see that the dress, Day-Glo orange, near-ultraviolet purple, some acid green, and a little magenta in a retro-Hawaiian parrots-and-hula-girls print, came across as a real attention-getter. Over on one of the San Francisco channels, the videotape was being repeated in slow motion, the million crystal trajectories smooth as fountain-drops, Zoyd in midair with time to rotate into a number of positions he didn't remember being in, many of which, freeze-framed, could have won photo awards someplace. Next came highlights of his previous attempts, at each step into the past the color and other production values getting worse, and after that a panel including a physics professor, a psychiatrist, and a track-and-field coach live and remote from the Olympics down in L.A. discussing the evolution over the years of Zoyd's technique, pointing out the useful distinction between the defenestrative personality, which prefers jumping out of windows, and the transfenestrative, which tends to jump through, each reflecting an entirely different psychic subtext, at about which point Zoyd and Prairie began to drift away.

"Give you a nine point five, Dad, your personal best — too bad the VCR's busted, we could've taped it."

"I'm workin' on it."

She looked at him evenly. "We really need a new one."

"All I need's the money, Trooper, I can't even keep enough groceries in this place."

"Oh, no. I know what that means. Fat talk! What am I supposed to do? Isn't me that's leaving all these cakes and pies and stuff layin' around, candy bars in the freezer, Nestle's Quik instead of sugar, eeoo! What chance have I got?"

"Hey, all's I was talkin' about was money, kid. Who's been makin' you crazy with fat talk?"

The girl's head on its long smooth neck and vertebrae gave a small precision turn and tilt, as if slipping into an adjustment that would allow her to talk with her father. "Oh . . . maybe one or two remarks lately from the Big I."

"Oh great, yes, the well-known punker diet expert — named himself after what again, some robot?"

"After Isaiah Two Four, a verse in the Bible," shaking her head I-give-up slowly, "which *your* friends his hippie-freak parents laid on him in 1967, about converting from war to peace, beating spears into pruning hooks, other idiot peacenik stuff?"

"Well both of you just better watch 'at shit, 'd it ever occur to you maybe ol' R2D2's just cheap, and doesn't want to buy you any more food than he has to? What's he doing? What *does* he let you eat?"

"Love is strange, Dad, maybe you forgot that."

"I know love is strange, known it since 1956, including all those guitar breaks. You're in love with this individual, well, maybe *you* forget, I already know him, I can remember all you guys trick or *treatin'* not so long ago and let me tell you, any kid who shows up at the door as 'Jason' from *Friday the 13th* [1980], please, take it from an old mental case, he's in some trouble."

Prairie sighed. "Everybody was Jason that year. He's a classic now, like a Frankenstein, and so what, I don't see how you could have any kind of a problem with that. Isaiah has always admired you, you know."

"What?"

"For jumping through all those windows. He's studied every inch of all your videotapes. Says you were nearly speared a couple of times."

"Nearly, ah. . . ."

"Glass falls straight down out of the window frame," she explained, "in these big sharp spears? heavy enough to go right through ya? Isaiah says all his friends have remarked on how awesomely cool you always look, how unaware of the danger."

White and nauseated, he was still able to peer dubiously out of one eye. No point telling her about the fake window today, she looked so sincere, even, unnaturally, admiring, good time to just dummy up. But was it true, was it possible, had he been that close to death or major surgery each previous fun-filled time? How, then, unless he could count on sugar windows from here on in, could he expect to bring in any more revenue this way? Heck — he should have been working for a Joey Chitwood-type thrill show all this time and making some real money.

"... and I think you and Isaiah could even do some business," Prairie had evidently been saying, " 'cause I know he'd be willing, and all you'd have to do's keep an open mind."

Zoyd didn't know what she was talking about, but forced himself to think chirpy. "Long as he don't open it for me," having then to dodge the athletic shoe, luckily without her foot in it, that came whizzing past his ear.

"You are judging him by his haircut, his haircut alone," shaking her finger, trying for something between neighborhood scold and soap-opera Chief of Psychiatric. "You've turned into exactly the same kind of father that used to hassle you, back when you were a teen hippie freak."

"Sure I was at least as heavy duty of a menace to the public as your boyfriend is today, but never did any of us in my generation show up late at night at somebody's door in no hockey mask, carryin' around all these lethal blades, even somethin' looked like a pruning hook? and you're telling me we can do business? What business, summer-camp renovation?" He started throwing Cheetos at her, scattering vividly orange crumbs all over.

"He's got a good idea, if only you'd listen, Pop."

"Pop this." Zoyd ate a Chee-to he'd been planning to throw. "Of course I can listen, I hope I can still do that, what kind of uptight father do you take me for, why, he might even turn out to be a fine young man despite all the evidence, look at Moondoggie, for example, in *Gidget* [1959], after all...."

"Isaiah!" hollered the girl, "let's move it mah man, no telling how long he's even gonna be in this good of a mood," and out of another dimension, where he'd been waiting in orbit, emerged Isaiah Two Four, who today, Zoyd noticed, had his long Mohawk colored a vibrant acid green, except at the tips, where some magenta shade was airbrushed on. Now these happened to be Zoyd's two all-time favorite colors, and Prairie, who had given him enough T-shirts and ashtrays in the quaint sixties combo, knew it. Was this some weird effort to be nice?

Isaiah, in their greeting, wanted to slap and dap, having always somehow believed that Zoyd had seen combat in Vietnam. Some of this was bush-vet and jailyard moves Zoyd recognized, some was private choreography he couldn't keep up with, though he tried, Isaiah throughout humming Jimi Hendrix's "Purple Haze." "Hey, so, Mr. Wheeler," Isaiah at last, "how you doing?"

"What's this 'Mr. Wheeler,' what happened to 'You lunch meat, 'sucker'?" this line having climaxed their last get-together, when, from a temperate discussion of musical differences, feelings had swiftly escalated into the rejection, on quite a broad scale, of most of one another's values.

"Well then, sir," replied the NBA-sized violence enthusiast who might or might not be fucking his daughter, "I must've meant 'lunch meat' only in terms of our joint strange fate as mortal sandwich, equally exposed to the jaws of destiny, and from that perspective what's it matter, rilly, that you don't care for the musical statements of Septic Tank or Fascist Toejam?" jiveassing so obvious that Zoyd had no choice but to thaw.

"By the same token, I could easily overlook as trivial your spirited advocacy of the Uzi as a means of resolving many of our social problems."

"That's gracious of you, sir."

"Eats, you guys," Prairie coming in with a gallon of guacamole and a giant-size sack of tortilla chips, Zoyd wondering if soon there ought not to appear as well, aha there it was — a cold six-pack of Dos Equis, ah *right!* Popping one open, beaming, he observed once again in his daughter the sly, not yet professionally developed gift of staging a hustle, something she must surely have got from him, and he felt himself begin to glow, unless it was the guacamole, in which she'd gone a little heavy tonight on the commercial salsa.

Zoyd's reference to the Uzi submachine gun, "Badass of the

Desert," as it is known in its native Israel, had been appropriate. Isaiah's business idea was to set up first one, eventually a chain, of violence centers, each on the scale, perhaps, of a small theme park, including automatic-weapon firing ranges, paramilitary fantasy adventures, gift shops and food courts, and video game rooms for the kids, for Isaiah envisioned a family clientele. Also part of the concept were a standardized floor plan and logo, for franchising purposes. Isaiah sat at the cable-spool table, making diagrams with tortilla chips and pitching his dreams — "Third World Thrills," a jungle obstacle course where you got to swing on ropes, fall into the water, blast away at surprise pop-up targets shaped like indigenous guerrilla elements . . . "Scum of the City," which would allow the visitor to wipe from the world images of assorted urban undesirables, including Pimps, Perverts, Dope Dealers, and Muggers, all carefully multiracial so as to offend everybody, in an environment of dark alleys, lurid neon, and piped-in saxophone music . . . and for the aggro connoisseur, "Hit List," in which you could customize a lineup of videotapes of the personalities in public life you hated most, shown one apiece on the screens of old used TV sets bought up at junkyard prices and sent past you by conveyor belt, like ducks at the carnival, so your pleasure at blowing away these jabbering, posturing likenesses would be enhanced by all the imploding picture tubes. . . .

Zoyd was barely ahead of the white water here, nearly taken under by the surge of demographics and earnings projections the kid was coming up with. Dazedly he realized that at some point his mouth had fallen open and remained so, he didn't know for how long. He shut it too abruptly and clipped his tongue, just as Isaiah arrived at the line, "And it won't cost you a penny."

"Uh-huh. How much *will* it cost me?"

Isaiah gave him the five-figure California orthodontia, plus full eye contact. Zoyd need only stand ready to cosign for a loan —

Zoyd allowed himself a lengthy and mirthless chuckle. "And who'll be doing the lending?" expecting some address in a distant state, obtained from a matchbook cover. Turned out to be the Bank of Vineland Itself. "You didt'n, uh, threaten 'em, nothin' like 'at?" Zoyd needling the long-shadowed youth.

Isaiah just shrugged and went on, "In consideration, you get all the construction and landscaping work."

"Wait a minute, why don't your parents cosign?"

"Oh. . . . I guess 'cause they've always been into, you know, nonviolence?" There was something wistful in the way he said this. It wasn't just that his folks were vegetarians, they also discriminated *among* vegetables, excluding from their diet everything red, for example, the color of anger. Most bread, having been made by killing yeasts, was taboo. Zoyd, no shrink, nonetheless wondered if the kid wasn't doing unto Prairie what was being done unto him at home, in terms of food craziness.

"And . . . your folks don't know about this yet?"

"Sort of wanted it to be a surprise?"

Zoyd cackled. "Parents love surprises," and he caught Prairie giving him a weird look, like, Oh yeah? here, try this —

Instead, "We were all gonna go camping out for a few days, OK? Basically the band and a couple of other girls?"

Isaiah played with a local heavy-metal band called Billy Barf and the Vomitones, who'd been having trouble lately finding work.

"Go see Ralph Wayvone, Jr., over at the Cuke," Zoyd advised, "his sister's getting married down the City next weekend, the band suddenly ain't gonna show, and he sounds a little desperate for a replacement."

"Uh . . . well maybe I'll do it now, can I use your phone?"

"Think it's in the bathroom, last time I looked."

Alone, he and Prairie happened to get eye contact. She'd never been a squirmer, not even as a baby. Finally she said, "So?"

"He's a OK fella, but no bank's gonna let me cosign no loan, come on."

"You're a local businessman."

"They'll call it gypsy roofer, and I owe too much money all over the place anyhow."

"They *love* it when you owe money."

"Not like I owe it, Prairie — if the whole project went belly-up, they'd take the house." A point that may even have begun to get through, when Isaiah came running out of the bathroom yelling, "We got the gig! We got it! Awesome! I can't believe it!"

"Me either," Zoyd muttered. "You're going to a full-scale Italian wedding and do what? 'Fascist Toejam's Greatest Hits'?"

"It could need some reconceptualizing," Isaiah admitted. "I, like, implied we were Italian, for one thing."

"Well you might want to learn a few of the tunes, but you'll settle in, try not to worry," chortling to himself as Prairie and Isaiah went out the door, yes always glad to help out, my boy, a crime-family gig, whatever, no no, don't bother to thank me. . . . Zoyd had played a few mob weddings in his career, nothing the kid couldn't handle, and besides the eats would more than make up for any awkward episodes, so it wasn't as if he were running a mean trick on his daughter's boyfriend, whom he was still not 100 percent crazy about, or anything like that. And as a problem to be addressed, Isaiah was more like a vacation from deeper difficulties, chief among which, all of a sudden, was the recrudescence of Hector Zuñiga in Zoyd's life, a topic, as he lit a joint and settled in front of the soundless Tube, that his thoughts unavoidably found their way back to.

IT was a romance over the years at least as persistent as Sylvester and Tweety's. Although Hector may from time to time have wished some cartoon annihilation for Zoyd, he'd understood from early in their acquaintance that Zoyd was the chasee he'd be least likely ever to bag. Not that he credited Zoyd with anything like moral integrity in resisting him. He put it down instead to stubbornness, plus drug abuse, ongoing mental problems, and a timidity, maybe only a lack of imagination, about the correct scale of any deal in life, drug or nondrug. And though not as obsessed these days about turning Zoyd — they'd had that crisis long ago — Hector still, for no reason he could name, liked to keep on popping in every now and then, preferably unannounced.

He showed up first in Zoyd's life shortly after Reagan was elected governor of California. Zoyd was living down south then, sharing a house in Gordita Beach with elements of a surf band he'd been playing keyboard in since junior high, the Corvairs, along with friends more and less transient. The house was so old that all of its termite clauses and code violations had been waived, on the theory that the next moderate act of nature would finish it off. But having been put up back during an era of overdesign, it proved to be sturdier than it looked, with its old stucco eaten at to reveal generations of paint jobs in different beach-town pastels, corroded by salt and petrochemical fogs that flowed in the summers onshore up the sand slopes, on up past Sepulveda, often across the then undeveloped fields, to wrap the San Diego Freeway too. Down here, a long screened porch faced out over flights of rooftops descending to the beach. Access from the street was by way of a Dutch door, whose open top half, that long-ago evening, had come to frame Hector under a ragged leather hat with a wide brim, peering through sunglasses, the darkening Pacific in pale-topped crawl below. Out on the street, wedged into most of the front seat of a motor-pool Plymouth, waited Hector's partner in those days, the seriously oversize field agent Melrose Fife. Zoyd, whose luck it happened to've been to answer Hector's knock, stood trying to understand what this individual with the outlaw hat and cop sideburns was talking about.

After a bit, Corvairs lead guitar and vocalist Scott Oof wandered in from the kitchen to join them, leaning on the doorjamb playing with his hair. "Maybe later," Hector greeted him, "you could explain this all to your friend here, 'cause I don't know if I've been gittín through. . . ."

"¿*Qué?*" replied Scott wittily. "*No hablo inglés.*"

"Whoa." Hector's front-door smile tightened up. "Maybe I should get my pardner up here for this. See him, out there in the car? You can't really tell till he stands up, but he is so big, that nobody ever wants to get him out of the car, 'cause once he's out, you dig, he ain't alwayss that easy to git back in?"

"Don't mind Scott," Zoyd hastily, "he's a surfer — so long, Scott — he had a little run-in a few years ago with some, uh, young gentlemen of Mexican origin, so sometimes —"

"In the parking lot at the Taco Bell in Hermosa, yes a memorable series of evenings, much celebrated in the folklore of my people" — this being in the early days of a Ricardo Montalban impersonation that would over the years grow more refined.

"You've come to take revenge?"

"Please. For-give me," Hector producing from an inside pocket, access to which now also afforded a leisurely view of a service .38 in an armpit rig, his federal commission in a fancy tooled flip-open leather case.

"Nobody here's into nothing federal," Zoyd didn't think.

Van Meter, back in those days sporting a profile that mandated at least a stop-and-frisk, ran in frowning. "What's wrong with Scott? he just split out the back."

"What I'm really here about," Hector had been explaining, "is the matter of drugs."

"Thank God!" screamed Van Meter, "it's been weeks, we thought we'd never score again! oh yes, it's a miracle —" Zoyd kicking him frantically — "who sent you, are you the dude that knows Leon?"

The federale showed his teeth, amused. "Subject you refer to is temporarily in custody, though sure to be back before very long in his accustomed spot beneath the Gordita Pier."

"Aaaaaa . . . ," went Van Meter.

"No, no my man but that is precisely the sort of corroborating detail that we value so highly," snapping, like a magician, a crisp five-dollar bill, half a lid of Mexican commercial in those days, from behind Van Meter's ear. Zoyd rolled his eyes as the bass player grabbed at the money. "And there's always plenty more in our imprest fund for good-quality product. For make-believe bullshit, of course, we pay nothing, and in time we grow annoyed."

That fatal five-spot was not the last Purchase-of-Information disbursement in the neighborhood. In those years there were so many federal narcs in the area that if you were busted in the South Bay you actually stood less chance of its being the local Man than some fed. All the beach towns, plus Torrance, Hawthorne, and greater Walteria, were in on some grandiose pilot project bankrolled with inexhaustible taxpayer millions, appropriate chunks of which were finding their way to antidrug entities up and down every level of governance. Zoyd, to be sure, made a point of never pocketing any of Hector's PI money personally, though he was content to go on eating the groceries, burning the gas, and smoking the pot others obtained with it. Now and then he would get fooled on some minor dope purchase, sweet basil in a heat-sealed bag, a small vial of Bisquick (yep, he'd murmur, still making stupid mistakes and how about yourself?) and he'd feel really tempted, sometimes for days, to turn the dealer in to Hector. But there were always good reasons not to — it would happen that one was a cool person who needed the money, another a distant cousin from the Middle West, or a homicidal maniac who would take revenge, so forth. Each time Zoyd failed to inform on these people, Hector grew furious. "You think you're protectín them? They just gonna fuck you over again." The edge in his voice was frustration, everything about this Gordita assignment was just really fucking frustrating, all these identical-looking beach pads beginning to blend together, resulting in more than enough mistaken addresses, earlymorning raids upon the innocent, failures to apprehend fugitives who might have only fled across an alley or down a flight of public steps. The arrangements of hillside levels, alleyways, corners, and rooftops created a Casbah topography that was easy to get lost in quickly, terrain where the skills of the bushwhacker became worth more than any resoluteness of character, an architectural version of the uncertainty, the illusion, that must have overtaken his career for him ever to've been assigned there in the first place.

"Situations back then," Zoyd hammered it on in, these many years later, "relationships, sure got tangled up in that house, with more and also less temporary love partners and sex companions, jealousy and revenge always goin' on, plus substance dealers and their go-betweens, and narcs who thought they were undercover trying to pop them, couple-three politicals fleein' from different jurisdictions, good deal of comin' and goin' 's what it was, not to mention you actin' like it was your own personal snitch Safeway, just drop in, we're open 24 hours."

They were sitting at a table in the rear of the restaurant at Vineland Lanes, Zoyd after a lot of lost sleep having decided to show up after all. He ordered the Health Food Enchilada Special and Hector had the soup of the day, cream of zucchini, and the vegetarian tostada, which upon its arrival he began to take apart piece by piece and reassemble as something else Zoyd could not identify but which seemed to hold meaning for Hector.

"Lookit that, lookit your food, Hector, what have you done?"

"At least I'm not droppín it all over the place, includín my shirt, like I was out in some parkín lot." Yes, a certain emphasis there for sure, and this after their having shared, maybe not many, but still a parking lot or two, even some adventures therein. Zoyd guessed that at some point since their last get-together Hector, as if against a storm approaching over his life's horizon, had begun to bring everything indoors. Stuck out in the field at GS-13 for years because of his attitude, he had sworn — Zoyd thought — he'd go out the gate early before he'd ever be some *cagatintas*, a bureaucrat who shits ink. But he must have cut some deal, maybe it got too cold for him — time to say goodbye to all those eyeswept parking lots back out under the elements and the laws of chance, and hello GS-14, leaving the world outside the office to folks earlier in their careers, who could appreciate it more. Too bad. For Zoyd, a creature of attitude himself, this long defiance had been Hector's most persuasive selling point.

What the federal computers this morning had not brought to Hector's attention was that the alleys today were scheduled for junior regional semifinals. Kids were in town from all over the northern counties to compete on these intricately mortised masterpiece alleys, dating back to the high tide of the logging business in these parts, when the big houses framed all in redwood had gone up and legendary carpenters had appeared descending from rain-slick stagecoaches, geniuses with wood who could build you anything from a bowling alley to a Carpenter Gothic outhouse. Balls struck pins, pins struck wood, echoes of collision came thundering in from next door along with herds of kids in different bowling jackets, each carrying at least one ball in a bag plus precarious stacks of sodas and food, each squeaking open the screen door between lanes and restaurant, letting it squeak shut into the next kid, who'd squeak it open again. Didn't take many of these repetitions to have an effect on Zoyd's lunch companion, whose eyes were flicking back and forth as he hummed a tune that not till sixteen bars in did Zoyd recognize as "Meet the Flintstones," from the well-known TV cartoon show. Hector finished the tune and looked sourly at Zoyd. "Any of these yours?"

Here it was. OK, "What are you sayin', Hector?"

"You know what I'm sayín, asshole."

Zoyd couldn't see a thing in his eyes. "Who you been talking to?"

"Your wife."

Zoyd began stabbing and restabbing his enchiladas with a fork while Hector waited him out. "Uh, well how's she doing?"

Hector's eyes were moist, and popping out some. "Not too good, li'l buddy."

"Tryin' to tell me what, she's in trouble?"

"You catch on fast for an ol' doper, now try this one, you ever heard of defunding? Maybe you noticed on the news, on the Tube, all these stories about Reaganomics, a-an' cutbacks in the federal budget and stuff?"

"She was on some program? Now she's off it?" They were talking about his ex-wife, Frenesi, years and miles in the past. Why, besides the free lunch, was Zoyd sitting here listening to this? Hector, leaning forward bright-eyed, had begun to show signs of enjoying himself. "Where is she?"

"Well, we *had* her under Witness Protection."

Not hearing the stress on *had* right away, "Oh bullshit, Hector, that's for Mob folks trying to be ex-Mob 'thout havin' to die first, since when are you usin' that Mafia meat locker for politicals, thought you just took 'em put 'em in the booby hatch like they do over there in Russia."

"Well, technically it was a different budget line, but still run by the U.S. Marshals, same as with the Mob type of witness."

Man could crush him with just a short tap dance over the computer keys — why was Hector being so unnaturally amiable? All that could possibly be restraining the tough old doorkicker was kindness, unfortunately a trait he was born so short on that nobody living or dead had ever observed it anywhere near him.

"So — she's in with all these Mob snitches, the money disappears, but you still have her file, you can punch her up when you need her —"

"Wrong. Her file is destroyed." The word hung in the wood space, between percussive attacks from next door.

"Why? Thought you guys never destroyed a file, 'th all 'ese little fund, defund, refund games —"

"We don't know why. But it's no game in Washington — *chále ése* — this ain't tweakín around no more with no short-term maneuvers here, this is a *real* revolution, not that little fantasy handjob you people was into, is it's a groundswell, Zoyd, the wave of History, and you can catch it, or scratch it." He eyed Zoyd with a smug look which in view of what he'd been doing to his tostada, over, by now, most of the tabletop, lacked authenticity. "The man who once shot the old Hermosa Pier durín a lightnín storm," Hector shaking his head. "Listen, K mart this week has full-length mirrors on sale, and I'm nobody's charm-school professor, but I'd urge you to get one. Might want to start upgradín your image, li'l buddy."

"Wait a minute, you *don't know why* her file was destroyed?"

"Is why we're gonna need your help. The money's good."

"Oh, shit. Yah, hah, hah, hah, you lost her's what happened, some idiot back there wiped out the computer file, right? Now you don't even know where she is, and you think I do."

"Not exactly. We think now she's headín back here."

"She wa'n' spoze to Hector, that was never part of the deal. I wondered how long it was gonna take — twelve, thirteen years, not bad, you mind if I call the Guinness Book Hot Line with this, it has to be a world record for fascist regimes keepin' their word."

"Still simmerín away with those same old feelings, I see — figured you'd be mellower by now, maybe some reconciliation with reality, I dunno."

"When the State withers away, Hector."

"*Caray,* you sixties people, it's amazing. Ah love ya! Go any-where, it don't matter — hey, Mongolia! Go way out into small-town Outer Mongolia, *ése,* there's gonna be some local person about your age come runnín up, two fingers in a V, hollerín, 'What's yer sign, man?' or singín 'In-A-Gadda-Da-Vida' note for note."

"Satellites, everybody hears everything, space is really some-thing, what else?"

The dope cop permitted himself an Eastwood-style mouth-muscle nuance. "Don't be disingenuous, I know you still believe in all that shit. All o' you are still children inside, livín your real life back then. Still waitín for that magic payoff. But no prob, I can live with that . . . and it ain't like you're lazy or afraid to work, either . . . impossible to tell with you, Zoyd. Never could figure out how innocent you thought you were. Sometimes you looked just like a hippie bum musician, for months at a shot, as if you never turned a buck any other way. Rill puzzlín."

"Hector! Bite yer tongue! You tellin' me I — I *wasn't* innocent, me behavín' like a saint through it all?"

"You behaved about like everybody else, pardner, sorry."

"That bad."

"I won't aks you to grow up, but just sometime, please, aks

yourself, OK, 'Who was saved?' That's all, rill easy, 'Who was saved?' "

"Beg pardon?"

"One OD'd on the line at Tommy's waitín for a burger, one got into some words in a parkín lot with the wrong gentleman, one took a tumble in a faraway land, so on, more 'n half of 'em currently on the run, and you so far around the bend you don't even see it, that's what became of your happy household, you'd've done better up against the SWAT team. Just in the privacy of your thotz, Zoyd. As a exercise, li'l kinda Zen meditation. 'Who was saved?' "

"You, Hector."

"*Ay se va,* go on, break your old *compinche's* heart. Here I thought you knew everything, it turns out you don't know shit." Grinning — a stretched and terrible face. It was the closest Hector got to feeling sorry for himself, this suggestion he liked to put out that among the fallen, he had fallen further than most, not in distance alone but also in the quality of descent, having begun long ago concentrated and graceful as a sky diver but — the tostada procedure was minor evidence — he growing less professional the longer he fell, while his skills as a field man depreciated. He had come, with these falling years, simply to rely on going in, trying to neutralize whoever was there with a repertoire of assault that still ran from stupefy to obliterate, and if they were waiting for him one time and got in the first move, *ay muere,* too bad. Hector sadly knew this wasn't anywhere near the samurai condition of always being on that perfect edge prepared to die, a feeling he'd known only a few times in his life, long ago. Nowadays, with his old fighting talents lapsed, what looked like simple impulse or will might as easily have been advanced self-hatred. Zoyd, the big idealist, liked to believe that Hector remembered everybody he'd ever shot at, hit, missed, booked, questioned, rousted, doublecrossed — that each face was filed in his conscience, and the only way he could live with such a history was to take these chances with his own bad ass, upping the ante as he moved into his late midcareer. This theory at least had kept Zoyd from lying around hatching plots to assassinate Hector, as others had been known to waste hours of potentially productive lives doing. Hector was the kind of desperado whose ideal assassin was himself — he could choose the best method, time, and place and would always have the best motives for it of anyone.

"So, let me guess, I'm spoze to be some early-warning alarm, some invisible beam she can walk through and break, so you get a few minutes' edge but meanwhile I'm the one gets interrupted, or come to think of it, broken, somethin' like that?"

"Not at all. You can go on with your life, such as it is. Nobody runnín you, you don't call in, we don't call unless we need you. All's you got to do's be there, in place — be yourself, as your music teacher probably used to tell you."

Late hit, Zoyd thought, not like him, what's wrong with the li'l fella today, with this edge on everything? "Well sounds like a breeze, and you mean I get paid for it too?"

"Special Employee scale, maybe even a bonus."

"Used to be a twenty, as I recall, limp and warm from some agent's wallet his kid gave him for Christmas. . . ."

"Sure — you'll find today it can be well into the low three figures, Zoyd."

"Wait a minute — bonus? What for?"

"Whatever."

"Can I have a uniform, a badge, a piece?"

"You gonna do it?"

"Bullshit Hector, you givin' me a choice?"

The federale shrugged. "It's a free country. The Lord, as they call him around my office, created all of us, even you, with free will. I think it's weird you don't even want to find out about her."

"You're one sentimental hombre, you meddlin' ol' Cupid ya. Well maybe you can relate to this — it took me a long time even to get to where I am on the whole subject o' her, now you want to post me right back down into it again, but guess what, I don't want to go back 'n' waller in all 'at."

"How about your kid, then?"

"Yes, Hector. What about her? I really need to hear some more federal advice right now about how I should be bringin' up my own kid, we know already how much all you Reaganite folks care about the family unit, just from how much you're always in fuckin' around with it."

"Maybe this ain't gonna work after all."

"It does seem," Zoyd careful, "like that you're spending a lot on one long-ago federal case everybody's forgotten."

"You should see how much. Maybe it goes beyond your ex-old lady, li'l buddy."

"Far, far beyond?"

"I used to worry about you, Zoyd, but I see I can rest easy now the Vaseline of youth has been cleared from your life's lens by the mild detergent solution of time, in its passing. . . ." Hector sat slumped in zomoskepsis, or the contemplation of his soup. "I should charge you my consultancy fee, but I already checked your shoes, so I'll give you this for free." Was he reading strange soup messages? "Your ex-old lady, up till they terminated her budget line, was livín in a underground of the State, not like th' old Weatherpeople or nothín, OK? but a certain kind of world that civilians up on the surface, out in the sun thinkín 'em happy thotz, got no idea it's even there. . . ." Hector was usually too cool to be much of a lapel-grabber, but something in his voice now, had Zoyd been wearing a jacket, might have warned of an attempt. "Nothín like that shit on the Tube, nothín at all . . . and cold . . . colder than you ever want to find out about. . . ."

"That case, I got no problem staying out of the way, 'specially anybody she's been runnin' with, and good luck yourself, pal."

"I don't need that from you, Zoyd, you're just as fucked as you ever were, and you picked up a mean streak too."

"Nothin' meaner than a old hippie that's gone sour, Hector, lot of it around."

"You pussies set yourselves up for it," Hector advised, "don't be complainín this far down the line, it's only business, and we're both gonna make out, all's you do's sit tight while I do the work."

"Hope you don't need a yes or no right away."

"Time is of the essence, you're not the only one I'm tryín to coordinate here." Shook his head sadly. "We been out cruisín different boulevards for years now, did you send one Christmas card, or ask about Debbi, or the kids, or what's been happenín to my consciousness? Maybe I'm Mormon now, how would you know? Maybe Debbi talked me into goín on a retreat one weekend and it changed my life. And maybe you should even be thinkín about your spirit, Zoyd."

"My —"

"Takes a little discipline's all, wouldn't kill you."

"I'm sorry, Hector, how are Debbi and the kids?"

"Zoyd, if only you hadn't been such a asshole all your life, just skippín along through the wildflowers, so forth, thinkín you were so special, that you didt'n have to do what everybody else did. . . ."

"Maybe I don't. You think I do?"

"Hey, all right fuckhead, try this — *you are goín to have to die?* Yeah-heh-heh, remember that? Death! after all them yearss of nonconformist shit, you're gonna end up just like everybody else anyway! *¡Ja, ja!* So what was it for? All 'at livín in the hippie dirt, drivín around some piece of garbage ain't even in the blue book no more, passín up some *really serious bucks*'t you could've spent not just on y'rself and your kid but on all your beloved bro and sister hippie fools who could've used it as much as you?"

A waitress approached with the check. Both men — Hector by reflex and Zoyd then startled into it — sprang toward her and collided, and the girl, alarmed, backed away, dropping the document, which then got batted around by the three parties until at last fluttering into a revolving condiment tray, where it ended up half submerged in a big fluffy mound of mayonnaise gone translucent at the edges.

"Check's in the mayo," Zoyd had time to note, when all at once, out past the street door, came a convergence of sirens, purposeful shouting, then heavy boots, all in step, thumping their direction.

"*¡Madre de Dios!*" an oddly panicked, high-pitched Hector was up and running for the kitchen — luckily, Zoyd noted, having left a twenty on the table — now with a platoon of folks come crashing in after him, what *was* this, all wearing identical camo jumpsuits and crash helmets with the word NEVER stenciled on. Two stayed by the door, two more went over to check the bowling alley, the rest went running on after Hector into the kitchen, where there was already a lot of screaming and clanging.

Dude in a white lab coat over Pendleton shirt and jeans now came strolling in between the two doorpeople, heading for Zoyd, who beamed insincerely, "Never saw him before."

"Zoyd Wheeler! Hi, caught you on the news last night, fabulous, didn't know you and Hector were acquainted, listen, he hasn't been quite himself, signed in with us for some therapy, and now, frankly. . . ."

"He broke out."

"We'll catch up eventually. But if you have any further contact, you'll give us a call, hmmm?"

"Who are you?"

"Oh. Sorry." He handed Zoyd a card that read, "Dr. Dennis Deeply, M.S.W., Ph.D. / National Endowment for Video Education and Rehabilitation," someplace down north of Santa Barbara, a struck circle around a TV set, above the Latin motto *Ex luce ad sanitatem,* with a printed phone number crossed out and another ballpointed in. "That's our local number, we're staying at the Vineland Palace till we catch Hector."

"Nice per diem. You guys're federal?"

"Bisectoral, really, private and public, grants, contracts, basically we study and treat Tubal abuse and other video-related disorders."

"A dryin'-out place for Tubefreeks? You mean . . . Hector. . . ." And Zoyd remembered him humming that Flintstone theme to calm himself down, and all those "li'l buddy"'s, which as they both knew was what the Skipper always liked to call Gilligan, raising possibilities Zoyd didn't want to think about.

Dr. Deeply shrugged eloquently. "One of the most intractable cases any of us has seen. He's already in the literature. Known in our field as the Brady Buncher, after his deep although not exclusive attachment to that series."

"Oh, yeah, that was ol' Marcia, right, and then the middle one's name was —" till Zoyd noticed the piercing look he was getting.

"Maybe," said Dr. Deeply, "you should give us a call anyway."

"I didt'n say I could remember *all* their names!" Zoyd yelled after him, but he was already halfway out the door, soon to be joined by the others and then, presently, gone, and without having caught Hector, either.

Hector, who it now seemed was some sort of escaped lunatic, was still at large.

ZOYD hit Phantom Ridge Road about an hour later than he wanted because of Elvissa up the hill's blown head gasket, which brought her down at 6:00 A.M. to borrow his rig, for which it had taken Zoyd then a while to scout up a replacement. This turned out to be a Datsun Li'l Hustler pickup, belonging to his neighbor Trent, with a camper shell whose unusual design gave the vehicle some cornering problems. "Long as you don't try it with the tank anywhere between empty and full," Trent suggested, he thought helpfully. But it was actually the camper shell, covered all over with cedar shakes in some doper's idea of imbrication and topped by a pointed shake roof with a stovepipe coming out, that seemed to be the problem.

Zoyd very carefully hooked a right and was soon climbing switchbacks up a ridge of as yet unlogged second-growth redwoods, on whose other side lay Phantom Creek. The fog here had burned off early, leaving a light blue haze that began to fade the more distant trees. He was heading for a little farm on the creek road, where he had a sideline in crawfish with a bush vet and his family. They'd go harvest the little 'suckers from up and down Phantom and a couple of adjoining creeks, and Zoyd would bring the good-eating crustaceans back down 101 to a string of restaurants catering to depraved yuppie food preferences, in this case California Cajun, though the critters also got listed here and there as Ecrivisses à la Maison and Vineland Lobster.

RC and Moonpie, real names left back along their by now erased-enough trail since the war, were as happy to see the money as the kids were to be out doing the work — Morning, the biggest, splashing down the middle of the creek, with the others carrying jars and sacks of twenty-penny nails, and fastening a piece of bacon to the bottom of every knee-deep pool they came to. By the time they got back to where they'd started, there'd be frantic invasions of crawdads, all milling around unable to get the bacon loose.

Procedure then was to bring out a minnow bag on a stick, hit the crawdad on the nose with the stick, and catch it, as it jumped, in the bag. Sometimes the kids would even allow their parents to come along and help out.

Zoyd had known the family since the early seventies, having in fact met Moonpie on the night of the day his divorce became final, which also happened to be the night before his very first window jump, in a way both part of the same letter of agreement. He was drinking beers in a longhairs' saloon called the Lost Nugget down on South Spooner in Vineland, looking for a way not to think about Frenesi or the life together that had just officially come to an end with no last-minute reversals, and Moonpie, equally young and lovely back in those days, seemed to Zoyd's crippled receptors just the ticket. That is until RC emerged from the can, with the deep eyes, the mortally cautious bearing, that told of where else he'd been. He slid back to the bar, dropped a hand on Moonpie's shoulder that she pressed for a moment with her cheek, and nodded at Zoyd with a please-don't-piss-me-off look of inquiry. Zoyd, already well into second thoughts anyway, instead spent the rest of that evening, and in fact many other nights down the years to come, not to mention daylight beer breaks, freeway meditations, and toilet-seat reveries, obsessing about his wife — he never would get too comfortable with "ex-wife" — and managing to bum out everybody inside a radius even these days considered respectable.

Zoyd's dream album someday would be an anthology of torch songs for male vocalist, called Not Too Mean to Cry. He had arrived in this recurring fantasy at the point where he'd take advertising space, late at night on the Tube, with a toll-free number flashing over little five-second samples of each tune, not only to sell records but also on the chance that Frenesi, up late some 3:00 A.M. out of some warm Mr. Wonderful's bed, would happen to pop the Tube on, maybe to chase the ghosts away, and there'd be Zoyd, at the keyboard in some outrageous full-color tux, someplace along the Vegas Strip, backed by a full house orchestra, and she'd know, as the titles scrolled by, "Are You Lonesome Tonight," "One for My Baby," "Since I Fell for You," that every one of these disconsolate oldies was all about her.

Frenesi had ridden into his life like a whole gang of outlaws. He felt like a schoolmarm. He was working gypsy construction jobs by day and playing at night with the Corvairs, never anyplace near the surf but inland, for this sun-beat farm country had always welcomed them, beer riders of the valleys having found strange affinities with surfers and their music. Besides a common interest in beer, members of both subcultures, whether up on a board or behind a 409, shared the terrors and ecstasies of the passive, taken rider, as if a car engine held encapsulated something likewise oceanic and mighty — a technowave, belonging to distant others as surf belonged to the sea, bought into by the riders strictly as-is, on the other party's terms. Surfers rode God's ocean, beer riders rode the momentum through the years of the auto industry's will. That death entered into their recreation more than into the surfers' helped shape an attitude, nonetheless, that had brought the Corvairs their share of toilet and parking-lot trauma, police interventions, sudden midnight farewells.

The band played up and down valleys still in those days unknown except to a few real-estate visionaries, little crossroads places where one day houses'd sprawl and the rates of human affliction in all categories zoom. After work, unable to sleep, the Corvairs liked to go out and play motorhead valley roulette in the tule fogs. These white presences, full of blindness and sudden highway death, moved, as if conscious, unpredictably over the landscape. There were few satellite photos back then, so people had only the ground-level view. No clear bounded shape — all at once, there in the road, a critter in a movie, too quick to be true, there it'd be. The idea was to enter the pale wall at a speed meaningfully over the limit, to bet that the white passage held no other vehicles, no curves, no construction, only smooth, level, empty roadway to an indefinite distance — a motorhead variation on a surfer's dream.

Zoyd had grown up in the San Joaquin, ridden with the Bud Warriors and later the Ambassadors, gone on many an immortally lunatic "grudge run," as Dick Dale might say, through the pre-suburban citrus groves and pepper fields, lost a high percentage of his classmates, blank rectangles in the yearbooks, to drunk driving or failed machinery, and would eventually return to the same sunny, often he could swear haunted, landscape to get married, one afternoon on a smooth gold green California hillside, with oak in darker patches, a freeway in the distance, dogs and children playing and running, and the sky, for many of the guests, awriggle with patterns of many colors, some indescribable.

"Frenesi Margaret, Zoyd Herbert, will you, for real, in trouble or in trippiness, promise to remain always on the groovy high known as Love," and so forth, it may have taken hours or been over in half a minute, there were few if any timepieces among those assembled, and nobody seemed restless, this after all being the Mellow Sixties, a slower-moving time, predigital, not yet so cut into pieces, not even by television. It would be easy to remember the day as a soft-focus shot, the kind to be seen on "sensitivity" greeting cards in another few years. Everything in nature, every living being on the hillside that day, strange as it sounded later whenever Zoyd tried to tell about it, was gentle, at peace — the visible world was a sunlit sheep farm. War in Vietnam, murder as an instrument of American politics, black neighborhoods torched to ashes and death, all must have been off on some other planet.

Music was by the Corvairs, these days calling themselves surfadelic, though the nearest surf at the moment was at Santa Cruz, forty miles away over farm roads and murderous mountain passes, and they had to contend with the traditional beer-rider haughtiness of the area — still, in later years, try as Zoyd might to remember everything at its most negative, truth was there'd been no brawls or barfing or demolition derbies, everybody had got along magically, it was one of the peak parties of his life, folks loved the music, and it went on all night and then the next, right on through the weekend. Pretty soon bikers and biker chicks, playing at villainy, were showing up in full regalia, then a hay wagon jammed full of back-to-nature acidheads from up the valley out on an old-fashioned hayride, and eventually the sheriff, who ended up doing the Stroll, a dance of his own day, with three miniskirted young beauties to a screaming electric arrangement of "Pipeline" and who was kind enough not to go near, let alone investigate, the punch, but did accept a can of Burgie, it being a warm day.

All through it, Frenesi was smiling, serene. Zoyd would be unable to forget her already notorious blue eyes, glowing under a big light straw hat. Little kids ran up, calling her name. She and Zoyd were sitting together on a bench under a fig tree, the band on a break, she was eating a cone of rainbow-patterned fruit ice whose colors miraculously didn't seep together, leaning forward to keep it off her wedding dress, which had also been her mother's and grandmother's. A tortoise cat who kept appearing from nowhere would walk directly under the dripping cone, get hit with ice-cold drops of lime, orange, or grape, meow as if surprised, squirm in the dust, roll her eyes around insanely, run off at top speed, and then after a while amble back to repeat the act.

"Did you notice my cousin Renée? Do you think she's having a good time?" Renée had just broken up with her boyfriend, but undeterred by depression had driven up from L.A. figuring maybe a party was what she needed. Zoyd remembered her, among the roster of his in-law aunts, uncles, and cousins, as a tall florid girl in a minidress that bore the image, from neck to hemline, of Frank Zappa's face, thus linking her in Zoyd's mind somehow with Mount Rushmore.

He smiled, squinting back, like a schoolmarm who still couldn't believe her luck. A breeze had come up and begun to move the leaves of their tree. "Frenesi, do you think that love can save anybody? You do, don't you?" At the time he hadn't learned yet what a stupid question it was. She gazed up at him from just under the brim of the hat. He thought, At least try to remember this, try to keep it someplace secure, just her face now in this light, OK, her eyes quiet like this, her mouth poised to open. . . .

Mean or not, he hadn't cried about it for a long time. The years had kept rolling, like the surf he used to ride, high, calm, wild, windless. But increasingly the day, the necessary day, presenting its demands, had claimed him, till there was only one small bitter amusement he refused to let go of. Now and then, when moon, tides, and planetary magnetism were all in tune, he went venturing out, straight up through the third eye in his forehead, into an extraordinary system of transport whereby he could go gliding right to wherever she was, and incompletely unseen, sensed just enough to be troublesome, he then would haunt her, for as long as he could, enjoying every squeezed-out minute. A vice, for sure, and one he had confessed only to a handful of people, including, it may have turned out unwisely, their daughter, Prairie, this very morning.

"Oh," sitting over a breakfast of Cap'n Crunch and Diet Pepsi, "you mean you *dreamed* —"

Zoyd shook his head. "I was awake. But out of my body."

She gave him a look that he didn't, so early in the day, attend to the full risk of, telling him she trusted him not to be running some cruel put-on. They'd been known not to share a sense of humor on many topics, her mom in particular. "You go there and — what? You perch somewhere and look, you keep flying around, how's it work?"

"It's like Mr. Sulu laying in coordinates, only different," Zoyd explained.

"Knowin' exactly where you want to go." He nodded, and she felt some unaccustomed bloom of tenderness for this scroungy, usually slow-witted fringe element she'd been assigned, on this planet, for a father. What mattered at the moment was that he knew how to visit Frenesi out in the night, and that could only mean he must feel a need for her as intense as Prairie's own. "Where's it you go, then? Where is she?"

"Keep tryin' to find out. Try to read signs, locate landmarks, anything that'll give a clue, but — well the signs are there on street corners and store windows — but I can't read them."

"It's some other language?"

"Nope, it's in English, but there's something between it and my brain that won't let it through."

Prairie made a sound like a game-show buzzer. "*I'm* sorry Mr. Wheeler. . . ." Let down and suspicious, she drifted away again. "Say hi to 'em up on Phantom Creek, OK?"

He took a left at the row of mailboxes, went strumming over a cattle guard, parked out by the horse barn, and walked in. RC was over in Blue Lake running chores, but Moonpie was around, looking after Lotus, the baby. The crawdads were in an old Victorian bathtub that doubled as a watering trough. Together Zoyd and Moonpie netted them out and weighed them on a seed, feed, and fertilizer scale, and he wrote her a postdated check he'd still have to scramble, this day already so advanced, to cover.

"Somebody at the Nugget the other night," baby on her arm, giving him now a straight, worried look, "askin' about you. RC thought he knew him, but wouldn't tell me anythin'."

"Latino gent, semi-Elvis haircut?"

"Yep. You in some trouble, Zoyd?"

"Moon darlin', when am I out of it? He mention where he was staying, anything like that?"

"Mostly just sat starin' at the Tube in the bar. Some movie on channel 86. He was talkin' to the screen after a while, but I don't think he was loaded or nothin'."

"Rill unhappy dude, is all."

"Wow. Comin' from you. . . ." Seeing Zoyd's odd smile, the baby echoed, "Comin' fum *you!*"

They transferred the crawdads to tubs of water in the back of the camper, and soon Zoyd was lurching and sloshing back down the road. He noticed Moonpie and Lotus in the rearview mirror, watching him around the curve, till the trees hid them.

So, fucking Hector again. Zoyd had only missed him that night by not showing up at the Lost Nugget, his usual hangout, having chosen instead a booth way in the back of the Steam Donkey, just off the old Plaza in Vineland, a bar that dated well back into the fog of the last century. Van Meter'd put his head in after a while, and they'd sat becoming slowly awash in Lucky Lager, snuffling over the olden times.

"Educated pussy," Zoyd sighed, "don't know why, f' some reason I must've been a easy mark. She was a filmmaker, went to Berkeley, I was working on people's gutters, she rilly freaked when she found out she was pregnant."

It was a long time ago, old as Prairie, who for a while had been a topic of debate. Frenesi was getting free advice both ways. Some told her it was the end of her life as an artist, as a revolutionary, and urged her to get an abortion, not that easy to come by in those days unless you drove south of the border. If you wanted to stay north of it you had to be rich and go through a committee exercise with gynecologists and shrinks. Others pointed out to her what a groovy chance this would be to bring up a child in a politically correct way, though definitions of this varied from reading Trotsky to her at bedtime to including LSD in the formula.

"But what hurts," Zoyd went on, "is how innocent I thought she was. Fuckin' fool. I wanted to wise her up, at the same time protect her from ever knowin' how shitty things could get. Was I stupid."

"You're blaming yourself for the line of work she got into?"

"For not seeing too much. For thinkin' we'd get away with it, thinkin' we'd beat them all."

"Yep, you really fucked up," Van Meter having himself a good chuckle. Their friendship over the years was based in part on each pretending to laugh at the other's hard luck. Zoyd sat there nodding How true, how true. "So worried about Hector you didn't even know the *other* federal guy was porkin' your wife till she was long gone! What a trip, man!"

"Appreciate the support ol' buddy, but I was still happy to be out of Hector's way back then 'thout gittin' my ass in too major of a sling." But he understood that like all suffering Tubeheads he must have really thought, as he and the baby were making their getaway, that that was it, all over, time to go to commercials and clips of next week's episode. . . . Frenesi might be gone, but there would always be his love for Prairie, burning like a night-light, always nearby, cool and low, but all night long. . . . And Hector, in his actorly literalness and brown-shoe conformity while also being insane, would never trouble his environment again. Damn fool Zoyd. Sent so gaga by those mythical days of high drama that he'd forgotten he and Prairie might actually have to go on living years beyond them.

All the rest of the day it seemed like he was getting funny looks everywhere he went. The swamper at Redwood Bayou, getting the place ready for lunch, disappeared into the back where the phone was as soon as Zoyd came in the door. The waitresses at Le Bûcheron Affamé gathered over in a corner murmuring, casting him slow over-the-shoulder looks it was hard even for him to take as anything but pitying. "Hi ladies, how's the warm duck salad today?" But nobody came forth with much more than mentions of ubiquitous though unnamed Hector. Back on the freeway, Zoyd kept a defensive eye out in all directions, no telling where the Tube-maddened Detox escapee might pop up. At his next stop, Humbolaya, amid stomach-nudging aromas from the Special of the Day, tofu à la étouffée, Zoyd hustled use of the office phone to call Doc Deeply on the direct line in to his wing of the Vineland Palace.

"NEVER," answered the perky female voice on the other end.

"Huh? I didt'n even ask you yet."

Her voice dropped half an octave. "This is about Hector Zuñiga — maybe you'd better hold." After a short recorded program of themes from famous TV shows, on came the mellifluous Dr. Deeply.

"Don't want to alarm you, Doc," Zoyd said, "but I think he's stalkin' me."

"You've . . . had these feelings for some time?" In the background, on some stereo, Zoyd could hear Little Charlie and the Nightcats singing "TV Crazy."

"Yeah, in Hector's case fifteen or twenty years. Some guys's in the *joint* for longer 'n that."

"Look, I can put my people on standby, but I don't think we can protect you around the clock, or anything." About then Chef 'Ti Bruce put his head in the door hollering "You still on?" and seeming anxious to have Zoyd out of there, when formerly it had been their custom to linger over beignets and chicory coffee.

Crawfish business done, Zoyd's next stop was out to the Old Thumb peninsula to Rick & Chick's Born Again, an auto-conversion shop located among log piles and county motor pools. The owners, Humboldt County twins, had found Jesus and their seed money at about the same time, during the fuel panic of the seventies, when, to get a tax break for bringing out the first U.S. passenger diesel, GM took its 5.7-liter V-8 Cadillac engine and, in some haste, converted it. In the season of purchaser disenchantment that followed, engine experts, including Rick and Chick, found they could make on the order of $2,500 per job reconverting these ill-considered mills from diesel back to gasoline again. Soon they'd expanded into bodywork, put in a paint shed, and begun doing more customizing and conversion, eventually becoming a byword up and down the Coast and beyond the Sierras of the automotive second chance.

Standing with the twins as Zoyd pulled up were the legally ambiguous tow-truck team of Eusebio ("Vato") Gomez and Cleveland ("Blood") Bonnifoy, all in a respectful tableau observing a rare, legendary (some believed only folkloric) Edsel Escondido, sort of a beefier Ford Ranchero with a complexity of chrome accents, including around that well-known problem grille, now pitted by years of salt fog, which Vato and Blood had just finished winching to earth from V & B Tow's flagship F350, *El Mil Amores*. Zoyd wondered what script possibilities were tumbling through the partners' heads. It was some elaborate game of doubles they played with the twins every time they came in here, the basic rule being never to say out loud where the vehicle in — often deep — question had really come from, nor even to suggest that the legal phrase "act of conversion" might here be taking on some additional sense.

Today, inspired by a wave of Bigfoot sightings down in the Mattole, Vato had nearly convinced the skeptical lookalikes that the Escondido had been found abandoned in a clearing, its owners frightened off by Bigfoot, in whose territory the car had then sat, anybody's prize, making its retrieval by the boys, who'd just happened to be out in that part of the brush, an adventure full of perilous grades, narrow escapes, and kick-ass four-wheeling all the way, followed at each turn by the openmouthed Rick and Chick, upon whom at last Blood, usually the closer in these proceedings, laid, "So Bigfoot bein' force majeure, we got the legal salvage rights." Dazed, the twins were nodding at slightly different rates, and another story of twilight reconfiguration, soon to be the talk of the business, was about to get under way.

Zoyd, already jumpy enough from people's reactions to him all day, was not reassured at seeing the gathering break up at his approach into short edgy nods and waves. They were having one of those four-member eyeball permutations that finally nominated Blood as the one to talk to Zoyd.

"This is somethin' about Hector again, right?"

"We heard he was back," Blood said, "but this ain't him, Blood, it's, uh, somebody else. And me and my partner were just wondering if you were planning to sleep on the base tonight?"

Here came another of those deep intestinal pangs. Zoyd knew that long ago in Saigon, Blood had more than once heard this warning from elements of the Vietcong in whose interest it was to keep him alive and in business. "Well shit. If it i'n' Hector, then who is it?"

Vato came over, looking as serious as his running mate. "They're federal, Vato, but it ain' Hector, he's too busy keepín ahead of that posse from the Tubaldetox."

Zoyd suddenly felt like shit. "I better see about my kid." Rick and Chick made mirror-image go-ahead gestures at the phone. "That Jikov 32, that Skoda carburetor you 's lookin' for, it's in my front seat, see what you think."

Prairie worked at the Bodhi Dharma Pizza Temple, which a little smugly offered the most wholesome, not to mention the slowest, fast food in the region, a classic example of the California pizza concept at its most misguided. Zoyd was both a certified pizzamaniac and a cheapskate, but not once had he ever hustled Prairie for one nepotistic slice of the Bodhi Dharma product. Its sauce was all but crunchy with fistfuls of herbs only marginally Italian and more appropriate in a cough remedy, the rennetless cheese reminded customers variously of bottled hollandaise or joint compound, and the options were all vegetables rigorously organic, whose high water content saturated, long before it baked through, a stone-ground twelve-grain crust with the lightness and digestibility of a manhole cover.

Zoyd happened to catch Prairie on a meditation break. "You OK over there?"

"Somethin' wrong?"

"Do me a favor, stay till I get there, all right?"

"But Isaiah and the band were coming by to pick me up, we're goin' camping, remember? Sheez, all that shit you smoke, your brain must be like a Etch-A-Sketch."

"Uh huh, don't get alarmed, but we are facing a situation where a quick mouth, even a leading example such as your own, won't be nearly as much use today as a little cooperation. Please."

"Sure this ain't pothead paranoia?"

"Nope and now I think of it could you ask the young gentlemen when they git there to stick around too?"

"Just 'cause they look evil, Dad, doesn't mean they're any good for muscle, if that's what you're thinkin'."

Feeling unprotected on all flanks, Zoyd went speeding in, running lights and ignoring stop signs, to Vineland, where he just made it to the door of the bank at closing time. An entry-level functionary in a suit who was refusing admission to other late-comers saw Zoyd and, for the first time in history, nervously began to unlock the door for him, while inside colleagues at desks could be seen making long arms for the telephone. No, it wasn't pothead paranoia — but neither was Zoyd about to step inside this bank. A security guard sauntered over, unsnapping his hip holster. OK. Zoyd split with a that's-all-folks wave, having luckily parked Trent's rig just around the corner.

Prairie wouldn't be off work for a couple of hours. Zoyd needed cash and also some advice about a quick change of appearance, and both were available from the landscape contractor Zoyd did some lawn and tree work for, Millard Hobbs, a former actor who'd begun as a company logo and ended up as majority owner of what'd been a modest enough lawn-care service its founder, a reader of forbidden books, had named The Marquis de Sod. Originally Millard had only been hired to be in a couple of locally produced late-night TV commercials in which, holding a giant bullwhip, he appeared in knee socks, buckle shoes, cutoff trousers, blouse, and platinum wig, all borrowed from his wife, Blodwen. "Crabgrass won't be'ave?" he inquired in a species of French accent. "Haw, haw! No pro*blem!* Zhust call — The Marquis de Sod. . . . 'E'll wheep your lawn into shepp!" Pretty soon the business was booming, expanding into pool and tree service, and so much profit rolling in that Millard one time thought to take a few points instead of the fee up front. People out in the non-Tubal world began mistaking him for the real owner, by then usually off on vacation someplace, and Millard, being an actor, started believing them. Little by little he kept buying in and learning the business, as well as elaborating the scripts of his commercials from those old split 30's during the vampire shift to what were now often five-minute prime-time micromovies, with music and special effects increasingly subbed out to artisans as far away as Marin, in which the Marquis, his wardrobe now upgraded into an authentic eighteenth-century costume, might carry on a dialogue with some substandard lawn while lashing away at it with his bullwhip, each grass blade in extreme close-up being seen to have a face and little mouth, out of which, in thousandfold-echoplexed chorus, would come piping, "More, more! We love eet!" The Marquis, leaning down playfully, "Ah cahn't 'ear you!" Presently the grass would start to sing the company jingle, to a, by then, postdisco arrangement of the *Marseillaise* —

> A lawn savant, who'll lop a tree-ee-uh,
> Nobody beats Mar-
> Quis de Sod!

Millard was known for spreading work around generously, and for paying in cash and off the books too. Half the equipment lot today was filled by a flatbed rig from someplace down in the Mojave, whose load was a single giant rock, charred, pitted, streaked with metallic glazes. "Wealthy customer," explained the Marquis, "wants it to look like a meteorite just missed his house."

Zoyd eyed it gloomily. "Askin' for trouble, those folks. Messin' with Fate."

They went on back to the office. Blodwen, hair full of pens and pencils, peeping away at the computer, glared at Zoyd. "Elvissa just called in looking for you, your rig's been impounded." Ah shit, here it was. Elvissa had been in the Vineland Safeway and when she came back out to the lot had found more law enforcement than she'd seen since her old marching days, surrounding the pickup she'd borrowed that morning from Zoyd as if expecting it to pull a weapon on them. Elvissa tried to find out what was going on, but had no luck.

"Listen, Millard, m'man, think I may need a disguise, and soon — can I trouble you for a professional tip or two?"

"What'd you do, Zoyd?" Blodwen wanted to know.

"Innocent till proven guilty, whatever happened to that?"

"All's I'd like to know is will they be after your money," a familiar question around here, the subcontractor accounts collectively having more attachments on them than a vacuum cleaner, "More liens," Zoyd had once suggested, "than the Tower of Pisa," to which Blodwen had answered, "More garnishes than a California burger — spouses, ex-spouses, welfare, the bank, the Lost Nugget, haberdasheries in faraway zip codes, it's what you all get for leading these irregular lives."

"Looks like it's what *you* get," Zoyd had remarked.

"Is why most of you ringdings keep gettin' paid off the books," she'd advised, making a face Zoyd remembered from teachers in elementary school. She wasn't a bad person, though Zoyd theorized that she'd've been happier if they'd gone to Hollywood. Millard and Blodwen had met in a San Francisco theater group, she doing pretty-girl walk-ons and he thinking about specializing in Brecht — one night in the Haight somebody had some acid, and after careening for a while through the sixties, they alit from their anarcho-psychedelic spin twenty miles up a mud obstacle course referred to as a road only by those who'd never been near it, deep in the Vineland redwoods in a cabin by a stream from whose bed they could hear gold-bearing cobblestones knocking together at night. When the business took off they'd rented a house in town, but had held on to the place in the mountains, where they'd first come back to Earth.

"Little busy just this second," Millard handing Zoyd an envelope with a sum of greenbacks within, "later would be better — say Hon, what's the Eight O'Clock Movie?"

"Um, oh, it's Pat Sajak in *The Frank Gorshin Story.*"

"Say about ten, ten-thirty?"

"Yikes, got to call Trent, he needs his rig."

Trent, a sensitive poet-artist from the City, had moved up north here for his nerves, which at the moment were not at their most tranquil. "Armed personnel carriers," Trent trying to scream and keep his voice down at the same time, "persons in full battle gear stomping through vegetable patches, somebody said they shot

Stokely's dog, I'm in here with a thirty-aught-six I don't even know how to load, Zoyd, what's gooeen *ahn?*"

"Wait, easy pardner, now it sounds like CAMP," meaning the infamous federal-state Campaign Against Marijuana Production, "but it ain't quite the season yet."

"It's you, fucker," Trent blubbering now, "they're usin' your place for a headquarters, everything's thrown out in the yard, they sure must've found your stash by now. . . ."

"Do they know what I'm driving?"

"Not from me."

"Thanks Trent. Don't know when —"

"Don't say it," Trent warned, sniffling, "see you whenever," and hung up.

Zoyd thought his best bet might be to find an RV park some-place and try to blend in. He reserved a space a few miles out of town up Seventh River under a fake name, praying nobody was listening in on this phone. Then, gingerly, proceeded in the cedar-shake eyesore to Bodhi Dharma Pizza, which he could hear tonight before he saw it. All the occupants of the place were chanting, something that, with vibes of trouble to come, he recognized — not the words, which were in Tibetan, but the tune, with its bone-stirring bass, to a powerful and secret spell against invaders and oppressors, heard in particular a bit later in the year at harvest time, when CAMP helicopters gathered in the sky and North California, like other U.S. pot-growing areas, once again rejoined, operationally speaking, the third world.

As Zoyd was about to pull into the lot, the first thing he saw through the front window was Hector standing tensely up on a table, completely surrounded by chanting pizza customers and staff. Zoyd kept driving, found a public phone, and called Doc Deeply at the Vineland Palace. "I don't know how dangerous he is or how long I can stall him, so try to make it soon, OK?"

Back inside Bodhi Dharma Pizza, Hector was furiously on de-fense, eyes inflamed, haircut askew. "Zoyd! ¡Órale, carnal! Tell these people how much I don' need this shit!"

"Where's my kid, Hector?"

Back in the employees' toilet, as it turned out, where Prairie had locked the door. Zoyd went and stood hollering back and forth with her, trying to keep an eye on Hector at the same time, while the deep chanting continued.

"He says he knows where my mom is." Her voice wary.

"He doesn't know where she is, he was askin' me the other day, now he's tryin' to use you."

"But he said, she told him that — she really wants to see me. . . ."

"He's bullshittin' you, Prairie, he's DEA, his business is lying."

"Please," Hector called, "could you do somethín about the glee club here, 'causs it's makín me, I don' know, weird?"

"You're abducting my kid, Hector?"

"She wants to come with me, asshole!"

"That true, Prair?"

The door opened. Big fat tears were rolling down her cheeks, with little swirls of violet eye makeup. "Dad, what is it?"

"He's crazy. He escaped from the Detox."

"You better know how to protect her, Wheeler," the federale getting frantic now. "You better have some resources, you're gonna wish she *was* with me before too long, *ése,* I ain't the only stranger in town today."

"Yeah you must mean that army up at my place — tell me Hector, who is that?"

"Anybody less of a fool would know already. It's a Justice Department strike force, they got military backup, and it's beín led by your old pal himself, Brock Vond, remember him? Man who took your ol' lady away from you, hah, *cabrón?*"

"Well, shit." Zoyd had just assumed all along they were Hector's people, DEA plus their local dope-squad tagalongs. But Brock Vond was a federal prosecutor, a Washington, D.C., heavy and, as Hector had so helpfully recalled, the expediter of most of Zoyd's years of long and sooner or later tearful nights down in places like the Lost Nugget. Why, at this late date, would the man be coming after Zoyd full-scale like this, unless it had something to do with Frenesi, and the old sad story?

"And you might as well forget about goín home, chump, 'cause you got no more home, paperwork's already in the mill to confiscate it under civil RICO, 'causs guess what, Zoyd, they found marijuana? in yer house! Yah, must've been two ounces of the shit, although we're gonna call it tons."

"Dad, what's he talkin' about?"

"They're up 'ere all right, Trooper."

"My diary? My hair stuff, my clothes? Desmond?"

"We'll get 'em all back," as she moved beside him into a one-arm embrace. He believed what he was saying, because he couldn't quite believe the other yet. Trent could've been taking some artistic liberties, right? Hector could be having a Tubal fantasy provoked by watching too many cop shows?

"Then I still need to know," Zoyd addressed the beleaguered narc up on the table, "why Brock Vond and his army is doin' this to me."

As if their chanting had been recitative for Hector's aria, everyone now fell silent and attended. He stood beneath a stained-glass window made in the likeness of an eightfold Pizzic Mandala, in full sunlight a dazzling revelation in scarlet and gold, but at the moment dark, only tweaked now and then by headlights out in the street.

"It ain't that I don' have Hollywood connections. I know Ernie Triggerman. Yeah and Ernie's been waitín years for the big Nostalgia Wave to move along to the sixties, which according to his demographics is the best time most people from back then are ever goín to have in their life — sad for them maybe, but not for the picture business. Our dream, Ernie's and mine, is to locate a legendary observer-participant from those times, Frenesi Gates — your ex-ol' lady, Zoyd, your mom, Prairie — and bring her up out of her mysterious years of underground existence, to make a Film about all those long-ago political wars, the drugs, the sex, the rock an' roll, which th' ultimate message will be that the real threat to America, then and now, is from th' illegal abuse of narcotics?"

Zoyd squinted. "Oh, Hector. . . ."

"I'll show you the figures," Hector raved on, "even with a 1% penetration we're oll gonna be rich forever off of this, man!"

"About this 'we,' " Zoyd was wondering, "have you brought Cap'n Vond on board this project yet, you and this Ernie?"

Hector was looking down at his shoes. "We didt'n finalize it."

"Y'haven't been in touch with him at all, right?"

"Well I don't know who is, *ése* — nobody's returnín calls."

"I don't believe this, you wantin' to be in the world of entertainment, when all along I had you pegged as a real terrorist workin' for the State? When you said cuttin' and shootin' I didt'n know you were talkin' about film. I thought th' only kind of options you cared about were semi- and full automatic. Why, I'm lookin' at Steven Spielberg, here."

"Risking a lifelong career in law enforcement," put in the saintly night manager, who called himself Baba Havabananda, "in the service of the ever-dwindling attention span of an ever more infantilized population. A sorry spectacle."

"Yah, well you sound like Howard Cosell."

"So Brock Vond taking over my place, Hector, that's got nothin' to do with your movie scheme, that correct?"

"Unless . . . ," Hector looking almost bashful.

Zoyd saw it coming. "Unless he's out looking for her too?"

"For," in a low suave croak, "let us say, motives of his own."

At which point, finally, in through the doors front and rear of Bodhi Dharma Pizza came the NATO-camouflaged guys and gals of the Tubaldetox goon squad, to bring Hector gently "back to where we can help you," cajoling him through the crowd, who'd begun to chant again. Doc Deeply, grooming his beard, strode over, high-fiving Baba Havabananda on the way.

"Can't thank you enough, anything we can do —"

"Long as he'll be out of my face for a while."

"Don't count on it, we're only minimum-security down there. We can keep him under observation, but if he wants to, he can be back on the street inside of a week."

"I got a contract!" Hector was screaming as they loaded him into the Tubaldetox paddy wagon, which went screeching off just as Isaiah Two Four and his friends came screeching in.

The boy loomed over them, frowning, unfrowning, frowning again as Zoyd and Prairie filled him in and the other Vomitones made dangerous sounds. Finally, "This wedding gig down in the City . . . what if Prairie came with us for a while? Get her out of the area?"

"These are like armed forces, Isaiah, you want that responsibility?"

"I'll protect her," he whispered, looking around to see who was listening.

Prairie was, and getting annoyed. "What is this? Typical males, you're handin' me back and forth like a side of beef?"

"How about *pork?*" Isaiah, slightly to Zoyd's relief, at least this unwise, now actually trying to poke her playfully in the ribs while she smacked his hand away. Good luck, young fella.

"You already know how to live on the road," Zoyd said. "Do you think you might be safer if you kept movin'?"

She came into his arms. "Dad, our house. . . ." She wasn't crying, fucked if she'd cry. . . .

"Will you stay over with me tonight? Can Isaiah come get you in the morning?"

Hector was right, she admitted later, she had been ready to go with him and find Frenesi. "I love you, Dad. But it's incomplete." They were lying in bunk beds in the back of Trent's eccentric camper, listening to the foghorns down the river.

"You're Tubed out worse 'n Hector if you think your mom and me'll ever get back together."

"You keep saying. But if you were me, wouldn't you do the same?"

He hated questions like that. He wasn't her. She could make him feel so old and tainted. "Maybe what you really want's just to get out of the house."

"Uh-huh?"

Fair enough. "Well good timing, 'cause it looks like there is no house, this li'l Smurfmobile here's it."

"Did you know this was gonna happen? Someday? You did, didt'n you."

Zoyd hrrumphed. "Well — there was supposed to be a deal."
"When?"

"You were still a baby."

"Yeah so is that why you never got married again, was that part of your deal, that I was never supposed to have a mom —"

"Whoa, there, Trooper, who was I gonna hook up with, who

were all 'ese ladies kickin' in my door all the time? Thapsia? Elvissa? Don't matter? Just so's you can say you have some mom?"

"But all you ever date is this, sorry but rilly B material, in terms of family skills, girls you pick up when they're out on eating binges at the Arctic Circle Drive-In, girls from these weird after-hours clubs whose whole wardrobe is like totally black, girls who inject cough syrup with biker boyfriends named Aahhrrgghh — in fact lots of them girls I see in *school* every day? Know what I think?" She'd rolled out of her lower bunk to stand and look him in the face, level. "Is that, deal or no deal, you must have always loved my mom, so much that if it couldt'n be her, it wouldt'n be anybody."

No, that hadn't been part of the deal. The clarity of her gaze made him feel fraudulent and lost. About all he could manage was "Wow. You think I really am crazy, don't ya?"

"No, no —" quickly, her head dropping just for the moment, "Dad, that's exactly the way I feel too, that . . . she's the only one for me." Then shaking back her hair, looking up again, stubborn, sure, out of Frenesi's blue eyes. The moment may have called for him to embrace her, but her remarks, by now familiar, about the role of jailbait in his emotional life warned him that this time he'd better refrain, even now when he most needed some kind of hug himself — only nod instead and try to look competent, call her Trooper, maybe sock her on the shoulder for morale . . . but have to lie there nevertheless, a foot and a half overhead, and let her find and follow her own way to sleep.

In the morning, full of marsh birds, cigarette smoke, and television audio, down the two sand grooves of the access road came the Billy Barf and the Vomitones Official Van, with elaborate nukehappy cyberdeath graphics all over the outside and a ring of welded-together miniature iron skulls for a steering wheel, at which sat Isaiah Two Four. Other dimmer faces bloomed behind the tinted bubble windows. Zoyd had no clear idea of what Prairie might be going into, felt helpless, didn't even know if he'd missed something last night and she was really going away for good. They'd agreed to keep in touch through Sasha Gates, Zoyd's ex-mother-in-law, who lived down in L.A.

"Stay out of that joint, ol' pothead," Prairie said.

"Keep 'em legs together," he replied, "teen bimbo." Somebody put a Fascist Toejam cassette, 300 watts of sonic apocalypse, on to the van stereo, Isaiah gallantly handed Prairie up into the lurid fuchsia padding of this rolling orgy room, where she became indistinct among an unreadable pattern of Vomitones and their girlfriends, and quickly, in an arc unexpectedly graceful, they had all turned outward, tached up, engaged, and like a time machine departing for the future, forever too soon for Zoyd, boomed away up the thin, cloudpressed lane.

BUT just before she left, Zoyd had slipped Prairie a strange Japanese business card, or as some would call it, amulet, which, leery as always of anything that might mean unfinished business from the olden hippie times, the girl at first had been reluctant even to touch. Zoyd had received it years ago, in return for a favor. At the time he was working a Hawaiian cruise gig for Kahuna Airlines, a non-sked flying out of LAX's East Imperial Terminal, a gig he'd stumbled into in the turbulent last days of his marriage, out on one more desperate attempt, transpacific this time, to save the relationship, as he saw it, or, as she saw it, once again come messing with her privacy, red-eyeing in to Honolulu on a charter flight in an airplane of uncertain make that was not only the flagship but also the entire fleet of a country he had not, till then, heard of. If Frenesi was half expecting him, it was not in the condition he arrived in, taken over by an itch he could no longer control to see how she spent her evenings. "Me, I get through OK," practicing in front of a stained and cracked mirror in the airplane lavatory, whispering in the jet throb and structural creaking, "just worryin' about you, Frenesi," standing there miles above the great ocean making these faces at himself.

At first it had seemed like a terrific idea, a perfect break for them both, at a critical time. Sasha had been there too, to see her off on the flight, she and Zoyd handing the half-asleep Prairie back and forth, arms to arms, like a rehearsal of arrangements to come. It was a rare cooperative moment for the in-laws, in their mutual uneasiness, Sasha never having known really what to make of Zoyd, settling instead for a reflex headshake whenever they met, with an embarrassed laugh that seemed to mean, "You are so inappropriate for my daughter that even you must see it and be as amused as I am — we're adults after all, and we can certainly share a chuckle, can't we Zoyd." But they were to find themselves, amazingly, on the same side of the law after all, which meant no custodial battles ever, for as they both came to learn, no judge would waste the time deciding whose rap sheet was more disreputable — if it was a choice between a lifelong Red grandmother and a dope fiend father, Prairie would end up as a ward of the court, and no question, they had to keep her out of that. Like it or not, they would be forced, now and then anyway, to coordinate their lives.

"Feel like Mildred Pierce's husband, Bert," is how Zoyd described his inner feelings to Frenesi, having located her finally at the gigantic Dark Ocean Hotel, a towering dihedral wallful of 2,048 rooms with identical lanais cantilevered into blue space, all facing the Pacific. Far below, tiny figures rode the curl of the tiny surf, sunned upon the beach, frolicked in tiny glowing aqua pools set in tropical groves of deep green.

From any distance an observer would have noticed, here and there upon the great bent facade, folks on their lanais out taking the breezes, eating room-service banquets, smoking the local cannabis, fucking in semipublic.

"Appreciate the comparison Zoyd, although as you see I'm alone, yes quite alone, not that there aren't enough good-looking guys around. . . ."

"Ain't pickups I'm thinkin' of, or we could've had this li'l get-together *long* ago."

"Oh? When, exactly?"

"Nah, forget it."

"Wait a minute, you come barging in here —"

"Yeah and on my own ticket too," almost adding, "my mommy didt'n pay for it," but seeing she was expecting it, he let the wave go by uncaught.

In fact what he'd done was check in right next door to her, so that they were standing on adjacent lanais hundreds of feet above sea level having this adult discussion, each holding a can of beer, Frenesi in a bikini and Zoyd in an old pair of baggies — except for the lethal altitude, it could have been year before last, back in Gordita Beach. Above them somewhere another couple were screaming at each other, out of control. Their voices, punctuating, helped to calibrate Zoyd and Frenesi's own, though they could share no smug look meaning, "at least we're not that bad," because they knew better.

Zoyd couldn't help wondering, almost aloud, where Brock Vond, her charismatic little federal boyfriend, might be. Hiding under the bed in her room, copping rays down on the beach at Waikiki? Zoyd didn't want to be disappointed. It was ignorance of U.S. Attorney Vond's whereabouts, after all, a kind of reverse presence, that had helped fetch Zoyd across the Pacific Ocean in a plane whose airworthiness only grew, in memory, more doubtful.

Sasha had been no help either. "You can't bring me into this. I'm not going to fink on my own daughter, am I? Even if I knew anything in the first place, which I don't — why would she tell me?"

"Well — you're her mom."

"You got it."

"OK then, how about Brock Vond, who we both know for what he is, exactly the kind of criminal fascist you've been takin' honest shots at all your life — are you gonna be loyal to somebody like that? All's I'm askin'," dropping into gentler, con-man tones, "is didn't you ever meet him? See him face-to-face?"

Sasha could hear the pleading, close enough to whining to make her careful. This poor sap could too easily settle for any least shadow of pain, seemed to want to suffer every hurtful detail. Dummy. Why waste his time so? He looked old enough to've been through it before, but who knew, maybe this was his maiden voyage into the green seas of jealousy. She might have asked him, but her job these days, it seemed, was just to hold her tongue, keep it sharpened and ready but withheld in a sheath of silence. Doubly frustrating because she was furious as hell with her daughter. Frenesi's involvement with Brock, politically, was appalling enough, but she'd also once again failed to take care of business, and Sasha was as angry as she'd ever been at Frenesi's habit, developed early in life, of repeatedly ankling every situation that it should have been her responsibility to keep with and set straight. Far as Sasha could make out, this eagerness to flee hadn't faded any over the years, with its latest victim being Zoyd.

Who at the moment was pretending to have a look around Honolulu. "So — I don't see Superfuck anyplace, what happened, Steve McGarrett couldn't solve a case, had to call him in on it?"

"Zoyd, better lay off, we don't want any trouble."

That she could have said "we" so easily had him suddenly short of breath, numb, drawing blanks. "Trouble? Me? Hey —" unbuttoning the native shirt he'd bought, flapping his arms, "I'm clean, lady! I ain't gonna shoot some asshole just 'cause he's fuckin' my wife, 'specially if it's a federal rap," while he really wanted just to double over in a clenched bodyfist right in front of her face . . . except that she would only shift away those eyes of blue painted blue, as the Italian oldie goes, shift them away to sea, weather, any prop in visual reach, for deploying that blue whammy was just as good — she knew it — as touching, or taking touch away.

She withdrew into her room, slid the glass door shut, pulled the drapes. He stayed outside, contemplating the airspace between him and the ground. He was almost pissed off enough to do the deed on himself, almost. . . . He finished off the beer in his hand and with what he imagined as cold scientific interest dropped the empty can, observing it all the way down, particularly the convergence of its path with that of a pedestrian far below, a surfer carrying a board over his head. Seconds after the beer can hit the board, Zoyd heard the faint clank of impact, as the can meanwhile bounced away into a nearby pool and sank, leaving no proof of its visit but the ding on the board, whose perfect geometry the surfer was now examining closely, with suspicions extending well beyond Earth's orbit.

Back inside his room, first thing Zoyd looked for was a connecting door to Frenesi, but no such luck. He lay on the bed, flipped on the Tube, lit a joint, took out his cock, and imagined her beyond the drywall barriers that could as well have been the years to come, seeing her at least as clearly as he would later, again and again, on the astral night flights he would make to be near and haunt her as best he knew how, seeing her now taking off her bikini, top and bottom, then unhooking her earrings, an act, because of how it revealed her nape, that had never failed to stir

Zoyd's heart. She headed for the shower, feeling soiled, no doubt, by her encounter with him. Apprentice ghostly peeper, he went right along, watching the bathing ritual he'd once grown to take for granted, fool, now able only to fine-tune the way the steam came and went around her body, being limited, given his own incorporeal state, to the lightest of physical forms. . . .

As sex fantasies go, this one, especially for vile-minded Zoyd, was pretty bland. More like an ex fantasy. No outfits, accessories, or scenarios beyond this pure interaction of woman, water, soap, steam, and Zoyd's own unseen restlessly throbbing eye, registering it all. Getting accustomed to the only future they would have. What didn't enter into this was that Frenesi had in reality repacked her bags immediately and checked out, so quietly that Zoyd, preoccupied with jerking off, never noticed.

It wasn't till later, when he tried to get flowers delivered to her room, that he learned she was gone. He had to break down, cry, and divulge most of the story before he could get an assistant manager to admit that Frenesi had gone to the airport and had mentioned catching the next flight back to L.A. "Well, shit," said Zoyd.

"You're not going to do anything, mm, weird, are you?"

"How's that?"

"Hawaii is where men from California bring their broken hearts, seeking exotic forms of self-injury not so readily available on the mainland. Some specialize in active volcanoes, others in cliff diving, many go for the classier swimming-out-to-sea option. I can put you onto several travel agents who offer Suicide Fantasy packages, if you're interested."

"Fantasy!" Zoyd was sniffling again. "Who said anythin' about make-believe, dude? Don't you think I'm serious about this?"

" 'Course, of course, but please, just —"

"Only thing that holds me back," Zoyd blowing his nose at length, "is the indignity of lying there all splattered by the pool and in my last few seconds on Earth hearing Jack Lord say, 'Book him, Danno — Suicide One.' "

The assistant manager, long used to this kind of talk, let Zoyd ramble on for a while, then tactfully disengaged. Soon evening had swept in and wrapped the islands. After a short unintended beer nap, Zoyd got up, put a white suit he'd borrowed from Scott Oof on over his Hawaiian shirt, rolled up the cuffs of the pants, which were a little long, left open the jacket, too tight and also too long, giving it a zoot-suit effect, put on shades and a straw hat he'd got at the airport, and hit the street in search of someplace he could sit in on a keyboard instrument, preferably with people he knew. That he was not headed for the airport owed as much to the indecipherability of the fine print on his ticket, a special excursion offer nobody at the airline said they'd ever heard of, as to a strange cheery fatalism that had often, instead of tears, been known, as now, to overwhelm him. Fuck her, he chirped to himself, today's your release date, let ol' Brock have her, let him take her on into that lawyers' world where they can get away with anything and get everything they want, and someday when the little bastard is running for national office, there together on the evening news they'll be, and you can pop a beer and toast the screen and think of that last time up on the balconies, her turning away, sashaying ass in that tiny flowered bikini bottom, hair swinging, the window sliding, no look back. . . .

He bounced slowly from one Honolulu bar to another, allowing himself to trust to the hidden structures of night in a city, to a gift he sometimes thought he had for drifting, if not into intersections of high drama and significant fortune, at least away, most of the time, from danger. At some point he found himself back in the toilet of the Cosmic Pineapple, a then-notorious acid-rock club, conferring with a bass player he'd worked with, who told him about the lounge-piano opening at Kahuna Airlines.

"A gig of death," his friend assured him, "nobody knows how they stay in business, and that's not the only mystery, either." There were unconfirmed reports of incidents high above the planetary surface that no one talked about in any but the most careful euphemisms. The list of passengers who arrived was not always identical to the list of those who'd departed. Something was happening, in between, up there.

"Sounds like just what I'm lookin' for," Zoyd figured, "who do I see?" Turned out to be a 24-hour number in the Yellow Pages,

with a display ad whose biggest type read ALWAYS HIRING. Zoyd
called them at about 2:30 A.M. and was signed up on the spot for
a dawn takeoff to L.A. He had just time enough to get back to
the hotel and check out.

Each 747 in the Kahuna Airlines fleet had been gutted and
refitted as a huge Hawaiian restaurant and bar, full of hanging
island vegetation, nightclub chairs and tables instead of airplane
seats, even a miniature waterfall. In-flight movies included *Hawaii*
(1966), *The Hawaiians* (1970), and *Gidget Goes Hawaiian* (1961),
among others. Zoyd was presented with a thick tattered fake book
full of Hawaiian tunes, and on the lounge synthesizer, a Japanese
make he'd heard of but never played, he found a ukulele option
that would provide up to three orchestral sections of eight ukes
each. It would take several flights across the Pacific Ocean and
back before Zoyd felt easy with this by no means user-friendly
instrument. The critter liked to drift off pitch on him, or worse,
into that shrillness that sours the stomach, curtails seduction, poi-
sons the careful ambience. Nothing he could find in the dash-one
under the seat ever corrected what he more and more took to be
conscious decisions by the machine.

Many would be the starry night, transparent dome overhead,
subpurple neon outlining the baby-grand synthesizer, that Zoyd's
fingers would creep the keys in auto mode while his mind occupied
itself with sorrows attending the ongoing self-destruction of his
marriage. Layovers in L.A. usually were only long enough for
phone calls she didn't return, seldom for visits to Prairie and her
grandmother, but never even the sight of Frenesi, who would have
already slipped out. On westbound flights, Zoyd's job at the keyboard, like that of the hula dancers, flame eaters, cocktail waitresses, and bartenders, was to keep passengers from thinking about
what lay in store for them on the Honolulu end, the luggage
misconnected and untraceable, the absent bus links to hotels which
had already lost everybody's reservations, the failure of Jack Lord
to show up, as promised in the brochure, for photo opportunities.
Kahuna's all but unpredictable scheduling produced arrival times
lost in midwatch hours when airport security grew eager to play
roles with disagreeable subtexts, harassing the single women,

sweating the dopers, abusing the elderly and foreign, staring, needling, trying to get something going. Where were the traditional local cuties with the flower leis, one for each deplaning neck? "For you?" the armed, uniformed gents all broke out into high barks of laughter. "At this hour? What for?"

And then there was the sky — something going on in between air terminals. Zoyd had been hearing rumors since that first Cosmic Pineapple encounter, and then later from coworkers such as Gretchen the make-believe Polynesian cocktail waitress, to whom he had introduced himself with an arpeggiated E flat 7th and some original material that went

> Whoa! Come 'n' let me roll that
> Little grass skirt,
> In the Zig Zag, of my em-
> Brace!
>
> Light on up, with th'
> Flame of love, take
> The frown right, off o' your face!
>
> Put it in a roach clip,
> Pass it to and fro,
> In between your lips and let th'
> Good smoke flow, oh
>
> It won't cost much, and
> It ain't gonna hurt, just
> C'mere with that uh little, grass skirt!

— long before the final bars of which she would usually have escaped his clutches, halfhearted, let's face it, to begin with, a social approach, considering the fog of postmarital misjudgment he was groping around in all the time back then, not so hopelessly offensive, anyway, that Gretchen wouldn't allow him points for going to the trouble. They presently had reached a keel even enough for her to start confiding things she'd heard, and after a while things she'd witnessed as well. Aircraft that came alongside and, matching course and speed exactly to those of the jet, hung there, fifty feet away, windowless, almost invisible, sometimes for hours. "UFO's?"

"Not —" she hesitated, the grass skirt, which was actually polyester, rustling rhythmically, "what *we'd* call a UFO. . . ."

"Well who would?"

"Just that they looked too familiar . . . up from Earth, for sure, not in from . . . out there or nothin'."

"You ever see who was flyin' 'em?"

Her eyes flickered in every direction they could before she murmured, "I'm not crazy, ask Fiona, ask Inga, we've all seen 'm."

He played four bars of "Do You Believe in Magic?" and squinted up at her, eyes mostly lingering on the synthetic skirt. "Will I see them, Gretchen?"

"Better hope you don't," but as she was soon to add, he must not've been hoping hard enough, because on their very next flight out of LAX, about 37,000 feet above the middle of the ocean, the festive jumbo was taken, the way a merchant's ship and cargo might be by pirates, an easy target, an aluminum shell dainty as a robin's egg to the other, which was solid, smaller, of higher mass and speed. As Gretchen had foretold, not exactly a UFO. The captain took what evasive action he could, but the other matched his maneuvers exactly. Finally they stood, side by side above the tropic of Cancer, between them, some twenty meters across, a flow of savage wind, as, slowly, not telescoping out, but assembling itself from small twinkling pieces of truss-work, the other spun across to them a windproof access tunnel, with a cross section like a long teardrop, that locked firmly on to the forward hatch of the Boeing.

In the plane, passengers milled among the resined hatch-cover tables, the plastic tikis and shrubbery, clutching their oversize paper-parasoled drinks, Zoyd attempting to keep up a medley of peppy tunes. Nobody knew what was going on. Arguments started. Through the port-side windows could be observed the burnished seams, the glowing engines of the other. Last sunlight lay in bands at the horizon, and some of the windows had begun to ice up, not in the quiescent way of frost on a kitchen window on Earth, but in a stressed clash of jet-speed geometries.

When the hatch at last sighed open, the intruders entered the flying nightclub with elite-unit grace, automatics ready, faces dim behind high-impact shields, all business. Everyone was ordered to a seat. The captain came on the PA. "This is for our own good. They don't want all of us, just a few. When they get to your seat number, please cooperate, and try not to believe any rumors you hear. And till we get the rest of you where your tickets say you're going, all drinks are on the Kahuna Airlines Contingency Fund!" which brought loud applause but would prove, in the drawn-out litigation attending this incident, to have been an appeal to a fictional entity.

Gretchen dropped by the synthesizer just to take a breather. "This is fun," Zoyd said. "First time I ever heard the cap'n's voice. If he can sing 'Tiny Bubbles,' I'm out of a job."

"Everybody's nervous and drinking. What a bummer. Kahuna Airlines done it again."

"This doesn't happen on the majors?"

"There was some kind of a industry-wide agreement? It would have cost more than Kahuna wanted to spend. The word they all use is 'insurance.' "

Night fell like the end of a movie. The alcohol flowed torrentially, and soon it was necessary to switch over to a reserve tank of inexpensive vodka, located in the wing. Some passengers fell unconscious, some glazed out, others kicked off their shoes and partied, notwithstanding the grim shielded troopers working slowly, methodically among them. As Zoyd was segueing into the main title theme from *Godzilla, King of the Monsters* (1956), he was distracted by a voice somewhere behind and slightly below him. "What it is, bro! OK if I — sit in?" He saw somebody in a blond hippie haircut, floral bell-bottoms, and tropical shirt, with a dozen or so plastic leis piled up around his face and shoulders, plus some pitch-black goggle-style shades and a straw hat, holding a banjo-ukulele of between-the-wars vintage. The hair turned out to be a wig, borrowed from Gretchen, who had also suggested Zoyd for sanctuary.

"Man's after you, eh," smoothly, finding a lead sheet with, inevitably, uke diagrams on it. "How about this?"

"Uh-huh!" the strange ukulelist replied. "But it'd be easier — in the key of G!" Ukulele talk, all right, the new sideman proceeding to turn in a respectable rhythm job on the old Hawaiian favorite "Wacky Coconuts," though when Zoyd took the vocal he got confused enough to have to go back to the tonic and wait.

Can't ya hear . . . them . . .
(vumm) Uh Wack-ky Coconuts,
(hm) Uh Wack-ky Coconuts,
Thumpin' in a syn-copated island,
Melodee . . .
Con-tinuouslee. . . .

Yes one by one those
(vum) Wack-ky Coconuts,
(vum) Wack-ky Coconuts,
Fallin' on m' roof like th' beat of some
Jungle drum . . . (mm!)
Vum-vum vum!

Why won't those
Ol' Wack-ky Coconuts, find some other place?
Why should I remain in Wack-
Ky Coconuts' embrace? Must be wacky 'bout

(vum!) Wack-ky Coconuts,
(vum!) Oh, those loco nuts,
They're the coconuts
For me!

The pursuers moved along among the boogeying and the cataplectic, none of them giving the strumming fugitive much of a look, in search, it seemed, of some different profile. Further, Zoyd noticed that every time he hit his highest B flat, the invaders would grab for their radio headsets, as if unable to hear or understand the signal, so he tried to play the note whenever he could, and soon was watching them withdraw in a blank perplexity.

Zoyd's odd visitor, with ritual economy, held out a business card, iridescent plastic, colors shifting around according to cues that couldn't always be sensed.

"My life — looks like you saved it!" The card read,

Takeshi Fumimota
ADJUSTMENTS
Phone Book, Many Areas

"That's you? Takeshi?"

"Like Lucy and Ethel — if you're ever in a jam!" He played a few bars on the uke. "At the point in your life when you really need this, you will — suddenly remember! that you have this card — and where you have stashed it!"

"Not with my memory."

"You'll remember." It was then that he simply faded into the environment, became invisible in what would be a nightlong party that now, with the departure of their visitors, had shifted into high.

"He-e-e-y," Zoyd spoke to the room, "I heard of job skills like that, but don't know that I'd care to associate with that heavy-duty type of a hombre, nothin' personal understand, that is o' course if you're still someplace you can hear me. Hah?" No reply. The card went into a pocket, then another, into a long sequence of pockets, wallets, envelopes, drawers, and boxes, surviving bar-rooms, laundromats, doper's forgetfulness, and North Coast winters, till the morning, not knowing if he'd ever see her again, when he suddenly remembered where it was after all the years and gave it to Prairie, as if she were supposed to be the one to have it all along.

HOME between shifts, Frenesi sat with a cup of coffee at a kitchen table in an apartment in the older, downtown section of a pale humid Sun Belt city whose almost-familiar name would soon enough be denied to civilian eyes by federal marker pens, sunlight streaming in unmitigated by tree leaves, feeling herself, like a tune that always finds its home chord again, drawn, taken in, tranquilized by hopeful rearrangements of the past, many of them, like today's, including her unknown daughter, Prairie, last seen as a baby smiling half-toothless at her, trusting her to be back that evening as usual, trying to wiggle out of Zoyd's arms, that last time, and into Frenesi's own. For years, whenever she and Flash moved in anyplace new, in a reflex superstition by now like sprinkling salt and water in every room, her thoughts would go to Prairie, and to where, in each new arrangement, she would sleep — sometimes the baby, sometimes a girl she was free to imagine.

Down the block, circular saws were braying metallically *eee-yuh! eee-yuh!* among hammerfalls, truck engines, truck stereos, not much of it registering now as Frenesi entertained images of a nubile teen Prairie, looking something like herself, in some California beach pad, wearing centerfold attire and squirming in the embrace of some surf bum with a downy mustache, named Shawn or Erik, among plastic swag lamps, purring audio gear, stained hamburger sacks, and squashed beer cans. But if I saw her on the street someplace, she reminded herself, I wouldn't even know her . . . one more teenage girl, no different from any of the mall rats she saw at work every day out at Southplex, one of four shopping malls, named for points of the compass, that bracketed the city, hundreds of these girls a day, whom she watched on the sly, nervous as a peeper, curious about how they moved and spoke, what they were into — that desperate for any detail, however abstractly Prairie so far away might share it with her generation.

She couldn't talk about much of this to Flash. Not that he "wouldn't understand" — two of his own kids were also somewhere denied him — but there was a level past which his attention began to wander. He might have been crazy enough to think she was somehow trying to rewrite all their history, being known to say things like, "Aw, it was just a judgment call, hon. Say you'd've tried to stay away, could've been even worse," eyebrows up and cocked in a way he knew women read as sincere, "old Brock come after you then no matter where you took her, and —" a sour grin, "ka-pow!"

"Oh, come on," she objected, "not with some little baby."

"Son of a bitch was fairly irate, that first time you tried to split, first time I ever heard your name, in fact. He totally lost it there for about a week." Brock Vond's screams, from the sealed upper floors of the looming federal monolith in Westwood, could be heard down echoing in the tranquillity of the veterans' graveyard as well as out on the freeway above the traffic noise, regardless of the hour. Nobody in that crisis knew what to do with Brock, who clearly needed some R and R over at "Loco Lodge," a Justice Department mental resort in the high desert. But none of the new Nixonian hires in internal affairs could even discover how to process him out there. Finally, after what to some had been far too long, he quieted down enough to pack up on his own one day and head back to D.C., where he was supposed to've been all along, so the paperwork on him just got shredded in California. But it was to be a while yet before reports stopped coming in from lunch counters and saloons, often known to have strictly enforced attitude codes, in unlikely West Coast locales, of disruptions by a, some said "wild-eyed," others "terminally depressed," Brock Vond. Many informants said they'd expected him to take off his clothes and do something unspeakable.

"Well, what a wacko!" commented Frenesi. They were sitting in their new kitchen — light shades of wood, Formica, houseplants, better than some places they'd been in, although the fridge here might have a bum thermostat. She took his hand and tried to catch his eyes. "Just the same, later on, I could have run. Just taken her, taken my baby, and fuckin' run."

"Yep," head stubbornly down, nodding.

"And it really matters, and don't say judgment call either, 'cause this isn't the damn NFL."

"Just tryin' to help." He squeezed her hand. "It sure wa'n't easy for me, you know, Ryan and Crystal . . . meant me givin' extra handouts on that chow line for the duration, just to find out their new *names,* way back when."

"Yeah. Great duty." Each sat recalling Brock Vond's reeducation camp, where they'd met. "Do you ever dream about it?"

"Uh-huh. Gets fairly vivid."

"Heard you," she said, "one or two nights," adding, "even all the way across town."

They then had a good mutual look. Her blue eyes and the clear child's brow above had always had power to touch him, he felt it now simultaneously in the heels of his hands, in his lower gums, and in the chi spot between his navel and his cock, a glow, a good-natured turn to stone, some hum warning of possible overflow into words that, if experience was any guide, would get them in trouble.

From Frenesi's side of the table, Flash was an absorber of light, somebody she had to look for to see and work to know, to whom she tithed too much of her energy, especially the times he was "across town," his phrase for out chasing other women. He liked to prowl the shady office complexes in the downtowns of these Sun Belt cities, looking for educated ladies in business suits who craved outlaw leather. No question, a pain in the ass — but alone, she thought, she would perish, too exposed, not resourceful enough. She thought, It's too late, we're locked into this, imagining often a turn of the conversation that would allow her to say, "All those guys — Flash, I knew it hurt you, I hated it, I'm sorry." But he would say, "Promise me you'll never do it again." She'd say, "How can I? Once they find out you're willing to betray somebody you've been to bed with, once you get that specialist's code attached to you, don't have to be glamour beefs like high treason anymore, they can use you the same way for anything, on any scale, all the way down to simple mopery, anytime they want to get some local judge tends to think with his dick, it's your phone

that rings around dinnertime, and there goes the frozen lasagna."
And he would have no answer, and it would be Frenesi who'd
bravely bring up impossibilities. "Fletcher, let's get the hell out of
this, on our own, for good . . . find a place? Buy it?" Sometimes
she even said it out loud. His answer was always not "Let's do
that" but "Sure . . . we could do that. . . ." And soon there'd be
only another posting, another defective rental the stipend check
would barely cover. Was anybody even looking anymore? Had
she ever believed in the federal promises of protection? Some fairy-
tale fleet of unmarked government cars circulating in round-the-
clock shifts, watching over them all asleep in their beds, making
sure their witnesses would all stay protected forever?

Silence in the place, their son, Justin, asleep in the Tubelight.
Prairie, who hadn't ever been there. The philodendron and the
parlor palm, wondering what was going on, and Eugene the cat,
who probably knew. Frenesi took her hand away from Flash's and
they all got back to business, the past, a skip tracer with an ob-
sessional gleam in its eye, and still a step or two behind, appeased
for only a little while. Sure, she knew folks who had no problem
at all with the past. A lot of it they just didn't remember. Many
told her, one way and another, that it was enough for them to get
by in real time without diverting precious energy to what, face it,
was fifteen or twenty years dead and gone. But for Frenesi the past
was on her case forever, the zombie at her back, the enemy no
one wanted to see, a mouth wide and dark as the grave.

When the sixties were over, when the hemlines came down and
the colors of the clothes went murky and everybody wore makeup
that was supposed to look like you had no makeup on, when
tatters and patches had had their day and the outlines of the
Nixonian Repression were clear enough even for the most gaga
of hippie optimists to see, it was then, facing into the deep autumnal wind of what was coming, that she thought, Here, finally —
here's my Woodstock, my golden age of rock and roll, my acid
adventures, my Revolution. Come into her own at last, street-
legal, full-auto qualified, she understood her particular servitude
as the freedom, granted to a few, to act outside warrants and
charters, to ignore history and the dead, to imagine no future, no

yet-to-be-born, to be able simply to go on defining moments only, purely, by the action that filled them. Here was a world of simplicity and certainty no acidhead, no revolutionary anarchist would ever find, a world based on the one and zero of life and death. Minimal, beautiful. The patterns of lives and deaths. . . .

What she hadn't been able to imagine, in the improvident rush of those early days, was that Nixon and his gang would also pass, Hoover die, even charades one day be enacted in which citizens could pretend to apply for and if found worthy read edited versions of their own government dossiers. Watergate and its many spinoffs ended the gilded age for Flash and Frenesi. She remembered him staying home for weeks, watching the hearings all day and then again on the public channel at night, on the floor with his face right up in the Tube, as intense as she ever saw him, all that summer pissing and moaning in front of the twitching little screen. He saw the retrenchment coming, the little or no per diem, the vouchers returned, denied, withdrawn — no more airport Ramada Inn suites, gran turismo-type auto rentals, PX privileges, cafeteria freebies, costume allowances, or, in all but operational emergencies, even collect calls. The personnel changed, the Repression went on, growing wider, deeper, and less visible, regardless of the names in power, office politics far away now determined the couple's posting to new addresses and missions, each another step away from costly pleasures, from boldness of scale, with less reason even to carry a weapon, becoming tangled in an infinite series of increasingly squalid minor sting operations of steadily diminishing scope and return, against targets so powerless compared to those who were setting them up that some other motive, less luminous than that of the national interest, must have been at work. Each time there'd be another script for them to learn, dumber than the last, actual detailed lines they had to practice with each other even though they wouldn't always work together. Flash would disappear for long stretches, he never volunteered where, and sometimes, sure, it could have been other women. Frenesi had run a quick estimate in her mind of how likely, barring a surprise confession, she'd be ever to find out, and decided there was no point worrying. She came to believe it was his way of expressing how he felt about what they had ended up doing with their lives, and who for.

"Tough to admit," she tried once to confide to him, "that those first couple college jobs were as good as it's ever gonna get."

"Another pussy routine," speculated Flash.

"Fletcher —"

"Oh, *I'm* sorry! I meant 'vagina,' of course!"

One of Flash's big sorrows was that once, not long ago, he'd been as outlaw as they come, grand theft auto, hard and dangerous drugs, small arms and dynamite and epic long hauls by the dark of the moon. But then he got caught, and his little teen wife left him, and the court took his babies away, and Flash was turned, left with no choice but to work his way up on their side of the law, soon finding that nobody trusted him enough to bring him all the way inside any structure of the governance. So there he had to hang, on the outside, part of the decoration, clinging with all the others he ran or was run by, gargoyles living on a sheer vertical facade. He knew they would only let him go where nothing would be damaged if he should turn again. It would mean a twenty- or thirty-year orbit around the lurid neon planet of adolescence — an entire adult career to be spent as a teenager under surveillance, none of whose "family" would ever believe in him.

In his DMV and jail photos, in Christmas Polaroids, in old crowd scenes too low-resolution to see whose face it was, Flash appeared always the same, unsmiling, a lean, prematurely drawn young man, alert and drug-free, with some local stylist's idea of a haircut. Trapped long ago into making believe he always knew what he was doing, he'd found it working so well at the start that soon he was keeping up the act even when there was "nobody else around," as Wilson Pickett might say. His family obligations were clear enough these days, if not always compelling enough, and so, unable to imagine the three of them ever parting, he soldiered through his duties with what looked like cheerful stoicism, except that underneath he remained a flaming and extravagant complainer, having learned how to use this aggressively, to negotiate for some of what he wanted from the world. His whammy was indignation — believing he'd been injured, he was able with the force of his belief to convince strangers with no possible connection to the case at hand that they were guilty. Out on the highway, especially, he'd been known to go actively chasing down motorcycle police, forcing them over to the shoulder, jumping out to pick fights. The unfortunate trooper would cower sidesaddle in his bike seat, squirming, thinking, This is crazy, but unable to find the button on his transmitter . . . strange. . . . "Furthermore, just 'cause they let you ride around on this li'l — lookit this piece of shit, I seen mopeds't could shut this 'sucker down, what *is* this, who *makes* it, Fisher-Price? Mattel? zis Barbie's Motorbike or some shit?" In some men such querulousness might indicate a soft streak a yard wide, but not in Flash, a vigilante of civil wrongs, settling things with his lethal and large-caliber mouth.

Many in the snitch community approved, being long unhappy with the old informant image of weasel-like furtiveness. "Why should we lurk around like we're ashamed of what we do?" Flash wondered. "Everybody's a squealer. We're in th' Info Revolution here. Anytime you use a credit card you're tellin' the Man more than you meant to. Don't matter if it's big or small, he can use it all."

Frenesi let him rave on. Her childhood and adolescence had been full enough of taps on the phone, cars across the street, name-calling and fights in school. Not exactly a red-diaper baby, she'd grown up more on the fringes of the political struggle in Hollywood back in the fifties, but the first rule was still that you didn't talk about anybody else, especially not about their allegiances. Her mother then had worked as a script reader and her father, Hub Gates, as a gaffer, always under dreamlike turns of blacklist, graylist, secrets kept and betrayed, grown-ups acting like the worst kind of kids, kids acting like they knew what was going on. As house receptionist, Frenesi'd had to learn to keep straight a whole list of fake names, and who used which to whom. Whatever it was, she hated and feared it, one set of grown-ups bitterly against another, words and names she didn't understand, though she knew when Sasha was between jobs or when Hub was fired off a picture, the two of them looking at each other a lot but not talking that much — a good time, Frenesi learned, to keep out of the way.

Frenesi the baby had come along a little after World War II ended, her name celebrating the record by Artie Shaw that was all over the jukeboxes and airwaves in the last days of the war, when Hub and Sasha were falling in love. Frenesi had a version of how they'd met, an upsweep come partly unpinned, a jaunty angle of sailor hat over eyebrow, jitterbug music, a crowded endless dance floor, palm trees, sunsets, warships in the Bay, smoke in the air, everybody smoking, chewing gum, drinking coffee, some all at the same time. A common awareness, as Frenesi imagined it, no matter whose eyes should meet, of being young and alive in perilous times, and together for a night.

"Oh, Frenesi," her mother would sigh when presented with this costume drama, "if you'd been there, you'd chirp a different tune. Try being a woman who also happens to be political, in the middle of a global war sometime. Especially with all those revved-up gentlemen around. I was one confused cookie."

She'd come down by old 101 from the redwoods to the City, a teenage beauty with the same blue eyes and wolf-whistle legs her daughter would have, out on her own early because of too many mouths to feed at home. Her father, Jess Traverse, trying to organize loggers in Vineland, Humboldt, and Del Norte, had suffered an accident arranged by one Crocker "Bud" Scantling for the Employers' Association, in plain sight of enough people who'd get the message, at a local ball game, where he was playing center field. The tree, one of a stand of old redwoods just beyond the fence, had been cut in advance almost all the way through. Nobody in the stands heard saw strokes, wedges being knocked loose . . . nobody could believe, when it began to register, the slow creaking detachment from the lives around it as the tree began its descent. Voices found at last only reached Jess in time for him to dive out of the way, to save his life but not his mobility, as the redwood fell across his legs, crushing them, driving half of him into the earth. There was then guilt money from the Association — cash in a market bag, left in the car — a small pension, a few insurance checks, but not enough to keep three kids on. They had a local attorney for the damned, sure no George Vandeveer, working on the case, but not hard enough or near enough to Scantling to matter.

Sasha's mother, Eula, was a Becker, from Beaverhead County, Montana, who'd been bounced as a baby upon the knees of family friends known to have shot at as well as personally dropped company finks, styled "inspectors," down mine shafts so deep you might as well say they ran all the way to Hell. Meeting Jess had been blind fate, she wasn't even supposed to be in town that night, ran into some girlfriends who talked her into going down to the IWW hall in Vineland, where they knew some fellows, and the minute Eula walked in, there he was, and as she found out not long after, the real Eula Becker too. "Jess introduced me to my conscience," she liked to say in later years. "He was the gatekeeper to the rest of my life." Wobblies, sneered at by the property owners of Vineland, and even some renters, as I-Won't-Works, were not known as nest builders or great marriage material, but Eula, meeting herself, discovered what she really wanted — the road, his road, his bindlestiff life, his dangerous indenture to an idea, a dream of One Big Union, what Joe Hill was calling "the commonwealth of toil that is to be." Soon she was with him in somber mill towns among logged-off slopes, speaking on the corners of mud streets lined with unpainted shacks and charred redwood snags, no green anywhere, addressing strangers as "class brother," "class sister," getting arrested at free-speech fights, making love in the creekside alders at the May Day picnic, getting used to an idea of "together" that included at least one of them being in jail in any given year. She would remember the first time she was shot at, by Pinkertons in a camp up along the Mad River, more clearly than the birth of her first child, who was Sasha. With Jess's crippling, she arrived at last at the condition of cold, perfected fury she had been growing into, as she now understood, all these years. "Wish I could just pick up my bindle and come along with you," she told Sasha when she left, "there's nothing much for us in this town anymore. All we can do about it now is just stay. Just piss on through. Be here to remind everybody — any time they see a Traverse, or a Becker for that matter, they'll remember that one tree, and who did it, and why. Hell of a lot better 'n a statue in the park."

Sasha left for the City, got work, began sending back what she could. She found a rip-roaring union town, still riding the waves of euphoria from the General Strike of '34. She hung around with stevedores and winch drivers who'd been there to roll ball bearings under the hooves of the policemen's horses. By the time the war came along she'd worked in stores, offices, shipyards, and airplane plants, had soon learned of the effort to organize farm workers in the valleys of California, known as the Inland March, and gone out there for a while to help, living on ditch-banks with Mexican and Filipino immigrants and refugees from the dust bowl, standing midwatch guard against vigilante squads and hired goons from the Associated Farmers, getting herself shot at more than once, writing home about it. "Something, isn't it?" Eula wrote back. Growing up, Frenesi heard stories of those prewar times, the strike at the Stockton cannery, strikes over Ventura sugar beets, Venice lettuce, San Joaquin cotton . . . of the anticonscription movement in Berkeley, where, as Sasha was careful to remind her, demonstrations had been going on before Mario Savio was born, not only in Sproul Plaza but against Sproul himself. Somewhere Sasha had also found time to work for Tom Mooney's release, fight the infamous antipicket ordinance, Proposition One, and campaign for Culbert Olson in '38.

"The war changed everything. The deal was, no strikes for the duration. Lot of us thought it was some last desperate capitalist maneuver, a way to get the Nation mobilized under a Leader, no different than Hitler or Stalin. But at the same time, so many of us really loved FDR. I got so distracted I quit working for a while even though there were these incredible jobs everywhere, just 'cause I had to try to think it through. You can imagine how much help I got."

"What about other women?" Frenesi wondered.

"My, what you'd call, sisters in the struggle, ooh no, no, my poor deluded pumpkin, forget that. They were all preoccupied. Having affairs while the husbands were overseas, trying to handle the kids *and* the mother-in-law, working or just playing too hard to want to talk any politics. No time either for night school, fellow students, teachers sorta thing. So finally when here came your father, in his government-issue uniform, not a tailor-made stitch on him, pant cuffs so high you could see his socks with the extra packs of smokes tucked into 'em —"

"Platters spinning, mellow reed sections," Frenesi would speculate, "I love it! Tell me more!"

"Oh, the joints were jumping those nights. Uniforms all over the place. Wild and rowdy like the Clark Gable movie. Bars that would stay open all day and night, trumpet and saxophone music blasting at you out of doorways, big crowds at the hotel ballrooms . . . Anson Weeks and his Orchestra at the Top of the Mark . . . all over downtown, these rivers of uniforms and short dresses. I was living on fried donuts and coffee with no cream, finally had to go out looking for work again."

And was soon adopted, in a way that may've been sexually, though not otherwise, innocent, by a small band with a steady engagement in the Tenderloin. Every night sailors and soldiers came crowding in to dance with San Francisco girls till the windows got light, to the music of Eddie Enrico and his Hong Kong Hotshots. "That's right, I was the girl vocalist, always could carry a tune, sang the babies to sleep at home and they never complained, 'course when I sang the 'Star-Spangled Banner' at the playoffs my junior year, our chorus teacher, Mrs. Cappy, came over shaking her head real slow — 'Sasha Traverse, you're no Kate Smith!' — but it didn't bother me, I wanted to be Billie Holiday. Not a burning ambition, more of a pleasant daydream. And then out of nowhere this professional, Eddie himself, telling me I *could* sing . . . nope, he wasn't trying to get me into bed, too much trouble already with ex-wives and road girlfriends suddenly showing up in town, etcetera. I trusted his opinion, he'd labored for years in all the big bands — he was back east playing congas with Ramón Raquello the night they interrupted 'La Cumparsita' with the news from Mars. Finally, just about the time the City was starting to boogie-woogie, he got together this band of his own. If he thought I could sing, well, I could. I did. Who'd be listening that close? These folks wanted a good time."

Turned out that as long as she kept her hair washed and stayed on pitch, she was just another instrument, and it could've been just about anybody, happened to be Sasha, high-heeling in to the

Full Moon Club that morning looking for a waitress job she'd heard about at another little nightspot the day before. That was her life then, hitting all the nightspots, only it was during the day. The Full Moon wasn't much of a place, but she'd already seen worse. She found the owner working on some plumbing behind the bar, and soon he had her passing him wrenches. One of the Hong Kong Hotshots came groping in, looking for his wallet. Sasha noticed he wasn't Chinese, but neither was anybody else in the band, Chinese references in those days being code for opium products, and the Hotshot personnel coming from Army bands, like the 298th, stationed in the area, or civilians too young or too old to be in the service, so that the little ork combined youthful high spirits, the experience of age, and that cynical professionalism Army bands are widely known for.

"Pardon me," the wallet seeker addressed Sasha, "are you here about the canary gig?"

The what? she wondered, but said, "Sure, what do I look like, the plumber?"

The owner angled his head up between some pipes. "You sing? why'dn't you say so?" The musician, who was Eddie Enrico himself, sat down at the piano, and there Sasha was all of a sudden singing "I'll Remember April," in G. Why'd she pick that? it changed key a hundred times. But this band must have been desperate for a warbler, because Eddie didn't try to make her fuck up, helping her along instead, telegraphing all the chord changes, keeping her gently steered in case she lost track of the melody. When they finished — together — the owner gave her the 0-0. "You got anything a little more, ah, fashionable to wear?"

"Sure. I just wear this when I go looking for waitress jobs. Which would you prefer, my gold lamé or the mink strapless?"

"OK, OK, only thinkin' of the boys in uniform." So was Sasha, though Eddie and she were already four very fast bars into "Them There Eyes." She unbuttoned a button on her dress, took off her hat and draped her hair like Veronica Lake over one of them there eyes, and once more they got through together with nothing much going wrong. "I'll ask my wife," the owner said, "maybe she can find somethin' snazzy."

She sang at the Full Moon for the duration. Sometimes the boys and girls, instead of dancing, all came pressing close around the bandstand, and stood there, holding each other, swaying in time to the music. As if they were really listening. At first it made her nervous — why wouldn't they dance? whose idea was this rapt silent swaying? — but then she found it was helping her hear her way around the music. The last spring and summer of the war, San Francisco really began to whoop and holler, as troops came redeploying through town on the way to the Pacific, including Electrician's Mate Third Class Hubbell Gates, who was assigned to a long-hull Sumner-class destroyer brand-new out of the yards, which then steamed across the ocean to Okinawa just in time to get hit, in its first fifteen minutes of action, by a kamikaze, and had to put back into Pearl for refitting. By the time she was ready again, the war was about over, and Hub more than eager for some romance in his life.

"He listened to me," Sasha declared, "that was the amazing fact. He let me do my thinking out loud, first man ever did *that*." After a while her thoughts started falling into place. The injustices she had seen in the streets and fields, so many, too many times gone unanswered — she began to see them more directly, not as world history or anything too theoretical, but as humans, usually male, living here on the planet, often well within reach, committing these crimes, major and petty, one by one against other living humans. Maybe we all had to submit to History, she figured, maybe not — but refusing to take shit from some named and specified source — well, it might be a different story.

"She thought I was listening," Hub liked to put in at this point, "hell, I would have listened to her read the collected works of — what's his name? Trotsky! Sure, just to have some time with your mother. She thought I was some great political mind, and all's I was thinkin' was the usual sailor-on-liberty thoughts."

"Took me years to find out how completely I'd been fooled," Sasha nodding, mock-serious. "Toughest truth I ever had to face. Your father's never had a political cell in his system."

Smiling, "Will you listen to that? What a woman!"

Not for the first time, Frenesi found she'd been switching her eyes back and forth, as if cutting together reverse shots of two actors. She had already been through a few of these what Hub called "exchanges of views." They ended with everybody screaming and throwing household items, edible and otherwise. She knew her parents liked to proceed backward, into events of the past, in particular the fifties, the anticommunist terror in Hollywood then, the conspiracy of silence up to the present day. Friends of Hub's had sold out friends of Sasha's, and vice versa, and both personally had suffered at the hands of the same son of a bitch more than once. To Sasha the blacklist period, with its complex court dances of fuckers and fuckees, thick with betrayal, destructiveness, cowardice, and lying, seemed only a continuation of the picture business as it had always been carried on, only now in political form. Everyone they knew had made up a different story, to make each of them come out looking better and others worse. "History in this town," Sasha muttered, "is no more worthy of respect than the average movie script, and it comes about in the same way — soon as there's one version of a story, suddenly it's anybody's pigeon. Parties you never heard of get to come in and change it. Characters and deeds get shifted around, heartfelt language gets pounded flat when it isn't just removed forever. By now the Hollywood fifties is this way-over-length, multitude-of-hands rewrite — except there's no sound, of course, nobody talks. It's a silent movie."

Bitter, probably, she had a right to be, but she'd learned to cover it with deliberate cool flippancy learned from watching Bette Davis movies, something Frenesi must have picked up on early because each time she happened to catch one on the Tube, she could often warp back into infant memories of a giant unfocused being holding her up at arms' length and booming lines like, "Well! You ahh — quitethelittlebundle, ahhn't you? Yes!" Laughing, delighted, enfolding her. No point having a sourpuss baby around the house.

Frenesi had absorbed politics all through her childhood, but later, seeing older movies on the Tube with her parents, making for the first time a connection between the far-off images and her real life, it seemed she had misunderstood everything, paying too much attention to the raw emotions, the easy conflicts, when something else, some finer drama the Movies had never considered worth ennobling, had been unfolding all the time. It was a step in her political education. Names listed even in fast-moving credits, meaning nothing to a younger viewer, were enough to provoke from her parents groans of stomach upset, bellows of rage, snorts of contempt, and, in extreme cases, switches of channel. "You think I'm gonna sit and watch this piece of scab garbage?" Or, "You want to see a hot set? Watch when she slams that door — see that? Shook all over? That's scab carpentry by some scab local the IA set up, that's what scabs do to production values." Or, "That asshole? thought he was dead. See that credit there?" getting right up beside the screen to zero in on the offending line, "That fascist fuck," tapping the glass over the name fiercely, "owes me two years of work, you could've gone to college on what that SOB will always owe me."

Up and down that street, she remembered, television screens had flickered silent blue in the darkness. Strange loud birds, not of the neighborhood, were attracted, some content to perch in the palm trees, keeping silence and an eye out for the rats who lived in the fronds, others flying by close to windows, seeking an angle to sit and view the picture from. When the commercials came on, the birds, with voices otherworldly pure, would sing back at them, sometimes even when none were on. Sasha would be out on the porch long after nightfall, knitting, sitting, talking with Hub or a neighbor, not a freeway within earshot, though the treetop whistling of the mockingbirds covered blocks, reedy, clear, possible for a child to fall asleep right down the middle of. . . .

In the years since she'd departed the surface of everyday civilian life, Frenesi had made it a point, maybe a ritual, whenever business brought her to L.A., to drive out east of La Brea, down into those flatland residential blocks, among the pale smudged chalet-roofed bungalows and barking dogs and lawn mowers, to find the place again, and cruise the block in low the way the FBI had all through her childhood, looking for Sasha but never seeing her, never once in the yard or through a window, till one visit there was new machinery in the carport and a Day-Glo plastic trike and a scatter of toys on the front lawn, and she had to go cash in more favors than she'd been planning to just to find out where her mother had moved — into a small apartment, as it turned out, not far away at all. Why? Had she been holding on to the house as long as she could, hoping Frenesi would come back home, but one day, from the weight of too many years or because she'd found out something fatal about her daughter, had given up at last on her, just given up?

Believing that the rays coming out of the TV screen would act as a broom to sweep the room clear of all spirits, Frenesi now popped the Tube on and checked the listings. There was a rerun of the perennial motorcycle-cop favorite "CHiPs" on in a little while. She felt a rising of blood, a premonitory dampness. Let the grim feminist rave, Frenesi knew there were living women, down in the world, who happened, like herself, to be crazy about uniforms on men, entertained fantasies while on the freeway about the Highway Patrol, and even, as she was planning to do now, enjoyed masturbating to Ponch and Jon reruns on the Tube, and so what? Sasha believed her daughter had "gotten" this uniform fetish from her. It was a strange idea even coming from Sasha, but since her very first Rose Parade up till the present she'd felt in herself a fatality, a helpless turn toward images of authority, especially uniformed men, whether they were athletes live or on the Tube, actors in movies of war through the ages, or maître d's in restaurants, not to mention waiters and busboys, and she further believed that it could be passed on, as if some Cosmic Fascist had spliced in a DNA sequence requiring this form of seduction and initiation into the dark joys of social control. Long before any friend or enemy had needed to point it out to her, Sasha on her own had arrived at, and been obliged to face, the dismal possibility that all her oppositions, however just and good, to forms of power were really acts of denying that dangerous swoon that came creeping at the edges of her optic lobes every time the troops came marching by, that wetness of attention and perhaps ancestral curse.

Just for its political incorrectness alone, Frenesi had at first reacted to Sasha's theory with anger, then after a while had found it only annoying, and nowadays, with the two of them into their second decade of silence, good only for a sad sniffle. She swung the TV set around now, lay down on the sofa, undid her shirt, unzipped her pants, and was set to go when all at once what should occur for her but the primal Tubefreek miracle, in the form of a brisk manly knock at the screen door in the kitchen, and there outside on the landing, through the screen, broken up into little dots like pixels of a video image, only squarer, was this large, handsome U.S. Marshal, in full uniform, hat, service .38, and leather beltwork, with an envelope to deliver. And his partner, waiting down beside the car in the latening sunlight, was *twice* as cute.

She recognized the envelope right away. It was the stipend check she'd been looking for like a late period since last week. It hadn't been in the mail at all, it was in this rugged lawman's big leather-gloved hand, which she made a point, nearing the Big Four-Oh these days and still at it, of touching as she took the check.

He raised his sunglasses, smiled. "You haven't been down to th' office yet, have you?" The U.S. Marshal administered and serviced Witness Protection, and in most of her assignments over the years there had been this matter of a courtesy call, as if to the home embassy in each new foreign country.

"We just moved in," putting a stress on "we" to see what would happen.

"Well *we* haven't seen, uhm," consulting some leather-covered field book, "Fletcher, either."

He'd had one hand up on the doorjamb, leaning and talking, the way boys had to her in high school. She'd remembered to zip her pants on the way to the door, but had only done up a button or two of her shirt, no bra on, of course. She angled her head to look at the time on his tanned wrist, inches from her face. "He ought to be back any minute."

He put the shades back down, chuckled. "How about tomorra, soon after eight A.M. 's you can?" The phone in the other room began to ring. "Maybe that's him now. Maybe calling to say he'll be late, why don't you get it?"

"Nice talking to you. Till tomorrow, I guess."

"I can wait."

She was already halfway to the phone, looked back at him over her shoulder but didn't ask him in. At the same time, there was no way she could order him to leave, was there?

It was Flash, calling from the field office where he worked, but not to say he'd be late, he never did that, just came in when he came in. "Don't git alarmed, but now — you had any visitors today?"

"Marshal just came to deliver the check in person, did seem a little unusual."

"It came? Outstanding! Listen, could you go out, soon 's you can, cash it, honey, for us, please?"

"Flash, what's up?"

"Don't know. Dropped by the terminal room, got talkin' to that Grace, you know, the Mexican one I 's pointin' out to you that time?"

With the big boobs. "Uh-huh."

"Said she wanted me to see somethin' funny. But it wa'n't too funny. Turns out, a lot of people we know — they ain't on the computer anymore. Just — gone."

It was the way he was saying it, with that only semicontrolled Johnny Cash type of catch or tremor she'd learned to tune in on, a 100 percent reliable omen. It meant what he liked to call profound feces, every time. "Well, Justin's due in any minute. Should I be packin' up?"

"Um first git the cash if you could, my sweet thing, and I'll be back there soon 's I can."

"You old snake charmer," as she hung up.

The marshals had split, doggone it, but here, charging up the outside stairs, pipe railings ringing, came Justin, with his friend Wallace, and Wallace's mom, Barbie, gamely puffing along behind. Frenesi grabbed her kid briefly, trailing part of a wet kiss along his bare arm as he flew past with Wallace, on into the alcove he'd made his room.

"Herd o' locusts," Barbie sighed.

Frenesi was standing by at the automatic-drip machine. "Hope you don't mind it this long in the pot."

"Better the longer it sits." Barbie worked part-time at the

courthouse, and her husband full-time at the federal building, for different arms of the law, and sometimes she and Frenesi looked after each other's kids, though they lived on opposite sides of town. "You're still on for Monday then, right?"

"Oh, sure," oh sure, "listen, Barb, I hate to ask, but my card keeps getting kicked out of the cash machine, nobody knows nothin' about it, my account's OK, but the bank's closed and I just got this check, um I don't suppose —"

"Last week would've been better, we 'as countin' on a bunch of vouchers to come through, now they tell us, guess what, lost in the computer, surprise."

"Computers," Frenesi began, but then, paranoid, decided not to repeat what she'd heard from Flash. She made up something about the check instead, and while the boys watched cartoons, the women sat in the breeze through the screen door, drank coffee, and told computer horror tales.

"Feel like old-timers grouchin' about the weather," Barbie said. Flash came in just as she and Wallace were heading out.

"Barbie! Oohwee! Let's see!" He took her left hand, twirled her around, then pretended to inspect the hand. "Still married, huh."

"Yep, and J. Edgar Hoover's still dead, Fletcher."

"Bye, Mr. Fletcher!" Wallace hollered.

"Say, Wallace, catch 'at game yesterday? What'd I tell you?"

"Still glad we didn't bet — that was my lunch money."

"Flash?" hollered both women at once. Flash stood out on the landing and watched till they were in the car and pulling away. Still waving, "She act funny at all?"

"No, uh-uh, why?"

"Her old man's some honcho down at the Regional Office, right?"

"Flash, it's a desk job, he's in administrative support."

"Hmm. I seem nervous to you? Oh — the check, 'd you cash it yet? 'Course not — why'm I even asking? My life story here. Well can I please have a look at it?" He squinted, angling it around. "Looks funny. Huh? Don't you think?"

"I'll get on it," she promised, "right after we eat. Now tell me about who isn't on the computer, that's making you so crazy."

He'd brought home a quickly compiled list, all independent contractors like themselves. Frenesi got out a couple of frozen, or with the state the fridge was in actually semithawed, peperoni pizzas, put the oven on to preheat, and made a fast salad while Flash opened beers and read off the names. There were Long Bihn Jail alumni, old grand-jury semipros, collectors of loans and ladies on strings who'd been persuaded to help entrap soon-to-be excustomers, snitches with photographic memories, virgins to the act of murder, check bouncers, coke snorters, and ass grabbers, each with more than ample reason to seek the shadow of the federal wing, and some, with luck, able to reach its embrace and shelter.

Or so they must have believed. But now, no longer on the computer, how safe could any of them be feeling? "You're sure now," she pressed, "you know for a fact ol' what's-her-name checked it out."

"Did it myself, type the name in, comes back 'No Such File,' all right? You want me to go beat her up, will that help?"

"This serious?"

"Fuckin' A." Which was about when Justin came wandering in, cartoons having ended and his parents now become the least objectionable programming around here, for half an hour, anyway — and just as well, too, because the last thing either parent needed right now was an argument, or what passed for one with them, a kind of alien-invasion game in which Flash launched complaints of different sizes at different speeds and Frenesi tried to deflect or neutralize them before her own defenses gave way.

"Say, Justintime, how's 'em Transformers, makin' out OK?"

"And how was everything over at Wallace's?"

The kid put on a genial smile, waved, put his hand to his ear like Reagan going, "Say again?" "How about a few questions," Justin pretending to look around the room, "Mom? You had your hand up?"

"We're just getting you back for all those questions you used to ask us" — Flash adding "Amen!" — "not too long ago."

"I don't remember that," trying not to laugh, because in fact he did, and wanted to be teased.

"Must be gettin' old, man," said Frenesi.

"Nonstop questions nobody could answer," Flash told him, "like, 'What is metal?'"

"'How do you know when you're dreaming and when you're not?'" Frenesi recalled, "That was my favorite."

Frenesi put the pizzas in, and Flash wandered away to eyeball the Tube. A little later, when they were eating, as if out of nowhere, Flash said, "Two possibilities I can see."

She knew he meant the computer list. One of these two possibilities was that the missing people were dead, or else hiding from whoever wanted them that way, a worst-case scenario that, neither wishing to interrupt the appetite of their son, who scarfed pizza under the same suspension of physical law that allows Dagwood Bumstead to eat sandwiches, would have to go unsaid. But she hazarded another. "Maybe they went the other way, surfaced, went up in the world again?"

"Yep. But why's it happening?"

Justin, pizza slice hovering on route to his face, said, "Maybe they all got their budget lines axed out."

Flash gave him a quick head-take, as if awakened by a practical joke. "Used to be a kid right here, what happened?"

"What've you been hearing, Justin?"

He shrugged. "Keep tellin' you guys, you should watch MacNeil and Lehrer, there's all this budget stuff goin' on all the time, with President Reagan, and Congress? It's on now, if you're interested. Can I be excused?"

"I'll," Flash looking over quizzically at Frenesi, "be, uh, right in. . . . Darlin', do you think that could be it? They're droppin' people from the Program, too many mouths to feed?"

"Nothing new." It was a time-honored way to keep the wards and snitches and special employees at each other's throats, competing for the ever-dwindling imprest funds, kept aware, never overtly, that with the Justice Department in regular contact with what it was still calling "Organized Crime," the list of names was negotiable, all too negotiable.

"But not on this scale," Flash waving the printout. "This is a massacre."

She looked around this place they'd never fully moved into — had they? — so why this sad feeling of imminent goodbye?

"I'll try to cash this down at Gate 7," she told him, "quick 's I can." She got out into deep sunset, airport traffic in the distance, downtown beginning to cast a glow, and in Flash's motor-pool Cutlass Supreme headed for the small community known as Gate 7, which had grown up over the years at the edge of the giant invisible base beyond. According to signs along the ancient freeway system, which ran through towering halls of concrete, echoing, full of shadows, there were at least a hundred of these gates, each intended to admit — or reject — a different category of visitor, but nobody knew for sure exactly how many there were. While some stood in isolation, hard to drive to, heavily protected, seldom used, others, like Gate 7, had generated around themselves service areas, homes, and shopping plazas.

The Gate 7 Quik Liquor and Deli, hunkering down among the off- and on-ramps of its exit, was jammed. It was Friday and a shift had just ended, the parking lot was a zoo, so Frenesi had to park along the frontage strip, near an unlit street lamp. Inside the place, men and women in uniforms, civvies, suits, party outfits, and work clothes milled and clamored, holding sixpacks in their teeth, balancing children and monster-size snack bags, reading magazines and tabloids, all, it seemed, looking to get checks cashed. Frenesi queued up under the fluorescent lights, in air-conditioning heavy with car exhaust, and could just make out at the far end of the line two part-time high-school girls, one ringing up purchases, one bagging. Neither, when she got there half an hour later, was authorized to cash her check. "Where's the manager?"

"I'm the acting manager."

"This is a government check, look, you do this all the time, you cash checks from the base, right?"

"Yah, but this here's no base check."

"They're in the federal building downtown, their phone number's right on the check, you can call them up."

"After office hours, ma'am. Yes *sir,* can I he'p you?" The line behind Frenesi had grown longer and less patient. She looked at the girl — a smug mouth, a bad attitude. She wanted to say, kid, better watch 'at shit. But she was about the same age as Prairie would be . . . working at this checkout maybe for the rest of her life, and with Frenesi's days of federal empowerment and one-phone-call conflict resolution years behind her and fading fast, she was no longer in any position to throw her weight around. . . . Humiliated, helpless, she came out sweating into the grayly overborne night, traffic smell, not enough street light, in the air a distant unlocalized rumbling from somewhere deep in the base.

She drove on downtown, being extra careful because she felt like doing harm to somebody, found a liquor store with a big Checks Cashed sign, got the same turndown inside. Running on nerves and anger, she kept on till she reached the next supermarket, and this time she was told to wait while somebody went in back and made a phone call.

It was there, gazing down a long aisle of frozen food, out past the checkout stands, and into the terminal black glow of the front windows, that she found herself entering a moment of undeniable clairvoyance, rare in her life but recognized. She understood that the Reaganomic ax blades were swinging everywhere, that she and Flash were no longer exempt, might easily be abandoned already to the upper world and any unfinished business in it that might now resume . . . as if they'd been kept safe in some time-free zone all these years but now, at the unreadable whim of something in power, must reenter the clockwork of cause and effect. Someplace there would be a real ax, or something just as painful, Jasonic, blade-to-meat final — but at the distance she, Flash, and Justin had by now been brought to, it would all be done with keys on alphanumeric keyboards that stood for weightless, invisible chains of electronic presence or absence. If patterns of ones and zeros were "like" patterns of human lives and deaths, if everything about an individual could be represented in a computer record by a long string of ones and zeros, then what kind of creature would be represented by a long string of lives and deaths? It would have to be up one level at least — an angel, a minor god, something in a UFO. It would take eight human lives and deaths just to form one character in this being's name — its complete dossier might take up a considerable piece of the history of the world. We are digits in God's computer, she not so much thought as hummed to herself to a sort of standard gospel tune, And the only thing we're good for, to be dead or to be living, is the only thing He sees. What we cry, what we contend for, in our world of toil and blood, it all lies beneath the notice of the hacker we call God.

The night manager came back, holding the check as he might a used disposable diaper. "They stopped payment on this."

"The banks are closed, how'd they do that?"

He spent his work life here explaining reality to the herds of computer-illiterate who crowded in and out of the store. "The computer," he began gently, once again, "never has to sleep, or even go take a break. It's like it's open 24 hours a day. . . ."

THE Wayvone estate occupied a dozen hillside acres south of San Francisco, with a view of the Bay, the San Mateo Bridge, and Alameda County through the smog on certain days, though today was not one of them. The house, dating from the 1920s, was in Mediterranean Revival style, presenting to the street a face of single-story modesty while behind it and down the hill for eight levels sprawled a giant villa of smooth white stucco, with round-topped windows and red tile roofs, a belvedere, a couple of verandas, gardens and courtyards, a hillside full of fig and olive trees, apricot, peach, and plum, bougainvillea, mimosa, periwinkle, and, everywhere today, in honor of the bride, pale plantations of jasmine, spilling like bridal lace, which would keep telling nose-tales of paradise all night, long after the last guests had been driven home.

Emerging from a pool the size of a small reservoir in plaid swim trunks from Brooks Brothers, unable even at first glance to be mistaken for any of the white marble statues surrounding it, Ralph Wayvone, Sr., caped himself with a towel stolen not that long ago from the Fairmont, ascended a short flight of steps, and stood looking out over a retaining wall that seemed in the morning fog to mark the edge of a precipice, or of the world. With only a few tree silhouettes, and both the freeways and El Camino Real miraculously silent, for just these moments Ralph Sr., appreciative of peace as anybody, could take another of what he'd come to think of as microvacations on an island of time fragile and precious as any Tahiti or one of them.

Registering upon strangers as the kind of executive whose idea of power is a secretary on her knees under his desk, Ralph in fact was more considerate of others than at times was good for him. He liked, and was genuinely attentive to, the platoons of children who always showed up at family gatherings like the one today. The kids picked up on this, appreciated it, and flirted back. Friends he valued for their willingness to talk to him straight said things like, "Your problem, Ralph, is you're not enough of a control freak for the job you're in," or, "You're supposed to allow yourself the illusion that what you do matters, but it don't look like you really give a shit." His shrink told him the same things. What did Ralph know? He looked in mirrors and saw somebody in OK shape for his age, he went and put in his regular time at the spa and the tennis court, had in his mouth some high-ticket dental work, with which he ate carefully and in style. His lovely wife, Shondra, what could he say? His kids — well, there was still time, time would tell. Gelsomina, the baby, was getting married today to a college professor from L.A., of a good family with whom Ralph had done complaint-free and even honorable business. Dominic, "the movie executive," as Ralph liked to call him, had flown in the night before from Indonesia, where he was line producer on a monster movie whose budget required readjusting on an hour-to-hour basis, so he'd been spending a lot of time on the phone, expensive but maybe managing to confuse whoever happened to be tapping it. And Ralph Jr., who was expected someday to take over Ralph Wayvone Enterprises, had driven down for a day off from his duties as manager of the Cucumber Lounge roadhouse up in Vineland.

"One thing you have to know," Ralph confided to his namesake the day the kid turned eighteen and got his ventunesimo party three years early, at the time a sensible move given the many talents then surfacing in his character for getting into trouble, "before you get too involved, is that we are a wholly-owned subsidiary."

"What's that?" inquired Ralph Jr. In olden times the father might have shrugged, turned without further talk, and gone away to enjoy his despair in private. The two Wayvones were down in the wine cellar, and Ralph could have just left him there, among the bottles. Instead he took the trouble to explain that strictly speaking, the family "owned" nothing. They received an annual operating budget from the corporation that owned them, was all.

"Like the royal family in England, you mean?"

"My firstborn son," Ralph rolling his eyes, "if it helps — please."

"I'd be like — Prince Charles?"

"*Testa puntita,* do me a favor."

But young Wayvone's anxious face was now smoothed by the sight of a dusty bottle of wine, a 1961 Brunello di Montalcino, put away the year he was born to be drunk this day of transition to adulthood, though his own share of it was to meet the same porcelain fate as the cheaper stuff he went on to drink too much of.

Gelsomina, being a daughter, didn't of course get any bottle. But did he hear her complaining? This wedding today was costing Ralph more than he'd paid for the house. After a full-scale nuptial Mass, the reception feast here would feature lobster, caviar, and tournedos Rossini, along with more down-home fare such as baked ziti and a complicated wedding soup only his sister-in-law Lolli, among her many virtues, knew how to make. The wine would run a full range from homemade red through Cristal champagne, and hundreds of dolled- and duded-up friends, relatives, and business acquaintances would populate the hillside, most of them in a mood to celebrate. The only piece of uncertainty, not a problem really, was the music, with the San Francisco Symphony on tour overseas, the society combo Ralph Sr. had booked originally having run into a little snag in Atlantic City, where their engagement had been involuntarily extended till they made up what they owed the Casino as the result of several foolish wagers, and these last-minute replacements, Gino Baglione and the Paisans, whom Ralph Jr. had hired up north without ever hearing, still an unknown quantity. Well — they had better be excellent, that's all Ralph had to say, or rather think, as the fog now began to lift to reveal not the borderlands of the eternal after all, but only quotidian California again, looking no different than it had when he left.

The band arrived at around midday, after two days of leisurely detours through the wine country, coastal Marin, and Berkeley. They had at last ascended a confusing network of winding streets, putting the last touches to their costuming and makeup, the glossy black, short synthetic wigs, the snappy mint-colored matching suits of Continental cut, the gold jewelry and glue-on mustaches, just before rolling to a stop at the main gate of the exclusive community of Lugares Altos and all being ordered out of the van and subjected each to a discrete bodyfrisk, plus scans for metal objects down to badge size and for electronic devices active and passive. Young Ralph was waiting nervously at the Wayvone parking area, where everybody piled out again. The Vomitone ladies, Prairie included, had likewise made an effort to tone down their extravagance of image, with the help of wigs, clothes, and makeup borrowed from their straighter friends. Billy Barf, whose acquaintance with anything Italian was limited to the deuteragonist of Donkey Kong and a few canned-pasta commercials, insisted on speaking with his imperfect idea of an ethnic accent until Isaiah Two Four, detecting not only its inauthenticity but also its potential for insult, drew the young band eponym aside for a word or two, though Ralph Jr., who had talked Californian all his life, had only taken it for some kind of speech impediment. "You guys have done this before, right?" he kept asking as they off-loaded their instruments, amps, and digital interfaces and proceeded down to a huge airy tent at the edge of a small meadow, where liveried servants bustled everywhere, setting out glassware and napery, hauling tons of shaved ice, high-rent hors d'oeuvres, flowers, and folding chairs, discussing at top volume the fine points of chores they had all performed around here a thousand times already.

"Wedding gigs are our life," Billy assured him.

"Just be cool, OK?" Isaiah murmured.

"Yah, rilly," cackled Lester, the rhythm guitarist. "You blow this, Bill, we all gonna git wasted."

They got through the first set on inoffensive pop tunes, rock and roll oldies, even one or two Broadway standards. But during the break, a large emissary with a distinct taper to his head, Ralph Sr.'s trusted lieutenant "Two-Ton" Carmine Torpidini, arrived with a message for Billy. "Mr. Wayvone's compliments, says thank you for the contemporary flavor of the music, which all the young people have enjoyed fabulously. But he wonders if in the upcoming set you might play something the older generations could more readily relate to, something more . . . Italian?"

More than eager to please, the Vomitones led off the set with a medley they'd been practicing of Italian tunes on a common theme of transcendence — a salsa treatment of "More" from *Mondo Cane* (1963), slowing to 3/4 with "Senza Fine," from *Flight of the Phoenix* (1966), and to wrap it an English-language version, in Billy's nasal tenor, of the favorite "Al Di La," from any number of television specials.

No one was more surprised than Billy when Two-Ton Carmine appeared once again, this time with hurried breathing, flushed face, a look of excitement, as if he sensed a chance to do some of the untidy work he received his paycheck for. "Mr. Wayvone says he was hoping he wouldn't have to go into too many details with you, but that he was thinking more along the lines of 'C'e la Luna,' 'Way Marie' — you know, sing-along stuff, plus maybe a little opera, 'Cielo e Mar,' right? Mr. Wayvone's brother Vincent, as you know, being a very fine singer. . . ."

"Yah," Billy now with a slow and blunted sort of comprehension, "uh, well. Sure! I think we have those arrangements —"

"In the van," muttered Isaiah.

"— in the van," said Billy Barf. "All I have to do's just —" sliding one arm out of his guitar strap. But Carmine reached over, removed the guitar from Billy's grasp, and began to turn it end over end, so as to twist the strap, now around Billy's neck, tighter and tighter.

"Arrangements." Carmine laughed, embarrassed and mean. " 'Way Marie,' what kind of arrangement do you need? You gentlemen are Italian, are you not?"

The band sat silent, feckless, watching their leader being garrotted. Few Anglos, some Scotch-Irish, one Jewish guy, no actual Italians. "Well, then, how about Catholic?" Carmine went on, punctuating his remarks with sharp yanks on the strap. "Maybe I could let yiz off with ten choruses of 'Ave Maria' and a Act of Contrition? No? So tell me, while you can, what's goin' on? Didn' Little Ralph say nothin' ta yiz? Hey! Wait a minute! What's this?" In the course of having the head on which it sat shaken back and forth, Billy's "Italian" wig had begun to slide off, revealing his real hairstyle, dyed today a vivid turquoise. "You guys ain't Gino Baglione and the Paisans!" Carmine shook his head, cracked his knuckles. "That's false pretenses, fellas! Don't you know you can end up in small-claims for that?"

Seeing that Billy Barf, enjoying a surrender to panic, had forgotten all about the quick-release clips at the ends of the guitar strap he was being strangled with, Isaiah came over and popped them loose for him, allowing the bandleader to stagger away trying to croak some air back into his lungs. "Actually," Isaiah began, "I'm a percussion person, my job is to take hard knocks and rude surprises, line 'em up in a row in some way folks can dance to, 's all I do, rilly, but as a connoisseur and from the story your face seems to tell a recipient of some of Life's hard knocks yourself, you can see the present crisis may not be worth emotional investment on the scale you contemplate, not to mention the bruises on Gino aka Billy here's neck, which will have him wearing bandannas for weeks, with crossover implications musically and also generating with numerous ol' ladies hickey suspicions you can well imagine, no, far from bein' a hard knock here, why, it's not even a brushstroke on Life's top cymbal, come on! Eh!"

"Ah," blurted the oversize gorilla, hypnotized, "yes you're right, kid, and I'm disappointed to say so 'cause I was all set for a multiple confrontation."

"Good," Billy Barf somewhere behind an amp, searching frantically for the keys to the van, "you're talking it out, that's good."

Fortunately Ralph Wayvone's library happened to include a copy of the indispensable *Italian Wedding Fake Book,* by Deleuze & Guattari, which Gelsomina, the bride, to protect her wedding from such possible unlucky omens as blood on the wedding cake, had the presence of mind to slip indoors and bring back out to Billy Barf's attention. Inconveniently by then, Billy, keys in fist, was on his single-minded way up to the parking area, so that the new bride, in her grandmother's wedding gown, was observed to go running after a non-Italian musician with unusual hair — not a breach of decency, according to more traditional-minded elements close to Ralph Wayvone, to be left unavenged. So despite the revival of music, dancing, and good cheer and the salvation of Gelsomina Wayvone's wedding day, this latent threat was enough to paralyze Billy for the rest of the gig, convinced as he now was that a hit order had gone out on him from the highest levels.

"Hey, 'f they want to ice you, Bill, they gonna do it," advised the Vomitones' bass player, who went by the professional name Meathook. "Best you can do's get you a li'l .22 caliber assault rifle and a full-auto drop-in fer it, when they come for you you can at least take a couple with you."

"Naw," disagreed the horn virtuoso 187, who'd named himself after the California Penal Code section for murder, "only wimps depend on machinery, what Bill needs is some close-combat skills, some knife, 'chuks, li'l jeet kune do —"

"Fun time's over, Bill, either leave town or hire some heavy security," put in Bad, the synthesizerist.

"Isaiah mah man, help me out here," Billy pleaded.

"On the other hand," Isaiah said, "they loved 'Volare.'"

During all this commotion, Prairie was up the hill a level or two, standing semidistraught in front of an ornately framed gold-veined mirror, one of a whole row, in a powder room or ladies' lounge of stupefying tastelessness, having an attack of THO, or Teen Hair Obsession. While the other Vomitonettes were running around with hair color or wigs, all Prairie'd had to do to look straight was brush hers. "Perfect!" tactful Billy had told her, "no-body'll look twice."

She stared into her reflection, at the face that had always been half a mystery to her, despite photos of her mother that Zoyd and Sasha had shown her. It was easy to see Zoyd in her face — that turn of chin, slope of eyebrows — but she'd known for a long time how to filter these out, as a way to find the face of her mother in what was left. She started picking again at her hair, with a coral plastic ratting brush a friend had shoplifted for her. Mirrors made her nervous, especially all these, each set over a marble sink with mermaids for tap handles, in a space lit like a bus station, walls covered in gold velvet with a raised heraldic pattern, pink and cream accents everyplace, a fountain in the middle, some scaled-down Roman repro, concealed speakers playing FM stereo locked to some easy-listening frequency in the area, seething quietly, like insect song.

Prairie tried bringing her hair forward in long bangs, brushing the rest down in front of her shoulders, the surest way she knew, her eyes now burning so blue through the fringes and shadows, to creep herself out, no matter what time of the day or night, by

imagining that what she saw was her mother's ghost. And that if
she looked half a second too long, it would begin to blink while
her own eyes stayed open, its lips would start to move, and then
speak to her stuff she was sure she'd rather not hear. . . .

Or maybe that you've ached all your life to hear but you're still
scared of? the other face seemed to ask, lifting one eyebrow a
fraction more than Prairie could feel in her own face. Suddenly,
then, behind herself, she saw another reflection, one that might've
been there for a while, one, strangely, that she almost knew. She
turned quickly, and here was this live solid woman, standing
a little too close, tall and fair, wearing a green party dress that
might have gone with her hair but not with the way she carried
herself, athletic, even warriorlike, watching the girl in a weirdly
familiar, defensive way, as if they were about to continue a conversation.

Prairie shifted the brush around so the pointed handle was now
its business end. "Problem, ma'am?"

All at once, from the stranger's battered cowhide shoulder bag,
which she'd set down right next to Prairie's earth-toned canvas
one, on the tile counter, came a thin piping tune in three-part
harmony, all sixteen bars of the theme from "Hawaii Five-O,"
which it then kept repeating, potentially forever.

"Excuse me, but would that be one of Takeshi Fumimota's old
business cards in your bag there, by any chance?" the woman
meanwhile digging down in her own bag to find and come out
with a small silvery unit, still chiming the stop-frame hula dancer,
the hundred different shots of the water, Danno looking through
the hole in the glass, McGarrett on the building.

"Here —" Prairie handing over her iridescent oblong, "my dad
gave me this."

"Scanner here's still programmed to pick 'em up, but I thought
these old-timers had all been called in by now." She shut off the
music right after the part that goes,

Down in the streets of Honolu-lu,
Just bookin' folks and bein' patched through, what a
Lu-wow! . . . Hawa-
Ii Five-Oh!

Putting out her hand, "I'm Darryl Louise Chastain. Me and Takeshi are partners."

"Name's Prairie."

"Just for a minute in the mirror there I thought you were somebody you couldn't possibly be."

"Uh-huh, well, I know I've seen you before too — whoa, wait a minute, was that *DL* Chastain, I always thought it meant Disabled List, sure it's you, you look different, my grandma showed me old snapshots of you. You and my mom."

"Your mom." Prairie saw her taking a breath in a controlled and deliberate way she recognized from the Bodhi Dharma Pizza Temple. "Oh, mercy." She nodded, faintly smiling, one side of the smile maybe a little higher than the other. "You're Frenesi's kid." She said the name with some effort, as if she hadn't pronounced it out loud for a while. "Your mom and me . . . we ran together, back in the old days."

They went outside and found a quiet piece of terrace and Prairie told DL about her mother's rumored return, and the DEA guy who might be crazy and his movie scheme, and the seizing of her home by a paramilitary force from the Justice Department.

DL looked serious. "And you're sure that name was Brock Vond."

"Yep. My dad says that he's bad shit."

"He's both. We still have some unbalanced karma, me and Brock. Now it sounds like you've got some too." She laid the Japanese amulet on the tabletop between them. "Takeshi calls these things *giri* chits, sorta karmic IOU's. Takes a lot of speed, gets grandiose, wants to base a world currency system on them, so forth — but if you present one to him, he's got to honor it. Were you planning on using this?"

"I'm feeling like Dumbo with that feather, I would clutch to anything right now. Why? What can your partner do for me? Can he find my mom?"

Which put DL in a pickle. Years with Takeshi, and she was still finding out what he could do. And couldn't. If Frenesi really was surfacing, anybody could find her. But with Brock Vond out tearing up the pea patch too, her movements might be less certain.

And whatever story DL told this kid must not, maybe could never, be the story she knew. She temporized. "Is, it's been what, 15 years, just about your lifetime, full of playin' make-believe, acting on faiths in things that sound crazy now, lying, turning each other in, too much time passed, everybody remembering a different story —"

"And you want to hear mine before you'll tell me yours."

"Knew you'd understand." A liveried waiter passed by with a tray full of champagne in glasses, and Prairie, who didn't even like beer, and DL, who objected philosophically to all drugs, each took one. "Frenesi Gates," DL touching her glass to the girl's, and a chill rode Prairie's shoulders.

Rising from the distant meadow came the music of the Vomitones, twanging and crashing their way through a suite from *Tosca*. "Well — my dad and my grandma both tell the same story. I cross-examine 'em, try to trick 'em, but except for picky details and memory loss from dope and so on, either it's true or they got together long ago and cooked something up, right?" waiting for DL to tell her she was too young to be so paranoid. But DL only smiled back over the rim of the slender glass. "OK — my mom made movies for that Revolution you guys tried to have, she was on the run, warrants out on her, FBI put her pictures in the post office, Zoyd was her cover for a while, and then they had me . . . and we were a family until the feds found out where she was and she had to disappear — go underground." There was a small defiant tremor in her voice.

Underground. Right. That's the story DL should have known they'd tell the kid. Underground. Now, how could DL tell her what *she* knew, and how could she not? "Brock Vond," very carefully, "had his own grand jury back then. They were all over the place, popping antiwar people, student radicals, getting indictments, including at least one against your mother. There's no statute of limitations, so it's still in force."

Prairie made an I-don't-get-it face. "You saying he's still chasing her, 15 years down the line, taxpayers' money, not enough real criminals around?"

"My best guess from what you tell me is, is that your mom is in some deep shit, Brock's after her, and if he came and took away your house, then he's after you too, maybe as a bargaining point against her." But this was going to be like trying to explain rape to a child and not talk about sex.

"But why?" Yeah. The girl's eyelids, in the afternoon shade, lay half open as she hung, so filled with innocence, with stupefied daughterly need, on each word, each space between words. But DL only gazed back, as if Prairie was supposed to be figuring things out too. Prairie hated to admit it, but so far what it sounded like was something dangerously personal between Brock Vond and her mother, territory she was as nervous about stepping into as DL appeared to be. Up on the table the other night at Bodhi Dharma Pizza, Hector had been screaming something about Brock Vond "taking away Zoyd's old lady." Prairie must have thought he meant making an arrest, forcing her mother to flee, something like that. But then what else?

In the orange sunlight, guests in gowns from the upper reaches of Magnin's and ruffled shirtfronts, tuxes, and tails, throwing ever longer shadows up the hillside, wandered, grouped and regrouped, ate, drank, smoked, danced, fought, staggered to the mike to do guest vocals with the band. Prairie found her glass empty, and a little bit later, a full one in its place. At some point this older guy showed up, looking a little ragged, kissed DL's hand, and tried a grab for her ass that she must have been expecting because he never made contact, lurching instead past Prairie and nearly over a low wall onto the buffet table the next level down. "Shondra and the kids look wonderful," DL remarked as he came slowly back, and she introduced Prairie to their host, Ralph Wayvone. "I don't want to be the one to piss in the punch bowl," DL added, "but better you know sooner than later, Prairie here has just had a run-in with your old pinochle partner Brock Vond."

"*Porca miseria.*" Ralph had a seat. "Just when I was starting to forget all that. Even thought *you* might be finally letting go of it. Wrong again, huh?"

"Maybe it won't let go of me."

"The past —" darting his eyeballs around. "Shrink says I'm supposed to be leaving it behind. He's right. Isn't he?"

"Well, Ralph," DL drawled, "matter of fact, see, Brock ain't *in* the past right now, he's in the present tense again, badassin' around up in Vineland County, actin' like a li'l fuckin' army o' occupation."

"Hey — I got nothing to do with pot growers, all right? You know that. As soon as I saw all this drug hysteria coming, I diversified on out of that whole market. Plus it's a Republican Justice Department, come on. I'm copacetic with all these people."

"Yeah — sometime they might not know how to stop. Anyway, I doubt it's pot, 'cause it's still too early in the season. Brock's not answering his calls, apparently, and nobody knows just what's goin' on, except there's a nut case leading a heavily armed strike force loose in California."

Ralph Wayvone swayed to his feet, looking glum. He patted DL's arm a couple of times. "I'll have 'em get on the computer, make a few phone calls. You be around?"

"Heading up the mountain, got to rendezvous with Takeshi."

"Say hello." He headed off into the house. Sunset was coming, and the two women still had a list of things to make up their minds about.

"You think I'm one of these kids on Phil Donahue," Prairie blurted, "shows up at some woman's door fifteen years later goin' 'Mommy, Mommy!' Hey. I have my privacy, had to fight for it sometimes, I know what that's worth, I ain't about to go bargin' in on hers."

"But Prairie, that would be small shit next to this Brock problem. He's dangerous."

"Can't we find her before he does?" So blatantly longing that DL had to stare down at her feet, like an amateur tap dancer.

"You ought to at least have Takeshi's input on this. Any reason you can't come with me?"

She took the amulet Zoyd had given her and moved it inside the perimeter of DL's scanner unit, and the McGarrett theme piped up again, melody, obbligato, and accompaniment. "I'll have to trust you."

"You'll have to trust yourself. If it feels too weird, don't, 's all."

"Come on and meet Isaiah."

They found him up in the van with Meathook, snorting a couple of lines just to perk up for what looked like some late-night overtime. "He-e-e-y, there she is!" Isaiah with a wet grin. "Great news, Ralph Jr. just hired us to play at the Cucumber Lounge. Things work out, we could be the house band."

"So you'll be heading back to Vineland now?"

He frowned, a huge hand on her shoulder, trying to solve a puzzle. "You're not gonna come?" He looked over at DL, and Prairie introduced them and told him about the amulet and the Japanese guy who was now obliged to help her. "But I promised your dad —"

"Just tell him what happened with the card he gave me and it'll be all right. Plus the longer I stick with you guys the more I could get you in trouble. APB's out on the van, I don't know. . . ." Isaiah was looking over at DL, eyebrows going like wings trying to pick up some lift. "She's cool, rilly," Prairie said.

"You sing?" is what Meathook wanted to know, his upper lip glistening and loose.

"If you're good boys," DL beamed, "I'll sing you the story of my life." So it was that as a breeze came up to send all the leaves in the landscape flickering, as low-voltage lighting bloomed along the walks and through the trees in citric green and yellow, and as Ralph Wayvone, for whom the gun-moll anthem was a great favorite, danced a kind of fox-trot with his newlywed daughter, DL came sauntering up to the mike in front of the reassembled Vomitones, having with kunoichi deftness removed an Uzi from its owner's sheath — "Hi, handsome, mind if I borrow this?" — to use as a prop, and, twirling it like a six-gun in a movie, taking time steps and shaking her hair around, sang, to the band's accompaniment,

> Just a floo-zy with-an U-U-zi . . .
> Just a girlie, with-a-gun . . .
> When I could have been a mo-del,
> And I should have been a nu-un. . . .
>
> Oh, just what was it about that
> Little Israeli machine? . . .

Play all day in the sand,
Nothin' gets, jammed, under-
Stand . . . what I mean —

So Mis-ter, you can keep yer len-ses,
And Sis-ter, you can keep yer beads . . .
I'm ridin' in Mercedes Ben-zes,
I'm takin' care of all my needs. . . .

I'll lose my blues, in some Jacuz-zi,
Life's just a lotta good clean fun,
For a floo-zy with-an U-U-zi,
For a girlie, with-a-gun. . . .

Ralph loved it, screaming, "One more time!" DL tossed the weapon back to the bewildered gunsel, Isaiah slowed the rhythm down
and on the final eight bars hit every other beat with a heavy
rimshot, an old show-tune tactic American audiences are condi-
tioned to meet with wild applause, which is what happened, along
with cries of "Who's your agent?" and "Are you married?"

Though all the Vomitones were eager to continue, DL, with
regrets, left the mike and with Prairie and Isaiah made her way
up through the low lights and night awakenings of jasmine to
where she'd parked her car, a black '84 Trans-Am with extra
fairings, side pipes, scoops, and coves not on the standard model,
plus awesomely important pinstriping by the legendary Ramón of
La Habra in several motifs, including explosions and serpents.

"Megabad, rilly," delighted Isaiah crooned. "What'll this do?"

"Just cruisin' or on a good night?"

"Prairie, if I teach you real quick to play drums — ?"

She looked up from her seat at him, towering against light smog
that only a few stars shone through. "When you see my dad —"

"Sure. We go up and eyeball your house too, if you want."

"Sorry about it, Stretch Pants."

"Be all right again soon." He knelt to kiss her goodbye through
the window. "Only a couple more commercials, just hold on,
Prair."

DL allowed the youngsters another beat and then hit the ignition, producing a menacing yet musical exhaust that sent Isaiah
Two Four into head-clutching ecstasy. The Trans-Am backed,

turned, and, to the stately Neo-glasspack wind chorale, combustion shaped to music, varying as she shifted gears, departed, the sound diminishing down the long maze of switchbacks, pausing for the gate, resuming the melody, blending finally into the ground hum of freeway traffic far below.

D ESCRIBED in *Aggro World* as "a sort of Esalen Institute for lady asskickers," the mountainside retreat of the Sisterhood of Kunoichi Attentives stood on a promontory dappled in light and dark California greens above a small valley, only a couple of ridgelines from the SP tracks, final ascent being over dirt roads vexing enough to those who arrived in times of mud, and so deeply rutted when the season was dry that many an unwary seeker was brought to a high-centered pause out in this oil painting of a landscape, wheels spinning in empty air, creatures of the hillside only just interrupting grazing or predation to notice. Originally, in the days of the missions, built to house Las Hermanas de Nuestra Señora de los Pepinares — one of those ladies' auxiliaries that kept springing up around the Jesuits in seventeenth-century Spain, never recognized by Rome nor even by the Society, but persisting with grace and stamina there in California for hundreds of years — the place had acquired extensions and outbuildings, got wired and rewired, plumbed and replumbed, until a series of bad investments had forced what was left of the sodality to put it up for rent and disperse to cheaper housing, though they continued to market the world-famous cucumber brandy bearing their name.

By the 1960s the kunoichi, looking for some cash flow themselves, had begun to edge into the self-improvement business, not quite begun to boom as it would in a few more years, offering, eventually, fantasy marathons for devotees of the Orient, group rates on Kiddie Ninja Weekends, help for rejected disciples of Zen ("No bamboo sticks — ever!" promised the ads in *Psychology Today*) and other Eastern methods. Men of a certain age in safari outfits and military haircuts and quite often the grip of a merciless nostalgia could always be counted on to show up with ogling in mind, expecting some chorus line of Asian dewdrops. Imagine their surprise at the first day's orientation session, when the Sisters, all wearing ninja gear and unpromisingly distant expressions, filed onstage one by one. Not only were most of them non-Asian, many were actually black, a-and Mexican too! What went on?

"There it is," DL said, "check it out." They had rounded a curve, and under the bright moon the forest fell away and the land went sloping down in pastures and then thickets of alder to where a creek rushed and fell, and up beyond that, high on the other side, there stood the Retreat. Steep walls weather-stained over old whitewash did not so much tower above the rolling, breaking terrain as almost readably reflect it, as if they shone at all their different angles like great coarse mirrors, beneath ancient tile roofs gone darkening and corroded under the elements, with windows recessed into shadow and seeming to bear no relation to any set of levels that might be inside. As they got closer, Prairie saw archways, a bell tower, an interpenetration with the tall lime surfaces of cypresses, pepper trees, a fruit orchard . . . nothing looked especially creepy to her. She was a California kid, and she trusted in vegetation. What was creepy, the heart of creep-out, lay back down the road behind her, in, but not limited to, the person, hard and nearly invisible, like quartz, of her pursuer, Brock Vond.

DL was known at the gates outer and inner, getting long looks Prairie couldn't interpret. By the time they got up to the reception building, there was a welcoming committee standing in the lamp-lined drive, all in black *gi*, headed by a tall, fit, scholarly-looking woman named Sister Rochelle, who turned out to be Senior Attentive, or mother superior of the place. "DL-san," she greeted her longtime disciple and antagonist. "What new mischief now?" DL bowed and introduced Prairie, at whom Sister Rochelle had been gazing as if she knew her but was pretending for some reason that she didn't. They entered a small tiled courtyard with a fountain. Owls called and swooped. Women lay naked in the moonlight. Others, all in black, stood together in the gallery shadows. "Any interest from law enforcement here?" inquired Sister Rochelle.

DL's line should've been something like, "Oh, you working for them now?" delivered emphatically, but she only waited quietly in what Prairie would learn was the standard Attentive's Posture, her eyes lowered, her lip zipped.

"So will the sheriff break down the gate right away, do you think, or wait till Monday morning? This ain't *The Hunchback of Notre Dame* here, and even if she's not some kind of escapee, there's the Ninjette Oath you took, clause Eight, you'll recall, section B? 'To allow residence to no one who cannot take responsibility for both her input and her output.' "

"Like earn what you eat, secure what you shit, been doin' it for years," Prairie said, "what else?" Not in the first place the sort of kid to take stuff personally, getting ESP messages that around here it might not even be considered cool, she had been tending to the line of her spine and quietly meeting the woman's neutral but energetic gaze. "Well then maybe you have some kind of work-study program here, list of courses, price schedule, maybe pick something cheap, be a live-in student, work off the fees?" detaching from their eye contact long enough to look around, as if for chores that needed doing, trying to wish some deal into being.

The Head Ninjette seemed interested. "Can you cook?"

"Some. You mean you don't have a cook?"

"Worse. A lot of people who think they're cooks but are clinically deluded. We're notorious here for having the worst food in the seminar-providing community. And we're looking at another herd next weekend, and we try different staff combinations, but nothing works. The karmic invariance is, is we're paying for high discipline in the Sisterhood with a zoo in the kitchen. Come on, you'll see."

Out in the evening, she led Prairie and DL around a few corners and down a long trellised walkway toward the rear of the main building. Suppertime was over and some postprandial critique now vehemently in progress. People huddled, intimidated, by the back entrance, out which came an amazing racket, giant metal mixing bowls gonging and crashing around on the flagstone floors, voices screaming, for background the local 24-hour "New Age" music station, gushing into the environment billows of audio treacle. Inside, something ruined was still smoldering on the back of a stove. Folks stood around next to pots that would need scouring. There lay throughout the deep old kitchen a depressing odor of stale animal fat and disinfectant. The chef who was supposed tonight to have been in charge crouched with his head in an oven, weeping bitterly.

"Hi guys," caroled Sister Rochelle, "what y'all doin'?"

Holding their nightly self-criticism hour, of course, in which everybody got to trash the chef of the day personally for the failure of his or her menu, as well as plan more of the same for tomorrow.

"I did what I had to," the chef blubbered, iron and muffled, "I was true to the food."

One of the stoveside loungers looked over. "What are you calling 'food,' Gerhard? That meal tonight wasn't food."

"What you cook's stomach trouble with fat on it," fiercely added a lady holding a meat cleaver, with which she struck a nearby chopping block for emphasis.

"Even your Jell-O salads have scum on them," put in a stylish young man in a couturier chef's toque from Bullock's Wilshire.

"Please, enough," whimpered Gerhard.

"Total honesty," people reminded him. This meanspirited exercise, thought to be therapeutic, was part of everyone's assignment back here to what Gerhard called "indefinite culinary penance."

"Isn't that kidnapping?" Prairie would wonder later.

No — they had all signed instruments of indenture, releases, had all arrived somewhere in their lives where they needed to sign. They spoke of scullery duty as a decoding of individual patterns of not-eating, seeing thereby beyond dishes, pots, and pans each uniquely soiled, beyond accidents of personality to a level where you are not what you eat but how. . . . At first Prairie had no time to appreciate many of these spiritual dimensions, because she was running her ass off nonstop. The penitents in the kitchen, weird-eyed as colonists on some galactic outpost, greeted her arrival as a major event. As it turned out, none of them could fix anything even they liked to eat. Some here had grown indifferent to food, others actively to hate it. Nevertheless, new recipes were seized on like advanced technology from beyond the local star system. After checking out the vegetable patch, the orchards, the walk-in freezers and pantries of the Retreat, wondering if she was violating some Prime Directive, Prairie taught them Spinach Casserole. And it proved to be just the ticket to get these folks going again as a team.

"What *were* you going to serve them?" she couldn't help asking.

"Dip," chirped a Mill Valley real-estate agent.

"Smores," chuckled a Milpitas scoutmaster, "with maple syrup."

"New England Boiled Dinner," replied an ex-institutional inmate with a shudder.

The secret to Spinach Casserole was the UBI, or Universal Binding Ingredient, cream of mushroom soup, whose presence in rows of giant cans there in the ninjette storerooms came as no surprise. Deep in the refrigerators were also to be scavenged many kinds of pieces of cheese, not to mention cases full of the more traditional Velveeta and Cheez Whiz, nor was spinach a problem, with countless blocks of it occupying their own wing of the freezer. So next day the classic recipe was the vegetarian entrée du jour at supper. For the meat eaters, a number of giant baloneys were set to roasting whole on spits, to be turned and attentively basted with a grape-jelly glaze by once-quarrelsome kitchen staff while others made croutons from old bread, bustling about while the spinach thawed, singing along with the radio, which someone had mercifully retuned to a rock and roll station.

DL popped her head in in the late afternoon and looked around. "Just what I thought — a teenage charismatic."

"Not me," Prairie shrugged, "it's 'ese recipes."

"Um, and those purple things, on the rotisserie?"

"Just somethin' out of the TV section. What's up?"

"Sister Rochelle wonders if you have a minute."

Prairie went along watchfully, at her own tempo, making a point of inspecting a few assembled casseroles as well as checking the baloney spin rate before leaving the kitchen, reminding herself of a cat. Upstairs, in the Ninjette Coffee Lounge, the Head Ninjette, with a mug of coffee in her hand, slowly emerged, as they conversed, from invisibility. It seemed to the girl that this must be a magical gift. She learned later that Rochelle had memorized, in this room, all the shadows and how they changed, the cover, the exact spaces between things . . . had come to know the room so completely that she could impersonate it, in its full transparency and emptiness.

"Could I learn to do that?"

"Takes a serious attention span." A look sideways. "Then the question of why should you want to?" Her voice was even, with a slow hoarseness suggesting alcohol and cigarettes. Prairie also thought she heard some distant country notes that Rochelle was suppressing on purpose, in favor of something more invisible.

Prairie shrugged. "Seems like it could come in handy."

"Common sense and hard work's all it is. Only the first of many kunoichi disillusionments — right, DL? — is finding that the knowledge won't come down all at once in any big transcendent moment."

"But Zen folks, like where I work, say —"

"Oh, that happens. But not around here. Here it's always out at the margins, using the millimeters and little tenths of a second, you understand, scuffling and scraping for everything we get."

"So don't get into it unless you mean it?"

"Well you ought to see how many gaga little twits we get up here, 'specially your age group, nothing personal, looking for secret powers on the cheap. Thinking we'll take 'em through the spiritual car wash, soap away all that road dirt, git 'em buffed up all cherry again, come out th' other end everybody hangin' around the Orange Julius next door go 'Wow!' 's what they think, like we'll keep 'em awake all weekend, maybe around dawn on Sunday they'll start hallucinating, have a mental adventure they can mistake for improvement in their life, and who knows? Or they get us mixed up with nuns or ballet?"

The girl made a point of looking at her watch, a multicolored plastic model from a Vineland swap meet. "Givin' those baloneys fifteen minutes a pound, think 'at's about right?"

DL smirked. "Not goin' for it, Rochelle-*ane*."

The Senior Attentive shifted gear. "Prairie, we subscribe to some outside data services here, but we also maintain our own library of computer files, including a good-size one on your mother."

Where Prairie had been, "your mother" in that tone of voice usually meant trouble, and she wasn't sure if this woman, who looked sort of middle-class, knew how it sounded. But Prairie was shaking with the need to find out anything she could, the way some girls she knew got about boys, his family's name in the phone book, anything. "Would it," slowly (should she bow?), "be OK if —"

"How about after supper?"

"Ohm mah way, as my Grampa the gaffer always sez." Not a minute too soon, she returned to find a number of casseroles beginning to redline, baloney glazes to decompose. Pretending to be setting an example, Prairie slid over to one of the work counters, wrestled a hot baloney into place, quickly sharpened a knife, and began to carve the object into steaming, purple-rimmed slices, which she arranged attractively on a serving platter, generously spooning more shiny grape liquid over the top, to be carried in and set on one of the mess-hall tables, where eaters would serve themselves — except for the people in assertiveness programs, of course, who sat over at their own table and each got a separate plate with the food already on it.

From the mess hall next door an ambiguous murmuring, part hunger, part apprehension, had grown in volume. Prairie grabbed a kettle of institutional tomato soup, carried it on in, and for the next couple of hours she also schlepped racks of newly washed cups and dishes in and bused dirty dishes out, cleaned off tabletops, poured coffee, going from one set of chores to another as they arose, sensing partial vacuums and flowing there to fill them, unable to help noticing that people were taking seconds on the Spinach Casserole, and the baloney too. Later she scrubbed out pots and pans and helped put stuff away and swab down the stone floor of the kitchen and scullery. By the time she got upstairs to the Ninjette Terminal Center and found out how to log on, the midsummer sunset had come and gone and the sounds of an evening koto workshop mixed with the good-nights of courtyard birds.

The file on Frenesi Gates, whose entries had been accumulating over the years, often haphazardly, from far and wide, reminded Prairie of scrapbooks kept by somebody's eccentric hippie uncle. Some was governmental, legal history with the DMV, letterhead memoranda from the FBI enhanced by Magic Marker, but there were also clippings from "underground" newspapers that had closed down long ago, transcripts of Frenesi's radio interviews on

KPFK, and a lot of cross-references to something called 24fps, which Prairie recalled as the name of the film collective DL said she and Frenesi had been in together for a while.

So into it and then on Prairie followed, a girl in a haunted mansion, led room to room, sheet to sheet, by the peripheral whiteness, the earnest whisper, of her mother's ghost. She already knew about how literal computers could be — even spaces between characters mattered. She had wondered if ghosts were only literal in the same way. Could a ghost think for herself, or was she responsive totally to the needs of the still-living, needs like keystrokes entered into her world, lines of sorrow, loss, justice denied? . . . But to be of any use, to be "real," a ghost would have to be more than only that kind of elaborate pretending. . . .

Prairie found that she could also summon to the screen photographs, some personal, some from papers and magazines, images of her mom, most of the time holding a movie camera, at demonstrations, getting arrested, posing with various dimly recognizable Movement figures of the sixties, beaming a significant look at a cop in riot gear beside a chain-link fence someplace while one hand (Prairie would learn her mother's hands, read each gesture a dozen ways, imagine how they would have moved at other, unphotographed times) appeared to brush with its fingertips the underside of the barrel of his assault rifle. Gross! Her Mom? This girl with the old-fashioned hair and makeup, always wearing either miniskirts or those weird-looking bell-bottoms they had back then? In a few years Prairie would almost be that age, and she had an eerie feeling miniskirts would be back.

She paused at a shot of DL and Frenesi together. They were walking along on what might have been a college campus. In the distance was a pedestrian overpass, where tiny figures could be seen heading both ways, suggesting, at least for a moment, social tranquillity. The women's shadows were long, lapping up over curbs, across grass, between the spokes of cyclists. Catching the late or early sun were palm trees, flights of distant steps, a volleyball court, few if any glass windows. Frenesi's face was turned or turning toward her partner, perhaps her friend, a suspicious or withheld smile seeming to begin. . . . DL was talking. Her lower teeth flashed. It wasn't politics — Prairie could feel in the bright California colors, sharpened up pixel by pixel into deathlessness, the lilt of bodies, the unlined relaxation of faces that didn't have to be put on for each other, liberated from their authorized versions for a free, everyday breath of air. Yeah, Prairie thought at them, go ahead, you guys. Go ahead. . . .

"Who was that boy," DL was asking, or "that 'dude,' at the protest rally? With the long hair and love beads, and the joint in his mouth?"

"You mean in the flowered bell-bottoms and the paisley shirt?"

"Right on, sister!"

"Psychedelic!" Slapping hands back and forth. Prairie wondered who'd taken the picture — one of the film collective, the FBI? Before the stained deep crystalline view she fell into a hypnagogic gaze, which the unit promptly sensed, beginning to blink, following this with a sound chip playing the hook from the Everlys' "Wake Up, Little Susie," over and over. Prairie remembered that she had to be up before sunrise, to prep for breakfast. As she reached toward the power button, she said good night to the machine.

"Why good night yourself, gentle User," it replied, "and may your sleep be in every way untroubled."

Back down in the computer library, in storage, quiescent ones and zeros scattered among millions of others, the two women, yet in some definable space, continued on their way across the low-lit campus, persisting, recoverable, friends by the time of this photo for nearly a year, woven together in an intricacy of backs covered, promises made and renegotiated, annoyances put up with, shortcuts worn in, ESP beyond the doubts of either. They would probably have met at some point, though who'd have been willing to bet they'd stick? The turbulence of the times was bringing all kinds of people together into towns like Berkeley, lured, like DL, by promises of action. In those days DL was just cruising up and down 101 looking for girl motorcycle gangs to terrorize, drinking drugstore vodka out of the bottle, hustling guys named Snake for enough double-cross whites to get her to the next population center offering a suitable risk to her safety. The night before she met

Frenesi she had chased the entire membership of Tetas y Chetas M.C. northward through the dark farm country around Salinas, vegetables fallen in profusion from the trucks and then squashed and resquashed by traffic all day making the night streaming against her face smell like a giant salad. Finally she ran out of gas and had to let them go. By then she was close enough to Berkeley, and had been hearing enough on the radio, to want to go look in. She couldn't have said, then or later, what she thought she was looking for.

What she found was Frenesi, who'd been out with her camera and a bagful of bootlegged ECO stock since dawn, finally ending up on Telegraph Avenue filming a skirmish line of paramilitary coming up the street in riot gear, carrying small and she hoped only rubber-bullet-firing rifles. Last time she looked she'd been at the front edge of a crowd who were slowly retreating from the campus, trashing what they could as they went. When the film roll ended and she came up out of the safety of her viewfinder, Frenesi was alone, halfway between the people and the police, with no side street handy to go dodging down. Hmm. Shop doors were all secured with chain, windows shuttered over with heavy plywood. Her next step would've been just to go ahead and change rolls, get some more footage, but to go rooting around in her bag right now could only be taken as a threat by the boys in khaki, who'd come close enough that even above the lingering nose-wrenching ground note of tear gas she could still begin to smell them, the aftershave, the gunmetal in the sun, the new-issue uniforms whose armpits by now were musky with fear. Oh, I need Superman, she prayed, Tarzan on that vine. The basic stone bowelflash had come and gone about the time DL showed up, all in black including helmet and face shield, riding her esteemed and bad red and silver Czech motorcycle, the Che Zed, overdesigned in every part, up onto which she gathered Frenesi out of danger, camera, miniskirt, equipment bags, and all, and carried her away. Skidding among piles of street debris and paper fires, over crumbled auto glass, trying not to hit anybody lying on the pavement, up onto some sidewalk and around the corner at last and down the long hillside to the Bay flashing in the late sun they escaped, in a snarling dreamrush of speed and scent. With her bare thighs Frenesi gripped the leather hips of her benefactor, finding that she'd also pressed her face against the fragrant leather back — she never thought it might be a woman she hugged this way.

Biker rapture, for sure. They sat devouring cheeseburgers, fries, and shakes in a waterfront place full of refugees from the fighting up the hill, all their eyes, including ones that had wept, now lighted from the inside — was it only the overhead fluorescents, some trick of sun and water outside? no . . . too many of these fevered lamps not to have origin across the line somewhere, in a world sprung new, not even defined yet, worth the loss of nearly everything in this one. The jukebox played the Doors, Jimi Hendrix, Jefferson Airplane, Country Joe and the Fish. DL had taken off the helmet and shaken out her hair, which lit up in the approaching orange sunset like a comet. Frenesi, jittery, starving, and gaga all at once, was still trying to figure it out. "Somebody sent you, right?"

"Cruisin' through, was all. You sure sound paranoid."

Frenesi gestured with her burger, trailing drops of separating ketchup and fat, each drop warped by the forces of its flight into swirling micropatterns of red and beige, and — "It's the Revolution, girl — can't you feel it?"

DL narrowed her eyes, wondering, What have we here. She felt like an adult come upon a little kid alone at a dangerous time of day, not yet aware of her mom's absence. "I could see you were just all revved up," she told Frenesi, though months later. "I couldn't help teasin' you. You were bein' so —" but let it go, pretending she couldn't think of the word. It probably wasn't *revolutionary*, invoked in those days widely and sometimes lovingly and enjoying a wide range of meaning. Frenesi dreamed of a mysterious people's oneness, drawing together toward the best chances of light, achieved once or twice that she'd seen in the street, in short, timeless bursts, all paths, human and projectile, true, the people in a single presence, the police likewise simple as a moving blade — and individuals who in meetings might only bore or be pains in the ass here suddenly being seen to transcend, almost beyond will to move smoothly between baton and victim to take the blow instead, to lie down on the tracks as the iron rolled in or look into the gun muzzle and maintain the power of speech — there was no telling, in those days, who might unexpectedly change this way, or when. Some were in it, in fact, secretly for the possibilities of finding just such moments. But DL admitted she was a little less saintly — "Is the asskicking part's usually what I'm lookin' for," watching Frenesi, waiting for disapproval. "But somebody told me it don't mean much unless I make what they call the correct analysis? and then act on it? Ever hear of that one?"

Frenesi shrugged. "Heard of it. Maybe I don't have the patience. I have to trust the way this makes me feel. Feels right, DL. Like we're really going to change the world this time," looking back in the same go-ahead-say-something way. But DL was smiling lopsidedly to herself. Backlit by the last of the sun, Frenesi in dazed witness, her face had become possessed by that of a young man, distant, surmised — Moody Chastain, her father. Later, when they got to showing each other pictures of their lives, there he was, same face in silver and dye, confirming the earlier gleaming moment — the halo of fresh-drawn copper, the ghostly young hero who'd come to her rescue, the whoop-de-do that day, Revolution all around them, world-class burgers, jukebox solidarity, as the sun set behind Marin and the scent of DL's sweat and pussy excitation diffused out of the leather clothing, mixed with motor smells.

Moody. He'd once been a junior Texas rounder, promoting bad behavior all over the Harlingen, Brownsville, McAllen area. For a while he and a small gang had managed to migrate as far as Mobile Bay, spreading apprehension from Mertz to Magazine, but he was soon back in his native orbit, handing out to all the ladies Dauphin Island orchids kept fresh with the beer in an ice tub in the truckbed and resuming his ways, which included driving fast, discharging firearms inappropriately, and passing around open containers, till a sheriff's deputy friendly with the family suggested a choice between the Army now or Huntsville later. The war then approaching was never mentioned directly, but, "Well, what'll I get to shoot?" Moody wanted to know.

"Any weapon, any caliber."

"I mean, *who* do I get to shoot?"

"Whoever they tell you. Interesting thing about that, way I see it, you don't have nearly the legal problems."

Sounded good to Moody, who went right down and joined up. He met Norleen while he was at Fort Hood at services in the same narrow wood church they got married in, just before he shipped out. It was about mid-Atlantic, surrounded by nothing that did not refer, finally, to steel, vomiting for days, imagining the horizon outside, the unnatural purity, before he understood how terrified he was. It was the first time in his career he couldn't climb in the truck and head for some borderline. He felt himself about to go crazy in this deep overcrowded hole, but he hung on, he tried to see through his fear, and when it came it was like finding Jesus — Moody saw, like the comics or Bible illustrations, a succession of scenes showing him the way he had to go, which was to imagine the worst and then himself be worse than that. He must torture the violent, deprive the greedy, give the drunks something to stagger about. He would have to become a Military Policeman, be as bad as he had to be to make it, using everything he knew from those rounder days. And so he did, pulling his first MP duty in London, on and about Shaftesbury Avenue, accessorized in virgin white, known, in military slang in those days, as a "snowdrop."

Darryl Louise was born right after the war, in Leavenworth, Kansas, after Moody, having made it through alive, was assigned to the Disciplinary Barracks there. In the years of war he'd done a lot of shooting, some wounding, a little killing, but despite his love of weaponry, he'd come to see bombs, artillery, even rifles, as too abstract and cold. The peacetime Moody wanted to get more personal now. Though he was already licensed to use life-threatening come-alongs, to crack heads and dislocate shoulders, he didn't really light up till he discovered the judo and jujitsu of the defeated Jap, then enjoying a postwar surge of interest. From then on Moody practiced when he could, wherever he happened to be posted, getting the best of East and West Coast schools of thought, working eventually part-time as an instructor with his own group of students. When DL was five or six she started tagging along with him down to the dojo.

"Could've been my mama thought he was slippin' around. Maybe I was supposed to keep an eye on him."

"Hmm-mm, I can see why." The snapshot Frenesi happened to be looking at showed Moody in his full-dress uniform, ribbons and medals and patches and fourragères, holding already oversize eight-month-old DL and grinning in the sunlight. There were palm trees behind them, so it couldn't't've been Kansas anymore.

"Way it looks," Frenesi said, when they could say things like this comfortably, "is that he went over. A wild kid who ended up being that deputy sheriff."

"Uh-huh," nodding, sparkling, "and guess who he took it out on." DL had noticed as she got older that her mother, Norleen, was apt to be in and out of their housing unit of the moment on mysterious "chores," her word for something else that years later DL surmised could have been boyfriends. Among Moody's problem areas was a practice of bringing home with him emotional elements of his work. The morning after one of their bigger gorounds, DL started hollering at her mother. "Why're you puttin' up with his shit?" But Norleen could only gaze tearfully back, needing to talk, all right, but not to her child, whom she must have thought she was protecting.

"Wait a minute," Frenesi broke in, "he beat on your mother?"

She got that who-the-fuck-are-you stare back. "Never heard of that where you come from?"

"He ever do it to you?"

She smiled tightly. "Nope. That was just it." Nodded, her jaw forward. "The son of a bitch, you see, wouldn't even work out with me — not even in public at the dojo, not even when we got to be the same size and rank. He would never get into the ring with me."

"He knew better."

"Oh, I wouldt'n've kicked his ass *that* hard. . . ." She kept a straight face while Frenesi grinned. "I'm serious, you don't let things like how you feel about your daddy get in the way. Not professional, bad for your spirit."

"What about your mom, why *did* she put up with it?"

Best Norleen could ever do was "It's his job," but DL still didn't

get it. "He loves us, but sometimes he has to be like 'at." Her face
that morning had been swollen, distorted enough to frighten the
girl, as if her mother were slowly turning into some other creature,
one that might even wish her harm.

"You mean, they're tellin' him to?"

Norleen answered with one of those sighs DL had by then
learned to dread, a beaten saddening surrender of breath. "No,
but they might 's well be. Just how it is. Men are runnin' it, they
don't ask us, better learn it now 'cause it doesn't end when you
grow up either, Darryl Louise."

"You mean *everybody* has to —"

"Ever'body darlin'. Can you reach me that big spoon over
there?" But years later, DL on a rare visit, her mother by then
divorced and living in Houston, Norleen finally told her, "Why,
the man had me scared spitless. What was I supposed to do? I
didn't even know how to shoot any o' them ol' stupid guns he
kept around. And I'm telling you, *you're* lucky you made it 's far
as you did. I know that something — Somebody — was lookin'
out for me."

And by then DL was able easily to sit attentive, pressureless,
through the Christer commercial that followed, one she'd already
heard more than once over the phone. She was finally acknowledging her mother's soul, one more side benefit of life in the martial
arts. The discipline had steered her early enough away from the
powerlessness and the sooner or later self-poisoning hatred that
had been waiting for her. Somewhere further along, she'd been
given to understand, she would discover that all souls, human and
otherwise, were different disguises of the same greater being —
God at play. She respected Norleen's love of Jesus even though
she'd had her own way to go since she was a girl, even before the
Department of Defense, that well-known agent of enlightenment,
ever thought of cutting Moody's orders for Japan.

This was during the lull between Korea and Vietnam, but the
troops on R and R could still keep Moody plenty busy. Norleen
was often out, running those chores of hers, so DL was left on
her own. She started to ditch the dependents' school, intending to
go look for an instructor in unarmed combat, usually winding up

hanging around pachinko parlors and making shady acquaintances, picking up enough of the language to find built into it a
whole charm school's worth of rules for getting along socially over
here.

One day, in the ringing crepitation of millions of steel balls,
ingeniously waxed pins, and spheriphagous "tulips," she grew
aware of a gap in the web, a local redirection of interest. She
looked around. He was dressed plainly and had the air of a servant.
Bowing, precise, he asked, "You eat *soba*?"

Bowing back, "You buyin'?"

His name was Noboru, and he claimed to have the gift of seeing
in a person what she was truly destined to be. "Don't get me
wrong!" between slurps, "you have definite *shodan* potential at
the game, but pachinko is not your destiny. I want you to come
and meet my teacher."

"You're — some kind of guidance counselor?"

"Been out searching a long time. The sensei asked me to."

"Wait — I've been around the circuit enough to know it's the
pupil who's supposed to go lookin' for the teacher. What kind of
a no-class setup is this here?" But she'd been having no luck on
her own, so maybe it was what her Aunt Tulsa liked to call "a
message from beyond."

Throughout their first interview, Inoshiro Sensei, as feared, kept
one hand on DL's leg while using the other hand to chain-smoke.
The pitch was take-it-or-leave-it simple. In her pachinko playing
his agent Noboru, with his infallible gift, had detected an advanced
ruthlessness of spirit, which the master, going then secretly to
observe, had confirmed. DL wondered if being already taller than
most Japanese adults, plus her eye-catching head of hair, came
into it at all. "There are things I am obliged to pass on. Skills no
one owns, but which must be carried forward."

"I'm not even Japanese."

"One of my major karmic missions this time around is to get
outside of Japanese insular craziness, be international *assukikaa,
ne?* Come on," announced the sensei, "we're going dancing!"

"Huh?"

"See how you move!" They proceeded, DL squinting and

frowning, to a water-trade joint around the corner called The Lucky Sea Urchin, where they danced some back-street two-step and DL waved off everything but 7-Up. It wasn't as if these jokers were accosting her at a real stable time of her life. At the school on the base, girls were given only a sketchy governmental account of puberty and adolescence. DL's were both turning out to be like vacationing on another planet and losing her traveler's checks. Not long before this her period, a major obsession by then, had arrived at last, plus lately she felt washed under by these long, sometimes daylong, waves of inattention, everybody looking at her weirdly, especially boys. The sensei had scowlingly little sympathy for any of this, however. In the traditional stories, a few of which DL would come to hear before she left Japan, the apprenticeship is harsh and long, someplace scenic up in the mountains where the student is put to work at menial outdoor tasks, learning patience and obedience, without which she can learn nothing else, and this alone, in some stories, takes years. What DL got from Inoshiro Sensei was more like the modernized crash course. Man here was clearly under some time pressure so heavy she didn't want to know, having herself decided it was a romantic terminal illness, an older woman someplace. . . . For ancient dark reasons, he could not return to the mountains, probably had killed somebody back there over this woman, and now, while she lay dying far away, he must live penitent, earthbound, down here in the ensnarling city, longing for her and the mist and the wind-shaped trees. . . .

The sensei ran DL all over the map on incomprehensible, some would say pointless, fool errands. He blindfolded her with tape and dark glasses and took her on the Yamanote Line, riding around for hours switching subways, at last unsealing her eyes, handing her a stone of a certain shape and weight, and leaving her well lost, with instructions to get back to his house before nightfall, using only the stone. He gave her messages she didn't understand to take to people she didn't know, at addresses harshly drilled in, that would turn out either not to exist or to be something else, like a pachinko parlor. He also enrolled her in a small dojo nearby run by a former disciple. She would put in half her time on traditional forms and exercises, then slip outside, around the corner and down the alley, to a rendezvous more felonious than illicit.

Meantime, all her school ditching had become a problem at home. The truancy squad was now in her face as part of a daily routine. Moody ignored it till they finally came to bother him at work, in front of other men, including officers, not the best way to send him home with a smile on his lips. For a week and a half he would already be screaming as he came up the front path, silencing birds, sending neighbor dogs, cats, and children fleeing indoors, and it would go on, out the screened windows and across the neat little yards, on through suppertime, prime time, and beyond, blunt, embittered, what the sensei would have called lacking in style. Norleen as usual kept silent, trying to stay out of the way, though sometimes on impulse she was known to actually bring them coffee right in the very fierce middle of it. And as usual Moody made no least move upon his daughter, who might by now, far as he knew, be able to do him some real harm. To tell the truth, these days, pushing twenty years in the service, he was starting to kick back some, working a regular daytime shift for a couple years now, manipulating paper that only represented the adrenaline and guts of what he used to do, putting in less and less time at gym, track, pool, or dojo, content to sit behind his increasing embonpoint with a personalized coffee mug wired permanently to his right index finger and shoot the shit with numberless cronies from head-bashing days who dropped by all the time. He'd lost his old enthusiasm for unarmed combat, and DL found no way, reasonable or at the top of her voice, to get him to see where her own love of the discipline was taking her. She did tell them both, trying to sound dutiful, about the dojo, but not about Inoshiro Sensei, having sworn to keep silent and already feeling the depressing weight of Moody's suspicions. "I ever find you 'th one 'nem little slant-eyed jerkoffs," as he expressed it, "he gets killed, and you get a Clorox douche, you understand me?" DL hated with all her heart to say so, but she did.

Another message from beyond, no doubt. She saw a pattern. He was settling for spoiling, snarling, aiming his belly at her like a great smooth bomb snout and calling her Trash, Gook-lover, and, mystifyingly, Communist too. Norleen nibbled her lip and from under her lashes sent sorrowing looks that said, Why keep getting him worked up, he'll take it out on me. "I was just sadistic enough," DL admitted, years later, to herself and then to Norleen's face, "so mad at you for all 'at knucklin' under, that sure I provoked him. Also I 's wonderin' what it would take to get you to fight him back."

Norleen shrugged. The central air-conditioning pursued its dark slow pulsing, traffic breathed along the freeways, trees outside just managed to stir in the moist subtropical air. " 'Course you knew all the while I was seeing Captain Lanier. . . ."

"What? Mama, his CO?" Well no, she sure hadn't known till now, how would she?

"He paid for the divorce, too."

DL shook her head, bewildered. "No shit?"

Norleen, born-again, mannerly and all, laughed like a girl with a garden hose in her hand. "No shit."

And DL guessed that Moody'd known about it all along, too. The Captain would have kept him reminded. Men had ways. She'd been living her childhood in a swamp full of intrigue, where, below, invisible sleek things without names kept brushing past, barely felt sliding across her skin, everybody pretending the surface was all there was. Till one day she had a moment. There just came flowing over her the certainty that only when she was away from them, learning to fight, did she feel any good. The sensei, for all his lechery, high-speed frenzies, temperamental snits and low-tolerance ways, had become a refuge from what lay breathing invisible somewhere back in the geometric sprawl of yards and fences and dumpsters of Dependents' Housing, more than ready to rise from its crouch and take her over. So instead of waiting for something dramatic enough to give her an excuse, which could be too dangerous, DL one day when they both happened to be out of the house just filled a small army bag with what she needed, turned much of the fridge's contents into sandwiches and packed them in a big number 66 market bag, stole a bottle of PX Chivas Regal for the sensei, and without any last look in at her room, went AWOL.

When she arrived at the sensei's house, she found most of the alley filled by a white Lincoln Continental whose ample dimensions had been beefed up further with armor plating, radar, gun pods, and command turrets. Nearby a detachment of smirking crew-cut young fellows in black suits and shirts, white neckties, black shades, posed and sauntered. She knew enough to keep out of the way, hunker down, wrap her hair in a scarf, wait in a shadow till she saw an elderly man in a suit and homburg hat come out the door with Inoshiro Sensei. They bowed, then clasped hands in a way not fully visible. The visitor was hustled by his *kobun* into the car, which then was carefully backed out of its tight squeeze. Pedestrian traffic resumed as if after a rainstorm, one more view of Edo.

Inside, DL found the place littered with foam plastic sake containers. They'd been sending out for it all day. Noboru was unconscious, but DL thought the sensei had a grip on himself. She asked him, respectfully, for asylum. He seemed amused. "Do you know who was just here?"

"Yakuza."

"You're too young for such things, Blondie!"

" 'Even a crying baby dummies up when she hears the name Yamaguchi-gumi,' " she recited in Japanese.

Sympathetic but leering, he reached for her. Mistake, sensei. She was immediately in a Vanishing Stance, surfaces loaded, ready to let him have it in any variety of ways, all depending on him. "Relax! Only testing you!"

"Uh-huh, tell me, sensei, if you're that tight with the Mob, and I'm working for you, does that mean —"

"Our connection is of very old *giri*, lot of details, Japanese names, you'd lose track. The war figures in heavily. But you and I, we're connected only by bonds of master and disciple, free to disconnect at any time. If you could leave your parents' house that lightly, you'll have no trouble leaving me."

What was this? Guilt? "You want me to go back?"

He cackled and fell into sounding not quite decipherable. "You will go back. Till you do, stick around!"

From then on she was able to devote herself full time to ninjitsu, including the forbidden steps outside its canons taken — it seemed long ago — by the sensei, through which the original purity of ninja intent had been subverted, made cruel and more worldly, bled of spirit, once eternal techniques now only one-shot and disposable, once greater patterns now only a string of encounters, single and multiple, none with any meaning beyond itself. This was what he felt he had to pass on — not the brave hard-won grace of any warrior, but the cheaper brutality of an assassin. When DL finally tumbled, she brought it to his attention.

"Sure," he told her, "this is for all the rest of us down here with the insects, the ones who don't quite get to make warrior, who with two tenths of a second to decide fail to get it right and live with it the rest of our lives — it's for us drunks, and sneaks, and people who can't feel enough to kill if they have to . . . this is our equalizer, our edge — all we have to share. Because we have ancestors and descendants too — our generations . . . our traditions."

"But everybody's a hero at least once," she informed him, "maybe your chance hasn't come up yet."

"DL-san, you are crazy," he diagnosed gently, "seeing too many movies, maybe. Those you will be fighting — those you must resist — they are neither samurai nor ninja. They are *sarariman*, incrementalists, who cannot act boldly and feel only contempt for those who can. . . . Only for what I must teach you have they learned respect."

He taught her the Chinese Three Ways, Dim Ching, Dim Hsuen, and Dim Mak, with its Nine Fatal Blows, as well as the Tenth and Eleventh, which are never spoken of. She learned how to give people heart attacks without even touching them, how to get them to fall from high places, how through the Clouds of Guilt technique to make them commit *seppuku* and think it was their idea — plus a grab bag of strategies excluded from the Kumi-Uchi, or official ninja combat system, such as the Enraged Sparrow, the Hidden Foot, the Nosepicking of Death, and the truly unspeakable *Gojira no Chimpira*. Despite the accelerated schedule, some of the moves Inoshiro Sensei taught DL would only make sense ten years or more from now — requiring that much rigorous practice every day for her even to begin to understand — and until she did understand, she was forbidden to use any of them out in the world.

As days and weeks passed, DL found herself entering into a system of heresies about the human body. In an interview with *Aggro World* years later, she spoke of her time with Inoshiro Sensei as returning to herself, reclaiming her body, "Which they always like to brainwash you about, like they know it better, trying to keep you as spaced away from it as they can. Maybe they think people are easier to control that way." The schoolroom line was, You'll never know enough about your body to take responsibility for it, so better just hand it over to those who are qualified, doctors and lab technicians and by extension coaches, employers, boys with hardons, so forth — alarmed, not to mention pissed off, DL reached the radical conclusion that her body belonged to herself. That was back when she was still thinking about ninjitsu. After a few years she didn't think so much but would just keep working out every day, finding the time and space, often at high cost, but every day of her life.

As the sensei had predicted, she did go back to Norleen and Moody, at least for a while. There had always been channels between the yakuza and the American military, and so eventually everybody knew where she was and that she was safe. Both parents, for their own reasons, were just as happy to have her out of the house just then, and the only reason DL had to resume her role as dependent minor at all was that the CO's wife found out about him and Norleen and proceeded to make life unquiet till Moody and the family were Stateside again.

A few years later, competing by then, DL heard about the Sisterhood of Kunoichi Attentives at some meet, "You know, the way you do. Hitchhiked up as far as the end of the gravel, did the last few miles on foot. Back then they let anybody who showed up crash here for free. Early days, more idealistic, not so much into money." She and Prairie were out taking a break, down by the creek. It was a couple of weeks after their arrival, with Prairie by now an old hand in the computer room as well as the kitchen. "Yeah now it's group insurance, pension plans, financial consultant name of Vicki down in L.A. who moves it all around for us, lawyer in Century City, though Amber the paralegal has been taking over most of his work since the indictment." DL seemed a little on edge. Her partner, Takeshi Fumimota, was due in for some kind of health checkup, they'd arranged to meet here, but he still hadn't shown.

"Are you worried?" Prairie, though at heart not a nosy kid, did want to give her the chance to talk, if it would do any good.

"Nahh, the ol' son of Nippon can take care of himself."

"Uh, so how'd you guys meet?"

"Aauuhhgghh!" First time outside of Saturday-morning cartoons Prairie had ever seen anybody scream with this intensity.

"Gee, thought it was a pretty innocent question. . . ."

HOW did we meet," DL's voice finding some agitated soprano level. "Well! Through Ralph Wayvone, really. I had been spending years and years of my life with these fantasies of taking revenge on Brock Vond. I wanted to kill him — one way or another he'd taken away the lives of people I loved, and I saw nothing wrong with killing him. I was that off-center, it afflicted me, wrecked my judgment." At first she'd thought Ralph was some kind of groupie. She'd noticed him, among the spectators, always wearing a suit. He finally approached her in a coffee shop in Eugene, where she had been staring dejectedly, apparently for some time, at a plate with four rubber scampi, rushed in fresh from the joke store down the street and covered as completely as possible with tomato sauce. She became aware of Ralph, looming over her food and glaring at it.

"How can you eat that?"

"Just what I ask myself. Anything else?"

Her visitor sat down across the table, clicked open an armored attaché case, and produced a folder with an 8 × 10 of a face she knew, a Fresson-process studio photograph of Brock Vond, looking like he'd just had a buffer run all over him, the high smooth forehead, the cheeks that still hadn't lost all their baby fat, the sleek and pointed ears, small chin, and slim little unbroken nose. This photo was clipped to some stapled pages, where she saw federal seals and stampings. "It's all from the FBI. Perfectly legit." He glanced at some ultrathin expensive wristwatch. "Look — you want him . . . we want him . . . say yes, both our wishes will come true."

She'd already checked out the cut and surface texture of Ralph's suit. "Well," she inquired, "what's ol' Brock up to these days?"

"Same public servant he always was, only bigger. Much, much bigger. He figures he won his war against the lefties, now he sees his future in the war against drugs. Some dear friends of mine are quite naturally upset."

"And he's too big for them? Please, you've got to be *rilly desperate*, comin' to me."

"No. You've got the motivation." At her look, "We know your history, it's all on the computer."

She thought of the white armored limo at Inoshiro Sensei's house, long ago. "Then you know how personal this is. If you want real ninja product, that could get in the way. . . . I assume you're buying skills and not just feelings here?"

"Buy, sure, but how about give? The one thing you truly want, huh? A good crack at a evil man? I know 'cause I see it in your eyes."

She didn't exactly shift her eyes away, didn't react much to this lowlife flirtatiousness, either, but there it was — he had her number, and it looked like he'd gotten it from the FBI. What was going on here? Did Ralph have a line into their NCIC computer? If they knew Brock was a target of Ralph's friends, why fail to protect one of their own? Unless of course the unfortunate setupee here was more likely DL herself, attempted assassination of a federal officer, some time in the Bureau of Prisons' mindfucking system perhaps. . . .

Ralph Wayvone, master of telepathic anxieties, tried to be helpful. "They wouldn't need any fancy excuse, Miss Chastain, they just go in, get anybody they want, do the paperwork later — what, you ain't figured that one out yet? I'd known you was such a little kid I'd o' brought yiz a Barbie doll."

"Yeah but why me? Thought you folks were more into pistols, dirks, car bombs, 'at sort of thing."

"I have heard," Ralph almost misty-eyed, "there's this touch that you can put on somebody, so lightly they don't feel it then, but a year later they drop dead, right when you happen to be miles away eating ribs with the Chief of Police."

"That would be the Vibrating Palm, or Ninja Death Touch." She went on to explain, in tones carefully free of exasperation, about the procedure, and how serious a matter it was. You didn't, for example, just go around putting it on people you didn't like. It was useless without a long history of training in martial disciplines, took years to master, and when used was a profoundly moral act. But at some point she realized she was also pitching herself to him. So did he. Patting her hand, "You're telling me I don't have to worry."

"In my time, Mr. Wayvone, I was the best."

"I remember," he said, instead of "So they tell me," but she didn't catch it. He'd heard about her in fact years before on the YakMaf grapevine, early dojo rumors, something extraordinary said to be happening at a certain regional elimination meet. So he'd driven across the Mojave all night one night to see her in action. From a dank cement arena her hair had blazed at him like the halo of an angel of mischief. In the Rolodex of Ralph's memory, young DL would be flagged that brightly. He was actually then to follow her for a time, meet to meet through the South and West, along a circuit of grim, early ex-Nam faces, motels always miles from the venue and down the wrong freeway, shoptalk, drinking, possession of weapons, T-shirts featuring skulls, snakes, and dangerous transportation. Ralph never thought of the look on his face as the helpless stare of an older man through a schoolyard fence, but as more the alert beaming of a micromanager. And sometimes he was right. In DL's case, the time he'd invested had yielded him a file he knew he'd make use of one day, and so it had come to pass.

He'd presented DL, however, with a crisis. She knew she'd been slowly poisoning her spirit, drifting further into her obsession with Brock Vond. Here was Ralph, promising resolution and release. What was she complaining about? Only that acts, deeply moral and otherwise, had consequences — only the workings of karma. One unfelt touch to the correct piece of Vond anatomy could commit her to a major redirection of her life. There was no question that she'd ever be free of Ralph. A girl did one Death Touch job and right away people started getting ideas. Whatever she chose to do would get her in trouble. She promised to give him her decision at dinner the next evening, and then she got the hell out of town, leaving the last of Ralph's tails near Drain, Oregon, beside a late-model Oldsmobile with steam pouring from beneath its hood.

She had to switch cars again before she got to L.A., then took the bus out to a bank branch on mid-Wilshire where she had once providentially stashed a packet of documents that would now give her a choice among identities, paid cash on Western Avenue for a '66 Plymouth Fury, bought a wig at a place across the street, went into a certain ladies' gas-station toilet on Olympic legendary in the dopers' community, and emerged a different, less noticeable person. The car radio, tuned to KFWB, was playing the Doors' "People Are Strange (When You're a Stranger)" as she injected herself into the slow lane of the eastbound freeway and settled in, hating to let any of it go, Banning, the dinosaurs, the Palm Springs turnoff, Indio, across the Mojave, to be redreamed in colors pale but intense, with unnaturally fine sand blowing in plumes across the sun, baby-blue shadows in the folds of the dunes, a pinkish sky — holding on, letting go, redreaming each night stop the less easterly places she'd been in all day, coming slowly unstuck, leaving for the United States, trying not to get emotional but still hanging on the rearview mirror's single tale of recedings and vanishing points as we hang on looks our lovers give.

On inertial navigation, knowing she'd know what she was looking for when she found it, DL didn't stop till the outskirts of Columbus, Ohio, which she first beheld around midday in a stunning onslaught of smog and traffic. By this time she was used to the car and its unorthodox push-button shifting, having made the analysis "stick shift = penis" and speculating that a push-button automatic might at least appear more clitorally ladylike, or, as DL might've put it, regressive, if there'd been anybody anymore to talk to, which of course there wasn't. She took a little apartment and found a job at a vacuum cleaner parts distributor's, typing and filing.

Columbus must have promised a life that some residual self, somewhere in the stifling dark, had wanted always. "Superman could change back into Clark Kent," she had once confided to Frenesi, "don't underestimate it. Workin' at the *Daily Planet* was the Man o' Steel's Hawaiian vacation, his Saturday night in town, his marijuana and his opium smoke, and oh what I wouldn't give. . . ." An evening newspaper . . . anyplace back in the Midwest . . . she would leave work around press time, make a beeline for some walk-down lounge, near enough to the paper that she could feel vibrations from the presses through the wood of the bar. Drink rye, wipe her glasses on her tie, leave her hat on indoors, gossip in the dim light with the other regulars. In the winter it would already be dark outside the windows. The polished shoes would pick up highlights as the street lamps got brighter . . . she wouldn't be waiting for anybody or for anything to happen, because she'd only be Clark Kent. Lois Lane might not give her the time of day anymore, but that'd be OK, she'd be dating somebody from the secretarial pool. They'd go out for dinner sometimes to this cozy Neapolitan joint down by some lakefront, where the Mussels Posillipo couldn't be beat. "So instead of being able to fly everyplace," her friend had replied, "you'd have to climb into some car you're still making payments on, drive on out, you, Clark Kent, to the scene of some disaster, blood, corpses, flies, teen technicians wandering around stoned, eyewitnesses in shock. . . . Superman never has to get involved with any of that. Why should anybody want to be only mortal? Better to stay an angel, angel." DL, more generous in those days, only thought her friend had missed the point.

In Columbus she spent days in shopping centers, Ninja Steno, assembling an invisibility wardrobe — murky woolens, dim pastels, flat shoes with matching purses, beige hose, white underwear, surprised how little of a chore it was — the blandest of accessories would call out to her from shop windows, the misses' sections of discount stores were acres of abundance waiting to be picked through. She had by now grown into a relationship with the Plymouth, named her Felicia, bought her a new stereo, was washing her at least twice per workweek plus again on weekends, when she also waxed the vehicle. She swam and did t'ai chi and continued to practice the exercises she had learned in Japan. She grew used to her disguised image in the mirror, the short haircut with the rodent-brown rinse, the freckles subdued under foundation, the eye makeup she'd never have worn before, slowly becoming her alias, a small-town spinster pursuing a perfectly diminished life, a minor belle gone to weeds and gophers before her time.

So that when they came and kidnapped her in the Pizza Hut parking lot and took her back to Japan, she wasn't sure right away that being sold into white slavery would turn out to be at all beneficial as a career step. They took her with a matter-of-factness that made her feel like an amateur. Her little car was left alone in its space, sometimes, across miles and years, to call out to her in a puzzled voice, asking why she hadn't come back. She fought, but whoever it was had sent experts that specialized in not damaging young women. The story she heard eventually was that a certain client would pay a fee in the hefty-to-whopping range for an American blonde with advanced asskicking skills. "No telling what's going to turn men on," whispered her bunkmate Lobelia as they waited in a hotel in Ueno to be brought to auction, " 'specially the ones we're gonna meet."

Dense transport and travel clamored all day, all night long. The rickety hotel, almost a disposable building, was pressed shuddering between the Yamanote Line and Expressway 1. The girls ate yakitori from the carts on Showa and were permitted out, in supervised groups, only to shop at the pitches under the tracks. Some of these girls, the market being what it was, were boys, of whom DL's friend Lobelia was among the most glamorous. "Wow," she had introduced herself, "are you a mess," launching then unbidden into a verbal hair-to-toenails makeover for DL, who at some point ducked her head, murmuring, "Guess I should be writing some of this down."

Lobelia paused and blinked. "Sugar, I'm trying to help. Think about it — you'll be up there on the block, how are you gonna feel if all they sell you for's a dollar ninety-eight?"

"Pretty cheap."

"Exactly, which is why I'm saying you need the purple liner, and at *least* three different eyeshadows, trust me, I know what these customers like, and right now honey, I don't mean to be cruel, but —"

So when the big night came, DL went to her purchasers wearing a painting of yet another face she could hardly recognize as one of hers. The room seethed with odors of drinking, smoke, cologne. Koto and samisen music came from hidden speakers. Hostesses tiptoed, knelt, fetched, and poured. Outside, wind was beating on sheet metal, city traffic circulated in humid fricatives, neon colors, some of them unknown outside Tokyo, turned the streets to a high-gloss display of transgression and desire. But in here, light-tight behind rubberized drapes, the auction room kept its colors to itself, with a crew of moonlighting studio gaffers beaming merciful salmons and pinks at the girls in their eye-catching outfits, each chosen earlier from a giant walk-in, in fact drive-in, closet filled with every kind of getup any customer who'd passed through here'd ever found erotic, schoolgirl uniforms tonight being the big favorite, some enhancing an already youthful look, others worn for the less forthright nuances that make grown women in juvenile attire so widely irresistible, much attention being paid of course to details like school crests, belt styles, underwear, and pleats, for any all-but-invisible discrepancy here could easily wreck a sale. "Girl, you have never seen picky," as Lobelia put it, "till you've been in one of these Jap meat shows."

Though a few women had come to bid, the audience was nearly all male. The auctioneer was a popular television comedian. Older gentlemen with fingertip deficiencies could be noted circulating in the crowd, attentive as geishas, although to other signals. Prospective buyers chatted softly, paged through catalogues, scribbled on notepads. Out in the bar a baseball game was on, Central League playoffs, and a few guests had lingered till the traditional 8:56, when the transmission from the ballpark was abruptly cut off, in the middle of a double play, in fact. In commotion, voicing their displeasure, the last stragglers entered the room in a cloud of ambiguous smoke, the heavy jade-inlaid doors swung shut and were locked, the houselights were dimmed, the music track segued to romantic disco, the comic took the mike, and the auction was on.

Each girl had a number pinned to her outfit. When it was called, she had to step into a spotlight and do a basic tits-and-ass or beauty-pageant turn. The girl just before DL came from a high valley in northern Thailand, bartered as part of a heroin deal, dolled up tonight in black chiffon and mink eyelashes, about to enter a world where she would never again meet anyone who had ever heard of the place she'd been born in and taken from. She was sold for a million yen and slipped from kinder theatrical lighting down into the dark to join her new owner, feeling something warm but unyielding, like padded steel, slide around her neck, around one wrist . . . no one spoke to her. No one would, for days.

DL, remembering beauty-contest interviews back on the childhood Tube, thought *Just relax and have fun,* picked up the beat, and stepped out into the warm fall of light to let everybody have a look. The minute she appeared she could hear altered breathing and interjections in a number of tongues, but was oddly aware herself only of one electrician, poised silent near a small fill light . . . just out of her field of vision, his smoky and blurred presence more real to her than any bidder in the room, any future master. . . . How could that be? *Relax, have fun.* She smiled even with her eyes, Lobelia's eyes, alert now at nipples and clitoris, the price being bid upward deliriously. Suddenly she heard a new voice. Others may have recognized it too. There were no more bids. The hammer fell, she left the light, blind for an instant, adrift on treacherous runway in high heels, but then feeling the hand take her arm firmly as shackles and steer her instead off into the wings. . . .

When she could see, moving quickly into the chill of outdoors, into an alley where a long American automobile waited, she turned to have a look at her purchaser. Shades, black and white outfit, inches shorter but — she already knew by touch — faster and better. "Relax, lady," he warbled pleasantly. "I'm only the agent here." He opened a rear door. In a slither of tulle, she ducked and curled, alone, into the back seat. The man disappeared up front, doors latched solidly, and off she was driven into neon confusion. Waiting for her on the seat were fresh flowers — orchids. She lifted her chin. As a girl she had missed every single dance, including school proms, and this happened in fact to be her very first orchid corsage in her life.

Tonight's blind date turned out to be none other than Ralph Wayvone, who had a suite at the Imperial. They eyed each other across a spacious sitting room. She'd slid off her shoes first thing and now flexed her toes in the deep carpet. "You're pissed off, huh," she ventured.

Ralph was pouring champagne. He turned, holding the two

glasses, and DL noticed changes in his packaging. His suit fit like Cary Grant's, he appeared to have shaved sometime in the last hour, and he was wearing a pink tropical blossom in his lapel. He still smelled, however, like the far end of a men's toiletries section in a drugstore, and his haircut had been performed by someone who must have been trying to give up smoking.

A lightning storm had appeared far out at sea and now, behind them out the window, was advancing on the city, taking brightly crazed shots all along the horizon. Somewhere in here a stereo began to play a stack of albums from the fifties, all in that sweet intense mainstream wherein the tenor drowns of love, or, as it is known elsewhere, male adolescence.

"Couldint believe it was you," handing her the fluteful of champagne, beaded in the humid night, his voice slow, almost dazed. She twirled for him, as she had just before he'd bought her, and drank champagne.

"You sure paid a lot."

"Annual event, goes in a pension fund."

"Oh — you only pretended to buy me."

"Not exactly. Let's say you're here till you can get away again."

"You still want Brock Vond."

"Now more than ever." He had his lower lip out, trying to look sinned against.

"Please — I just needed a vacation from my life. You never heard of that?"

"Should I be reprimanding my intelligence people? Are they giving me faulty data on you? It don't sound to me like you're really all that hungry to get this little fuck. Like you've —" she was expecting "lost your nerve," but he thoughtfully went for "changed your attitude," instead.

She met his look. "Long as you're here in town, why not talk to some talent scouts, I'm not the only one knows 'is particular Oriental trick, you know."

"But you are the one who can execute." Tony Bennett had been singing "The Boulevard of Broken Dreams." Ralph touched her bare arm lightly. "Darryl Louise, think of who you are — mentioned in *Black Belt* before you were ten, the *Soldier of Fortune* interview, that centerfold in *Aggro World,* almost made runner-up in the Dangerous Teen Miss pageant in '63. . . ."

"Best I could do was Miss Animosity, why are you bringing up my rap sheet here?"

"All that great gift — you wanted to just escape it? Spend the rest of your life typin' up invoices and dodging the customer-service reps? I could cry."

"Could you. And would I have to deal with that?"

"Ahh, you cold cookie. . . . I can take ya, but I'll never break ya." He put down his glass, held his arms open. "Come on, Black Belt. Dance with an old gentleman."

Ralph had shifted — she could feel it — into a fifties time warp, and DL, once in his arms, found, surprised, that she could now think about her situation clearly for the first time since the Pizza Hut. Even putting champagne and orchids aside, here was the first human in her lifetime of running away who'd ever taken the trouble to come after her, not to mention publicly buy her, however much in play, for the sticker price of a Lamborghini plus options. How could a girl not be impressed? And as lagniappe she'd get the chance to ice detestable Brock Vond once and for all.

They drifted across the neutral carpeting, crooners crooned, and the storm came sweeping on. He was careful, mouth close to her ear, to speak only during instrumental breaks. "You might even get to like working for us. Our benefits package is the best in the field. You get to veto any assignment, we don't ask for weekly quotas, but we do run a cash-flow assessment on each of you quarterly. . . ."

"What's this, then, your leisure outfit, where's 'em gold chains, 'at endangered-species hat?"

"*Ufa, mi tratt' a pesci in faccia* — my dear Miss Chastain, who'd ever try to run a lady such as you, with your independent ideas plus all those lethal talents, do I look that stupid?"

Well, the problem of course was that he didn't look quite stupid enough. Had a certain luminous shade of skin not balanced out the wrong-length sideburns, the tightly rationed smile not likewise made up for the no-eye-contact eyes, why she'd most likely've passed on the venture and had to arrive at other, less hopeful arrangements. But it came about, after a night and a day of jack-hammer sex, amphetamines, champagne, and Chaliapin Steaks ordered up from Les Saisons, that she was sped by Lincoln limo, semen drying on her stockings and one earring lost forever, through rainglare and wet streets to the notorious Haru no Depaato, or Department Store of Spring, installed in a room of her own, and handed a large clutch purse stuffed full of yen, for transitional expenses till she went officially on the payroll.

"Your other clients," Ralph trying to be helpful, "they'll just be there for your cover, right?"

"Ralph, wow, I — I feel better already." In fact, she did, not because of the clients, who were no worse than expected, but because she was finally back getting some dojo time in, stretching, striking, working out with 'chuks and eagle catchers, meditating, finding inside herself the way back to shelter she'd wondered more than once if she'd lost for good. Outside the establishment, in the street, to keep herself in the mood, she paid special attention to car collisions, ambulances in a hurry, even bowls of severed shrimp heads in the noodle shops, as she and Ralph Wayvone went nailing down the scenario for Brock's assassination.

"He'll be flying in for a two-week international prosecutors' symposium, staying at the Hilton. We have a schedule of his free time, unless he's also one of those mischievous lads who like to play hooky. You'll wait, you'll live by his schedule — sooner or later he'll show up, he's a regular here whenever he's passing through."

"But he'll ID me, he'll remember."

"Not the way you'll be."

Uh-huh, the way she'd be . . . of all the jacking around she was getting, that makeover would prove to be the real shocker. Soon as the Depaato beautician staff got to work, the minute they brought out the wig she was to wear, dyed and styled precisely, she knew. And when she saw it on, a shivering crept all over her skin, as she looked at her own face on Frenesi's head. "Mr. Brock Vond," the girls assured her, "likes American girl, looking just this way, always the same," the little sixties outfits, the lurid makeup of the time. . . . But I'll have to wear shades, she thought, he'll see my own pale eyes and it won't work, surely he'll want hers, those fluorescent blue eyes of Frenesi's. . . . And so he would, but that was all taken care of too — when the time came, DL would be wearing tinted contact lenses.

"I knew it!" Prairie exploded. "My mother and this creep, and you better tell me how serious, DL —"

"Serious."

"So my dad and my grandma've been lyin' to me all the time? They told me she was on the side of the people — how could she've ever gone near somebody like this Brock guy?"

"I never could figure it either, kid. He was everything we were supposed to be against." But the shock had been different for DL — it was in finding out that he loved Frenesi but did not possess her, and was driven to fetishism in faraway countries as his only outlet, helpless to change — obsessed, though it gagged her to admit it, as DL. And Ralph, the fucker, must have known the whole story all along. Was he getting off on this? What kind of a sense of humor was that, anyway? Sometimes, waiting in her room, she'd wonder if this was all supposed to be some penance, to sit, caught inside the image of one she'd loved, been betrayed by, just sit. . . . Was it a koan she was meant to consider in depth, or was she finally lost in a great edge-to-edge delusion, having only read about Frenesi Gates once in some dentist's waiting room or standing in line at the checkout, whereupon something had just snapped and she'd gone on to make up the whole thing? And was now not in any Japanese whorehouse waiting to kill Brock Vond at all, but safely within a mental institution Stateside, humored, kindly allowed to dress up as the figure of her unhappy fantasies? For company while she waited she left the Tube on with the sound off. Images went rolling in and out of the frame as she sat, quiescent, sometimes teasing herself with these what-is-reality exercises, but keeping always balanced, right on that line, attentively breathing herself through the turn of the hours, the rise and fall of the five elements and the body organs governed, the combinations, the dance of husband-wife and mother-son laws. Today, of course, you can pick up a dedicated hand-held Ninja Death Touch calculator in any drugstore, which will track, compute, and project for you quick as a wink, but back then DL had only her memory to rely on and what she'd learned from Inoshiro Sensei, obliged early, she and her brain, to enter a system of eternal repayment humming along with or without her existence. Sensei called it "the art of the dark meridians," warning her repeatedly about the timing. "Perfect blow to the correct alarm point, but at the wrong time — might as well stay home — watch a Run Run Shaw movie!" She asked if she could visit him. They said no.

Meanwhile, Takeshi Fumimota was in and out of Tokyo for reasons of business connected with the mysterious obliteration of a research complex belonging to the shadowy world conglomerate Chipco. About a week after Brock Vond's arrival, Takeshi was standing at the edge of a gigantic animal footprint which only the day before had been a laboratory. From an insurance point of view, the place was totaled, though free of fatalities, the event having occurred precisely during an evacuation drill. Strange!

Looking through the dark morning drizzle, Takeshi couldn't even see over to the other side of the foot-shaped crater. From up here on the rim, about all he could make out were the yellow headlamps of the tech squads moving far below, taking samples of everything, every last splinter, for testing. Here and there edges of the footprint had begun to slide in.

As Takeshi made his way cautiously down, he found a network of plastic duckboards and temporary traffic lights already in place. Traffic was heavy. He paused at a turnout, poured himself another cup from his coffee thermos, and took another amphetamine capsule. "It's going to take a while," he chuckled aloud, drawing a stare or two, "to get to the bottom of this!" Another strange element, as his former mentor Professor Wawazume, eccentric CEO of Wawazume Life & Non-Life, had reminded him over the phone last night, was that recently Chipco had wanted a floater written in on an inland marine policy, against "damage from any and all forms of animal life." The demolished complex was located on a lightly traveled piece of coastline, and Chipco could certainly argue that something had come up out of the surf, put one foot in the sand for leverage, and stomped on the lab with the other.

Since it had happened at low tide, any second print on the beach would have got washed away when the tide came back in. "Clearly reptilian," the Professor had summed up, "or possibly the work of a — disgruntled environmentalist!" Takeshi, by the time he got to see it from the air, didn't want to rule out another secular possibility — a professional job. There were some fancy blasters around, studio special-effects people, Yank veterans of Vietnam, few yakuza maybe — Takeshi knew most of the boys and girls, though it wasn't always easy to keep track, and the work could get pretty sophisticated. Size 20,000 here could be an artifact from heel to claw-tip.

Having begun well inside the corporate embrace of Wawazume Life & Non-Life, high above the violet radiance of the city, through ghostly Marunouchi dusks he had dreamed of disengagement and freedom, of working as a *ronin*, or samurai without a master, out free-lancing in a dangerous world. By the time his life brought him here, down in the reeking beast-print, the hazy red, green, and yellow lights and striped barricades, the struggling in the mud and rain after a mystery that might at the end be only as simple as greed, become at least independent, though Professor Wawazume still kept sending a lot of business his way, no more corporate pin on his suit lapel, only the buttonhole unadorned, lordless, his one fixed address now a cubicle in outer Ueno he shared rent on, containing an armored file cabinet, a telephone, and the signed, framed photo of himself the Professor had given him when he left to go out on his own (an enlarged paparazzo shot, the Professor looking even more goofy than usual, lurching after a noted beauty in gold lamé, flip hairdo, and two-centimeter eyelashes outside a bar in Shinjuku, a lucent string of drool begun to descend from one corner of his mouth), Takeshi had already long been a nomad in the sky's desert, continuing to depart in kerosene fumes to seek another connection in another Pacific port, to nod to faces he had last seen coming out of the Yat Fat Building in Des Vœux Road, to check the body of the stewardess and what he could see out the window of the body of the airplane, and at last, when they began to lift, to commend himself to the gods of the sky. But despite his millions of passenger miles, he could never recall being in their domain, instead only groaning, laboring along, just above the webs of power lines, almost sharing expressway space, making unnumbered short hops between local airfields, places Takeshi had never heard of, invisible under industrial smoke and traffic exhaust, kept away from all promises of wild blue yonder.

He had arrived now at the bottom of the strange crater, far below sea level, after long detours and a sense of time forever lost. . . . Tech-squad people he'd tried to talk to had all, so far, been evasive. I knew it! he realized. I haven't been buying enough drinks! The rain clouds had settled in. Looking up, Takeshi could no longer see the rim he'd descended from. A group of Techs nearby had started shouting angrily at each other, their headlamp beams swooping and crossing. Takeshi recognized his acquaintance Minoru, a government bomb-squad expert. Not a genius, exactly, more like an idiot savant with X-ray vision. When the discussion moved on, Minoru remained, gazing at something cupped in his hands.

"Pretty strange today, Minoru-san!"

"Strange! Here, look at this!"

Familiar. "Eastern bloc, *ne?*"

"*Ē.* But now — watch!" Minoru rotated the fragment.

"*Hen na!*" But he allowed Minoru to ID the modification.

"South African!"

"*Motto hen na!*"

Finally Minoru waved and started away. "Never been in a hole like this one. Don't like it!"

"Let's go have drinks!" Takeshi called after him.

Whatever Minoru may have replied was lost in a sudden downrush of noise, a terrific roaring quite close by in the mist. Everyone Takeshi could see stood or crouched, looking up, not really poised to flee — where in this mud deathtrap was there to go? — but relaxing helpless under some imminent unthinkable descent . . . and *what was it,* appearing out of the cloud cover, causing a reflex wave of *oh*'s to sweep the paralyzed onlookers . . . what was this glistening surface of black scales, dripping with seawater and kelp, these giant talons, curving earthward?

"It's come back!" People began to scream and run. Others, producing cameras, tried to photograph the confusion, or angrily waved radiation meters and microphones at the approaching object. By the time Takeshi could even react, the mysterious visitor, smaller than at first supposed, had angled over toward a makeshift landing pad, where it turned out to be one of Chipco's fleet of customized jumbo passenger helicopters, whose underside its crew, a byword of practical jokery throughout the firm, had playfully disguised, with plastic sheet and fairings of appropriate textures, as a monster's sole. Everybody had been fooled!

The helicopter had come to evacuate everybody from the hole, immediately, according to an announcement over its speakers. Was this another joke? "Who cares?" Takeshi muttered out loud, "I'm ready! Enough work for one day!"

"I heard that," said Minoru, climbing on board with him. "Were you serious — about those drinks?"

"Sure." He had something on his mind — what was it?

"Think we can get — Singapore Slings?"

As they took off, rising up the mud cliffsides crumbling away now in dark roaring collapses, Takeshi remembered his car, still at the parking lot. Could he go to the rental company and plead force majeure yet again, thin as the excuse was by now? They ascended into deep clouds and flew in zero visibility for what could have been an hour or more. Passengers, mostly Techs and military, read tabloids and comic magazines, listened through earphones to pocket radios, played cards or go. Takeshi and Minoru headed aft to a small bar with a price list that made up in exorbitance for what it lacked in variety. There were no Singapore Slings, so they drank beer instead. As empties accumulated, rotor-throbbed into vibrations along the bar, Minoru grew more cryptic and sly. "I like it up here . . . it's like a toilet for me — a final, private space."

"Ah — you fly a lot?"

"Business — much of it offshore these days. Last year I was in the sky — more than I was on the ground!"

Takeshi reminded himself that whenever his companion wasn't actually trying to take apart strange bombs in person, he was irrevocably ordering someone else to.

"We haven't flown together," Minoru went on, beaming maliciously, "since Lhasa International, good old LHX!"

"Aw. Knew you'd bring that one up."

"Been on my mind — especially today! Maybe you can guess why!"

The helicopter came out into midafternoon sunlight. They were flying over some vast yellow-gray industrial reservation full of buildings whose only purpose was to shield the activities inside from viewers overhead. There were also areas set aside as parkland, and what looked like shopping and amusement centers. The PA came on. "We are approaching the famous Chipco 'Technology City,' home of 'Chuck,' the world's most invisible robot." Takeshi and Minoru tried to order two more beers, but the bar was closing. "How invisible," the voice continued, "you might wonder, is 'Chuck'? Well, he's been walking around among you, all through this whole flight! Yes, and now he could be right next to you — o-or you!" They began to descend, signs came on, Minoru sighed. "I'd rather stay up there!" The PA had begun to recite train information. Chipco had its own stop on the Tokaido Shinkansen, from which it would be a little under three hours to Tokyo.

On the train they got back to the Himalayan caper. There were similarities — assault on the inanimate, the Czech origins of both the initiator unit and the explosive, Semtex . . . and the dummy motive.

"So," Takeshi said, "you don't think this was self-inflicted."

"Who wrote the floater?"

"Professor Wawazume himself." Same as the Himalayan incident. They looked at each other, the two weary old hands, feeling as usual like jungle indigenous going in after a firefight to scavenge brass for pennies a ton. Far above them some planetwide struggle had been going on for years, power accumulating, lives worth less, personnel changing, still governed by the rules of gang war and blood feud, though it had far outgrown them in scale. Chipco was in it up to their eyeballs, and it looked like the Professor might have been fading some of the action. Nothing surprised either Takeshi or Minoru by now about the game, in which the everyday pieces were pirate ships of the stratosphere and Himalayas held for ransom.

"Those Himalayas!" Takeshi reminisced. "Right at the worst part, that sudden blizzard sweeping in —"

"— and we'd lost our way — everything white! Couldn't find the pass! The seconds were — ticking down!"

"Your wristwatch — with the turquoise numbers — only thing in the storm anybody can see! The bomber is already back in Geneva — with a perfect alibi! Suddenly — who do we run into, in that little shack — at the edge of infinity . . . literally!"

"Kutsushita-san!" Both men collapsed in laughter. "Everybody thought he'd drunk himself to death —"

"Instead he'd gone off to Tibet — to save his soul!"

"My first nuke assignment," Minoru recalled, after they'd finished laughing.

Takeshi nodded. "We called you — the Kid!" They had a nice spin in the time machine, but arrived at Tokyo Station with nothing about the present case any clearer. Minoru headed for a public phone while Takeshi waited, reaching for his Georgian silver snuff-box, where the *shabu* were. Minoru, growing agitated, made another call, hung up suddenly, and, with white now visible all the way around the irises of his eyeballs, came after Takeshi, who got ready to run the other way.

"Somebody we have to see! Right now! It could already be too late!" He grabbed Takeshi by the necktie and pulled him, protesting loudly, through the bustling station till they found a taxi. Minoru told the driver to go to the Tokyo Hilton International in west Shinjuku. There was a convention in town of prosecutors from all over the world, including Interpol heavies, big-city DA's, and restless global travelers, among whom Minoru could easily find half a dozen who'd tell him all about the initiator fragment, even get facsimiles while he waited of the sales slip, with the purchaser's current address, if he liked. Takeshi kept his hand on the door handle but forgot, each time the cab slowed, to jump out. It was '78, during a period of epic and bloody street war among all major factions of the yakuza, and no place public was safe from liability. Pedestrian life in Shinjuku shared the same nervous dread. Disco music coming out the club doors was all in minor keys tonight, the beat slower, undanceable. Through years of stately unfoldings of the deep actuarial mysteries that allowed him to go on making a living, Takeshi had come to value and watch closely in the world for signs and symptoms, messages from beyond, and even discounting the effects of drug abuse, nothing about the city seemed quite right tonight, as if a day already tough was about to start getting worse. . . .

At the Hilton, Minoru found the names on his list all conscientiously engaged in scheduled evening activities, one at a Yak Doc Workshop, another at a Plea-Bargaining Clinic, yet another at a symposium titled "Funding That First Election Campaign." Frustrated, they headed for the bar and sat drinking till somebody paged Minoru, who disappeared and remained that way. After a while Takeshi wandered off to the toilet, but could not immediately find his way back and after a couple of wrong turns walked into some sort of rear foyer, just off the street, where he could hear large V-8 engines idling. Two Americans in brown gabardine suits were arguing.

One of them was Brock Vond, who was saying, "We need time to round up some troops. Don't want them to know we found anything out, hm? They'll have their checkpoints between here and there, so what we need now is a plausible head and shoulders in the back seat. Who knows, Roscoe, you may even have to go in there."

"They'll ID me in two seconds, Brock. Naw, what we need —" Looking around rhetorically, he spotted the mentally confused Takeshi. "Hey — this could be just the customer. *Kombanwa*, m' friend, you speak English?" Which is when Takeshi actually saw Brock Vond for the first time, moving forward into the light, and thought for a terrified second or two it was himself and something radical, like death, had just happened. It was a stressed and malevolent cartoon of his face, of what he shaved and had long looks at, but its steady glide forward had him hypnotized. Brock slid a rectangle of white plastic into the breast pocket of Takeshi's suit jacket. "Your passport to an evening you'll never forget," whispered Brock, and "Don't say we never did nothing for you," added Roscoe. And there was Takeshi in the back seat of a strange oversize American car, locked in, being borne through the streets of Shinjuku southward, crossing the Expressway, into Roppongi, expecting street mines, storms of automatic-weapon fire, convinced he had stumbled into the middle of some Japanese gang-war drama with a couple of *gaijin* bit players in it.

The car let him off beside a building the size of a warehouse, whose only light was next to a metal door, illuminating a slot the size of the card he'd been given. The neighborhood was deserted. Takeshi tapped on the car window, but the car only revved up and moved out and was soon around the corner and gone. Takeshi looked at the card. Next to a logo of a pleasant-looking young woman in provocative attire, it said, in English, "GENTLEMEN TITS ASS CLUB / For the Connoisseur." It sounded like Takeshi's sort of place, yet he knew Brock and Roscoe were sending him in as a decoy. "A tough call," he admitted — "what would you have done?"

"Found a cab," Prairie said. "But then again. . . ." She'd finally got to meet Takeshi, who'd showed up in the dead of night talking a mile a minute and demanding to be put on the Puncutron Machine, a device he apparently believed had brought him back to life once. When they were introduced next morning at breakfast, she saw this shorter, older guy wearing a truly gross suit, in synthetic fabric but printed to look like some tweed of bright powder-blue flecks against a liver-colored background. The pants bagged at the knees. DL leaned lightly on his shoulder and looked down at him, a little apologetic. "Just got to keep an eye on his feet, you'll be fine," as Takeshi took Prairie's hand and leered genially. "Here," DL reaching over and swiftly brushing bangs down over his eyebrows while he tried, muttering, to push her away, "who's he remind you of?"

"Moe!" Prairie cried.

He winked. "What's she been tellin' ya, Toots?"

"All about it," said DL.

"Looks like I got here just in time." From then on he was not shy about putting in with color commentary on DL's version. Until, just before the dark metal door with the plastic key, he paused and wondered aloud, "Maybe we should just skip over the sex part here. . . ."

"She is just a kid," DL agreed.

"You *guys?*" Prairie protested.

"Heedlessly then — fingering its smooth rigid contours, I — took the plastic card and — thrust it into the slot, shuddering as — something whined and the object was — abruptly sucked from my fingers. . . ." After a brief scan it was stuck back out at him, like a tongue. Inside, he found the place all but vacated, little evidence of any night's business, no fumes of sake, no screened clatter of gaming tiles, or feminine crossings and glimpses. . . . Had there been a police raid? Had Brock already found his troops? From distant margins of the place voices could almost be heard. Suddenly he'd walked right into the middle of a piping of parlor-maids, easily a dozen of the charming soubrettes in scandalously short outfits of organdy and taffeta, who gathered around him like shiny birds of doom. He began to sweat with panic and also to get an erection. He was hustled along, daintily coerced with flashing burgundy nails, through room after room, barely able, in the delicate stampede of high heels, to keep from tripping, down deserted hallways, trying to be a sport, going, "Ladies, ladies!" and "What's all this?" But he was only cargo. Surrounded by airy petticoats and fluttering eyelashes, he was billowed at length into an elevator, and they all dropped suddenly, pressing together, till the doors opened onto a corridor lit by musk-scented black candles, with only one other door in it, down at the far end. As they were shoving him out of the elevator, the girls acknowledged him for the first time. "Have an enjoyable evening, Vond-san," they cried. "Don't be so nervous!" Then all together, rustling, breezy, they bowed and departed by elevator, reaching as the doors closed into necklines and stocking tops for cigarettes and matches and lighting up.

"Vond-san"? Must be — his lookalike, back at the Hilton! They thought he was this American! What should he do? He looked around for a button to summon back the elevator, but there was none, the walls were smooth. The one door at the end of the passage was covered in black velvet, with a silver doorknob. As carefully as he approached, he could still hear his shoes squeaking in this muffled place. Maybe it was all Minoru's idea of a practical joke. He tried to knock on the door, but the velvet surface absorbed the blows. He was supposed to turn the knob himself, open, step in. . . . There was DL, lying in bed, hat, long earrings, *miniskirt?* Incredible! This Vond character must be — a miniskirt man too! She smiled. "Hurry, Brock. Get those fuckin' clothes off."

Oboy, an assertive woman! Takeshi thought, I love it! "But that's not —" he began.

"Ssh. Don't talk. Undress. You're safe here."

Trembling in a way whorehouses seldom got him to do, Takeshi stripped, conscious of each article coming off, of the air and the weight of her watching against his skin. Somewhere the hour chimed. By the ancient system, it was the hour of the cock, "In more ways than one," as Takeshi in later years liked to interpolate in comical accents, predictably to DL's annoyance. A bird usually associated with the dawn, the cock, by the laws of the Death Touch, belonged to early night. By now the chi cycle of the victim would have arrived in the region of his triple warmer, considered wife to the bladder, which was thus endangered. In the Dim Mak method, the Needle Finger DL intended to use could be calibrated to cause a delay of up to a year in the actual moment of death, depending on the force and direction of its application. She could hit Brock Vond now, and months in the future be safely in the middle of a perfect alibi at the moment he dropped dead.

"Now *wait* a minute," Prairie interrupted, "you're right there in this superintimate situation with a guy taking his *clothes* off, and it's obviously Takeshi here, a stranger, but you're still calling him Brock?"

"It was 'ose contacts they made me wear," said DL, "to make my eyes as blue as your mom's — yours, for that matter. Cheapskates at the ol' Depaato wouldn't even spring for a pair that was in my prescription."

"You had on somebody else's contacts? Eeoo!"

"And I couldn't see shit. Brock and Takeshi were both about the same size and body format anyway, and my mind right then was switched onto more of a transpersonal mode."

"Payin' attention to what you were doing," Prairie guessed.

So much so that it wasn't till later that DL remembered the contact lenses, which had been repossessed almost as soon as the deed was done. The more she considered, the more thickly came the birds of creepiness to perch on her shoulders. She never found out for sure, but had come to believe that the lenses had been taken from the eyes of a dead person. That furthermore she had been intended to witness her own act of murder through the correction to *just this person's* eyesight. Likely a hooker, DL speculated, who'd been caught holding out, who'd spent her whole short life off the books, whose name, even names she'd used professionally, nobody remembered anymore. As lost now as she could get.

But whose countersight DL was looking through that hour as she straddled the naked man on the bed, found his penis and slipped it in, breathing with precision, conscious only of the human alarm points spread below, defenseless, along those dark meridians. No longer needing anyone's eyes, she went in by other sensors, direct to the point, opposing his chi flow, spiraling her own in with the correct handedness. Takeshi never felt it. It wasn't till he climaxed moments later and started screaming in street Japanese that DL, de-transcending, realized something might be amiss. She hung over the side of the bed, groping at her eyes, Takeshi with a softoff sliding out and away in some confusion. When he saw her face again, he was amazed at the sudden green paleness of her irises, as if something had drained away. She clenched her lids, blinked.

"Oh — God — oh, no —" faster than he could follow, she had rolled off the bed and taken a fighting stance with the door to her right.

"Hey, beautiful," Takeshi up on one elbow, "if it was something *I* did —"

"Who are you? No — never mind —" She turned and fled out the door, in her high-sixties outfit, observed as she went by any number of cameras, population now returning to the corridors, plausible copies, for DL, of known enemy faces, bearing old wrongs, old scores to settle, converging here around her sloppy, amateur attempt at homicide. . . .

Ralph Wayvone, who'd been patched in as a courtesy from the Imperial, followed DL's progress out to the street on his own monitor, as well as Takeshi's slow bewildered dressing and departure. "Better put somebody on that Japanese guy. Maybe we can help."

"Want me go get her?" inquired Two-Ton Carmine Torpidini.

Ralph appeared to think about it. "Let her go, we can always find her again . . . she'll know how much she owes us now."

The phone rang, Carmine took it. "Says that somebody tipped off our boy. So he must have sent in a stuntman."

Ralph kept watching the screen, watching her go, those long, beautifully-in-shape legs, that slowed-down martial-arts lope, finally with an extravagant "Mmwahh!" blowing her a kiss as she vanished. "So long, babe. I was hopin' you'd be the one. If you couldint nail him, who can?"

"He's *too* lucky," Carmine philosophized. "But he's livin' on borrowed time, 'cause a lucky streak don't last forever."

"Fuckin' Vond," Ralph Wayvone sighed, "he's the Roadrunner."

DL flew back to California, homing brainlessly in once again on the Kunoichi Retreat, where she'd been coming since her adolescence, then leaving, then coming back again, building a long-term love-hate affair with the Attentive staff, Sister Rochelle in particular. But this time Rochelle could see how awful she looked, and only assigned her to a cell and suggested gently that they talk the next day.

It would have given DL time to try and look quietly, frontally, at what she'd done. No use. She cried, failed to sleep, masturbated, snuck down to the kitchen and ate, snuck into the Regression Room and watched old movies on the Tube, smoking cigarette butts out of the public ashtrays till the birds woke up. By the time she dragged in to see the Senior Attentive, she was a sleepless wreck. The older woman reached, smoothed hair away from DL's sweating forehead. "I've done something so —" DL sat trembling, couldn't find a word.

"Why tell me?"

"What? Who else can I tell that'll understand?"

"Just what I wanted today, just when the cash flow's starting to turn around, just as I'm finding my life's true meaning as a businessperson, I might've known it, in you waltz and suddenly I've got to be Father Flanagan." She shook her head, pursed her lips like a nun, but sat and heard out DL's confession. Finally, "OK, couple questions. Are you sure you didn't, at the last instant, pull back?"

"I'm — not sure, no —"

"Paying attention," darkly, " 's the whole point, DL-san." The body transaction had been complex, referential, calling in not only chi flow and the time of day but also memory, conscience, passion, inhibition — all converging to the one lethal instant. The Senior Attentive gazed evenly at the bent nape, the averted face. "Just from your life pattern already, here's what I think. Living as always let's say at a certain distance from the reality of others, you descended —"

"I was taken!"

"— you were brought — down again into the corrupted world, and instead of paying attention, taking the time, getting prepared, you had to be a reckless bitch and go rushing through the outward forms, so of course you blew it, what'd you expect?"

And that was when DL remembered Inoshiro Sensei's remarks about those who never get to be warriors, who on impulse go in, fuck up, and have to live with it for the rest of their lives. He had *known* — he had seen it in her, some latency for a bungled execution at a critical moment, somewhere in her destiny — but how could he ever have warned her? DL realized she had been nodding solemnly for a while. "What I need to know," she whispered at last, "is, can it be reversed."

"Your life? Forget it. The Vibrating Palm, well yes and no. It depends on many variables, not least being how quickly it'll get seen to."

"But . . ." but what was she saying? "but I was just down there. . . ."

"Since you were here with us last, we've built up a good medical unit — couple of licensed DOM's on the staff now, some new therapy machines — and while we don't see *that* many Ninja Death Touch cases, your victim has a better chance the sooner you can get him up here."

"But how'll I ever find him again? I didn't think I'd — I wanted —" but DL thought better of it.

But Rochelle said, "Let's have it."

"I hoped there might be . . . ," a small failing voice, "some way I could stay?"

Out the window, screened by eucalyptus trees, could be seen once-white walls overgrown with ivy, a distant bight of freeway tucked into the unfolding spill of land toward "down there" — while up here the wind blew among the smooth gold and green hills, it seemed endlessly. Here was the deep quiescent hour, the bottom dead center of the day. The women sat in the Ninjette Coffee Mess and watched the caustics of sunlight flutter on the insides of their cups.

"If there were ninjitsu jury boards," Rochelle suggested, "you'd get your card pulled for what you say you did. Maybe this is the time, sister, that you'll finally start pulling your weight. We've always believed in your sincerity, but it can't get you much further — when do we ever see you concentrate, where's the attention span? Blithely driving off down the road in some little low-rent touring machine, showing up again in something from an assistant buyers' sale at Zody's beggin' to be taken back, on again off again over the years, no continuity, no persistence, no . . . fucking . . . attention. All we see's somebody running because if she stops running she'll fall, and nothing beyond."

"I thought you'd take me in no matter what I'd done."

"And if I wanted you to leave us forever, I'd just say 'Leave,' wouldn't I?"

"And I'd have to leave." For the first time in the interview the sun-haired girl raised her eyes to those of the motionless Headmistress — a compound look, flirtatious while at the same time pushing away, clearly desperate at, any thought of having to go find Takeshi again. "But if I bring him back up —"

Sister Rochelle rolled her eyes in mock surrender. "We should reward you by letting you stay forever? Oh, child. Thirty-year-old, hardcase, cold and beautiful child."

It was as much blessing as DL was likely to get. She asked for and was granted a few days to prepare. And had got to where she could stay away from other people's smokes, keep her hands off her pussy, and hypnotize herself to sleep when who should appear at the gate but Takeshi, looking for *her,* saving everybody the trouble.

Not that he hadn't been through some difficulties of his own, of course, beginning back in Tokyo with the swamp of primal fear he'd been fighting through since finding out what had happened, which hadn't taken him long. The morning after his adventure at Haru no Depaato he tried to call Minoru at his office in the antiterrorist subministry, but all he got was a lengthy runaround, including suggestions that the person no longer existed in the form Takeshi had known. After a while, no matter what extension he called, he was immediately put on hold and left there.

Takeshi went around all that day and the next feeling like a toxic dump. Symptoms of everything, particularly thoracic and abdominal ones, lanced through him. He quit ordering from room service because the sight of food now nauseated him. The final hammerstroke came when he got his suit back from the cleaners, the suit he'd worn to and from his encounter with DL, and found it full of holes, each five to ten centimeters across, in the front of the jacket and at the top of the pants, the edges ragged and black, as if burned and rotted through at the same time. He called the *dorai kuriiningu,* who were apologetic but unhelpful.

"Used perchloroethylene — like we do on everything! I was amazed — when all those holes started!"

"Started? Started what?"

"To get bigger! Only took a few seconds! Never saw anything like it!"

Sweating and aching, deeply apprehensive, Takeshi made an emergency appointment with one of the staff croakers at Wawazume Life & Non-Life, remembering to bring the afflicted suit with him. Dr. Oruni laid it out on an examining table and sent some automated scanning device over it while he and Takeshi watched a video screen in the next room, displaying the data in graph and print form. "These are all alarm points," the doctor showing with a cursor the pattern of holes. "Some strange, corrosive energy — very negative! Have you been in a fight?"

Takeshi remembered what he'd been trying all day not to —

the American girl — the way she'd stared, the terror and failure in her face just before she turned and fled. He told the doctor about their rendezvous in the Haru no Depaato while he ran Takeshi through an abbreviated physical, grunting darkly at everything he seemed to find. Nothing really showed up, though, till the urine scan. Doc Oruni pulled a bottle of Suntory Scotch out of a small refrigerator, found two paper cups, poured them 90% full, put his feet up on his desk, and dolefully surrendered to mystery. "There's no cancer, no cystitis, no stones. Proteins, ketones, all that — it's normal! But something very weird is happening to your bladder! It's like trauma, only — much slower!"

"We — can't be more specific?"

"Why, do you — think you can find this somewhere in some — actuarial table? And once you see the odds, and learn the name, it'll go away?"

"It — doesn't happen often, *ne?*"

"I've never seen it — only read articles, heard talk around the clubhouse — anecdotes. If you like, I'll send you to somebody who can give you details. . . ."

"Just whatever you can tell me, then?"

"Ever heard of the Vibrating Palm?"

"Yeah — been in there once or twice!"

"Not a bar, Fumimota-san. An assassination technique — with a built-in time delay! Invented centuries ago by the Malayan Chinese, adapted by our own ninja and yakuza. Today a number of systems are taught — same effect!"

"She did that to me?" *Effect?* "But I didn't feel anything."

"*Dewa* — there's your good news! Allegedly, the lighter the touch — the longer you've got to live!"

"Well — how long?"

The doc chuckled for a while. "How light?"

Takeshi rode the elevator down alone, fully taken over, through the descent, by the fear of death. Now he could feel each of his suffering alarm points, count different struggling pulses, imagine his chi flow, in turbulence — blocked, darkly reversed, stained, lost — slowly destroying his insides. Any time he went to piss now would be an occasion for terror.

"My own sleaziness — has done me in!" It was too late even for remorse over the years squandered in barely maintaining what he now saw as a foolish, emotionally diseased life. He came reeling out of the elevator under the combined influence of speed, Scotch, and some new tranquilizer nobody knew anything about but which the detail man had left a huge barrel of samples of in the waiting room, with a sign urging passersby to take as many as they wished, so what some might have called his glibness no doubt had its origins in the realm of the chemical.

Back at the hotel he found a ticket to SFX tonight on the red-eye, with a note from Two-Ton Carmine expressing sympathy for his recent inconvenience and the hope that once in San Francisco he would communicate with the enclosed phone number. What difference did it make? Takeshi shrugged. He packed a carry-on bag with two weeks' supply of amphetamines, a change of underwear, and an extra shirt and grabbed the hotel bus out to Narita.

The hours on the airplane were among the worst of his life. He drank steadily and, when he remembered to, popped green time-release capsules of dextroamphetamine plus amobarbital. He took some time to read through the stuffer for the tranquilizers he'd picked up at the doc's. Oh, ho, ho! Look at all these contraindications! Every variety of shit that was seething around already in his system, as a matter of fact, was prohibited. "Well!" out loud, "*that* being the case —" he ordered another drink and swallowed some more tranquilizers. His seatmate, a serious-looking *gaijin* businessman with a hand-held computer game that had up till now claimed his attention, looked over at Takeshi and then continued staring for a while. "You aren't committing suicide, are you?"

Takeshi grinned energetically. "Suicide? Nah! Uh-uh, buddy, just — trying to relax! I mean — don't you just hate flying? Huh? when you start thinking — about *all the possibilities*. . . ."

The young man, even though in a window seat, did his best to edge away. Takeshi went on, "Here, you want to try one of these? Huh? they — they're really *good*. Evoex, ever heard of them? Something new!"

"There's a hidden camera somewhere, right? This is a commercial?" The question rang almost prayerfully in these surroundings, the moonlit childhood-picture-book clouds out the rounded toy windows, the lambent fall of electric light on faces and documents, the affectless music in the earphones, the possibly otherworldly origins of Takeshi's madness. . . .

"You'd be — real interested in this!" Takeshi began, "maybe even — tell me what you think I should do — because frankly, I'm at my wit's end!" proceeding then to rattle out the whole story, sparing no medical detail. The suit-wearing juvenile was more than willing to listen to anything, as long as it delayed the moment, easily imagined, when Takeshi would produce a weapon and begin to run amok in the aisles.

When Takeshi paused at last, the American tried to be sympathetic. "What can you expect? A woman."

"No, no! Somebody thought I was — somebody else."

"Hmm. Maybe you thought *she* was somebody else."

Takeshi grew instantly paranoid, assuming, for some reason, that the young man was talking about his ex-wife, the film actress Michiko Yomama, currently starring as a light-comical obstetrician in the television series "Babies of Wackiness," a Japanese import currently and inexplicably blowing away all its U.S. ratings competition. If there was any connection between that homicidal hooker in the Haru no Depaato and Michiko, with her fragile smiles and gifts of disappearance, Takeshi couldn't see it. They'd been married, as a matter of fact, during a classical sixties acid trip, in which it became beyond clear to them both that in some other world they had been well acquainted. In this one, however, they only seemed programmed for unhappiness. One would find the other across a room and both would gaze awhile, sick with betrayal, remembering the deep and beautiful certainty beyond words, wondering why they should only have had a glimpse and where it might be now. After a few years, he moved out of the house. She moved to Los Angeles. The kids by now were safely established in different corporations. Takeshi and Michiko still kept up a slender sympathetic link — now and then, passing through L.A., he dropped in. "No," he replied to his seatmate's speculation, "at the time — I was only thinking about the fucking!"

The other man tightened his lips, frowning. "Mm-hmm." He

returned to his computer game, something called "Nukey," which included elements of sex and detonation, though the cheapness of its early sound chips reduced orgasm to a thin rising whine, broken into segments as if for breath, and made the presumably nuclear explosions, no more than symbolized here by feeble bursts of white noise, even less satisfying.

By the time he landed at San Francisco International, Takeshi had been up for three days, during which he had also not bathed or shaved. He looked at his face-stubble in a men's-room mirror. As long as I don't sleep, he decided, I won't shave. He paused at the sink, swaying a little. That must mean, he pursued the thought, that as soon as I fall asleep, I'll start shaving! Noticing a number of curious looks, he glided out again into the airport lobby, a centimeter or two above the actual floor surface, remembering just in time to zip his fly.

At the phone number in Carmine's note turned out to be Carmine himself. "Hey, Fumimota-san!"

Takeshi had started to shiver. A young woman with regular features, wearing a draped white gown, appeared out of the airport crowds, leaned her forearm on Takeshi's shoulder, whispered, "Watch the paranoia, please!" and disappeared again. "I went to the doctor. What else can you tell me?"

DL's name, and that of her intended target. "Hot antidrug celebrity right now, was on a Donahue, had a full page in *Vogue*, but he can't help you none, and he wouldn't if he could."

"What about her, then?"

"Your odds get better. Story we have is, she did it, she can undo it." Takeshi could hear small plastic percussions as Carmine, with fingers used to more ancient and less magical tasks, punched up the latest on DL Chastain, which he shared with Takeshi, along with directions up to the Ninjette Retreat. "Any problems, let us know, and sorry again about the mixup. Sayonara."

"Ciao." *Mixup?* He rented a car and checked into one of the airport motels, put on the air-conditioner and the Tube, hit the Search button on the remote, and lay watching the channels crank by, two seconds apiece, till at last on some high-numbered independent channel whom should he find, looking exceptionally good, but his ex-wife, Michiko, in a nightclub interior, apparently out on a date with a baby about a year old in a tuxedo, who was crawling around on top of their table, upsetting drinks, dumping ashtrays, squealing with pleasure, and drawing public attention. It was a "Babies of Wackiness" rerun, one he hadn't seen. He was only just able to watch it through. By the second commercial break he could feel a great bodylong wave of sorrow beginning to approach, to grow, to shake him apart. All that mostly sleepless night there would be tears in Takeshi's ears, snot in his mustache, and sinuses aching like love gone astray, though set next to the fact that he was technically dead, these were pretty minor.

Next day, feeling mysteriously better, he was back on the case, visiting widely separated Bay Area pharmacies with forged prescriptions for speed, purchasing a ukulele and the liver-and-blue suit he was wearing when Prairie met him, studying the road map like a racing form till he'd handicapped the alternate routes and imagined changes of plans associated with each, before at last turning eastward and beginning his ascent to the Retreat of the Kunoichi Attentives, an all-day hard-edged video game, one level of difficulty to the next, as the land rose and the night advanced. Enough of this, like travel in outer space, can begin to what they call "do things" to a man. By the time he arrived at the Retreat, high on that fateful California ridge, he was no longer in his right mind, and the object of more attention than he usually liked. All around the courtyard in the crescent shadows he thought he heard small-arms safeties being taken off. Even unarmed, any of these kunoichi was tough enough of a cookie to distribute him from here to Gardena with a minimum of effort. What stopped his forward progress for a second was the sight of DL, hair incandescent, gelid green eyes set on full power, head-on. Try to keep in mind, he memoed himself, this is the woman — who murdered you the other day! But he got a hardon instead and managed to forget everything except that night at the Depaato of Spring, the distant long-legged American girl astride him, riding him as she would a beast, hair backlit, face kept to itself, in shadow — playing his body meridians with the points of dark-lacquered fingernails . . . killing him in the process! Terrific! The thought should have discouraged his erection but, strangely, didn't.

"You forget, everybody!" he cried insouciantly, "I'm already dead!" as there in the perilous open, regarded no doubt over the sights of Uzis set on full automatic, under the stilled beaks of mountainside birds, Takeshi reached into his bag to produce only the ukulele, gals, no problem, and strum a four-bar intro before singing, as certification he was harmless,

JUST LIKE A WILLIAM POWELL

Oh it's like layin' bricks, without a trowel,
Like havin' a luau, with no fish 'n' poi,
When you're just like, a William Powell,
Lookin' for some, Myrna Loy!

Well, Lassie's got Roddy McDowall,
Trigger's got, Dale and Roy,
Asta's got William Powell, goin'
"Where th' heck's that, Myrna Loy?"

And just think of how Tarzan, would start to how-l,
If he only was hangin' out, with Cheetah and Boy —
I feel like th' alphabet, without a vowel,
Like Flatfoot Floogie, with only one Floy —

Guess I'll just, throw in the towel,
Aw I'll never find the, real McCoy,
Just another William Powell,
Lookin' for that Myrna Loy. . . .

There was a silence not so much stunned as divided on whether to mow the 'sucker down, and his uke with him, right on the spot, or a little later. In fact, if Takeshi was counting on anything, it may have been the cross-purposes he felt in the air, a suspicion that DL didn't enjoy unquestioning support.

During his song he'd been time-stepping sideways, closer to DL, who had been observing with a mixture of amusement and disgust. As he drew near and she saw his face emerge to her at last as from a faint morning haze, she understood that from the time they had collided in Tokyo, even with her running away, he had desired her. But she could not, in much detail, imagine his sexual motives any better now than then. She shook her head — "You fuckin' crazy?"

"Maybe I came up here," Takeshi replied, "to do *you* a favor, Freckles!"

"Hold!" Sister Rochelle came stalking into the courtyard to break up the unpromising tête-à-tête. "You," pointing at Takeshi, "are a fool, whereas you," turning to DL, "it personally disappoints me to say, aren't even that far along. It should have been obvious to me right from the jump. You deserve each other. Therefore you, Sister Darryl Louise, under pain of the most major sanctions, are commanded to become this fool's devoted little, or in your case big, sidekick and to try and balance your karmic account by working off the great wrong you have done him . . . is there anything you'd like to add on?"

"No sex," stipulated DL. Takeshi began to squawk. "And when is 'is jail sentence up?" she also wanted to know.

Sister Rochelle figured a year ought to be about right, the same amount of time DL's reckless Needle Finger was to have given Takeshi to live. "Make that a year and a day, and don't look at me like that, you came here seeking a life of sacrifice, DL-san, which reminds me, about your PX bill —"

Light applause from the shaded edges of the courtyard, where in twos and threes curious ninjettes had been pacing, whispering, touching. "And now," Rochelle nodding to Takeshi, "we'd better see about bringing *you,* back to life. Sister DL, you might want to observe."

"This —" protested Takeshi, "does she have to be in on it? Hasn't she done enough?"

"Yes as you keep pointing out," DL snapped. They went inside quarreling, in single file, ninjettes crowding in to look. Birds could once more be heard, but singing now without much spirit, their voices oddly earthbound and afflicted. The trio proceeded to the Retreat Clinic, Sister Rochelle's pride and joy, home of the notorious Puncutron Machine.

"Got to get that chi back flowing the right way, now."

Takeshi looked around. It was an airy structure, once a barn, redivided into treatment rooms here and there but dominated by the machine, some of whose extensions rose as high as two stories. One of many therapeutic devices sold freely in California at the time, the Puncutron, though not encouraging for many patients to look at, had in the health community its share of intense loyalists. Detractors included the ever-vigilant FDA, one step ahead of whom the Puncutron's producers had so far just managed to keep. It was clear that electricity in unknown amounts was meant to be routed from one of its glittering parts to another until it arrived at any or all of a number of decorative-looking terminals, "or actually," purred the Ninjette Puncutron Technician who would be using it on Takeshi, "as we like to call them, electrodes." And what, or rather who, was supposed to complete the circuit? "Oh, no," Takeshi demurred, "I think not!"

"Consider what your options are," advised the Head Ninjette, "and behave like an adult."

Another Attentive, young, pretty, and more interested in eye contact than is good for the concentration of a proper ninjette, had appeared, carrying a sheaf of forms on a clipboard. She handed Takeshi a ten-page menu of audiotapes, from among which he was supposed to choose something to listen to during his Puncutron session. There were hundreds of selections, each good no doubt for its own set of bodily reactions. . . . Would *The All-Regimental Bagpipes Play Prime Time Favorites* get him through better or worse than *Taiwanese Healthy Brain Aerobics*? Some choices! As he went scanning down the list, the possibility emerging that far from having been scientifically or even carefully selected, these tapes had all in fact been snatched pretty much at random out of the bargain cassette bins at a Thriftimart in one of the more out-of-the-way locations, and indeed, given the skills ninja were famous for, might not even have been paid for at the checkout, the others went on hooking him up to the sinister ebonite and brushed-gold apparatus, each of whose stylish electrodes could be adjusted in at least two degrees of freedom, to contact the body at, on, and occasionally in, particular organs and areas.

"Kind of — erotic, isn't it, Toots?" Takeshi, having disrobed, now trying to chat up the ninjette with the clipboard while pretending to ignore the equally pleasant-looking Ninjette Puncutech who was slowly, and here and there intimately, attaching electrodes.

"You're cute, in an old-movie way," admitted the flirty-eyed ninjette, "but I need these forms completed, here, and here."

"What about here — aw, come on, babe, I could be — killed on this thing! Least you folks could do is — grant a man's last wish —"

"Yer wiggleen!" warned the other ninjette, trying to adjust something around his head, "now hold *still*."

"Well here, maybe you'd . . . just want to put your leg . . . mmhh —"

"Oh I can't believe this," DL fuming, "does he even understand what we're doing for him? Hey scumbag, do you even —"

"Stop," wearily counseled the Head Ninjette, "all this jabbering, will you. Thanks. Calm? Professionalism?"

". . . OK, and the Acker Bilk album," Takeshi had been deciding, "and, let's see, *The Chipmunks Sing Marvin Hamlisch*?"

Hookup complete, Sister Rochelle stood grinning with the main switch in her hand. "Now then my good man, see if this doesn't do a Roto-Rooter job on those ol' meridians, get 'em hummin'!"

Hmmmm, well, yes it did, that is to some extent. In years to come DL would often have occasion to holler at him, "Should've just left you on the Puncutron" — so often, in fact, that it would turn into an endearment. When this session was done, the ninjettes disconnected him and took him on a gurney to a recovery room, unadorned except for flowers and a small black iron Buddha on a shelf. Here, crossed by a beam of sunlight, in the act of reaching up under a regulation ninjette lab coat, Takeshi, as if beneath a spell, dropped voluptuously off to sleep.

He went on an intensive program of Puncutron sessions, herbal therapy, brain-wave recalibrations. Some of these turned out to involve DL. They realized they were being, somehow, tuned to each other. Could be brain waves, could be chi, maybe good old ESP. They would lie hooked up side by side like actors in a brain-transplant movie while the Puncutron vibrated and Takeshi, his musical preferences mysteriously self-revised, now listened through earphones to soul-strumming Tibetan chants. He still had no idea who she was.

One night as he was lying in bed watching a "Bionic Woman"

episode, the Head Ninjette came in to turn down the volume and tell Takeshi another kind of bedtime story. "Hey! She was just about to —"

"Jaime Sommers will understand. This is important, so listen up. It takes place in the Garden of Eden. Back then, long ago, there were no men at all. Paradise was female. Eve and her sister, Lilith, were alone in the Garden. A character named Adam was put into the story later, to help make men look more legitimate, but in fact the first man was not Adam — it was the Serpent."

"I like this story," said Takeshi, snuggling into his pillow.

"It was sleazy, slippery man," Rochelle continued, "who invented 'good' and 'evil,' where before women had been content to just be. In among the other confidence games they were running on women at the time, men also convinced us that we were the natural administrators of this thing 'morality' they'd just invented. They dragged us all down into this wreck they'd made of the Creation, all subdivided and labeled, handed us the keys to the church, and headed off toward the dance halls and the honky-tonk saloons.

"Now — behind those jive Oscar Goldman shades you look bright enough to understand that I'm talking about Darryl Louise. For all her personal distance with people, she won't have an easy time out there with you, because she never does, and it might not be out of line if now and then you'd entertain a few kind moments of thought on her behalf."

Takeshi raised his shades and gave her the eye-to-eye, intrigued by the expression on her face. She could almost have been asking a favor. "My pleasure — but there was more?"

The Head Ninjette, using only her eyebrows, shrugged. "Don't commit original sin. Try and let her just be."

Easy for you to say, lady, he muttered, silently, later, not to her face, in fact leaving, driving away from the Retreat, from that ridge above the fir forest, just beyond the coastal clouds. He was taking DL back down, along the mud ruts to the paved country roads, down to the arterial, to the on-ramp to the Interstate, till she was all the way back inside the Mobility. Speeding down the freeway in a rented Firebird, they both realized it was the first time since the room in Tokyo that they'd been alone together.

She looked over at him. "So this is Victim's Compensation. Shouldn't you be giving me orders?"

He considered this for a while. "Not much I can think of, with that — no-sex clause and all!"

"Hey," came her speedy reply, "think how I feel about the one year."

Their first tiff. A while later, "Listen then! Why don't I just — let you out, at the depot of your choice! Buy you a ticket — back to the Retreat!"

She wouldn't look at him, but shook her head no. "Can't."

"They really won't let you back?"

"I show my face before the year's up, and the sanctions are extreme. Please don't ask what they are."

"Go ahead — it might give me a cheap thrill!"

"The Ordeal of the Thousand Broadway Show Tunes —"

"Stop, *stop*, changed my mind —"

"The Andrew Lloyd Webber Chamber of —"

"You mean they'd actually —"

"That, and worse."

They drove for a while in a silence not altogether tranquil, more like a deepening joint depression. Somber forested hills rolled by, and she watched him nervously till suddenly he flipped her a sidewise slice of a grin. "Fun, huh?"

She snorted — not quite a laugh. "Yeah — no sex."

He began to chuckle. "One year!"

For a few seconds the car drifted between lanes, as if no one was paying attention. "You hungry?" asked DL.

"No appetite — must be this drugstore Methedrine! Wait — here's a nice-looking exit! Look at that glow in the sky! YOUR MAMA EATS, how can we resist?"

"You're crazy," as they came wheeling in, "look at this place, listen to that jukebox, observe the machinery in this parking lot, *oh* no, I have many bitter experiences, *Mis*-ter Fumimota-*san*, with exactly this type of establishment, which has all the signs of t-r-o-u-b-l-e, and we'd best get back on that freeway, right, now."

"What do I have to worry about? You — you've got to be — my bodyguard!"

"No, uh-uh, you don't get it, a kunoichi's first rule is Try to stay *out* of trouble, both within herself and then in terms of the outside environment? Like what bars and stuff she'll walk into, and as your bodyguard, rilly —"

"OK, OK," discovering there was no way to go but around the back, where the parking lot was so poorly lit that they did not at once notice several persons reeling around the asphalt with spoons in their noses, and not the elegant little gold models, either, but full-size stainless coffee spoons, taken from this very roadside eatery. "Would help if — you could do something about our — visibility!" Takeshi grunted. "You folks — you're supposed to be good at that!"

"OK, there's a paint and body shop in Santa Rosa? handles a lot of ninja work, they'll do you a camouflage job on this short you can go park and smoke dope on the sheriff's lawn nobody'll see you — you want to ask for Manuel."

"Thinking about right now, Darryl Louise," as threading the maze of auto anatomy they rounded yet another corner. It was the first time he'd called her by her name.

"On the other hand," she suggested, "maybe this is all intentional, maybe we're meant to go in here."

"Maybe not — sounds like old-time hippie philosophy to me!"

"OK, how about 'I'll buy'?"

Takeshi zipped into an open space and killed the motor. By the time they got inside YOUR MAMA EATS and had a closer look, it was too late to do anything but make mental notes on where the exits were. They sat in a booth of scuffed turquoise plastic and tried to avoid eye contact with everybody, including each other. Turned out that YME was a famous barbecue joint in this area. The windows were painted black, and the counter ran all the way around a huge central pit where different hardwoods glowed and the cooks tended, basted, pulled, or sliced cuts of beef and pork, hot links, and ribs, woodsmoke being drawn out the vents lazily enough that some mixed with the cigar, cigarette, and joint smoke already in the air. Takeshi ordered the Galaxy of Ribs, and DL thought she'd have the Brisket Fantasy, but mainly what they were interested in was coffee.

Takeshi's watch, one of whose readouts was on Tokyo time,

beeped at him. "Holy smoke! Got to check in — with the Prof!" He found a pay phone out by the toilets and punched in a lengthy code. Professor Wawazume himself picked up. "First of all, your pal — Minoru, the bomb-squad guy — he never came back to work! Disappeared!"

"He knew something!" Takeshi darkly replied. "I should have found out what!"

"No problem!" cried the Professor in a mischievous tone that Takeshi, with some alarm, recognized.

"You don't mean that you —"

"*Hai!* Put the word out that Minoru told *you* everything! Just before his — mysterious fade-out!

"So now they'll come looking for me!"

"Exactly! Good thing you called in, *ne?*"

"Anything from the lab on that footprint?"

Yes, working feverishly around the clock, programmers at WL & N-L had come up with a Standardized Reflexology Analysis, based on the ancient idea that many meridians, or say major nerves, of the body come to dead ends upon the soles of the feet — the 3-D body is projected on the 2-D sole, a map of itself. All across the print left in the mud there had remained tiny electromagnetic signatures, some of them erased by the rain but enough there to provide a snapshot of what had been going on in all the major organs, including the brain, of whatever this foot had belonged to, at the instant it came down.

"Organs! Brain! You're saying —"

"Report reads — 'Consistent with the foot impression of a saurian creature on the order of — one hundred meters high'!"

"Let me recap — it wasn't an exploder's job, and you have now sent — whoever took care of Minoru — after me! does that — about cover it?"

"One more thing!" The Professor's voice was beginning to fade. In the interests of cost containment, Takeshi subscribed to the services of Cheapsat, an economy communications satellite that was not, like more expensive units, geosynchronous, or parked in orbit always above the same spot on the Earth — no, Cheapsat instead drifted continually backward through the heavens, always going over the horizon in the middle of people's phone calls, as it even now was doing. "The performance of Chipco!" Professor Wawazume desperately screaming down into inaudibility, "on the Tokyo Stock Exchange! It's suddenly become very — strange! Yes, 'strange,' that's the word! For example —" at which point the low-rent orbiter set, and Takeshi, cursing, had to hang up.

He came back to the booth to find, in the turquoise shadows, his space occupied by a young fellow he didn't recognize, one, moreover, who had been scarfing away at Takeshi's Galaxy of Ribs, which had only just arrived — smoky, fragrant, permeated with a notorious sauce waiting to jump the mucosae of yet another unwary diner — and were already half gone. There was barbecue drippings all over the table, along with half a dozen longneck empties. "Hey!" this late-teenage-looking individual, even shorter than Takeshi, jumped up, nose running, eyes bright, as if gone psychotropic on hot peppers and mustard, to introduce himself as Ortho Bob Dulang, hitchhiker and, as it turned out, Thanatoid.

"The pretty lady said it was OK to start in on yer ribs, there, pardner, hope 'at's all right 'th you." DL was looking on with a sociable and, to Takeshi's eye, entirely false smile. "Thanatoids don't get to see many major foods, such as ribs," Ortho Bob continued, "food within the Thanatoid community never bein' that big a priority."

"That would explain it, all right. Do you mind if I ask —"

"What's a Thanatoid. OK, it's actually short for 'Thanatoid personality.' 'Thanatoid' means 'like death, only different.'"

"Do you understand this?" Takeshi asked DL.

"Near as I can tell, they all live together, in Thanatoid apartment buildings, or Thanatoid houses in Thanatoid villages. Housing's modular and pretty underfurnished, they don't own many stereos, paintings, carpets, furniture, knickknacks, crockery, flatware, none o' that, 'cause why bother, that about right, OB?"

"Uhk ee ahkhh uh akh uh Oomb," said the kid through a big mouthful of Takeshi's food.

" 'But we watch a lot of Tube,' " DL translated. While waiting for the data necessary to pursue their needs and aims among the still-living, Thanatoids spent at least part of every waking hour with an eye on the Tube. "There'll never be a Thanatoid sitcom," Ortho Bob confidently predicted, " 'cause all they could show'd be scenes of Thanatoids watchin' the Tube!" Depending how desperate a sitcom viewer might be feeling, even this could've been marginally interesting had Thanatoids not long ago learned, before the 24-hour cornucopia of video, to limit themselves, as they already did in other areas, only to emotions helpful in setting right whatever was keeping them from advancing further into the condition of death. Among these the most common by far was resentment, constrained as Thanatoids were by history and by rules of imbalance and restoration to feel little else beyond their needs for revenge.

"Understand she gave you the Vibrating Palm," Ortho Bob surfacing at last from his meat inferno. Takeshi was about to fly into a dither when he recalled how, not so long ago, he'd bent the ear of his airplane seatmate on the very same topic — one, besides, that a Thanatoid in particular might enjoy hearing about. Ortho Bob stared brightly, expectantly, from one of them to the other with a "smile" Thanatoids, though no one else, considered pleasant enough.

"So —" Takeshi reaching for one of the fried peach pies DL had thought to order, checking the edges of the frame for lines of withdrawal and additional Thanatoids, "some rib joint, huh!"

"Yeah," the "smile" widening, " 'some rib joint,' you're part Thanatoid yourself, ain't you, Mister."

DL, the bodyguard, picked this point to jump in. "Prob'm with that, OB?"

"The difference," Takeshi was remarking, "being, I think, that I'm trying to go — the opposite way! Back to life!"

"Thought once the Palm was on you, that's it."

"She thinks she can reverse it — if she atones for it — in the correct way!"

"No offense, folks, but this sounds like . . . wishful thinkin', don't it?"

Takeshi snorted. "What else — have I got?"

"My mom would love this. She watches all these shows where, you got love, is always winnin' out, over death? Adult fantasy kind of stories. So you guys, it's like *guilt* against death? Hey — very Thanatoid thing to be doin', and good luck."

Ortho Bob was heading back up to the Thanatoid village at the confluence of Shade Creek and Seventh River, in Vineland County. If they could get him up there, he could find them a place to stay.

Takeshi cocked an eye at DL and told her the news from Tokyo, the likelihood that Wawazume'd have to pay off on the lab-stomping disaster, the formidable pursuit set in motion against them thanks to the Professor's clever strategy.

"Guess we could use some cover," said DL.

"You heard the — security office! Let's go, Ortho Bob-san!"

And it was this unscheduled layover in Shade Creek, as they recalled to Prairie years later, that got them into the karmic adjustment business. A whole town full of Thanatoids! It would provide an inexhaustible supply of clients, though most of them, owing to the cupidity of heirs and assigns, couldn't pay much. But as the lab-stomping case, though still wide open, grew less immediate, Takeshi and DL became slowly entangled in other, often impossibly complicated, tales of dispossession and betrayal. They heard of land titles and water rights, goon squads and vigilantes, landlords, lawyers, and developers always described in images of thick fluids in flexible containers, injustices not only from the past but also virulently alive in the present day, like CAMP's promise of a long future of devoted enforcement from the sky. After a while DL and Takeshi started renting a conference room in the Woodbine Motel, just across the creek from town, for weekends anyway, though the rest of the time they preferred a back corner in the sprawling Zero Inn, where anybody could wander through and contribute to the day's testimony.

But right at the beginning DL had to sit Takeshi down for an elbows-on-the-table talk. "It ain't a-zackly Tokyo here, you know, you can't just go free-lancin' in 'karmic adjustment,' whatever that is — nobody'll pay for it."

"Ha-ha! But that's where you're wrong, Carrot-head! They'll pay us just like they pay the garbage men from the garbage dump, the plumbers in the septic tank — the mop hands at the toxic spill!

They don't want to do it — so we'll do it for them! Dive right down into it! Down into all that — waste-pit of time! We know it's time lost forever — but they don't!"

"Keep hearin' this 'we.' . . ."

"Trust me — this is just like insurance — only different! I have the experience, and — better than that, the — immunity too!"

She was afraid of what that meant. "Immunity from . . . ," her eyes wavering to the skylight and windows, she gestured outside, at the unseen insomniac population of Shade Creek. "Takeshi-san . . . they're ghosts."

He winked lewdly. "Do you want to — bite your tongue — or can I do it for you? That word — around here it's a no-no!" They were victims, he explained, of karmic imbalances — unanswered blows, unredeemed suffering, escapes by the guilty — anything that frustrated their daily expeditions on into the interior of Death, with Shade Creek a psychic jumping-off town — behind it, unrolling, regions unmapped, dwelt in by these transient souls in constant turnover, not living but persisting, on the skimpiest of hopes.

He led her to their window to have a look. They'd been up most of the night, and by now it was dawn. Although the streets were irregular and steeply pitched, the entryways and setbacks and forking corners, all angles ordinarily hidden, in fact, were some-how clearly visible from up here at this one window — naive, direct, no shadows, no hiding places, every waking outdoor sleeper, empty container, lost key, bottle, scrap of paper in the history of the dark shift just being relieved, was turned exactly to these windows from which Takeshi and DL looked down at the first yawners and stirrers, begun now to disengage from public surfaces. . . . "They seem so close . . . can they see us?"

"It's a trick — of the morning light!" Had they continued to watch from here as the sun rose, they would have seen the town begin to change, the corners of things to rotate slowly, the shadows come in to flip some of the angles inside out as "laws" of perspective were reestablished, so that by 9:00 A.M. or so, the daytime version of what was meant to be seen out the peculiar window would all be in place.

"Fumimota-san," DL turning from the window, the newly sun-filled streets below, "some of these folks don't look too good."

"What do you expect? What was done to them — they carry it right out on their bodies — written down for — all to see!"

"And by fixing each beef, that'll bring back the lost limbs, erase the scars, get people's dick to working again, that it?"

"No — and we don't restore youth, either! Why — you don't have enough else — to feel guilty about?"

"Yep — one foolish mistake, now I'm payin' it off for the rest of my life."

"Only — for the rest of mine, angel!" as up out of a calm and sunny ocean the killer sub *Unspeakable* briefly poked its periscope, eyeballed their vessel, ascertained that it was not the Love Boat, and withdrew. But they were learning, together, slowly, how to take evasive action, and at the moment it was down through an austere maze of Shade Creek alleyways and vacant lots for an extended breakfast and another day's business.

Ortho Bob came lurching over, looking as awful as the night he must have spent, wanting to talk some more about his case. He had been damaged in Vietnam, in more than one way, from the list of which he always carefully — though it might only have been superstitiously — excluded death. There were items enough on his get-even agenda, relief for none of which was available through regular channels. "Fuck the money, rilly," Ortho Bob had stipulated, "just get me some revenge, OK?"

"Go for the money," Takeshi pleaded, "it's easier." For example, revenge on whom? Ortho Bob, eager to help, had provided half a dozen names, which Takeshi was already running traces on. "Try to see my own problem," he said as the former grunt, who on Earth time would be 28 or so now, sat down and started eating waffles off Takeshi's plate. "The amount of memory on a chip doubles every year and a half! The state of the art will only allow this to move so fast!" In traditional karmic adjustment, he went on, sometimes it had taken centuries. Death was the driving pulse — everything had moved as slowly as the cycles of birth and death, but this proved to be too slow for enough people to begin, eventually, to provide a market niche. There arose a system of deferment, of borrowing against karmic futures. Death, in Modern Karmic Adjustment, got removed from the process.

"Ee-ee hukh ngyu huh ay!"

" 'Easy for you —' "

"I got it! Don't worry — if this doesn't work — we can always go for the reincarnation option!"

One of the waitresses, a non-Thanatoid who commuted from Vineland, came over with a tabloid called the *Meteor*. "Nice goin', you guys, can I have your autographs on this?" On page 3 was a photo of Takeshi and DL, a nighttime exterior, both of them casually dressed and looking even more paranoid than usual.

"This background — I think it's — Sydney, Australia!" Takeshi muttered to DL. "Were you — ever there?"

"Never — you?"

"Nope, maybe we've both got — amnesia! Or maybe it's a — composite photo! 'The shadowy Takeshi Fumimota, and — unnamed associate, vacationing — "Down Under" '! Always my favorite location," allowing his gaze, with a Grouchoic roll, to rest, long enough, upon her pelvic area. She smiled grimly.

This was about the lab and the footprint, of course — a deliberate leak to the *Meteor* and who knew where else. Takeshi tried to be cheerful. "At least they — didn't ID you!"

"You missin' a brain lobe, Takeshi? They're tryin' to smoke us out's what the message is, is that they'll go easy on me if I just turn you, got it, ya sleazy ol' Nip grease-job ya?"

He looked around frantically for the nearest drug, which turned out to be a recently mixed frozen mai tai, left unattended on a nearby table. "Wait a minute!" She grabbed his arm in midlurch. "Nobody drinks 'at shit fer breakfast, that could be a yakuza frappé right there." Appreciating her concern, Takeshi reached for DL's leg. "On second thought, drink right up, I keep forgetting, suicide used to be your old lifestyle."

She was referring to what he had a way of calling his "interesting work with airplanes" during World War II. "Though to be frank," she continued, "I can't imagine you in anybody's air force, let alone the kamikaze, who, I understand from the history books, were fairly picky about who flew for 'em."

"Lighten up! This'll all be — great advertising!"

"That thick head," she advised, "could be in some telescopic sight right now."

He lifted his shades, looking serious. "Getting you in trouble — it was never in my plans, DL-san. Maybe you should start to think — about beaming out of this, *ne?*"

She ran a hand through her hair, gave him a look. "Can't."

"It's a black hole! It's taken away thirty years of my life! I don't want it — to drag you in!"

"It's my job — I can't back out."

"Sounds like my — ex-wife!" He looked around, pretending to be crazy. "*Domo komarimashita!* What did I do, get married again and forget about it already?"

"You —" she could not believe this, "loudmouth and fool. Sister Rochelle plus a trained Oriental Medicine Team brought you back from the fuckin' *dead,* you twit, you think they go around doin' that for free? I'm your doctor bill, bright boy, you pay by havin' me in your life day in and day out, the person who once murdered you, OK, attached to you now by bonds of obligation far beyond what you, a disgrace to the folks who invented *giri,* can grasp, it seems."

Unflinching Takeshi, in what he hoped would not be taken as anything but the sociable gesture he meant it as, had been oscillating his eyeballs back and forth between DL's tits, which happened to be at the same altitude as his face.

"Enjoyin' yourself, aren't you, Takeshi. Mm, I'm happy for ya, you know, yes times like these, makes a gal want to, I don't know, forget all her ninjette vows?"

"Yes, yes?"

"And kill!" A few heads at nearby tables turned expectantly. Though sagging wasn't part of DL's job description, nevertheless how she'd love to just turn to liquid, relax — instead, since she'd been with Takeshi down here, she hadn't been able to sit and get into even the dustless-mirror phase before some other bullshit crisis would have her paged back once again out of the anterooms of clarity, back down the many levels to a malodorous, cheaply lit, nowhere-up-to-code assortment of spaces, one of which always had to include Takeshi or a situation he'd created, while he, guru of karmic adjustment, was out taking care of what he imagined to be business, and whilst she, mistress of invisibility, suffered but would, did, not cry after her lost simplicity — only desired it, as an insomniac might lust for sweet, potent sleep.

They went out of the restaurant and down a long viny arcade, among invisible birds and dew that still lay in the shadows, to their conference room. The little portable sign read OPEN KARMOLOGY CLINIC, WALK RIGHT IN, NO APPT. NECESSARY. Takeshi wore a suit and tie, DL a made-to-measure *gi* of raw silk from the Burlington Arcade in Nathan Road, Kowloon. They worked at a long banquet table set on a low platform among giant multicolored plastic houseplants that might've been alien moldmakers' whims, for nobody who saw them could really identify them, and in front of a mural-size map of Vineland County, flanked by U.S. and California flags on flagstands. There was a portable chalkboard, a coffee mess, a mike and amp. Takeshi and DL listened, taped, asked questions, took notes, trying for an image of informal gravity.

Waiting for them this morning were towaway teammates Vato and Blood, whom they'd met in the parking lot of the Woodbine Motel, late at night, thundering along in low in a Custom Deluxe named *Mi Vida Loca,* searching for likely units. The boys, when Takeshi and DL had appeared in their headlights, had been "scaling" the cars in this lot, as timber scalers will go through a piece of forest to estimate how many board feet of lumber it contains. Their task would seem to've been straightforward — simply choose, for towing away, the highest-priced rides first. But it depended, as either partner would've been quick to explain, on the *make* of high-priced ride — a Rolls Royce owner, for instance, would know how to turn the bothersome chore of redeeming his automobile into a lighthearted adventure, cheerfully paying all the exorbitant fees, some invented on the spot, and throwing in a big tip besides. On the other hand, towing away any Mercedes, even in the short run, was a losing proposition. No Mercedes driver would ever show up at V & B Tow at three in the morning in any mood for fun. Vato and Blood had recently been to a workshop down at a spa in Marin on this very subject, "Interpersonal Programming and the Problem Towee," in which the point had been made more than once that a Mercedes driver in redeeming his impounded ride shows no better manners than when he drives, trying first thing, in the marque's tradition of never signaling, an unannounced kick in the balls.

"Uh-huh," DL assured Vato, who, impressed with her looks, had been babbling along with no clear idea what he was saying.

"And sometimes," Blood now picking it up and directing his remarks to Takeshi, "you know, Doc, some fine units end up in our pound, and the owners never do claim 'm." He laughed in a make-believe crazy way that Takeshi heard as a *kiai*, or paralyzing scream just before an assault, but Blood only took him by the head and playfully began to twist it back and forth, like a lemon on a lemon squeezer. "Can't have somethin' like that sit around forever," now in a quieter, strangely intimate tone, "so we price it for quick sale."

" 'It,' " Takeshi between twists, "you keep saying 'that' and 'it.' "

"Say like — I'm talkin' about a Ferrari, all right?"

"You talking — about a Ferrari?"

"Was I getting specific?" He flipped Takeshi's head away like an empty lemon rind. "Next you be axkin' me the price."

"No offense."

"Sounds like the team I bet on last week," Vato put in.

"Raight on!" They ran through a Vietnam-style handclasp set to the tune of *2001: A Space Odyssey* (1968), going "Dum, dum, dum," in harmony, "DAHdahhhh!" slapping a high five, "Dum, dum, dum, daDAHH!" spinning around, slapping palms behind their backs and so forth while Takeshi and DL leaned against the front fenders of the truck, looking on. Vato produced a business card, for which Takeshi by reflex exchanged one of his own, "Allowín you anytime 24 hours to access the V & B Tow Preferred List, which gives a instant update on makes, models, years, conditions, special features."

"And say Doc," Blood added, "we also a little sleepy this time of night. . . ."

"Sure!" coming out with a handful of "white diamonds." And the fellows went on with their night's cruising after accounts towable. But next day they showed up unexpectedly at the Karmology Clinic with some input relating to Vietnam in general and Ortho Bob Dulang in particular, tales of who bought what in the Ton Son Nhut latrine while bats intercepted the legendary oversize mosquitoes, who entered wailing a hot bounded world they might, at the last moment, have recognized, and stoned bat-fishermen cast their hooked lines upward into the dark . . . and who only talked about and who did what to certain officers they all seemed to have in common, and why they had been led into the wrong place, and how many there were when the sun went down and how many when it came up . . . some of it was war stories, some just happy horseshit, and some was the stunned headlong certainty that precedes talking in tongues, though neither Vato nor Blood quite got to that.

As they came to know one another better, as the boys learned about the Death Touch, the Ninjette Retreat, the Puncutron Machine, the year and a day — and in time the rollover of the partnership for yet another year and a day, and so on — they remained among very few who did not offer DL and Takeshi any free advice, though between themselves the story was an object of lively commentary. Vato wanted it to be a sitcom. Whenever the topic came up, he made a point to laugh about it a lot, trying to fill in for a live studio audience.

" 'Pose it ain't that way," Blood objected, "maybe it's one them Movies of the Week where the dude has a incurable disease?"

"Nah, the way I like it is, is that she tells him everythín but he never checks any of it out to see if it's true, he just lets 'em all go ahead, fuckín around with needles, electricity, and shit, 'cause why bother, right, he don't know how much time he's got left. And she won't tell him . . . she ain't in the mood, nobody gets inside ten meters of her. Threaten her with a weapon? What if he fucks up and kills her, then he really has a problem."

Takeshi had in fact tried to entertain this upbeat scenario, though it hadn't entertained him much because he couldn't help seeing how wishful it was. What if, wild and unreasonable hope, she'd only been putting him on all the time, and this was her eccentric, even weird idea of flirting with him? Most of the time he couldn't believe she'd really Done It to him, because even this long way down the line he still had trouble believing in his own death. If she'd killed him, why stick around? If she hadn't, why put him, a complete stranger, through all this? It was driving him toward what, in fairly close to it now, he could detect as some state of literally mindless joy. There was no way he knew of to experience such joy and at the same time keep his mind. He wasn't sure this might not be her real mission — to make of his life a koan, or unsolvable Zen puzzle, that would send him purring into transcendence.

As time went by, that is, he did begin to wonder. But could not ask — she would only evade, turn her head away and smile, not in any sinister way but with a child's secretive semipro glaze, longing — though she only told him years later of how she used it to get her through — for the Retreat, the cloudy ridge, the high dark walls, where she could nest for a while with the others — not crippled sparrows but birds of prey, ragged from the storm, tired from the hunt, in for a little R and R — longing for the mountains, much as she'd once romantically imagined about her old teacher Inoshiro Sensei. This is what he had prepared her for — to inherit his own entanglement in the world, and now, with this perhaps demented Karmology hustle of Takeshi's, with the past as well, and the crimes behind the world, the thousand bloody arroyos in the hinterlands of time that stretched somberly inland from the honky-tonk coast of Now.

Vato and Blood were slouched in folding chairs when Takeshi and DL came in to open up shop, both humming back and forth in a strange free-form antiphony, sometimes falling silent, picking up the tune two and a half bars later exactly together, latently menacing, like a bee swarm. It was the famous V & B Tow Company Theme, based on the Disney cartoon anthem " 'I'm Chip!' — 'I'm Dale!' " sung originally by a chipmunk act that never quite achieved either the charisma or the recognition of Ross Bagdasarian's trio, Alvin, Simon, and Theodore. In Vietnam, Vato and Blood had worked mostly in the motor pool but now and then had to go out on convoys. In off of what was supposed to be a routine spin through the forests and turned instead into an outstandingly dark and death-laden time, having wandered one afternoon into a cement lounge deep within the Long Binh complex, reeking with attitude, they opened beers and settled in to watch the Tube. Some officer far away had determined that Disney cartoons would be just the right kind of entertainment for them, which was correct, if for the wrong reasons. As other loungers edged nervously away from the boys, suddenly on came Chip 'n' Dale, and an unmistakable flash of recognition. After listening to the chipmunk duo's Theme a couple of times, getting the lyric and tune down, Blood, turning to Vato during a commercial for re-enlistment, sang, "I'm Blood," and Vato immediately piped up, "I'm Vato!" Together, "We just some couple of mu-thuh-fuckers / Out —" whereupon a disagreement arose, Vato going on with the straight Disney lyric, "Out to have some fun," while Blood, continuing to depart from it, preferred "Out to kick some ass," turning immediately to Vato. "What's 'is 'have some fun' shit?"

"OK, OK, we'll sing 'kick some ass,' no problem." Singing, "I'm Vato —"

Still annoyed, "Uh, I'm Blood. . . ."

"We just some couple of —" at which point Vato maliciously sang "crazy bastards" instead of "motherfuckers." The two broke off and glared at each other. Over the next few years, as they were getting their business going, this was to keep happening — sometimes they managed to get from one end of the song to the other in perfect agreement, but most of the time they did not. The song became a kind of bulletin board for the partnership, a space on which they could hang these variations to remark on questions of the moment and plans of the day. The night before, for example, out in the truck, Blood had been singing, "End up eatin' some fast food that you *know* / Will taste like shit —" referring to an argument that had been going on all week about where to take the third partner at V & B Tow, Thi Anh Tran, to lunch for her birthday, whose date Blood, the company yenta, had found in her folder. Both agreed it would be a nice surprise, but where to eat?

Blood ruled out Chinese, Japanese, Vietnamese, Thai, and Polynesian. "She don't want to be eatin' that shit, that's all she ever
ate over there was zat shit, and exspecially not on her birthday,
Blood," said Blood.

"OK, Vato," said Vato, "then how about Mexican, take her
to Taco Carajo, startín at noon, live strollín mariachis, hot Mexican *antojitas* —"

"Hey maybe *you* can eat that shit —" The task seemed impossible — every eatery choice carried some risk of offense, and
neither wished to call down any Dragon Lady type of curses from
the woman who these days held in her exquisite hands every last
detail of V & B's finances, including many of interest not only to
the IRS but also to organizations that were much less coy about
theft. Though they went to elaborate lengths to deny it, Vato and
Blood were both afraid of her. In May of '75 they'd found her
languishing in Pendleton, along with thousands of others who'd
flooded in after the fall of Saigon, but their history went back
further, to their wartime association with Gorman ("The Specter")
Flaff's legendary operations in money orders and piasters, into
which they had bought at exactly the right moment in the Specter's
tangled financial saga to furnish them with the metaphysical edge
of seeming to have performed an angelic intervention. In return
they gained the superstitious Flaff's confidence, which turned out
to include naming them in his will to take over his obligations to
Thi Anh Tran.

"Don't remember we ever talked about it, Vato."

"Nope, we just did it, right?"

"There it is."

"We owed it to Flaff."

"Flaff owed it to her." He'd been springing for her education
at one of the Ecoles des Jeunes Filles in Saigon, plus a small al-
lowance check, for reasons there were only rumors about. One
story was he'd barbecued her family and felt guilty, but neither
part of that sounded much like the old Specter. Few months later,
out too close to the wrong woodline, that was it for Gorman. At
the base camp a chaplain was holding the letter for Vato and Blood
in which the name of Thi Anh Tran first came up. They drank

warm Cokes, sat down, Phantoms thundered over the jungle, helicopter blades beat the humid air. Years later, grown up and a certified CPA, there she was in Pendleton, in a 25-person army tent, all processed, just waiting, smoking Kools and listening to AM rock and roll. As a term of their sponsorship, they hired her as their bookkeeper, but soon, recognizing her worth, dealt her in for an equal share of the business. Now she had them both so nervous they'd do anything to avoid upsetting her.

"Say, Blood," said Blood to Vato, "Vietnamese bitch say she want to talk to you."

"Uh-oh," Vato muttered.

"You do somethin' wrong?"

Vato figured it must be that burger and fries he'd put on company plastic. He was in her office for ten minutes, with no sounds of any kind to be heard behind the door. Vato emerged shaking his head. Blood happened to be right there. "Well, uh, how you doin', Blood?"

"That Vietnamese bitch, you know what, she's really somethín," said Vato.

"You tellin' me? I know that."

"Yeah this time, she had some pistol, Vato."

"Pistol. What kind?"

"ChiCom MAC 10."

"No such thing. She *poinedt* it at you?"

"Who saw it? Did you see it?"

"I didt'n — did you?"

"I *saw* it, Vato."

After they finally decided to have the birthday luncheon at an upscale soul-food place called Once Upon A Chitlin, the question arose, who was going to ask her? They had to argue for half an hour before agreeing to do it together. But who'd go through first when she called, "Come in"?

"Vietnamese bitch say 'Come in,' " muttered Blood.

"Well go on ahead," Vato in a whisper.

"What's 'is 'go on ahead' shit?"

"Who is it?" called the woman behind the door.

"Us!" hollered the mercurial Vato.

"Shh-*shh!* Who *aksed* you?

"*She* didt, man —"

The door was opened by Thi Anh Tran, who peered up at the two of them. The ChiCom MAC 10 was nowhere, at least by any casual eye, to be seen. She was wearing a fawn jumpsuit of some loose cotton weave, accessorized in different shades of red — eyeglass frames, scarf, belt, and suede cowgirl boots that might have set her back somewhere in the mid three figures. Red designer barrettes held her hair sleekly back from an articulate brow and temples that often seemed ready to betray more than the shielded eyes ever would.

"She's not so bad," Vato suggested to Blood later that night, out on the road.

"What do you mean?"

"Aw, you know, if she did somethín with her hair, maybe wear some clothes that you could see some skin, right?"

Blood, whose amusement quota that month had not so far even been approached, allowed himself a snort and a half a chuckle. "You about to step on your dick once again."

"Thanks, it's what I get for doín like they tol' me in therapy I'm spoze to, tryín for total honesty with my ol' war buddy an' shit. We been through all this before, you know, I can take it once again."

"Plenty of times," Blood agreed.

"Meanín that I never learn, that what you're sayín?"

They were in full quarrel as the truck arrived at the freeway on-ramp. "Watch it Vato, that was a Greyhoun' *bus* right there —"

"Seen it, Blood."

The radio blurted at them. Vato had it coming out of speakers forward and aft, and Blood, surprised as usual, cringed under the decibels, and the truck wavered in and out of the lane. "Zat got to be so loud?"

Vato reached for the volume just as the radio thundered, "Hello, boys," in what, at a normal level, might have been an intriguing female voice.

Vato froze. "It's her! The Vietnamese bitch!"

"Vato and Blood, Vato and Blood, where are you, come in, please?"

"Mm, it do sound like her, the one you're thinking of, so why don't you go on ahead, pick up the phone."

It was an emergency call from up in Shade Creek. Thanatoids. V & B Tow was nearly alone on that stretch of 101 in its willingness to tow away vehicles associated with Thanatoids and, inevitably, Thanatoid stories. Tonight's had gone off the edge of a hillside road and was now in the top of an apple tree in the orchard just below.

"We goín the right way?" Vato pretended to ask his partner.

"You the navigator, you tell me." So Vato made a big point of getting the county map out of its compartment, shaking it open in crisp percussions.

After a while, "I can't see nothín, what is this?"

"Is nighttime's what it is," Blood replied, "Jello-O Brain."

"Hey! I'm gonna put the dome light on, all right?"

"Huh. 'Pose to be readin' that map, so why'n't you just use the map light."

"It's way under the dash, it throws this little spot of light, which to see anything you got to move the map around a inch at a time, is why, to answer your question, I don' want to use, no map light."

"Tell you what I don't want, Blood, is to be out in some uncontrolled space with less light on it than the space I'm in, you understand, which if you put that dome light on is what'll happen —"

"Hey! Just tell me — where's the flashlight, all right? I'll use that. Where is it, it ain't here."

"It's in th' electrical-equipment locker, where it spoze to be."

"In the back of the truck."

"It's electric, ain't it?"

This was all recreational bickering. By this time they'd been in business for a couple of years and already learned the roads of Vineland well enough to use in the dark, which now and then they'd been obliged to — the maps were usually just there for props as Vato and Blood went prowling everywhere the suburban lanes, the sand and grass tracks, the gullied-out mud nightmares. They had scrambled over slides, rigged tackle in the trees, winched out lots' worth of vehicles, from early-model toughmonkey Porsches out for a little all-terrain exercise to dapper fishing vans sporting four-color trout murals and CB call letters in glittery stick-on alphanumerics. They had seen things in the forest, and particularly up along Seventh River, whose naming aloud, in certain area taverns, was cause for summary octogenarihexation from the establishment, as well as for less formal sanctions in the parking lot.

They took the North Spooner exit and got on River Drive. Once past the lights of Vineland, the river took back its older form, became what for the Yuroks it had always been, a river of ghosts. Everything had a name — fishing and snaring places, acorn grounds, rocks in the river, boulders on the banks, groves and single trees with their own names, springs, pools, meadows, all alive, each with its own spirit. Many of these were what the Yurok people called *woge*, creatures like humans but smaller, who had been living here when the first humans came. Before the influx, the *woge* withdrew. Some went away physically, forever, eastward, over the mountains, or nestled all together in giant redwood boats, singing unison chants of dispossession and exile, fading as they were taken further out to sea, desolate even to the ears of the newcomers, lost. Other *woge* who found it impossible to leave withdrew instead into the features of the landscape, remaining conscious, remembering better times, capable of sorrow and as seasons went on other emotions as well, as the generations of Yuroks sat on them, fished from them, rested in their shade, as they learned to love and grow deeper into the nuances of wind and light as well as the earthquakes and eclipses and the massive winter storms that roared in, one after another, from the Gulf of Alaska.

For the Yuroks, who had always held this river exceptional, to follow it up from the ocean was also to journey through the realm behind the immediate. Fog presences glided in coves, dripping ferns thickened audibly in the gulches, semivisible birds called in nearly human speech, trails without warning would begin to descend into the earth, toward Tsorrek, the world of the dead. Vato and Blood, who as city guys you would think might get creeped out by all this, instead took to it as if returning from some exile of their own. Hippies they talked to said it could be reincarnation — that this coast, this watershed, was sacred and magical, and that the *woge* were really the porpoises, who had left their world to the humans, whose hands had the same five-finger bone structure as their flippers, OK, and gone beneath the ocean, right off around Patrick's Point in Humboldt, to wait and see how humans did with the world. And if we started fucking up too bad, added some local informants, they would come back, teach us how to live the right way, save us. . . .

The orchard Vato and Blood were looking for was on the other side of Shade Creek, meaning the usual difficult passage over the ruins of the old WPA bridge, where somehow, mysteriously, at least one lane was always open. Sometimes entire segments vanished overnight, as if floated away downriver on pontoons — detours were always necessary, often with the directions crudely spray-painted onto pieces of wall or old plywood shuttering, in the same bristling typeface as gang graffiti. There were always crews at work, around the clock. Tonight Vato and Blood had to wait while a truck piled high with smashed concrete and corroded iron rod went grinding back and forth by its own routes of beaten earth. Figures in fatigues and sometimes helmets could be seen, always in small groups, maybe Corps of Engineers, nobody was sure. They did not interact with the public, not even as flagmen. Drivers were left to decide how safe it was to proceed. Blood inched the rig forward, past great triangular rents in the pavements, through which, screened by a rough weave of reinforcing rods, they could see the river of midnight blue below. The work had been going on since the '64 storm, when the Seventh, cresting, had taken part of the bridge. Broken silhouettes had stood against the sky for all the years since.

Having crossed safely at last, they put on all their running lights, popped in the Bernard Herrmann cassette, and proceeded up the Shade Creek Valley road to that driving-through-the-night music from *Psycho* (1960), till they found the orchard and, with the help of spotlights, a Toyota in the treetops. As they watched, the front door opened and the driver began to get out, causing the car to oscillate wildly, apples to fall.

"Better just take it easy till we can find you a ladder," Vato called up.

"Won't matter, I'm a Thanatoid."

"Our insurance. What about the car?"

"Straight." By which he meant solid, three-dimensional, and not apt to vanish unaccountably between Shade Creek and the V & B pound, as Thanatoid units — cars returned, for reasons of road karma, from Totality — had been known to do, much to the perplexity of the partners. They found an orchard ladder in a shed, and soon the driver had descended, a stock model late-sixties longhair, power-forward-size but short on humor. "Well I'm a pilgrim," he identified himself, "who's taken ten years your time just to get this far. The network has been buzzing, like, 'for a while' with stories about this karmic adjuster working out of Shade Creek, who actually gets results? I've come to ask him to take my case."

"We know him, Blood, happy to run you on into town."

"*Sate* . . . your friend — he's here someplace?" Takeshi squinting around the conference room.

"No," Vato sounding a little nervous, "thought we'd better check it out first."

"What he's having trouble spittin' out," said Blood, "is you already know him, DL, he was gunned down in a alley at the beach in Trasero County ten years ago?"

She knew. "Ah," she knew all right, "shit." So here came the first chickens running point, soon to be squadrons darkening the sky, seeking a Home to Roost in that perhaps by now no longer existed.

"Weed Atman. Well. Poor fuckin' Weed. Guess I should've been wondering when he'd show."

"Mentioned some old runnin' mate of yours," Blood said.

"He still feels rilly bitter," Vato added, "he blames her for what happened."

Prairie was hearing this, in her turn, from DL in the sun-filled kitchen of the Kunoichi Retreat. "My mom *killed* a guy?" She was shivering, almost with excitement, but mostly with fear.

"Weed said somebody else had the gun, but he knew that Frenesi set it all up."

"Why would she? Who was he?"

"We were all sorta runnin' together for a while, down in Trasero, College of the Surf? Weed was a what you'd call campus revolutionary. But there was also a strong rumor he was workin' for the other side."

"Did you ask him which side he was on? He can tell you now, can't he? got no reason to lie?"

Takeshi snickered. DL said, "Afraid that ain't the way it works . . . but I appreciate it's important to you. It makes a difference what side *she* would have had to be on. . . ."

"You're trying awful hard not to say somethin', DL. First you tell me she's runnin' around on my dad with this federal megacreep, now you say she helped kill a guy? Does everybody know all about this and I'm just the dumb kid they wait to tell last?"

"Take that up with your father and Sasha. Only reason I'm tellin' you's if you put those facts together —"

"They spell Mother?"

"Prairie, she was working for Brock."

But the kid took no more than a beat and a half before, "Yeah? carried a badge, commission card?"

"She was an independent contractor. They all were, are. . . . That way if she ever got burned, the Man could deny knowledge."

"Why tell me? who cares?"

"Brock's on your case, figure that's a pretty compelling need to know. Prairie? Come on."

"OK, but do you mind if I take a second to process it, plus it's now also time for me to go set up for supper? Either of you happen to know what's in the 'Variety Loaf'?"

DL let her off the hook. "Thought the EPA confiscated all that."

It was tonight or never as far as Prairie was concerned. All the Variety Loaves, stacked in a distant niche of the freezer, had begun to glow, softly blue-green, like a night-light for the rest of the frozen food, not, as once supposed, safely dead but no, only, queerly, sleeping . . . o-or perhaps only pretending to sleep — gaahhh! Like everybody else in the kitchen, Prairie had a threshold for how long she could spend in that sinister freezer before some more than thermometric chill sent her back out into the less clearly haunted world, pulses thumping.

"OK — I need a crew in there, we're bringin' out all that Variety

Loaf, then we'll take a vote if it's safe to eat," raising her voice, "so be here, be near, or learn the meaning of fear! Ah right! Gerhard, Sister Mary Shirelle, Mrs. Lo Finto, the twins, let's go for the glow, you guys," and stepping in time to the music on the radio, which happened to be the theme from *Ghostbusters* (1984), off they went. But it wasn't long before a dispute arose as to the morality of disturbing the microenvironment of the freezer. "Bioluminescence is life," suggested the twins in hasty overlap, "and all life is sacred."

"Never eat anything that glows," pronounced Mrs. Lo Finto, an Italian mother who not only couldn't cook but actually suffered clinical kouxinaphobia, or fear of kitchens, her assignment back here being part of her therapy. They stood in the chill of the freezer, under a marginal light bulb, with the Variety Loaf providing a turquoise fill, bickering in parallel, eventually bringing a sample out to the kitchen.

"It does not look so bad in the daylight," Gerhard pointed out as work slowed and everyone gathered around the enigmatic foodstuff.

"That's 'cause you can't see it glow, dummy."

"Tradition among the tribes of Central Asia of ingesting luminescent molds as a spiritual practice —"

"But molds have rights too!"

Prairie had a few seconds' glimpse of how dishearteningly long this might go on, how inconclusive, time-wasting, and unspiritual it would all turn out anyway, just as a touch she knew brought her turning to see DL suited up, carrying some gear, in a hurry. It was as if a solemn bell had begun to ring. "Here's your back pack. 'Me gotta go,' as the Kingsmen always used to say, and you too."

"But —" the girl gesturing back toward the kitchen, the faces she'd come to know, all the meals yet unplanned, and DL's plain message that it was already old videotape. As they moved outside and down the vined fragrant colonnade, Prairie heard the beat of helicopters, more than one, close overhead, hovering, waiting. What the fuck?

They reentered the main building, running now — deeper, into corridors, down flights of ringing metal stairs. Takeshi joined them outside the Retreat wine cellar, bottles sticking out of at least four suit pockets.

"You're looting?" DL paused to inquire.

"Few random vintages, I was — pressed for time!"

"Undrinkable, of course, theft itself being the main thing with you, right, Takeshi."

"Check it out, Freckles! Here — '71 Louis Martini, *ne?* A legend! And this one's — some kind of French stuff!"

"Um, you guys. . . ."

"Gates are shut," DL reported, "figure a minute 'n' a half each with a bolt cutter, plus at least three Huey Cobras in the air, FFAR's, grenade launchers, Gatling guns, the works."

They arrived at the mouth of an oversize freight elevator, scrambled inside, and began to plunge earpoppingly hellward, aged fluorescent bulbs buzzing and flickering till the brakes caught just when it seemed too late, and they boomed to a stop and came out into a tunnel, deep underground, which led them under the creek bed and then slowly uphill for half a mile, where they exited at last into brightly sunlit terrain where they could hear in the distance the invading motor convoy and the blades of the helicopters, merged in an industrious roar that could as well have been another patch of developer condos going up.

They found the Trans-Am under camouflage netting down among some alder and moved out by way of old logging roads, zigzagging toward I-5, Takeshi consulting maps, DL driving, singing

> Oh, kick out, the jambs, motherfuck-er,
> 'Cause here comes, that Stove once again —
> You thought I was somethin' in Olathe,
> Wait till, you see me in Fort Wayne. . .

and Prairie huddled down in back, hanging on, wishing they could wake into something more benevolent and be three different people, only some family in a family car, with no problems that couldn't be solved in half an hour of wisecracks and commercials, on their way to a fun weekend at some beach.

THEY blasted down to L.A., heading back to the barn only semivisible and near as anybody could tell unobserved, Manuel and his auto alchemy team at Zero Profile Paint & Body of Santa Rosa having come up with a proprietary lacquer of a crystalline microstructure able to vary its index of refraction so that even had there been surveillance, the Trans-Am could easily, except for a few iridescent fringes, have been taken for empty roadway.

If Prairie had been expecting an old-movie private eye's office, seedy and picturesque, she wouldn't be getting it today. The Fumimota suite was located in a basic L.A. business/shopping complex of high-rises that stood on a piece of former movie-studio lot. Space devoted to make-believe had, it was thought, been reclaimed by the serious activities of the World of Reality. A lot of old-time oaters had been lensed here — she'd watched some, Saturday mornings on the Tube — but where stagecoaches had rolled and posses thundered, now stockbrokers whispered romantically about issues and futures into tiny telephone mikes no bigger than M&M's, crowds dressed to impress came and shopped and sat on tile patios eating lunch, deals were made high overhead in legal offices that weren't always legal, sharing these altitudes with city falcons who hunted pigeons in the booming prisms of sun and shadow below.

Prairie still had no idea of what "karmic adjustment" was supposed to be, but for the first time it began to seem plausible to her that Takeshi, if not what he said he was, at least might be more than the nose-twister and eye-poker he appeared. The place was full of computer terminals, facsimile machines, all-band transmitter/receivers, not to mention components scattered all over, printed circuits, laser units, DIP's, disk drives, power supplies, and test equipment —

"Hi-tech Heaven," her eyes wide.

"That'd be your first mistake," DL said. "Most of it's just props to make ol' Sleazebrain here look good."

"Please," Takeshi waving a palm-sized remote control. "What can we offer you?" In rolled a little robot fridge, with two round video screens side by side, each with an image of a cartoon eye that shifted and blinked from time to time, and a smile-shaped speaker for a mouth, out of which now came a synthesized medley of refrigerator tunes, including "Winter Wonderland," "Let It Snow," and "Cold, Cold Heart." Stopping in front of Prairie, humming and flexing small electric motors, it recited its contents.

"You said 'designer seltzer,' what's that?"

"Another stage in the marketing philosophy of the mid-1980s," replied the mobile cooler. "At the moment I have Bill Blass, Azzedine Alaïa, Yves St. Laurent —"

"Fine!" Prairie a little high-pitched, "that'll be, uh —" and *pow* there was the stylish seltzer, stone-cold in its YSL-logo container in the essentially Reagan-era fashion colors of gold and silver. One of the video eyes winked at her, and from the mouth emerged a shiny pink tongue of some soft, wobbling plastic. "Anything else?" the creature inquired in the kind of voice Prairie had come to mistrust even before she could talk.

"Thanks, Raoul," DL said, "we'll let you know."

The video eyes closed, and Raoul glided back to its recharge station, playing "I'll See You Again" and "Drink, Drink, Drink."

"Time machine's in the shop," Takeshi brightly, "otherwise we'd all — go for a spin!"

"Just had to R-and-R another tachyon chamber," DL amplified, "exactly a tenth of a second after the warranty ran out, the 'sucker blew, why they call it a 'time' machine, I guess?"

But Prairie had been sitting glazy at one of the screens, stroking some keys. "If I wanted to know where she was, say right this second —"

DL shook her head. "I really don't get this. The woman —"

"DL-san —" Takeshi had his eyebrows up.

"Go ahead," the girl getting to her feet. "She ran out on me. Probably to be with Brock Vond, is the way it looks. I'm the last person she wants to see. I leave anything out?"

"Plenty. Like all your friends in 'em Cobra gunships, who seem at the moment to be part of the package, you get her, you get them too?"

"In fact —" Takeshi pretending to run over to the window and anxiously check the sky, "why are we — even hanging around with this kid? She's dangerous!"

DL reached and looped a length of hair back behind Prairie's ear. "Until you get to see her . . . would you settle for watchin' her? It's the best I can do."

"You know I have to settle for what I can get," the girl whispered, keeping her eyes down because she knew DL was on to her and if their eyes met she'd just blow it.

Ditzah Pisk Feldman lived in a Spanish split-level up a pleasant cul-de-sac on the high-rent side of Ventura Boulevard, with pepper trees and jacarandas in the yard and a vintage T-Bird in the carport. She was divorced and solvent, with only about a half-hour commute to work. The girls were with their father for the summer. When DL had known her back in Berkeley, Ditzah and her sister Zipi were going around in battle fatigues with their hair in matching oversize Jewish Afros, spray-painting SMASH THE STATE on public walls and keeping plastic explosive in Tupperware containers in the icebox. "Pretending to be film editors," she told Prairie, "but we were really anarchist bombers." This evening she looked like your average suburban mom, though what did Prairie know, maybe it was another disguise. Ditzah was drinking sangria and wearing eyeglasses with fashion frames and a muumuu with parrots all over it.

It was just before prime time, with the light outdoors not quite gone, birds loud in the trees above a distant wash of freeway sound, the concrete surf. Ditzah led them across the patio to a workshop in back, with a Movieola machine and 16mm film all over the place, some on reels or cores, some in pieces lying around loose, and some in cans inside steel footlockers, which turned out to be the archives of 24fps, the old guerrilla movie outfit.

Back then they had roved the country together in a loose low-visibility convoy of older midsize sedans, pickups with and without camper shells, an Econoline van for equipment, and a dinged and chromeless but nonetheless kick-ass Sting Ray that served as a high-speed patrol unit, among all of which they kept in touch by CB radio, still then a novelty on the road. They went looking for trouble, they found it, they filmed it, and then quickly got the record of their witness someplace safe. They particularly believed in the ability of close-ups to reveal and devastate. When power corrupts, it keeps a log of its progress, written into that most sensitive memory device, the human face. Who could withstand the light? What viewer could believe in the war, the system, the countless lies about American freedom, looking into these mug shots of the bought and sold? Hearing the synchronized voices repeat the same formulas, evasive, affectless, cut off from whatever they had once been by promises of what they would never get to collect on?

"Never?" asked a local TV interviewer once, somewhere back in the San Joaquin.

And here came Frenesi Gates's reverse shot. Prairie felt the two women shift in their seats. Frenesi's eyes, even on the aging ECO stock, took over the frame, a defiance of blue unfadable. "Never," was her answer, "because too many of us are learning how to pay attention." Prairie gazed.

"Well, you sound like our own Action News Team."

"Except that we have less to protect, so we can go after different targets."

"But . . . doesn't that get dangerous?"

"Mm, in the short run," Frenesi guessed. "But to see injustices happening and ignore them, as your news team has been ignoring the repression of farm workers here in this county who've been trying to organize — that's more 'dangerous' in the long run, isn't it?" Aware at each moment of the lens gathering in her own image.

DL, on the other hand, obliged to approach life in 24fps with cold practicality, stayed as far out of camera range as she could. When she talked, it was about tactics and timetables, hardly ever politics, and then only as much as she had to. She made sure the rolling stock was always ready to roll, scouted each new location for rendezvous points and multiple ways out of town, and though preferring to plan their way around cops and cop sympathizers was not above keeping a pry bar handy beneath her driver's seat. If they did get caught it would have to be DL, as unit chief of security, who lingered behind to delay the pursuit.

"That night Sledge drove us right into the middle of a drug bust?" Ditzah cackled, "Me and Zipi smoking shit somebody marinated in DMT, couldn't keep a thought in our heads, we kept wanderin' off and you'd have to go find us —"

"Thought that was the hash in the hot fudge sundaes."

"No, that was Gallup, the hot fudge. . . ."

"Um," Prairie pointing at the screen, "who're all these folks?"

It was a slow pan shot of 24fps as constituted on some long-ago date the two women were unable now to agree on. An incoherent collection of souls, to look at them, a certain number always having drifted in and out — impatient apprentices, old-movie freex, infiltrators and provocateurs of more than one political stripe. But there was a core that never changed, and it included genius film editors Ditzah and Zipi Pisk, who'd grown up in New York City and, except for geographically, never left it. California's only reality for them was to be found in the million ways it failed to be New York. "Magnin's?" Zipi would smile grimly. "OK for a shopping center, somewhere on Long Island perhaps, very nice ladies' toilet of course, but please, this is no major store." Ditzah was the food kvetch — "Try and get a Danish *anywhere* out here!" They found West Coast people "cold and distant" as invariably as they remembered apartment living in the Big Apple being all "warm and neighborly."

This amused the others. "Are you kiddeen?" Howie, who took care of the paperwork, would snort. "I visited my sister back there, try to even get eye contact it's yer ass, babe."

"*We* are not the ones who have to encapsulate *our*selves inside our cars all the time," Zipi would point out, "are we? no, and our dogs and cats never have to get sent to shrinks, and *we* certainly do not come up out of the water, fuck somebody right there on the beach then go jogging away without even leaving their phone number," which had in fact happened to her during the girls' first or introductory weekend on the West Coast, the event, despite its air of the supernatural, having left both sisters with a certain attitude toward the surfing community, of which, because of his xanthocroid looks, they had singled out Howie as typical.

To watch them at work was to enjoy unthinking exhibitions of grace. Zipi edited with her nails and Scotch tape, Ditzah favored teeth and paper clips, and when it got to the Movieola stage, rarely was either sister more than a frame off. They liked to chain-smoke while they worked and to have two or three television sets, tuned to different channels, going at the same time, plus rock and roll, the more acid-oriented the better, on the radio, thus cutting and splicing in an environment you could call rhythmic. When Mirage, the unit astrologer, found out they were both Geminis, she started feeding them daily aspects. They learned to get up at strange hours, and when the Moon was void of course, not to work at all.

Frenesi and the Pisks had taken over what was left of the Death to the Pig Nihilist Film Kollective, based in Berkeley, a doomed attempt to live out the metaphor of movie camera as weapon. The Kollective's assets included camera bodies, lenses, lights and light stands, Movieola, hydraulic camera mount, fridgeful of ECO, and, at first anyway, a rump of the Kollective's more stubborn personnel, who had put some of the language of their old manifesto into 24fps's new one — "A camera is a gun. An image taken is a death performed. Images put together are the substructure of an afterlife and a Judgment. We will be architects of a just Hell for the fascist pig. Death to everything that oinks!" — which for many was going too far, including Mirage, on her feet to insist that pigs are really groovy, in fact far groovier than any humans their name ever gets applied to.

"Say 'roaches,'" suggested Sledge Poteet.

"Roaches are cool," protested Howie, who happened to have a joint in his mouth. Krishna, the sound person, put in with a stipulation that all life, even that of roaches, is holy. "Wait a minute," cried one of the original Death-to-the-Piggers, "that kind of talk invalidates our whole conceptual base, this is about shooting folks here, is it not?"

"Oh yeah? what's your sign, man?" Howie wanted to know.

"Virgo."

"It figures."

"Signism!" Mirage screamed. "Howie, that's worse than racism!"

"Worse than sexism," added the Pisks in unison.

"Ladies, ladies," boomed Sledge, gesturing with his 'fro pick, while Howie, eyes ablush, held out a smoldering joint of gold Colombian as a token of peace.

"Be groovy, everybody," advised Frenesi, who wasn't exactly chairing the get-together, only struggling as usual to keep outside the bickering. This outfit was nobody's anarchist fantasy. When DL came aboard, she and Sledge, with whom she shared a fondness for enlightenment through asskicking, immediately became the realist wing of 24fps, counterposed to the often dangerously absent dreamers Mirage and Howie. Frenesi and the Pisks soldiered on in the center, and the task of trying to keep everybody "happy" fell to Krishna. Frenesi would come back with half a dozen rolls of dysrhythmic young Californian women dancing at a rally, Zipi and Ditzah would fly into a rage at the impossibility of getting any of these hippie chicks to do anything on the beat ("It's tzuris I don't need!" "Tzimmes also!"), and it was always Krishna who found the right music, expertly manipulated the tape speed, and seemed to know what the Pisks wanted before they did, quickly getting a reputation in the unit for broad ESP skills. When backs were left uncovered and chores undone, when words got too ambiguous, it was Krishna who led everybody to the bathroom and served as counselor for as long as it took. Without her, Ditzah thought, no telling how much sooner it would all have come apart, exchanging with DL now a look that Prairie didn't miss.

Night and movies whirred on, reel after reel went turning, carrying Prairie back to and through an America of the olden days she'd mostly never seen, except in fast clips on the Tube meant to suggest the era, or distantly implied in reruns like "Bewitched" or "The Brady Bunch." Here were the usual miniskirts, wire-rim glasses, and love beads, plus hippie boys waving their dicks, somebody's dog on LSD, rock and roll bands doing take after take, some of which was pretty awful. Strikers battled strikebreakers and police by a fence at the edge of a pure green feathery field of artichokes while storm clouds moved in and out of the frame.

Troopers evicted the members of a commune in Texas, beating the boys with slapjacks, grabbing handcuffed girls by the pussy, smacking little kids around, and killing the stock, all of which Prairie, breathing deliberately, made herself watch. Suns came up over farm fields and bright-shirted pickers with the still outlines of buses and portable toilets on trailers in the distance, shone pitilessly down on mass incinerations of American-grown pot, the flames weak orange distortions of the daylight, and set over college and high school campuses turned into military motor pools, throwing oily shadows. There was little mercy in these images, except by accident — backlit sweat on a Guardsman's arm as he swung a rifle toward a demonstrator, a close-up of a farm employer's face that said everything its subject was trying not to, those occasional meadows and sunsets — not enough to help anybody escape seeing and hearing what, the film implied, they must.

At some point Prairie understood that the person behind the camera most of the time really was her mother, and that if she kept her mind empty she could absorb, conditionally become, Frenesi, share her eyes, feel, when the frame shook with fatigue or fear or nausea, Frenesi's whole body there, as much as her mind choosing the frame, her will to go out there, load the roll, get the shot. Prairie floated, ghostly light of head, as if Frenesi were dead but in a special way, a minimum-security arrangement, where limited visits, mediated by projector and screen, were possible. As if somehow, next reel or the one after, the girl would find a way, some way, to speak to her. . . .

And suddenly both women were going "Oh, fuck!" together and laughing, though not at anything funny. It was inside a courthouse lobby someplace and some little guy with a jocklike walk, wearing a suit, was crossing left to right. Ditzah rewound the film. "Guess who, Prairie."

"Brock Vond? Can you put it on pause, freeze it?"

"Sorry. We did transfer it all to videotape, and there are duplicates around, but the idea was to disperse the archives so they'd be safer, and I got stuck with all the film. Here, here's the little shaygetz again." Brock had convened his roving grand jury up in Oregon to look into subversion on the campus of a small community college, and 24fps had gone there to film the proceedings, or as much as they could find with Brock always changing venues and times on them at the last minute. They chased him from the courthouse, through the rain, to a motel, then to the fairground exhibition hall, the college and high school auditoriums, the drive-in-movie lot, finally back to the courthouse again, where Frenesi, by then not expecting him, just trying to shoot some old WPA murals about Justice and Progress if she could figure a way to compensate for the colors, which had darkened with the years since the New Deal, in the middle of a slow pan around the rotunda, happened to pick up in her viewfinder this compact figure in a beige double-knit, striding toward the staircase. Another camera eye on the same crew might've dismissed him as one more pompous little functionary. Zooming in a little on his face, she began to track him. She didn't know who he was. Or maybe she did.

She had used her faithful 16mm Canon Scoopic, bought new at Brooks Camera in downtown San Francisco, a gift from Sasha, with one built-in zoom lens, a control button in the end of the handgrip that you pushed with your thumb, and inscribed in the viewfinder a TV-screen shape so you could frame a shot for the evening news, though this one of Brock ended up on a bedsheet tacked to the wall of a motel room, lightproof drapes pulled against the subtropical glare, with most of the 24fps membership jammed in together to watch the Oregon rushes.

"So that's the Prosecutor, hmm?" Zipi Pisk sounding a little dreamy.

"That *was* the Prosecutor," Krishna pointed out serenely.

"Yeah you got some real pretty takes of this creep," DL semi-teased her friend. "What's goin' on?"

Brock was more photogenic than cute, with his buffed high forehead, modish octagonal eyeglass frames, Bobby Kennedy haircut, softly outdoor skin. He hadn't seen much of Frenesi's face with the Scoopic in front of it, but couldn't have missed her legs, long, bare, sleekly muscled, pale in the rainlight, in the courthouse echoes. And he could feel how she focused in on him, him alone — the lines of force. The roll ended, she withdrew her thumb, uncovered her face. "Ya got me," said Brock Vond, bringing out a Boyish Grin he'd been told was effective though not devastating. "Maybe I'll get a shot of you someday."

"Nothing the FBI won't already have . . . go check it out."

"Oh, all they care about is identifying faces. I'd want something a little more," trying not to stare too hard at those noteworthy legs, "entertaining, guess you'd say."

"Little . . . courtroom drama, maybe."

"There you go. Make you a star. We'd all have a real good time."

"Sounds like one more of those bullshit State degradation rituals, thanks anyway but I'll pass."

"Oh — you'd have no choice. You'd have to come." He was smiling.

She moved her pretty jaw a little forward. "I wouldn't come."

"Then a man in a uniform, with a big pistol, would have to make you come."

Frenesi should have just zinged him one — something — left the area and stayed out of the way for a while. That would have been correct procedure. She was wondering instead why she'd worn this little miniskirt today when it would have made more sense to wear pants.

Her silence in the dimmed motel room had deepened like a blush. "It's only a movie," she finally said. "Think the light's OK?"

" 'Sucker ain't worth no Zippo flame on a cloudy night," in the opinion of Sledge Poteet. Everybody in 24fps had their own ideas about light, and about all they shared was the obsession. Meetings convened to take care of business would turn into arguments about light that happened so often they came to seem the essence of 24fps. Against Howie's advocacy of available light because it was cheaper, Frenesi wanted actively to commit energy by pouring in as much light as they could liberate from the local power company. In the equipment van, among quartz lamps and PAR bulbs, color-temperature meters, blue filters, cable of different gauges, lamp stands, and ladders, were also grid-access devices, designed and taught her by Hub Gates, customized as occasion demanded by his daughter, "the young gaffer," as he liked to call

her, intended for draining off whenever possible the lifeblood of
the fascist monster, Central Power itself, merciless as a tornado
or a bomb yet somehow, as she had begun to discover in dreams
of that period, personally aware, possessing life and will. Often,
through some dense lightning-shot stirring of night on night, she
would be just about to see Its face when her waking mind would
kick in and send her spreading awake into what should have been
the world newly formatted, even innocent, but from which, as it
proved, the creature had not after all been banished, only become,
for a while, less visible.

"You don't think they know when we go in on those meters
and tie points and shit? Someday they'll be waitin' for us," predicted Sledge.

"Part of this business, Sledge," from DL.

"Uh-huh, but I'm the one gets y'all's ass out of town when it
happens." The other big ongoing debate around here was over the
claims of film against those of "real life." Would it be necessary
someday for one of them to die for a piece of film? One that might
never even get used? How about crippled or hurt? What was the
risk level supposed to be? DL would smile off at some angle, as
if embarrassed.

"Film equals sacrifice," declared Ditzah Pisk.

"You don't die for no motherfuckin' shadows," Sledge replied.

"Long as we have the light," Frenesi sounding so sure, "long
as we're runnin' that juice in, we're OK."

"Oh yeah? they just pull the plug on your ass."

"Shoot yer lights out, man," Howie giggled.

Frenesi shrugged. "That much less to carry." Nonchalant talk,
considering the dangers they'd already been in and out of, more
than most movie people saw in a whole career. Was she really
that superstitious or whatever it was — naive? — to think, this far
into the life she thought she'd chosen, of any protection for herself — did she really believe that as long as she had it inside her
Tubeshaped frame, soaking up liberated halogen rays, nothing out
there could harm her?

The informal slogan around 24fps was Che Guevara's phrase
"Wherever death may surprise us." It didn't have to be big and

dramatic, like warfare in the street, it could happen as easily where they chose to take their witness, back in the shadows lighting up things the networks never would — it might only take one cop, one redneck, one stupid mistake, everybody on the crew could dig it, though in the usual way it was too hard for most of them to believe in, even when they began to learn with their bodies the language of batons, high-pressure hoses, and CZ gas, and as the unit medical locker gradually amassed a painkiller collection that was the envy of bikers and record producers up and down the Coast. They were still young, exempt, and for DL, in charge of security, sometimes infuriatingly careless. Just as she was allowing herself to think they might be showing a learning curve on the subject, along came the events at College of the Surf down in Trasero County, and there they found themselves all the way up Shit's Creek, with all lines of withdrawal from the campus denied them. By the time of the last offer by bullhorn of safe passage, every road, watercourse, storm drain, and bike path was interdicted. All phones were cut off, and the news media, compliant as always, at a harmless, unbridgeable distance. On that last night, 24fps had exclusive coverage of the story, if anybody survived to bring it out.

THE shape of the brief but legendary Trasero County coast, where the waves were so high you could lie on the beach and watch the sun through them, repeated on its own scale the greater curve between San Diego and Terminal Island, including a military reservation which, like Camp Pendleton in the world at large, extended from the ocean up into a desert hinterland. At one edge of the base, pressed between the fenceline and the sea, shimmered the pale archways and columns, the madrone and wind-shaped cypresses of the clifftop campus of College of the Surf. Against the somber military blankness at its back, here was a lively beachhead of drugs, sex, and rock and roll, the strains of subversive music day and night, accompanied by tambourines and harmonicas, reaching like fog through the fence, up the dry gulches and past the sentinel antennas, the white dishes and masts, the steel equipment sheds, finding the ears of sentries attentuated but ominous, like hostile-native sounds in a movie about white men fighting savage tribes.

How it had come to this was a mystery to all levels of command, especially here, bracketed by the two ultraconservative counties of Orange and San Diego, having like a border town grown into an extreme combination of both, attracting the wealthy, who gathered around golf courses and marinas in houses painted the same color as the terrain, with vast floor areas but no more elevation than there had to be, flew in and out of private airfields, would soon be dropping in on Dick Nixon, just over the county line in San Clemente, without even phoning first, most of them solid Southern California money, oil, construction, pictures. Ostensibly College of the Surf was to have been their own private polytechnic for training the sorts of people who would work for them, offering courses in law enforcement, business administration, the brand-new field of Computer Science, admitting only students likely to be docile, enforcing a haircut and dress code that Nixon himself

' confessed to finding a little stodgy. It was the last place anybody expected to see any dissent from official reality, but suddenly here with no prelude it had begun, the same dread disease infecting campuses across the land, too many cases even in the first days for campus security to deal with.

But when traveling Movement coordinators began to show up, they could only shake their heads and blink, as if trying to surface from a dream. None of these kids had been doing any analysis. Not only was nobody thinking about the real situation, nobody was even brainlessly reacting to it. Instead they were busy surrounding with a classically retrograde cult of personality a certain mathematics professor, neither charismatic nor even personable, named Weed Atman, who had ambled into celebrity.

It was a nice day, everybody was out in Dewey Weber Plaza enjoying the sunshine, boys loosening their ties, even taking off their jackets, girls unpinning their hair and hiking their skirts up as far as their knees, a thousand students out on their lunch breaks, drinking milk, eating baloney-and-white-bread sandwiches, listening to Mike Curb Congregation records on the radio, talking about sports and hobbies and classes and how the work was going on the new Nixon Monument, a hundred-foot colossus in black and white marble at the edge of the cliff, gazing not out to sea but inland, towering above the campus architecture, and above the highest treetops, dark-and-pale, a quizzical look on its face. In the midst of a noontide scene tranquil enough to have charmed a statue, there arose, suddenly, the odor of marijuana smoke. That it was widely and immediately recognized later led historians of the incident to question the drug innocence of this student body, most of whom were already at least in violation of the California mopery statutes about Being In A Place where the sinister herb was burning. The fateful joint that day could have come, heaven knew, from any of the troop of surfer undesirables who'd lately been finding their way up the cliffside and in among the wholesome collegians, bringing with them their "stashes," consisting — up till now — mainly of stems and seeds, which because of a mysterious anomaly in surfer brain chemistry actually got them loaded but which produced in those they were trying to "turn on" only headaches, upper respiratory distress, shortness of temper, and depression, a syndrome that till now the college kids, not wishing to seem impolite, had pretended to find euphoric. But that day, at the mere distant spice-wind scent of the Joint in the Plaza, other states of mind all at once seemed possible. Like loaves and fishes, the hand-rolled cigarettes soon began to multiply, curls of smoke to become visible, all from the same bag of what drug-agency reports were to call "extremely potent" Vietnamese buds, perhaps, it was later suggested, brought in by somebody's brother in the service, since it sure wasn't surfer product.

As events were later reconstructed, when a young woman suddenly fell to her knees and began screaming at Jesus to deliver them all from the satanic substance, a disheveled young man in a beige suit, with eyeballs like a county map and a loose smile he could not, for the first time in his life, control, approached the distraught girl, attempting, in a spirit of benevolent therapy, to insert a lit reefer into her mouth, which drew the unsympathetic attention of her boyfriend. Others took sides or, bummed out, began also to scream and run around, while several went off to phone the police, so before long units from Laguna to Escondido were responding, what they lacked in coordination being more than made up for by their eagerness at a chance to handle, however briefly, some college-age flesh. It was the following confusion of long crowdwaves, carrying smaller bursts of violence that exploded like seeds in a surfer's cigarette, that Weed Atman, preoccupied with the darker implications of a paper on group theory he'd just been reading, came woolgathering and innocent into the midst of. "What's happening?" he asked.

"You tell us, you're tall enough."

"Yeah, High-Altitude, what's going on over there?"

Weed saw that he was the tallest person in his vicinity, if "vicinity" be defined as a domain bounded by a set of points partway to the next person of a height equal to or greater than his own, six three and a half, this distance varying linearly with the height — His thoughts were interrupted by a scuffle nearby. Three policemen, falling upon one unarmed student, were beating him with their riot sticks. Nobody was stopping them. The sound was clear and terrible. "What the hell," said Weed Atman, as a throb of fear went right up his asshole. It was a moment of light, in which the true nature of police was being revealed to him. "They're breaking people's heads?"

"How about over that way?"

"Line of cops — helmets, fatigues — carrying some kind of weapons. . . ." Suddenly Weed was the spotter.

"Man, let's split!"

"Somebody get us out of here!"

"Follow this big dude!"

"I'm just tall, that's all," Weed tried to point out, but it seemed he'd already been chosen, already too many were going to move exactly the way he did. And he was still reeling from his law-enforcement epiphany. Without thinking, become pure action for the first time since ascending a rock face one sunrise last year in Yosemite, he led them to safety, out the back way, past Greg Noll Lab and The Olympics Auditorium. Most of them kept on going, but a few stayed with Weed, making their way finally down to the Las Nalgas Beach apartment of Rex Snuvvle, a graduate student in the Southeast Asian Studies Department, who while being in-doctrinated into the government's version of the war in Vietnam had, despite his own best efforts, been at last as unable to avoid the truth as, once knowing it, to speak it, out of what he easily admitted was fear of reprisal. In his increasingly deeper studies he had become obsessed with the fate of the Bolshevik Leninist Group of Vietnam, a section of the Fourth International that up till 1953 had trained in France and sent to Vietnam some 500 Trotskyist cadres, none of whom, being to the left of Ho Chi Minh, were ever heard from again. What remained of the group was a handful of exiles in Paris, with whom Rex, in paranoid secretiveness, had begun to correspond, having come to believe that the BLGVN had stood for the only authentic Vietnamese revolution so far but had been sold out by all parties, including the Fourth International. What it stood for in his own mind was less simple. These men and women, few of whose names he would ever know, had become for him a romantic lost tribe with a failed cause, likely to remain unfound in earthly form but perhaps available the way Jesus was to those who "found" him — like a prophetic voice, like a rescue mission from elsewhere which had briefly entered real history, promising to change it, raising specific hopes that might then get written down, become programs, generate earthly sequences of cause and effect. If such an abstraction could have for a while found residence in this mortal world, then — of the essence to Rex — one might again. . . .

So did he envision himself counseling and educating Weed Atman, a dialogue in which together they might explore American realities in the light of this low-hanging Eastern lamp — but Weed, much to his dismay, turned out to be all but silent. At the Steering Committee meeting that night for the newly formed All Damned Heat Off Campus, or ADHOC, Weed just milled around. " 'To have said and done nothing is a great power,' " Rex quoted Talleyrand, " 'but it should not be abused.' " Weed smiled absently, absorbed by the beat of rock and roll music beamed by the megawatt in over the border from the notorious XERB. Girls everywhere, as if by magic, were become all thighs and dark eyelashes, and boys, seized as well by this geist that could've been polter along with zeit, had actually cut off pieces of hair from their heads and, too impatient to grow beards, glued it onto their faces. Innocent festivity ruled far into the night, not much by Berkeley or Columbia standards, maybe, though Rex did manage to place Weed in what looked like the emerging junta.

By all the laws of uprising, this one should have been squashed in a matter of hours by the invisible forces up on the base. Instead it flourished, as week after week amazingly went by, a small crescent-shaped region of good spirits in that darkening era, cheerful not in desperation or even defiance, but in simple relief from what had gone before, still innocent of how it could ever be stopped. Perhaps its very textbook vulnerability allowed it to be spared — why worry about anything that could so easily be brushed into the sea, like crumbs off a tabletop? At the same time, it was still too uncomfortably close to San Clemente and other sensitive locales.

Meanwhile, ominously, the education denied them now proceeded, as enough of them saw through to how deep, how empty was their ignorance. A sudden lust for information swept the campus, and soon research — somebody's, into something — was going on 24 hours a day. It came to light that College of the Surf was no institution of learning at all, but had been an elaborate land developers' deal from the beginning, only disguised as a gift to the people. Five years' depreciation and then the plan was to start putting in cliffside vacation units. So, in the name of the people, the kids decided to take it back, and knowing the state was in on the scheme at all levels, including the courts, where they'd never get a fair deal, they chose to secede from California and become a nation of their own, which following a tumultuous nightlong get-together on the subject they decided to name, after the one constant they knew they could count on never to die, The People's Republic of Rock and Roll.

The 24fps convoy rolled in the day after the official declaration. Cafés, beer taverns, and pizza parlors were ahum with intrigue. Young folks with subversive hair ran through the streets putting up posters or spray-painting on walls PR³, CUBA WEST, and WE'RE RIGHT UP THEIR ASS AND THEY DON'T EVEN KNOW IT! No hour day or night was exempt from helicopter visits, though this was still back in the infancy of overhead surveillance, with a 16mm Arri "M" on a Tyler Mini-Mount being about state of the art as far as Frenesi knew. Down at ground level, as things turned out, it was herself and the Scoopic. Not that she would have said she was working for Brock, exactly. When he took copies of the footage she shot, he paid no more than the lab costs. She told herself she was making movies for everybody, to be shown free anywhere there might be a reflective enough surface . . . it wasn't secret footage, Brock had as much right as anybody. . . . But then after a while he was not only seeing the outtakes, but also making suggestions about what to shoot to begin with, and the deeper she got into that, the deeper Brock came into her life.

Meantime, most of the members of 24fps thought she was into "a number," as they called it back then, with Weed Atman. Prairie had her suspicions too, just from the way Frenesi was filming him, initially at a night wingding that was supposed to be a general policy meeting. Led Zeppelin music blasted from the PA, bottles and joints circulated, one or two couples — it was hard to see — had found some space and started fucking. Up on the platform several people were screaming politics all at the same time, with constant input from the floor. Some wanted to declare war on the Nixon Regime, others to approach it, like any other municipality, on the topic of revenue sharing. Even through the crude old color and distorted sound, Prairie could feel the liberation in the place that night, the faith that anything was possible, that nothing could stand in the way of such joyous certainty. She'd never seen anything like it before. Then, in a shot of the whole crowd, she noticed this moving circle of focused attention as somebody made his way through, until a tall shape ascended to visibility. "Weed!" they cried, like a sports crowd in another country, the echo just sub-siding before the next "Weed!" By this stage of his career Weed looked exactly like the kind of college professor parents in those days were afraid would seduce their daughters, not to mention their sons. "Attractive in an offbeat way," was one of the com-ments in his COINTELPRO file, an already lengthy stack of doc-uments that eventually would oblige the Bureau, when they wished to move it about, to hang a WIDE LOAD sign on the back. His hair was approaching shoulder length, and tonight he wore a cowrie-shell necklace, white Nehru shirt, and bell-bottom trousers covered with four-color images of Daffy Duck. And oh how Frenesi, that throbbing eye, was lingering on him, and presently, in time to the music, zooming in and out every chance she got on Weed's crotch.

"Subtle," remarked DL.

"Nuanced," added Ditzah. "I give it a thumbs-up."

For somebody who spent as much time as he did with objects so abstract that most people went their whole lives without even hearing about them, Weed pursued a remarkably untidy personal life. Technically separated from his wife, Jinx, sharing custody of Moe and Penny, he was orbited as well by an undetermined num-ber of ex-old ladies and their relatives and kids, who showed up from time to time either in person or by way of certified mail, process servers, or else all together on one of Weed's infamous family weekend get-togethers, when everybody was supposed to wallow in retro-domestic Caring and Warmth, except of course for whoever the latest girlfriend happened to be — left to her own resources, she would usually, after a while, grow dazed with it. The kids ran thumping around, eating nonstop, the adults drank, took drugs, hugged, wept, had insights, marathoning through the night till breakfast, nothing ever resolved, false reconciliation abounding. All very jolly for Weed, naturally, being the one who got to set up and direct these extravaganzas, to preside beaming as two or more pleasant-looking women, in Weed's case often wearing provocative attire and getting physical about it, competed for his attention. Mysteriously, the various ladies kept going for this every time, and the kids loved it. If this was how adults were allowed to act, their own outlook might not be so bad.

Frenesi in fact had gone directly from a sinkful of dishes accumulated during one of these all-night love feasts right on to an early jet to Oklahoma City, where by now she was meeting Brock Vond for regular trysts in the waterbed suite of a motor inn out on South Meridian, by the airport. She hitched a ride up to LAX with Jinx and the kids, to whom she pretended she was headed for the Bay Area. "It was nice of all you guys not to gang up on me."

" 'Cause we've all been there," Jinx's smile unrelaxing.

"He doesn't strike me somehow as . . . real groovy husband material?"

"Oh — he thinks he is. Thinks being married will help anchor him to real life, so he won't go floating off into some other dimension?"

"Do you understand any of this math trip he's on?" After a pause, the two had a short laugh. "He tried once, but after a while he must've forgot I was there, just kept on writing equations and stuff."

" 'From the foregoing, it is intuitively obvious . . . ,' " Jinx doing his voice. "That's how soon I knew it was over. But as you probably found out, once you can stop him talking, he's all business. So, you know, you do kind of hang around."

"A lot of this is the politics too, Jinx, I hope you dig."

"Just don't tell me you're in love, OK?"

"Sister, I ain't even in line."

The kids were giggling in the back. "Funny, huh?"

Giggles. "We're just waitin'," said Moe.

"What for?"

"For one of you to say 'asshole,' " said Penny.

Flying to Oklahoma was like taking a shuttle to another planet. After a lunch hour of sex, they lay among plastic room-service litter in front of the Tube, which had just announced that the powerboat racing out by the dam at Lake Overholser had been suspended. Voices accompanied by weather maps kept breaking in with updates on a number of storm cells moving out in the landscape, surrounding the city. Ghostly predigital radar images appeared, of gray mother storms giving birth from their right-hand sides to little hook-shaped echoes that grew, and detached, to glide off on their own as murderous young tornadoes. Weather commentators tried to maintain the tradition of wackiness the job is known for, but could not keep out of the proceedings an element of surrender, as if before some first hard intelligence of the advent of an agent of rapture. Outside, from a remote camera, the sky was the underside of a beast, countless gray-black udder shapes crawling in in front of a squall line, behind it something distantly roaring, dangling immense stings veined with lightning, sweeping, destroying. . . . She felt electrically excited — more than his cock, just then, she needed his embrace. Fat chance. He'd been watching it all like a commercial, as if the Beast opposite the city were a coming attraction he had grown overfamiliar with.

What he seemed to want was to talk business. He had drafted, sent up, and was about to have authorized a plan to destabilize and subvert PR[3] with funding from one of the DOJ discretionary lines. "It's a laboratory setup," Brock argued, "a Marxist ministate, product of mass uprising, we don't want it there and we also don't want to invade — how then to proceed?" His idea was to make enough money available to set them all fighting over who'd get it. It would also, as Brock pitched it, have value as a scale model, to find out how much bringing down a whole country might cost.

She lay with her hair all messed up, lipstick smeared, arms and legs in a loose sprawl, nipples erect and, to the infrared-sensitive eye, glowing steadily. A peal of thunder from outside fell close enough to send a shuddering fine ache all across her skin. She wanted so to hold him. She had entered a brief time-out in the struggle, from which, if she'd chosen to, she also could have seen most, maybe all the way to the end, of what she could lose for this — OK, there he was, full-length, the whole package — for what? The fucking? Anything else?

On the screen, the weather crew had fallen queerly silent. At first Frenesi wondered if the sound had gone out, but then one of them laughed nervously and the others joined in. It would happen again before suddenly, unannounced, a preacher with a hand mike, in front of a great luminous cross, appeared on the screen in stylishly long sideburns and a leisure suit of some lurid brick-colored synthetic. "Looks like we're in the hands of Jesus again," he announced. "Someday, with the right man in the White House, there will be a *Depart*ment of Jesus, yes and a *Sec*retary of Jesus, and he'll be talking to you all, on a *nationwide hookup,* instead of this old ignoramus from the piney woods. No friends, I'm no expert, wouldn't know a suction vortex if it walked up and said bless you brother — ah but I do know how the men of science measure tornadoes, and that's on what they call the Fujita Intensity Scale. But folks, maybe today that name should be Fu-*Jesus*. . . ."

"Mind if I, uh —" Frenesi reaching and turning off the set.

"Your mathematician doesn't go in for that sort of thing?"

Frenesi put her ears back, and white triangles appeared at the corners of her eyeballs.

"Or does he? Maybe he's one of these servants of the Lord, with a holy mission to defy Caesar?"

"Think I covered that on one of those forms of yours."

"I read it," almost breathless, looking like a boy, "I watched all the film footage, too, but I never saw anything about his spirit. That's what I'd like to hear about sometime. I want his spirit, hm? I'm happy to leave his body to you."

"Oh, I don't know, Brock, he might be just your type."

He took off his glasses, smiled at her in a way she'd learned to be wary of. "Actually he is, and I'm sorry you had to find out this way. Remember last time, when I told you not to bathe, hm?

because I knew you'd be seeing him that night, knew he'd go down on you — didn't he? ate your pussy, hm? of course I know, because he told me. You were coming in his face and he was tasting me all the time."

Brock's homophobic sense of humor? She tried to remember if that was how it had happened, and couldn't . . . and what did he mean about "wanting" Weed's spirit?

"You're the medium Weed and I use to communicate, that's all, this set of holes, pleasantly framed, this little femme scampering back and forth with scented messages tucked in her little secret places."

She was too young then to understand what he thought he was offering her, a secret about power in the world. That's what he thought it was. Brock was young then too. She only took it as some parable about his feelings for her, one she didn't exactly understand but covered for with the wide invincible gaze practiced by many sixties children, meaning nearly anything at all, useful in a lot of situations, including ignorance.

Somebody had left a promotional magnum of Grand Cru de Muskogee Demi-Sec, made from a Concord grape variety imported from Arkansas, in a wastebasket full of ice. It had a nearly opaque, deeply purple color bordering on the ultraviolet and a body comparable to that of maple syrup, through which its bubbles, though multitudinous, were obliged to rise slowly and, alas, invisibly. But Brock, an aspiring gentleman, did the gallant thing and managed to choke down his share, even managing to toast Weed once or twice. She gave him the little-girl photofloods, 4800° of daylight blue, and whispered, "It's why you kill each other, isn't it?"

"Who?"

"Men. Because you can't love each other."

He shook his head slowly. "Missed the point again — you never get beyond that hippie shit, do you."

"Point I didn't miss," she finished the thought, "is you prefer to do it by forcing things into each other's bodies."

"I hope that's a mischievous look."

"Don't get many of them, do you?"

"It's Atman who's been putting you on this 'trip,' you're getting too old to be such a smartass on your own."

She smiled and raised her glass. "You got it, just a 'medium,' goes in these four holes, comes out this one. Hey, and let's not forget nostrils, huh?"

They lounged around the room, on and off the waterbed, becoming more grapey than drunk, and Brock just wouldn't give the Weed situation a rest. Outside, beyond the dense rubberized drapes, now a solid black rectangle rim-lit with a least glimmer of failed daylight, was the storm, the Event. Just when she thought they were nestled safe in the center of America — here were sounds in the air they couldn't have imagined, roars too deep for any Air Force jets from Tinker, some nonliquid clattering on the roof that could only be insects of a plague. Frenesi went to the window and pulled enough of one drape aside to have a look. At the sight of the black rolling clouds she caught her breath — she'd never seen a sky like this on Earth, not even with the help of LSD. With no warning, everything would pulse hugely with light, and the undersides and edges of the great clouds be hit with electric blue and now and then, all creviced in black, a terrible final red. In the last light out the window, near enough to see, a funnel cloud, its tip not yet touching the earth, swung slowly, deliberating, as if selecting a target below. She pulled the drapes open to allow a sword-shape of outside patio light, which had just come on, to fall across the bed, where Brock lay with his forearm over his eyes and his socks on. "You can figure it out, can't you?" he cried over the booming death-drone outside, "you have a smart-assed angle on everything else, why can't you see this one? Your boyfriend is in the way. In our way." Just quiet enough to register as deferent, sincere.

"Real easy, then — just take me off the case. Chances are he won't even notice."

"Anyone can deliver me his body," called Brock Vond across the room, "if that was all I wanted, you'd've been off it long ago."

There, as her mother used to sing, he said it again.

"Remember handing me all that shit in your office till I agreed to send in a written report? You said then there wouldn't be anything more."

"But you're right there literally in bed with him — perfect placement. He's the key to it all, the key log, pull him and you break up the structure," and the logs would disengage, singly and in groups, and continue on their way down the river to the sawmill, to get sawed into lumber, to be built into more America — Weed was the only one innocent enough, without hidden plans, with no ambitions beyond surmounting what the day brought each time around, he just went lurching on happily into his new identity as a man of action, embracing it as only an abstract thinker would, with the heedless enthusiasm of some junior doper discovering a new psychedelic, enjoying the unqualified trust of all who came inside his radius. With him gone and the others scrambling after the greenbacks in Brock's safe, PR^3 would fall apart.

"Never thought you'd try to hustle me like this, Brock."

"I didn't think you'd ever get into it with Atman, either," his voice just for the moment stressless, unprotected. "Plans change, I guess. . . ."

She understood as clearly as she could allow herself to what Brock wanted her to do, understood at last, dismally, that she might even do it — not for him, unhappy fucker, but because she had lost just too much control, time was rushing all around her, these were rapids, and as far ahead as she could see it looked like Brock's stretch of the river, another stage, like sex, children, surgery, further into adulthood perilous and real, into the secret that life is soldiering, that soldiering includes death, that those soldiered for, not yet and often never in on the secret, are always, at every age, children. She came and lay next to him, but not touching. The storm held the city down like prey, trying repeatedly to sting it into paralysis. She lay on one elbow, unable to stop gazing at Brock, pretending to herself that it made some difference to him whether or not she and Weed were fucking . . . just as she had to pretend that Brock was not "really" what he looked like to everybody else — namely, the worst kind of self-obsessed collegiate dickhead, projected on into adult format — but that someplace, lost, stupefied, needing her intercession, was the "real" Brock, the endearing adolescent who would allow her to lead him stumbling out into light she imagined as sun plus sky, with an 85 filter in, returning him to the man he should have grown into . . . it could've been about the only way she knew to use the word *love* anymore, its trivializing in those days already well begun, its magic fading, the subject of all that rock and roll, the simple resource we once thought would save us. Yet if there was anything left to believe, she must have in the power even of that weightless, daylit commodity of the sixties to redeem even Brock, amiably, stupidly brutal, fascist Brock.

At some point he must have gone drifting off to sleep, and she hadn't noticed. She watched over him, hers for a while, allowing herself to shudder with, even surrender to, her need for his bodily presence, his beauty, the fear at the base of her spine, the prurient ache in her hands . . . at last, so swept and helpless, she leaned in to whisper to him her heart's overflow, and saw in the half-light that what she'd thought were closed eyelids had been open all the time. He'd been watching her. She let out a short jolted scream. Brock started laughing.

AS a resident of the everyday world, Weed Atman may have had his points, but as a Thanatoid he rated consistently low on most scales, including those that measured dedication and community spirit. Even his first of many interviews with Takeshi and DL, continuing off and on over the years, had been enough to establish a detachment of attitude, a set of barriers neither found they could cross. We are assured by the *Bardo Thödol,* or *Tibetan Book of the Dead,* that the soul newly in transition often doesn't like to admit — indeed will deny quite vehemently — that it's really dead, having slipped so effortlessly into the new dispensation that it finds no difference between the weirdness of life and the weirdness of death, an enhancing factor in Takeshi's opinion being television, which with its history of picking away at the topic with doctor shows, war shows, cop shows, murder shows, had trivialized the Big D itself. If mediated lives, he figured, why not mediated deaths?

At first Weed went around feeling like a political defector. People pretending to be amateur students of the sixties kept showing up to fish for information and annoy him with entry-level chitchat. He was often obliged to be at functions not to his taste, wearing tuxedos it was impossible for the average Thanatoid to rent anyhow, owing to the usual complexities in the credit situation. Weed soon found he'd been 86'd from every tux outlet in Hollywood and on south, so he headed the other way, up over the passes and out the long desert arterials, out past the seed and feed houses and country music bars and Mexican joints with Happy Hours featuring 99¢ margaritas out of a hose, under the smog, the dribbling rain, the toxic lens of sky, to where folks, he hoped, were more trusting if less picky about what they wore, and where in fact formal dress, by some subterranean fashion law, turned out to be much less conventional. Soon he began showing up at Thanatoid service-organization affairs in ensembles of vivid chartreuse, teal, or fuchsia, the ties and cummerbunds hand-painted with matching motifs like tropical fruit, naked women, or bass lures. For tonight's tenth annual get-together, Thanatoid Roast '84, Weed sported a stretch tux in an oversize aqua and gold houndstooth check, with lime-green athletic shoes. Each year the community chose to honor a Thanatoid old-timer whose karma had kept up a suitably steady rhythm of crime and countercrime over the generations, with facts only grown more complicated, many original wrongs forgotten or defectively remembered, no resolution of even a trivial problem anywhere in sight. Thanatoids didn't exactly "enjoy" these long, resentful tales of injustice modulating, like a ballpark organ riff, to further injustice — but they honored them. Figures like tonight's Roastee were their Emmy winners, their Hall-of-Famers and role models — their own.

What an evening. They told obscure but rib-tickling Thanatoid jokes. They twitted one another for taking inordinate lengths of Earth time to clean up relatively penny-ante karmic business. Thanatoid wives bravely did their part to complicate further already tangled marriage histories by flirting with waiters, buspersons, and even other Thanatoids. Everyone drank and smoked furiously, and the menu featured the usual low-end fare, heavy on sugar, starch, salt, ambiguous about where the meat had come from, including which animal, accompanied by bushels of french fries and barrels of shakes. Dessert was a horrible pale chunky pudding. There was sparkling wine, to be sure, but all clues to its origin had been blacked out with felt-tip marker at some unknown stage in its perhaps not even entirely legal journey. As more of this was drunk, Thanatoids grew less shy about lurching up to the mike and reciting insult testimonials to the Roastee, or making with the quips.

"What do you call a Thanatoid with 'Sir' in front of his name? Knight of the Living Dead! How many Thanatoids's it take to screw in a light bulb? None — it gets too hot in there! What does a Thanatoid do on Halloween? Puts a fruit bowl on his head, two straws up his nose, and goes as a Zombie!"

The 1984 Thanatoid Roast was being held up north, at an old Thanatoid hangout, the Blackstream Hotel, which dated from the times of the early timber barons, hidden far from highways, up among long redwood mountainslopes where shadows came early and brought easy suspicion of another order of things . . . believed, through some unseen but potent geometry, to warp like radio signals at sundown the two worlds, to draw them closer, nearly together, out of register only by the thinnest of shadows. In the century since the place was built, tales of twilight happenings had accumulated, rooms, corridors, and wings taken on reputations for sightings, exorcisms, returns. Pilgrims enjoying a broad range of legitimacy had been around, so had Leonard Nimoy's "In Search Of" people and Jack Palance's "Believe It or Not," and deals, as you could always count on hearing, were in the works.

"And someday," the joker at the mike was saying, "maybe they'll even put Thanatoid Roasts on television, as a yearly comedy special, yeah, big names, network coverage — 'course *we* won't live to see it. . . ." The drummer gave him a couple of bass thumps and some slow mashed sizzling from the high-hat. Providing the music tonight was a local pickup group, including, on bass, Van Meter, who'd heard about it down at the Lost Nugget, would have tried to talk his running mate Zoyd into coming along and playing keyboard, except that nobody had seen Zoyd around for most of the week, and Van Meter didn't know if he should be getting worried yet or not. Zoyd had been staying with planters he knew up by Holytail, beyond the coastal ranges and the yearlong fogs, in a valley where growing conditions were ideal — about the last refuge for pot growers in North California. Access, at least by road, wasn't easy — because of the Great Slide of '64, you had to double back and forth along both sides of the river and take ferries, which weren't always running, and bridges said to be haunted. Zoyd had found a community living on borrowed time, as everyone watched the scope of the CAMP crop-destruction effort growing without limit, season after season — as more state and federal agencies came on board, as the grand jury in Eureka subpoenaed more and more citizens, as friendly deputies and secure towns one by one were neutralized, taken back under government control — all wondering when it would be the turn of Holytail.

The Vineland County sheriff, Willis Chunko, a squinty-eyed, irascible old media hand who showed up every autumn, as sure a precursor of the season as the Jerry Lewis telethon, posing on the evening news next to towering stacks of baled-up marijuana plants or advancing on some field shooting a flamethrower from the hip, had featured Holytail on his shit list for years, but the area was extraordinarily tough for him to penetrate. "It's Sherwood Forest up there," he would complain to the cameras, "they hide up in the trees, you never see 'em." No matter how Willis chose to arrive, Holytailers always had plenty of advance warning. The network of observers extended down to Vineland, with some lurking right outside the Sheriff's Department itself with rolls of quarters, ready to call in, others hooked up by CB radio in roving patrols on all surface routes, or scanning the sky from ridges and mountaintops with binoculars and converted fishing-boat radars.

As crops in the sun grew fatter, flowered, more densely aromatic, as resinous breezes swept out of the gulches to scent the town day and night, the sky over Vineland County, which had allowed the bringing of life, now began to reveal a potential for destroying it. Pale blue unmarked little planes appeared, on days of VFR unlimited nearly invisible against the sky, flown by a private vigilante squadron of student antidrug activists, retired military pilots, government advisers in civvies, off-duty deputies and troopers, all working under contract to CAMP and being led by the notorious Karl Bopp, former Nazi *Luftwaffe* officer and subsequently useful American citizen. During these weeks of surveillance, helicopter and plane crews were beginning to assemble each morning in a plasterboard ready room out in the flats below Vineland, near the airport, waiting for Kommandant Bopp to appear in the full regalia of his old profession and announce Der Tag.

Up in Holytail, the growers hung around at Piggy's Tavern and Restaurant, discussing, in an atmosphere of mounting anxiety, the general dilemma of when to harvest. The longer you waited, the better the crop, but the better, too, your chances of getting hit by the CAMP invaders. Storm and frost probabilities, and personal paranoia thresholds, also figured in. Sooner or later Holytail was due for the full treatment, from which it would emerge, like most of the old Emerald Triangle, pacified territory — reclaimed by the enemy for a timeless, defectively imagined future of zero-tolerance drug-free Americans all pulling their weight and all locked in to the official economy, inoffensive music, endless family specials on the Tube, church all week long, and, on special days, for extra-good behavior, maybe a cookie.

With surveillance farther up the watershed and over the ridge-lines quickening, so had the civic atmosphere down in Vineland taken on an edge, traffic downtown and in the lots at the malls grown snappish and loud with car horns and deliberate backfires, boat owners anxiously in and out of parts places several times a day, reports of naval movement, at least one aircraft carrier sighted on station just off Patrick's Point, and AWACS planes in the air round the clock now, not to mention the Continental charm of Kommandant Bopp all over the local news, as he, often in Nazi drag, declared his "volunteer" sky force at maximum readiness. Something waited, over a time horizon that not even future par-ticipants could describe. Once-carefree dopers got up in the mid-dle of the night, hearts racing, and flushed their stashes down the toilet. Couples married for years forgot each other's names. Mental-health clinics all over the county reported waiting lists. Seasonal speculation arose as to who might be secretly on the CAMP payroll this year, as if the monster program were by now one more affliction, like bad weather or a plant disease. The cook-ing in the cafés got worse, and police started flagging down every-body on the highways whose looks they didn't like, which resulted in massive traffic snarls felt as far away as 101 and I-5. A par-rot smuggler in an all-chrome Kenworth/Fruehauf combination known as the Stealth Rig, nearly invisible on radar, swooping by law enforcement with the touch-me-not authority of a UFO, showed up late one Saturday afternoon, parked beside 101 just across the bridge in unincorporated county, and sold out his entire load before the sheriff even heard about it, as if the town, already jittery, just went parrot-crazy the minute they saw these birds, kept drunk and quiet on tequila for days, ranked out in front of the great ghostly eighteen-wheeler, bundles of primary color with hangovers, their reflections stretching and blooming along the side of the trailer. Soon there was scarcely a house in Vineland that didn't have one of these birds, who all spoke English with the same peculiar accent, one nobody could identify, as if a single unknown bird wrangler somewhere had processed them through in batches — "All right, you parrots, listen up!" Instead of the traditional repertoire of short, often unrelated phrases, the parrots could tell full-length stories — of humorless jaguars and mischief-seeking monkeys, mating competitions and displays, the coming of humans and the disappearance of the trees — so becoming necessary members of households, telling bedtime stories to years of children, sending them off to alternate worlds in a relaxed and upbeat set of mind, though after a while the kids were dreaming landscapes that might have astonished even the parrots. In Van Meter's tiny house behind the Cucumber Lounge, the kids, perhaps under the influence of the house parrot, Luis, figured out a way to meet, lucidly dreaming, in the same part of the great southern forest. Or so they told Van Meter. They tried to teach him how to do it, but he never got much closer than the edge of the jungle — if that's what it was. How cynical would a man have to be not to trust these glowing souls, just in from flying all night at canopy level, shiny-eyed, open, happy to share it with him? Van Meter had been searching all his life for transcendent chances exactly like this one the kids took so for granted, but whenever he got close it was like, can't shit, can't get a hardon, the more he worried the less likely it was to happen. . . . It drove him crazy, though most of the time he could keep from taking it out on others, what muttering he did do just lost as usual in the ambient uproar of the day, often oppressive enough to force him out of the cabin on gigs like this, though it meant a long, intimidating drive upward through crowds of tall trees, perilous switchbacks, one-lane stretches hugging the mountainsides, pavement not always there — then a sunset so early he thought at first something must have happened, an eclipse, or worse. He nearly lost his way in the dark but was guided by its own pale violet glow at last to the Blackstream Hotel, which loomed up in an array of dim round lights that seemed to cover much of the sky. He'd heard about the place but had no idea it was this big.

Tonight all he'd brought was an ancient Fender Precision bass that he'd taken the frets off of himself back around '76, when he heard about Jaco Pastorius doing the same to a Jazz Bass. Van Meter had seen in the act further dimensions, the abolition of given scales, the restoration of a premodal innocence in which all the notes of the universe would be available to him. He filled in the grooves with boat epoxy and drew lines where the frets had been, just to help him through the transition. Now, years later, with all but murky outlines of that epiphany long faded, he figured fretless at least was a good choice for this crowd, who, though they didn't respond to much, seemed noticeably to perk up whenever Van Meter took long wavering woo-woo-woo-type glides on his instrument, something they could relate to, he imagined, though admittedly he didn't know that much about Thanatoids.

> They're ev'ry . . .
> Place that ya go,
> Down ev'ry
> Row that ya hoe,
> Somehow, ya
> Just ne-ver know, say it ain't so,
> Thanatoid World!
>
> They're ringin'
> Sales at the store,
> They're standin'
> Guard at the door,
> They're turnin'
> Tricks on the floor, that 'n' much more,
> Thanatoid World!
>
> They've got that,
> Tha-natoid stare,
> They've got that,
> Tha-natoid hair,
> They've, got, that, — *there's*
> A Tha-natoid, *there's*
> A Tha-natoid (where?)
> Right There!
>
> So if you're
> Desp'rate some night,

You never
Know but you might,
Just step on
In-to the light, clear out of sight,
Thanatoid World!

A kind of promotional jingle more than a song, and about as up-tempo as anything would get around here tonight, the 'Toids preferring minor chords and a dragged recessional pulse. Gestures in the direction of rock and roll were discouraged, though blues licks were allowed to pass. The band was a twist-era puttogether, two saxes, two guitars, piano, and rhythm. From somewhere mildew-prone and unvisited, the hotel staff had brought piles of old-time Combo-Ork arrangements of pop standards, including Thanatoid favorites like "Who's Sorry Now?," "I Gotta Right to Sing the Blues," "Don't Get Around Much Anymore," and the perennially requested "As Time Goes By." Van Meter had to keep forcing himself to slow down, not to mention the drummer, whose brightness of eye, wetness of lip, and frequent visits to the men's lounge suggested a personality at best impatient, and who now and then liked to explode into these ear-assaulting self-expressive solos, hollering "All right!" and "Party Time!" Despite his enthusiasm, the beat, as the evening went on, only grew slower. It was to be an all-night rallentando. Van Meter had played reds parties, where a number of bikers and biker women got in a room, took barbiturates, and nodded out, this being, basically, the party, which compared to this gig were evenings filled with vivacity and mirth. After a while just getting through 32 bars took a whole set. The dancing, rudimentary to begin with, tended toward gig's-end stillness, as conversation grew less and less meaningful to what few outsiders had blundered in, shunpike tourists who had only a dim idea tonight of just how far from the freeways they'd come.
"Chickeeta, what's with all these people?"
"See how slow they're moving, Dr. Elasmo!"
"It's Larry, remember?"
"Ups, rilly. . . ."
"Uh-oh, here comes one of them, now remember, it's not the office, OK?"

"Evening . . . folks . . . you . . . seem . . . to . . . be . . . from . . . out . . . of . . . town. . . ." It took some time to get said, and both Dr. Larry Elasmo, D.D.S., and his receptionist Chickeeta began to break in more than once, mistaking for pauses the silences between his words. Because Thanatoids relate in a different way to time, there was no compression toward the ends of sentences, so that they always ended by surprise. "Wait, I think I know you now," continued the slow-talking Thanatoid, who turned out to be Weed Atman in his eye-catching Spandex tuxedo, "we had appointments . . . kept rescheduling . . . years ago? Down south?"

"Maybe you saw one of Doctor's commercials?" Chickeeta suggested, while the embarrassed Dr. Elasmo went "Larry! Larry!" out of the side of his mouth. These days he ran a chain of discount dental franchises called Doc Holliday's, famous for its $49.95 OK Corral Family Special, advertising in all major market areas in the West — but back when he'd crossed Weed's path he'd been a low-rent credit dentist known around San Diego for his stridently hypnotic, often incoherent radio and TV commercials. Somehow, in Weed's deathstunned memory, Dr. Elasmo's video image had swept, had pixeldanced in, to cover, mercifully, for something else, an important part of what had happened to him in those penultimate days at College of the Surf, but faces, things done to him that he could not . . . quite. . . .

It was right at the steepest part of his curve of descent into irresponsibility, or, as he defined it at the time, love, with Frenesi Gates, and he was spending a lot of hours out on the freeway, going through the empty exercise of trying to fool Jinx, who was having a relapse into anger and hiring private detectives to keep an eye on everybody. One day, as Weed was heading for a strip of motels in Anaheim, doing about seventy, palms aching and dry, pulse knocking in his throat, awash in thoughts of incredibly seeing Frenesi again, whom should he notice, first in his mirror, then slowly drawing abreast in the lane to his left, but the well-known video toothyanker himself, in a long chocolate Fleetwood, clearly on his own horny way to an illicit rendezvous — a deep glittering sideswung gaze, flipping away to check the road, then back to stare at Weed again, the two of them blasting along at dangerous speed, up and down hills, around curves, weaving among flatbeds and motorheads, Weed at first pretending not to see, then, tentatively, nodding back. But there was only that stare, chilling in its certainty that *it knew who Weed was*. Soon, in beach-town bars and country saloons, in rock and roll hideaways up canyons full of snakes and LSD laboratories, anyplace inside a hundred-mile radius that Weed and Frenesi tried to slip away for a quiet minute, there at some nearby table would be the silent, staring Dr. Larry Elasmo, or a person wearing, like a coverall and veil, his ubiquitous screen image, grainy, flickering at the edges . . . usually in the company of a tanned and lovely young blonde who might or might not have been the same one as last time.

In some way, as it developed, the lascivious tooth physician enjoyed a franchise to meddle in the lives and with the precious time of people he didn't even know — one that Weed, beached these years beside the Sea of Death, still didn't understand. Somehow the Doc had been authorized in those days to send people, Weed included, a form that required them to come to his offices at a certain time. No-show penalties were never exactly spelled out, only hinted at. The place was all the way downtown, in a setting of old brick hotels, sailors' bars, aging palm trees towering above the streetlights — a stark sprawling maze of cheap partitions inside a gutted former public, perhaps federal, building, now stained and ruinous, its classical columns airbrushed black with fine grime on their streetward halves, except for the fluting, letters across the frieze overhead long chiseled away, no longer readable, ascended toward by a broad littered flight of steps that seethed with visitors on appointments, small business deals up and down at all levels and into the great echoing cement lobby, lined with geometric statues who loomed overhead, staring down like the saints of whatever faith this building had served.

Weed could have ignored the form in the mail, but he was haunted by that first gleaming whammy on the freeway, so he showed up on time and wearing a jacket and tie, but had to wait, as it turned out all day, in the bullpen just off the lobby, on a flimsy folding chair, nothing to read but propaganda leaflets and withered newsmagazines from months gone by, afraid even to go out and look for lunch. This was to happen again and again. Dr. Elasmo always ran late, sometimes days late, but each time he insisted Weed fill out a postponement form, including "Reason (explain fully)," as if it were Weed's fault. Weed felt more and more guilty as he became an old bullpen regular, one of a throng of what should plainly have been dental cases but always proved to be something else, none of them smiling, who passed nervously both ways through the gates in the railing that stood like a bar in a courtroom, an altar rail in a church, between the public side and the office penetralia full of their mysteries. Sometimes Dr. Elasmo would be rolling a table carrying a tray of shining — why couldn't Weed ever make them out clearly, was it the low-wattage light in the place? — dental equipment of some kind? "Welcome to Dr. Larry's World of Discomfort," he would whisper, going through the paperwork. There was a recurring message, one too deep for Weed, always about paper. "I can't accept this form. This will all have to be renegotiated. Rewritten. You'll figure it out." It was some long, ongoing transaction, carried on, like dentistry, in a currency of pain inflicted, pain withheld, pain drugged away, pain become amnesia, how much and how often . . . sometimes Ilse, the hygienist, stood waiting by a door into a corridor, leading, he knew, to a bright high room with a tiny window at the top, impossibly far away, some blade of sky . . . she was holding something . . . something white and . . . he couldn't remember. . . .

And Weed at the close of the workday would go back down the chipped and crumbling steps, back across a borderline, invisible but felt at its crossing, between worlds. It was the only way to say it. Inside, at that well-known address he could no longer remember, was an entirely different order of things. He was being exposed to it gradually during these repeated, required visits. Each time there he returned to PR[3] less sure about anything — deeply confused about Frenesi, whom he loved but didn't completely trust, because of gaps in her story, absences neither she nor anyone else in 24fps would explain. He was also being driven ever crazier by the swarm of disciples who clustered around him more thickly and frantically as days gathered and a feeling of crisis began to grow, all making the basic revolutionary mistake, boobish, cheerful, more devoted the louder he screamed at and insulted them. "Yes my guru! Anything — chicks, dope, jump off the cliff, name it!" Tempting, especially that part about the cliff — but even more seductive were the seekers of free advice. "Weed, how about picking up the gun? We know it's supposed to be wrong, but we don't know why."

Once he would have proclaimed, "Because in this country nobody in power gives a shit about any human life but their own. This forces us to be humane — to attack what matters more than life to the regime and those it serves, their money and their property." But these days he was saying, "It's wrong because if you pick up a rifle, the Man picks up a machine gun, by the time you find some machine gun he's all set up to shoot rockets, begin to see a pattern?" Between these two replies, something had happened to him. He was still preaching humane revolution, but seemed darkly exhausted, unhopeful, snapping at everybody, then apologizing. If anybody caught this change, it was much too late to make a difference. They still came trooping up the alley to Rex's place at Las Nalgas, like ducklings looking for a mother. Surf, somewhere hidden in the fog, didn't crash so much as collapse on itself, wetly over and over. Though he lived there, Rex didn't show up much at these gatherings anymore, having finalized his own plans to fly off to Paris and join whatever was left of the Vietnamese section of the Fourth International. "It'll never work," Weed told him, "you're an Anglo, who'll trust you?"

"Anybody who can rise above racist bullshit like that, I guess." Once deferent, these days Rex was getting bitter about his protégé, who hadn't turned out at all the way he'd hoped. Though Rex wouldn't have called it purity, he'd still expected from Weed more thought, less wallowing in the everyday. Rex himself saw the Revolution as a kind of progressive abstinence, in which you began by giving up acid and pot, then tobacco, alcohol, sweets — you kept cutting down on sleep, doing with less, you broke up with lovers, avoided sex, after a while even gave up masturbating — as the enemy's attention grew more concentrated, you gave up your privacy, freedom of movement, access to money, with the looming promise always of jail and the final forms of abstinence from any life at all free of pain.

"Kind of pessimistic?" Weed suggested.

"I don't see you giving up anything," Rex answered, and this, to both of them, seemed a clear sign that their fates were diverging. Rex had once owned this Porsche 911, as red as a cherry in a cocktail, his favorite toy creature, his best disguise, his personal confidant, and more, in fact all that a car could be for a man, and it's fair to say Rex had made a tidy emotional as well as cash investment — indeed, he would not have flinched from the word "relationship." He called it Bruno. He knew the location of every all-night car wash in the four counties, he'd fallen asleep on his back beneath its ventral coolness, with a plastic tool case for a pillow, and slept right through the night, and he had even, more than once, in scented petroleum dimness, had his throbbing manhood down inside one flared chrome carburetor barrel as the engine idled and with sensitive care he adjusted the pulsing vacuum to meet his own quickening rhythm, as man and machine together rose to peaks of hitherto unimaginable ecstasy. . . .

Long might the automotive idyll have gone on had the PR³ Exterior Bureau, in its search for allies in the world at large, not initiated talks with the Black Afro-American Division, who all wore shiny black Vietnam boots, black-on-black camo fatigues, and velvet-black berets with off-black wide-point stars on them ChiCom-style just to lounge around in, who showed up by invitation at the clifftop republic and got into an all-day argument with its indigenous, whom they kept referring to as children of the surfing class. They may have been the first black people ever to set foot in Trasero County, certainly the first that many of the PR³ inhabitants had ever seen, so that a good deal of rudimentary history had to be gone over before the discussion even caught up with the present day. As this ground on, Rex grew impatient — he wanted to talk Revolution. But the brothers from BAAD seemed content just to play Trash The Xanthocroid with what, given this crowd, were some pretty easy shots.

"But we're fighting the common enemy," Rex protested. "They'd just as soon kill us as you."

The BAAD contingent liked that one, and laughed merrily. "The Man's gun don't have no blond option on it, just automatic, semi-automatic, and black," replied BAAD chief of staff Elliot X.

"No! When the barricades are in the streets, we'll be on the same side of them as you!"

"Except that we don't have the fuckin' choice, we got to be there."

"That's it, that's just it! We're choosing to stand *with* you!"

"Uh, huh."

"What'll I have to do, to convince you guys," Rex with tears on his face, "that I would really go to the wall, that, shit, I would die for your freedom!"

There was a lull in the volume. Elliot X said, "What kind of car you drive?"

"Porsche" — he'd almost said "Bruno" — "nine-eleven, why?"

"Give it to us."

"You say, uh. . . ."

"Yeah, come on, revolutionary brother!"

"See you put that *Parsh* up where your mouth's at."

It is difficult in this era of greed and its ennoblement to recall the naturalness and grace with which Rex, way back then, smiling, simply produced from the depths of his fringe bag the pink slip and keys to the 911 and handed them on up to the podium, where Elliot X, mike in hand, a class act, went to one knee, like a performer to a fan, to receive them. The citizens of PR³ cheered and sang and voted magnanimously to make the Porsche a gift of the community, while the brothers began to negotiate internally about which of them was going to drive it away. Around sundown two delegations, black and white, proceeded to the parking lot for the formal handover. Rex, already well into second thoughts, holding back sobs, silently bade farewell to his old companion, to the desert washes and creek beds and mountain roads, the shopping plazas and green suburban streets they'd seen together. It stood in the last Pacific light, headlamps gazing at Rex reproachfully, no longer even Bruno, since it had been redesignated UHURU, for Ultra High-speed Urban Reconnaissance Unit.

"It's OK," Frenesi offered, "you did the right thing."

"I feel like shit." And what business was it of hers? He had no more illusions about infiltrators than he did about sunshine revolutionaries — or, for that matter, the fate of PR^3. But seeing how it was with Weed and Frenesi, he knew there'd be no point in issuing warnings. Once he said, "You're up against the True Faith here, some heavy dudes, talking crusades, retribution, closed ideological minds passing on the Christian Capitalist Faith intact, mentor to protégé, generation to generation, living inside their power, convinced they're immune to all the history the rest of us have to suffer. They are bad, bad's they come, but that still doesn't make us good, not 100%, Weed."

"What are you talking about?" Weed standing all the way up.

Rex was heading for the land of the May Events, and saw no reason not to say, "Weed — bail out."

"Yeah, then what?"

"Math. Discover a theorem."

Weed frowned. "Um — I don't think that's what you do with theorems."

"I thought they sat around, like planets, and . . . well, every now and then somebody just, you know . . . discovered one."

"I don't think so." They remained then, looking at each other directly, for longer than they ever would again. Neither one could know how few and fortunate would be any who'd be able to meet in years later than these and smile, and relax beneath some single low oak out on an impossible hillside, with sunlight, and the voices of children, "And we actually thought we were having it out over these points of doctrine," as some fine-looking young teener appears now from nowhere with a picnic spread, as they all sit and eat cracked crab and sourdough bread and drink some chilly gold-green California Chenin Blanc, and laugh, and pour more wine, "really obscure arguments, typewriters rattling through the windows all over campus, all night long, phone lines humming, amazing amounts of energetic youthful running around, and all for what?"

The pleasant package with the eats looks over. "I was beginning to wonder."

"Well, we were being set up all the time, it turned out. The FBI was in there like some little guy in a bar going let's-you-and-him-fight. Anonymous letters and phone calls, night riders, flat tires, job and landlord trouble, all made to look like it was coming from ol' what's his name here and the BLGVN/US."

She is aware of her importance here, shaded, safe, saved, a person for them both to pretend to explain things to, as a way of negotiating an agreeable version of history.

"Yes, old Rex here, he nearly 'blew me away.' "

"Rex!"

"Afraid so, kid."

"Kept saying, 'You get it yet? Huh? You get it?' I said, 'Get what?' He said, 'Oh well maybe you should get it now. Huh? You think now's a good time for you to *get it?*' I could see he was carrying something in his bag — one of those rough-out shoulder bags with all the fringe that guys carried for a while. Something concentrated, heavy, but you couldn't tell for certain. Could have been a part for his car."

"Rock specimens." The two of them chuckle at the distant memory. "Just a pair of innocent hippies, one with a service .38. Hard to say which was the bigger fool."

Weed had found himself a classical pigeon, with no exit but the one Rex was standing in and no resources beyond an old Case knife someplace in a box down the back of the crawl space, as he watched the object in Rex's purse, much as another man in a different context might want to watch the one in his pants, noting subtle rearrangements of pleats and ripples each time he moved, trying to guess length, diameter, and so forth. . . .

"What are you looking at?" Rex clearly agitated and getting more so.

"Nothing."

"You were looking at my bag. You think my bag is nothing?"

"You seem upset tonight, Rex, what is it?"

They both knew that what it was was Frenesi. She was spending more and more time in and out of Rex's place and hardly any with 24fps. After a series of consultations with others in the unit, DL had suggested to Howie, who admitted he could use a break from the Pisks' Trasero-heightened surfophobia, that he find a way to keep an eye on Frenesi. He borrowed an old surfboard for a prop and soon was dropping in at Rex's at least once a day. If Frenesi noticed, she didn't react. One night, having nodded out in one of the bedrooms in front of a rerun of "The Invaders," Howie became aware of some strange vibrational episode out in the living room, along with XERB at a volume not high enough to cover voices. He came blinking into the living room and saw Rex and Frenesi sitting close together on the couch, their eyes dark and moist, faces flushed. They'd been laughing, was what had brought Howie up out of a drugged sleep. "Howdy folks."

This look on her face he'd seen before, but didn't know what it meant. "Heard the news about Weed?"

Howie went on into the kitchen, opened the refrigerator, and stood gazing inside. "Nope, what happened?"

The two started laughing again, an amateur, ungainly sound, as if the forces they were letting out were new to them and just about as much as they could handle. "Hey!" cried Rex, "where do you think he is right now?"

"Home in bed," Frenesi with a high strangled slurring.

"All right! We could go do it right now. Huh?"

"We could make a plan and follow it, no impulses."

It? Howie wondered. In the far corner of the freezer he found a chocolate-covered banana from Hermosa Beach, all crystalline with undefrosted snow, and wandered back in. "Are you guys pissed off at Weed or something?"

The pair on the sofa exchanged a look, and Frenesi said, "Think we should tell him?"

"Sure," Rex with more angry laughter. "Who's old Howie gonna tell?"

"On second thought —" Howie began.

Too late. "Weed is an FBI plant," Frenesi told him. "His job was to lead us all someday up the wrong piece of trail and guess who'd be waiting."

"Oh come on, who says?"

"He does."

"Ack." Howie got instant dry mouth, and the frozen banana turned to sawdust. The glitter-eyed absence of humor in the room drew into its vacuum and down over his cringing soul the cold certainty that they weren't fooling. "Well look folks, if Weed really told you he's FBI, then you have to bring in the membership, everybody, call a meeting, get it all out."

"Oh, fuck, Howie," she was suddenly furious, "little kid games."

"They're killing us, man," Rex earnestly face to face, "locking us in those federal slams, regular and mental, packing us away, this is who he's been working for all the time. Pretending. Reporting back on us?"

"But," Howie losing faith in his argument, "if they're sneaky enough to plant somebody, they're also sneaky enough to lie about Weed, aren't they?"

"What do you want, Howie," Frenesi prancing back and forth like a rocker with a microphone, as if redirecting energy that might get her into mischief, "he told me himself, out loud, with his mouth."

"But why tell you?"

Oh, did she shoot him a look then — about the kindest thing it had to say was "Figure it out."

Howie, who knew he might cry if this kept on, said, "All a big fuckin' game, OK — so now he blew his cover, the game's over."

"Uh-uh," Rex almost leering, "now we're in sudden-death overtime."

Frenesi came and took Howie's face in her hand, gently, but reserving more vigorous options. "You've been living on the same planet as all of us — every night they pick us up, and they beat us, and they fuck us, and sometimes we die. Don't any of you kiddies understand, we either have 100% no-foolin'-around solidarity or it just doesn't work. Weed betrayed that, and it was cowardly because it was easy, 'cause he knew we can't shut anybody out, down the end of that road is fuckin' fascism, so we take 'em all, the hypocrites and double agents and summertime outlaws and all that fringe residue nobody else'll touch. That's what PR[3] started out as — so did we for that matter, remember? The All-Nite Shelter. The lighted doorway out in the Amerikan dark where nobody gets refused? Weed remembers."

She knew how to pick a lock as straightforward as Howie's. Embarrassed, he reached for the Tube, popped it on, fastened himself to the screen and began to feed. "What'd I tell you?" cried Rex. "Howie's cool."

"Howie, what do you think, can we put floods in here?"

"Huh? Have to unplug the stereo, is all. What you got in mind?"

"Nail him with my Scoopic, get up in his face with a radio mike, no mercy."

"It's takin' his soul, man," Howie reminded her.

"Already taken," Rex said.

Frenesi was on her own here, improvising. She knew she was messing with Rex, using him against Weed, wasn't sure if she wanted to, knew that Brock wanted her to, that had been clear since the day of the tornadoes, but how was she going to sit down, even lie down, and talk any of it over? Who with, anyway? She'd have to tell it, silently, to a DL who would miraculously forgive her, to the Sasha whom years ago it had been possible to tell anything. Make-believe interlocutors, dolls in a dollhouse. Frenesi had thought for a while that her need to talk would build out of control, till she was helpless to hold it in and she ended up as a crazy woman on a bus bench, along an endless flatland boulevard, talking out loud without rest, like an astronomer seeking life out in space, on a brave slender hope that somebody might begin to listen. But in practice she'd only kept getting up one morning after another till at some point she found she'd adapted well enough to what she was becoming. The house in Culito Canyon she was crashing at had a redwood deck with a table and chairs where she could sit out in the early mornings, drink herb tea and make believe — her dangerous vice — that she was on her own, with no legal history, no politics, only an average California chick, invisible, poised at life's city limits, for whom anything was still possible. Though she was lingering on the sunny side of 25 then, she still felt like some veteran blues singer, with a lifetime of playing toilets, owing money, and surviving violence already behind her, so that these early cool minutes on the deck, when she could find them, with an unseen delirium of birds, sun in the tops of trees, radio music, woodsmoke, and babies squealing from across the canyon, became what she held precious and often lived for. It was the only peace she was seeing in her life, with Brock sending down these increasingly nutzo directives, plus calling up in the middle of the night, to the dismay of housemates, demanding yet another Oklahoma rendezvous, and with Weed, whose fucking each time they met got wilder, less in his control, who with luck might make the Guinness Book someday but was meanwhile not picking up too many points for emotional maturity, harassing her round the clock, screaming at everybody else. As he became more hysterical, Jinx, now daily in his, not to mention Frenesi's, face, seemed to grow more grimly centered. A close reader of cues others never saw, she knew — it was in her unturning stare whenever she and Frenesi crossed paths — that Frenesi was close to her husband from motives other than sexual, and there were only a couple of things it could be. Jinx shared her anxieties with DL, who'd been driving up to a dojo in Redondo Beach with her once or twice a week. Despite the difference in their ranks, they found themselves able to work out for hours together and think only fractions of hours had gone by. Most of their communicating was by way of their bodies — when they talked it was strangely roundabout, reluctant. But they both saw, ghostly, denied, protected, another Frenesi, one they were prohibited access to. It hurt more for DL, of course — she might've expected it from a lover, but hell, they'd been *partners*.

Beginning the night she and Rex had publicly hung the snitch jacket on Weed, Frenesi understood that she had taken at least one irreversible step to the side of her life, and that now, as if on some unfamiliar drug, she was walking around next to herself, haunting herself, attending a movie of it all. If the step was irreversible, then she ought to be all right now, safe in a world-next-to-the-world that not many would know how to get to, where she could kick back and watch the unfolding drama. No problem anymore with talk of "taking out" Weed Atman, as he'd gone turning into a character in a movie, one who as a bonus happened to fuck like a porno star . . . but even sex was mediated for her now — she did not enter in.

Once, on a rare sleepover with Weed at a motel in Anaheim,

she awoke at a deep hour of the night to hear tiny voices that seemed to come from Weed's sleeping face, very high-pitched, with East Coast lowlife accents — "Hey, dat was a renege, you don't get dem points." "Ya can't meld dat one, Wilbur, ya buried it." And "Da bidduh goes double bete, let's see da cards," at least that's what it sounded like — the little voices faded now and then. It wasn't Weed himself — she could hear his breathing, regular and slow, no matter what the voices happened to be saying. "Hey, Wanda! Bring us anudduh six-pack, huh?" "Come on Wesley, feed da kitty!" What was going on? In the air-conditioned hour without a name, she leaned over his face, trying to see lips moving, ventriloquism. . . . She sniffed. Infinitesimal traces of cigar smoke and spilled beer. Abruptly the voices stopped, then broke panicked into an incoherent twittering — they'd seen her, looming in, and then she saw them, just about to shimmer out of paralysis into flight, one moment sitting by Weed's nose, curled at his nostrils, enjoying the breeze in and out, and the next all spooked and streaming down the sides of his face, nearly invisible now against the bedclothes — gaaahhh! was that one of them she *felt*? She rolled out onto the floor, cursing under her breath, put the lights on, and went and inspected every inch of the bed with a ball-peen hammer she happened to have in her purse. Innocent Weed slept on. She found nothing but a colorful smear on the pillow that resolved close up into a scatter of tiny patterned rectangles, each no more than an eighth of an inch long and flimsy — her most careful breath dispersing many of them to invisibility. In the morning they were all gone. It wasn't till years later, on a lunch hour, somewhere inside the rusticated grandiosity of an Indiana courthouse — not too far from Brock Vond's old hometown, as a matter of fact — trying to find out, as usual, about a stipend check, that she heard, in human frequencies, the same phrases she'd heard that night, and followed the voices to a judge's chambers, sunny, wood, undusted, where nobody looked up when she put her head in. The game turned out to be pinochle, and she understood then that years ago, in Anaheim, she had seen the famous worms of song, already playing a few preliminary hands on Weed Atman's snout.

*

Earlier in the day, the next-to-last day, Frenesi and Brock had met in a clifftop suite, under a vaporous and subtropical light falling through high windows, un-Californian light, belonging someplace else where the water table was above the ground and reptiles slipped into the swimming pools at night. They were in one unit of a rambling compound of decrepit, obsessionally Art Deco guest structures, curving walls corroded and flaking on their seaward faces, half-moon windows crossed by thin bars of pitted chrome, queer unusable prisms of space with no access. The prevailing color was blue, a somber ultramarine weather-chipped and scarred everywhere, as if by group assault, in pale graffiti. Just down past the trees was a sand beach, and then the sea.

He wore a pale suit, Frenesi loose bright pants and shirt and round wire-rims with ND-1 filters for lenses. This was supposed to be borrowed unofficial space. Neither had offered the other anything liquid — it was among the least of all the civilities allowed to lapse throughout Brock's profession as the Nixonian Reaction continued to penetrate and compromise further what may only in some fading memories ever have been a people's miracle, an army of loving friends, as betrayal became routine, government procedures for it so simple and greased that no one, Frenesi was finding out, no matter how honorable their lives so far, could be considered safely above it, wherever "above" was supposed to be, with money from the CIA, FBI, and others circulating everywhere, leaving the merciless spores of paranoia wherever it flowed, fungoid reminders of its passage. These people had known their children after all, perfectly.

"So it worked," she reported, "congratulations. Your key log just came loose and floated away. He's got no more credibility, only the fringe folks'll stay with him now."

Brock only looked back, smug, glittering, what she'd learned to call his upping-the-ante face. "No. Not enough." Light beat against the sea, landward and through the tall raked windows. "Tell me — hm? How was the mood on campus?"

"It's all coming apart. Suddenly everybody's got a payoff story to tell, total paranoia. Steering Committee is supposed to be meeting down at Rex's tonight. We're going to be filming it. Once we have him on film, whether he lies or whether he confesses, he's done for, it doesn't matter."

"Just from being on film." Almost affectionately.

"You'll see."

"No." And then he told her, carefully, in detail often crude enough to make her afraid, of Weed's visits to downtown San Diego for "therapy sessions," Brock called them — "Too much math, too many abstract ideas, so we gave him some reality, just enough, to counteract that, no worse than going to the dentist. Till after a while he could begin to see our side."

"Then it was true — he was working for you."

"Against you, hm? Your lies about him turned out to be truth?" Not nearly as shocked as he wanted her to be, Frenesi saw that if Weed had been fooling her, then so had Brock, by keeping it from her. The Boys. Absorbed by this line of thought, she hadn't even seen when Brock brought it out, but all at once there it was, perfectly in focus, complexly highlighted, mythical, latent and solid at the same time — a terminally opaque, property-room Smith, a Chief's Special, withheld from crucibles and collectors for missions just like this.

"Brock —"

"It's only a prop."

She looked carefully around the front. "It's loaded."

"When these little left-wing kiddie games come apart, things often turn dangerous."

"And you're thinking of my safety, Brock how sweet, but come on, it's only rock and roll."

His eyes were brimming with gelatinous tears, and his voice was higher in pitch. "Sooner or later the gun comes out."

"I don't believe that."

"Because you never had the gun . . . but I always did."

"I wouldn't know how to use it."

He laughed, an obnoxious retro-collegiate whinny. "It's all right. I only want you to get it to Rex."

"Rex?"

"He doesn't know it's from me, don't worry, he's still 'pure,'

I know distinctions like that are important to you. I just want it there, in place, part of the household, hm?"

"I can't bring a gun in the house."

"But you can bring a camera. Can't you see, the two separate worlds — one always includes a camera somewhere, and the other always includes a gun, one is make-believe, one is real? What if this is some branch point in your life, where you'll have to choose between worlds?"

"So either I pussy out or become a courier of death, wow, this is some swell choice you're giving me." Who *was* this jerk?

"Don't you even want to touch it? Just to know what it feels like?"

"Hard and maybe a little greasy, by the looks of it."

"But you still don't really know, hm? And you're frightened, but at the same time . . . a little curious. How heavy is it? What'll happen if I touch it there, or there. . . ."

"Let go of me, Brock," her bare legs struggling, flashing in the blurred sunlight as he brought her hand to rest upon the firearm. And then waited until he felt in her hand probable acquiescence, then took his hand away. And hers remained. "And," eyes lowered, "I'm supposed to walk up to Rex and just — is there like a message that goes with it or anything?"

"As long as it's physically his."

Men had it so simple. When it wasn't about Sticking It In, it was about Having The Gun, a variation that allowed them to Stick It In from a distance. The details of how and when, day by working day, made up their real world. Bleak, to be sure, but a lot more simplified, and who couldn't use some simplification, what brought seekers into deserts, fishermen to streams, men to war, a seductive promise. She would have hated to admit how much of this came down to Brock's penis, straightforwardly erect, just to pick a random example.

Her impulse was to deny his simple formula, to imagine that with the gun in the house, the 24-frame-per-second truth she still believed in would find some new, more intense level of truth, is what she was telling herself. Light this little 'sucker here about eight to one, soften the specular highlights, start in on a tight close-up . . . draw back, incorporating the lovely, deadly thing in the master shot of tonight's gathering, transfiguring the frame, returning at last to the invisible presences and unavoidable terms of which all she had up till now lit and made visible had been only the ghosts. . . .

Turned, and turning — the light from the sea, the rights and wrongs she'd picked up from Hub and Sasha, the tides of need that Brock, her inconstant moon, brought and took . . . he would have everything, the little fucker would get it all his way, because from then on, though they would still now and then pretend, both knew she had nothing more to negotiate with. He would not even spare her from the first thing she had sworn to him she'd never do — at some point she had to go up in front of his grand jury, in a city, days distant, where trolley cars ran beneath grimy black webbing that stretched in all directions, all converging in a desert-yellow plaza downtown, the cars painted yellow a shade sunnier than the pavement and trimmed in some tepid green — messenger cables, hangers, and trolley wires sprung from brackets on wood poles trembled and sang and cast shadows of intricate frogwork as sparks went crackling, nearly invisible in the day's glare. She was guided indoors, through low plasterboard corridors, with no way to see who else was sharing the subdivided building. The grand jury already knew her story. The testimony took days but was all pro forma. She tried to watch the white male faces, though without seeming too bold — to imagine them as they might have looked on film, these substantial and good citizens. Each morning she went in to them wrecked, breakfast having been two or three time-bomb tranquilizers and some instant coffee, on top of the previous night's drug combo, which had not exactly worn off by reveille. She woke in bedsheets smelling of vinegar, motel sheets at very first morning light, cold seeping through the inches of space beneath the metal door, another shape in the dark by the other bed, the smell of a cigarette, long minutes of knowing she was there but not who she was.

MR. VOND: How would you characterize the subject's be-
    havior in this final period?
MISS GATES: The last —

243

MR. VOND: The last few days of his life.

MISS GATES: More and more . . . unstable. By then, all he
wanted was out — but he felt he was trapped.

MR. VOND: Did he seem to you to be . . . in the control of
anyone else? Acting on orders, anything like that?

MISS GATES: He thought he was being coerced. He kept
saying that they were "forcing" him.

MR. VOND: And who did you understand "they" to be?

MISS GATES: I thought he meant — I don't know, the
people.

Not an answer the jury wanted, but for Brock they let it pass.
Nor a question that mattered to Frenesi. She had trouble understanding what they wanted. Maybe only her appearance before
them, nothing else. Nobody attempted to trace the path of the
gun. It was almost a supernatural term in the story — a creature
that appears only so that the deed will be done, and then vanishes.
No sign-out form, no log entries, no ballistics tests or serial numbers. But around suppertime that next-to-last day, there it was
inside Rex's fringed cowhide bag. Rex was supposed to be out
someplace, and for the first time in anyone's memory, the bag had
not gone with him. Instead it sat, with its suggestive protuberance,
lounging on the Indian-print sofa like a guest who has come to
stay.

Weed was wearing sandals with argyle socks, a departure from
the hip that Frenesi had just begun to find endearing, and drinking
one after the other spritzers of a fortified demographic wine, anal-
ogous to Night Train or Annie Green Springs, but targeted to the
barrio, known as Pancho Bandido. He sat on the floor, in an
awkward lotus he would never perfect, elbows on knees, head in
hands. "Only a little more aggravation," he greeted Frenesi, "and
you know what?"

"Well, maybe you can relax," is how the transcript of the surveillance tape had her talking, "because your troubles are at an
end, and you are out of it now."

He raised his head slowly to look at her. She had never seen
his eyes like this. "They sent you to tell me something, what was
it." Who, again, did she understand this "they" to be?

Not everybody in 24fps had shown up. Something was going

on up on campus, a rally or assembly, and DL was there with the Arri and Zipi with a wind-up Bolex to see what would develop. There had been no posters or announcements or indeed anyplace left for communication to come from, only the gathering, in falling dark and confusion without limit, around the fountain in the Plaza where PR³ers in their youth had frolicked stoned and nude. Now, with the black rearing silhouette of the Nixon Monument against the sunset, bullhorns with failing batteries quacking invisibly, suddenly no one recognized anyone's face, and each was isolated in a sea of strangers. A common feeling, reported in interviews later, was of a clear break just ahead with everything they'd known. Some said "end," others "transition," but they could all feel it approaching, something about how the smog was pressing from the sky, unmistakable as the waiting before some eclipse in earthquake weather.

Down in the beach house, Sledge Poteet, shades clamped on and hair picked into a black spherical bush, was holding booms and running cable for Krishna, while Howie, eyelids, from what he'd been inhaling, painted upper and lower in fluorescent rose liner, rigged lights and reloaded cameras for Frenesi, with Ditzah running around doing everything else. Frenesi was crouched beside Weed. "This will be your best chance, your most sympathetic forum, all you have to do is tell how it happened, how you think it *could* have happened, no one is judging you, Weed, the camera's only a machine . . . ," and so forth, movie sincerity. Howie kept kicking them, Frenesi would start to film, Weed would change his mind, Howie'd kill them again. This happened a few times. At some point Jinx showed up with Moe and Penny, giving Frenesi the ritual Searching Look. Moe headed for the Tube and Penny started for the kitchen but paused a moment by the Indian sofa.

"Did Rex forget his bag?" She had a look of concern — a little kid who really worried about other people. Her plump small hand lay fidgeting slowly on the hard object just a hide's breadth away.

"Oh, wow," Frenesi precisely intercepting, finding the point on the strap to take it by, "I'll give it to him, Penny, thanks," up onto her shoulder in a smooth single curve while also reaching to adjust the girl's bangs for her, but not so tenderly that Penny didn't pull away after a polite interval and, pushing her hair back off her forehead, run in to join Moe.

Weed, who might have known what was in the bag, had been watching her. By swooping on Penny she had admitted that she knew too. So what. But she was feeling lightheaded. Jinx, in from the kitchen with the Pancho Bandido bottle, looked nervous.

"Um . . . this is it for wine, you guys, I don't even see this where *I* shop unless it's over in the automotive section someplace. . . ." Jinx reported later that they'd stared at her with what looked to her like drug-dilated eyes, Frenesi on her feet in a controlled sway, Weed down in his broken lotus, for seconds that stretched till Frenesi nodded, managed a smile. "Say, Jinx."

The phone rang. It was DL for Frenesi, reporting in from up on the campus. The coast highway had been sealed off, marine units from Pendleton were moving into position to come up the cliffside, and rolling down from the base just above the campus were armed personnel carriers and a couple of tanks. The California Highway Patrol and the Trasero County sheriff were standing by. "Think I can score us a generator, but I don't know if there'll be any way out, not for much longer. Can you get up here?"

"Soon as we can . . . DL, are you OK?"

"Your boyfriend Weed's name has been coming up a lot. If he's still in town, he might want to think about not being."

"Yeah, he's —" she was aware then of the shouting from the other room. Rex was back. Rex and Weed, with Jinx putting in.

"Oh, shit." The last words DL was to hear from her friend for a while. Frenesi hung up and ran in to find Jinx moving the kids briskly out the door and Weed on his feet between them and Rex, who was shaking and white, with the bag over his shoulder and one hand resting on the heavy lump inside. The lights were on and both cameras were running, Ditzah with a battered old Auricon, Howie with the Scoopic.

Both of them turned to her. "Tell him!" Rex was almost in tears. "Tell this asshole we know everything."

What she would then have to bear with her all her life, what she would only succeed in denying or disguising for brief insomniac minutes here and there, was not only the look on his face — Ditzah took the close-ups while Howie kept further back, framing the three of them — but the way that what he was slowly understanding spread to his body, a long, stunned cringe, a loss of spirit that could almost be seen on the film, even after all the years between then and the screen in Ditzah's house in the Valley . . . some silvery effluent, vacating his image, the real moment of his passing. He had just time enough to say Frenesi's name before the frame went twisting and flying off his face, "Lot of shoving all at once," Ditzah recalled, "Howie happened to be changing rolls, but Krishna got all the audio — here —"

Rex screaming, "Don't you walk away from me!" the squeak of a screen door, feet and furniture thumping around, the door again, a starter motor shrieking, an engine catching, as Sledge then moved on out into the alley after them and Frenesi tried to find enough cable to get one of the floods on them and Howie got his new roll in and on his way out offered to switch places with Frenesi, who may have hesitated — her camera, her shot — but must have waved him on, because it was Howie, innocent and slow-moving, who emerged into the darkness and, while trying to find the ring to open the aperture, missed the actual moment, although shapes may have moved somewhere in the frame, black on black, like ghosts trying to return to earthly form, but Sledge was right there on them, and the sound of the shot captured by Krishna's tape. Prairie, listening, could hear in its aftermath the slack whisper of the surf against this coast — and when Howie finally got there and Frenesi aimed the light, Weed was on his face with his blood all on the cement, the shirt cloth still burning around the blackly erupted exit, pale flames guttering out, and Rex was staring into the camera, posing, pretending to blow smoke away from the muzzle of the .38. He would not after all be lucky enough to sit under that oak on that dreamed hillside someday with a miraculously saved Weed Atman, in some 1980s world of the future. The camera moved in on his face. "Howie found the zoom," Ditzah commented. "We realized we were all there in an alley face-to-face with an insane person with a loaded gun."

Up on the screen Rex was crying, "It should have been you, Frenesi, fuckin' whore, where are you?" Just behind the light harsh in his face and continuing to pour unwavering, Frenesi was silent. Prairie imagined her standing with nothing but the light between her and Rex and his hatred while he hung, tightening in pain all over, holding the gun but no longer in possession of it. He walked over to Weed's body, went down on one knee, laid the gun beside him. That's when Frenesi killed the light, that's how the shot ended, in a close-up of one of Rex's gleaming eyeballs, with the light she was holding reflected on it round and bright, and in the back-scatter — if Prairie only looked closely enough she would have to see her — Frenesi herself, dark on dark, face in wide-angle distortion, with an expression that might, Prairie admitted, prove unbearable.

The footage following was from up on the campus, the last hours of the People's Republic of Rock and Roll. There wouldn't be any single assault, Attica-style, but instead a scattered nightlong propagation of human chaos, random shooting, tear gas from above, buildings and cars set ablaze, everyone a possible enemy, too much of it in the dark after the electric power, along with the water, got cut off. There was smog but no moon or starlight. Out on a trailer parked in back of the Film Arts building, however, was a Mole-Richardson Series 700 generator, in more or less running order, although once he had some light to work by, Sledge couldn't help reaching into the engine, tweaking the idle and timing and shit. Strangers began to come cautiously in from the darkness. Miles in the distance, from faraway Anaheim Stadium, came the sounds of a Blue Cheer concert. To the 24fps crew it felt like the day after the end of the world, seeing what was there to be taken from the generously funded Film Arts Department, legendary Eclairs whose mere hourly rental would have meant weeks of scuffling, Miller heads, Fastaxes for slow motion, Norwood Binary light meters, at last the high-ticket production of their dreams, and it had to be in this trapped and futureless night.

They lit it on up, with lamps and luminaires, using the fastest film they had, a cache of 7242 from the Film Arts fridge, and a wide-open aperture so there wasn't the depth to it Ditzah would have liked, yet there she, DL, and Prairie sat prehypnotic before the shots of helicopters descending, kids dancing all tuned to the same station on the radio, a ratlike swarm of approaching troops in camouflage and blackface suddenly caught in the beams of arc lamps they proceeded to shoot out as Howie had prophesied, with the camera never pulling back, but standing against whatever came its way and often moving out into it. "She could get herself killed," Prairie cried.

"Yep," said Ditzah and DL together.

By morning there were scores of injuries, hundreds of arrests, no reported deaths but a handful of persons unaccounted for. In those days it was still unthinkable that any North American agency would kill its own civilians and then lie about it. So the mystery abided, frozen in time, somewhere beyond youthful absences surely bound to be temporary, yet short of planned atrocity. Taken one by one, after all, given the dropout data and the migratory preferences of the time, each case could be accounted for without appealing to anything more sinister than a desire for safety. At his news conference, Brock Vond referred to it humorously as "rapture." Fawning, gazing upward at the zipper of his fly, the media toadies present wondered aloud where, in his opinion, if it was OK to ask, Mr. Vond, sir, the missing students might have gotten to. Brock replied, "Why, underground, of course. That's our assumption in this, from all we know about them — that they've gone underground." Somebody from the radical press must have infiltrated. "You mean they're on the run? Are there warrants out? How come none are listed as federal fugitives?" The reporter was led away by a brace of plainclothes heavies as Brock Vond genially repeated, highlights dancing merrily on his lenses and frames, "Underground, hm? Rapture below. Yes, the gentleman in the suit and tie?"

Earlier, while the newshounds had all been across campus at the main gate, preoccupied with getting shots of coed cuties in miniskirts being handled by troopers in full battle gear in which leather recurred as a motif, none had noticed the small convoy of field-gray trucks, locked shut, unmarked, that had left out the back way without even pausing for the security at the checkpoint.

Threading a complex array of ramps, transition lanes, and suspiciously tidy country roads, the trucks eventually pulled up onto the little-known and only confidentially traveled FEER, or Federal Emergency Evacuation Route, which followed the crestline of the Coast Range north in a tenebrous cool light, beneath camouflage netting and weatherproof plastic sheet. It was a dim tunnel that went for hundreds of miles, conceived in the early sixties as a disposable freeway that would only be used, to full capacity, once.

The convoy's destination lay hours to the north, in a wet and secluded valley that had been the site of an old Air Force fog-dispersal experiment and later, before the apocalyptic grandeur of Kennedy-era strategic "thinking" found itself bogged, nukeless, in the quotidian horrors of Vietnam, intended as a holding area able to house up to half a million urban evacuees in the event of, well, say, some urban evacuation. A few dozen housing units, like model homes at the edge of newly subdivided acreage, had been put up just to give visitors a feel for the concept — all standard-issue Corps of Engineers jobs, some of them apartments meant for families, as the word was understood back then, some barracks for detached men, women, boys, and girls whose families might still be "temporarily unaccounted for." There was a mess hall, toilet and shower facilities, pool and Ping-Pong tables, a movie projector, softball diamond, basketball court. Water ran everywhere, redwoods and Sitka spruce went towering in ragged silhouette up to the ridgetops and over, and behind them, most of the year, gray regiments of cloud marched in from the coast.

DL in the meantime had come straggling back to Berkeley, to the workshop off San Pablo, with Howie and Sledge, either loyal to the end or just in shock, walking slack for her, and found they were just about all that was left of 24fps. DL by then was so crazy that half the time she didn't know who was there and who wasn't. This along with a chiming, way inside her ears, and a light that glowed at the edges of everything, both clearly signals to stand by, message follows.

It took them a while just to find out where Frenesi had gone. There'd been reports in from people who'd seen her taken off in the convoy, some of whom had tried to follow, only to come each time to a peculiar network of transition roads where no matter which combinations they used they were unable to gain access. But they had heard and glimpsed, somewhere in the terrain above them, the old FEER freeway, defects here and there in its camouflage, gray columns and guardrails, ruins from Camelot. Maps were available up and down the street, few agreeing, none getting too specific about what was inside the ragged polygon at the end of the classified freeway, labeled only "National Security Reservation."

DL and the boys took the flagship of the 24fps motor pool, a '57 Chevy Nomad with a four-wheel-drive option, raised up a couple of feet and equipped with big high-flotation tires, crash bars, and winches fore and aft. About the time they got onto the Richmond–San Rafael bridge, rain began to fall, and they hit San Rafael at prematurely dark and vaporous rush hour, all eight or ten lanes full of exhaust plumes drooping like tails of some listless herd. DL was driving, her bright hair confined in a loosely knit olive snood, plowing on ahead through the wet shift's-end dusk, sitting upright in serene metered fury, holding centered and in focus the image of the enemy, Brock Vond, and of the woman he had kidnapped — for Frenesi could not have gone willingly, no, this asshole of a cop had wanted her, so he'd decided he'd just take her and assumed nobody would do anything about it. Well, Brock, excuse me, Captain, but guess what.

Street estimates in Berkeley about the population of the camp in the mountains ran on the order of ten to a hundred, depending how the different sources felt seeing their nightmares about the Nixon regime coming true. Howie and Sledge were skeptical about proceeding this way on other people's guesswork. They peered at the maps, each with that enigmatic blank in the middle, like the outline of a state in a geography test, belonging to something called "the U.S.," but not the one they knew. "It's a hundred miles around, DL. If they see us coming, they have all the time in the world to take her and stash her someplace else."

"They won't see me." If Frenesi's realm was light, DL's was the dark. Most of those in 24fps had seen, or not seen, her pass without effort through areas infested with cops and cop weapons, rescuing along the way brothers and sisters and the vehicles they'd ridden in in, and come out the other side asking what's for lunch, with the blazing beacon of her hair, which the Man was never quite able to see, no more messed up than when she'd gone in. Sledge and Howie both believed in her invisibility, the same way in those days it was possible to believe in acid, or the imminence of revolution, or the disciplines, passive and active, of the East.

The sturdily enhanced Nomad, beginning now to run into some grades, rushed along in the rain, while the guys navigated, blinking little pocket flashes on and off, seeking a route of ascent to the Third, or Mesopotamian, Freeway implied by the other two that ran the lowlands to east and west. Through suburbs and pasture and forest they sped — from concrete to blacktop to macadam, at last to a gullied and boulder-strewn glacis, or defensive slope, behind a chain-link fence that they winched up enough of to get through. After locking the wheels and switching over to 4WD, "Hang on," advised DL, and away they began to roar, smoke, and climb, pops from the terrain sending everybody bouncing and banging their heads on the roof of the rig, the landscape out the windows seesawing violently around. Once or twice they nearly went over, but at last the Nomad scraped through a breach in the guardrail and gained the deserted old highway.

Every hundred feet or so, just off the shoulder, was a slender pole holding a medallion about the size of a party-size pizza, with a face on it, not something generalized to represent, say, the Ordinary American, but a particular human face, looking directly at the viewer with a strangely personal expression, as if just about to speak. Inscribed at the base of each pole, in some weathered metal gray as an old zinc wartime penny, was the story that went with the face.

"Virgil ('Sparky') Ploce, 1923–1959, American Martyr in the Crusade Against Communism. Lt. Col. Ploce was the first American of many who have attempted to clear from the face of our hemisphere that stubborn zit known as Fidel Castro. Undercover, posing as an ultrazealous Cuban Communist, 'Sparky' soon charmed his way into the bearded dictator's confidence. His plan was to have offered to Castro, and then lit for him, a giant Cuban cigar that actually contained an ingenious bomb of 'Sparky's' own design, made of plastic explosive, detonator, and a length of primer cord. Unfortunately for freedom-loving people everywhere, an accumulation of manufacturing errors had caused the head and the tuck of the cigar to appear virtually identical, so that when the fuzz-faced Latin tyrant bit off the wrong end and pulled out the primer cord with his teeth, security guards were immediately alert to the danger. Overseers of a typical Red Slave State, they apprehended and executed Lt. Col. Ploce on the spot." The face above this was young, clean-shaven, and short-haired, and seemed to be smirking.

As they discovered when they got moving and one by one new stone-colored medallions appeared through the rain, in their headlight beams, each of these folks' images had been given eyes designed to follow whoever was driving past, so the Nomad's progress was observed, perhaps appraised, by silent miles of oversize faces, set a little higher than the average passenger vehicle stood. Had they been meant somehow for the long jammed and crawling hours of flight from the City, something inspirational to look at, to assure them all in a way not immediately clear *it is not the end,* or *there is still hope . . .* ? was it only some travel game for the kids, to keep them occupied, to pass the time till the sudden light from behind, the unbearable sight in the mirror?

They arrived at the fence, about where the maps said it would be, well before dawn, during the hour of the rat, when the body sleeps deepest even if awake, still following the same cycle, most vulnerable. DL slipped into a black jumpsuit and ski mask. A cold wind blew down off a ridge someplace, bringing the smell of trees. Howie and Sledge gave her the old 24fps kissoff, "Be groovy or B movie," one minute watching the highlights spun off her pale eyeballs, the next trying to see where she'd gone.

Later, of course, doing the bookkeeping on this caper, filling in logs after the fact, she could appreciate how broadly she'd violated the teachings of her sensei. She had not become the egoless agent of somebody else's will, but was acting instead out of her own selfish passions. If the motive itself was tainted, then the acts, no matter how successful or beautifully executed, were false, un-

true to her calling, to herself, and someday there would be a
payback, long before which she would understand that by far the
better course would have been to leave Frenesi where she was.
She followed the fence till she saw lights, the bleary all-night
cyan blue flooding over everything, revealing a wide-open field of
fire between the gate and the nearest barracks, about a hundred
yards inside it. She moved quickly toward the sentry, keeping her
eyes on his own, which were aimed downward, reading to pass
the dark watch, till she was too close for it to matter anymore. It
was one of Inoshiro Sensei's proprietary whammies, based on a
well-known ninja invisibility technique known as *Kasumi*, or The
Mist. By wiggling her fingers precisely in his face, she selectively
blinded him to her presence — he could go on with his life, but
without DL in it. She was already inside, away along the fence,
becoming its harsh woven shadow, watching for patrols, scanning
the distant barracks, nocking and setting herself, archer and arrow,
her passage through the turquoise glare untimed, unthought. In
the building's penumbra, not even breathing hard, so elegantly
that you couldn't say jimmied, she more like Jamesed the side door
lock with a needle of antique ivory the sensei had given her long
ago, and slipped within, into night's last act, where dozens of
sleepers, alone and paired, lay on the wood floor on thin government mattresses, snoring, snuffling, calling out, flailing around,
and, what DL was looking for, wide awake — a face lit by reflection off the floor, one she then remembered from Berkeley, from
the old Death to the Pig Nihilist Film Kollective. "Just happened
to be passin' through, lookin' for Frenesi was all."
He hesitated, not long but long enough. "You here to bring her
out?"
"Want to come along, you're sure welcome."
"Oh thanks anyway, it's no worse in here than where I was."
"But you're a political prisoner."
He smiled out one side of his mouth. "I firebombed a car with
a bunch of FBI in it — they all got out OK, I figured, hey, groovy,
I total the car, they stay alive, so long dudes, have a nice violence-
free life — only they must've saw it different."
"You showed disrespect."

"If I split with you now, they'll put me on the Ten Most Wanted, have me back inside in a day — not worth it."

"Nice seein' you again, brother, and now it's time for a little rewind and erase on ya, nothing personal. . . ." In the green and blue shadows she repeated the procedure she'd used on the gate guard. Directed then by soft whispers, perhaps not themselves voices of the waking, from pallet to pallet among the sleepers, she came at last to a dim figure lying prone, her hands beneath her, pressing, squirming, sighing, wearing only a blue chambray work shirt with half the buttons missing, streaked dark with her sweat. DL, who already knew it wasn't Frenesi, went to one knee beside her, the girl crying out, shrinking away from the black apparition, hands across her breasts. "I'd love to," DL smiling behind her mask, "but I'm in sort of a hurry, maybe you could just tell me where she is."

The girl gazed, lips apart, wet fingers at her throat. "They took her to the Office." It was nearby, in the camp's administrative center. Hard to get into? You bet. The girl, under DL's coaxing, told her what she could, relaxing, dropping her hands to her lap.

Again DL violated procedure. Taking the small face in her hand, "And the reason you're in her bed finger-fucking yourself is that you love her, have I got that correct?"

Her wrists and arms growing tense, her averted face darkening with blood, "I can't stand it without her . . . think I'm dying." She sought DL's eyes in the ultramarine night.

DL went on ahead before the girl could react, leaned in, lifting the mask, and kissed her open mouth, soon enough feeling the unhappy little tongue come fluttering forward. DL let her have a quick nonlethal taste of the Kunoichi Death Kiss, which is ordinarily the setup for a needle swiftly thrust into the brainstem of the kissee but was here meant only in malicious play, to stun her victim into rethinking her situation. . . . Spanish guitars ringing in her mind, DL slipped the girl's shirt off and with a black-gloved finger traced a big letter Z — above, between, below her breasts. "*Hasta la próxima, querida mia,*" and over the señorita's balcony she did vanish, emerging, as a matter of fact, right between two sentries making their rounds, unseen, unheard, though perhaps, who could be sure, not unscented.

The administration building was all concrete and local river rock, in a Corps of Engineers style not noted for whimsy, raised up on a long sweep of steps at least as high as it was, with rows of white columns suggesting national architecture and deathless temple, intended to reassure, to discourage too many questions, to turn to use whatever residue of nation-love might be hidden among the tens of thousands of traumatized nuclear refugees it had been designed to impress. DL prowled its perimeter till she found a marshal on watch and before he even saw her got rid of his weapon and punched into a sequence of his trigger points the subroutine *Yukai na,* or Fun, a low-order limbic pleasure cycle that would loop over and over as long as the officer behaved himself. They strolled into the facility smooth as Daffy and Bugs and got on the elevator down to a subterranean complex known as the Office. It was as if they descended into the rodent hour itself, no way to tell how fast they were falling. DL felt herself counterpopping her ears and had to nudge the marshal, whose whole body by now was a shit-eating grin, to remind him to do the same.

They were down in the Cold War dream, the voices fading from the radios, the unwatchable events in the sky, the flight, the long descent, the escape to refuge deep in the earth, one hatchway after another, leading to smaller and smaller volumes. Sleeping compartments, water, food, electricity, curtailed possibilities, an extension to life in a never-ending hum of fluorescent light and recycled air. And right now, still this side of the Unimagined, also offering deep privacy for whatever those in command might wish to do to people they brought down here. Would the magnitude of the fear that had found expression in this built space allow them to use it in ways just as uncontrolled and insane . . . thinking it authorized them somehow?

The place smelled of office solvents, paper, plastic furniture, cigarette smoke in the carpeting and drapes. DL's guide brought her smartly through a set of right-angled turns at last to a door, around which she slid ninja-style, blocking the outside light, leaving the marshal purring and indisposed to move.

Frenesi told DL later that the dream she'd wakened from was one she'd mentioned to her friend before, the one, recurring for her almost on a lunar basis, that she'd named the Dream of the Gentle Flood. A California beach town, the houses tightly crowded, nearly all of glass, huge windows that were really glass walls, all trembling at the wind off the ocean, would be partly engulfed by a tidal wave, long announced, daylit transparent green, flowing smoothly in, with plenty of time for people to get to higher ground, bringing the sea in up the hillside exactly to the level of the house Frenesi was in, observing. Though everyone in town was safe, the beaches were gone, and the lifeguard towers and volleyball nets, and all the expensive beachfront houses and lots, and the Piers, all covered by the cool green Flood, which almost paralyzed her with its beauty, its clarity . . . for "days" she could watch nothing else, while around her the town adjusted to its new shoreline and life went on. Late at "night" she went out on her deck and stood just above the surf, looking toward a horizon she couldn't see, as if into a wind that might really be her own passage, destination unknown, and heard a voice, singing across the Flood, this wonderful song, the kind you heard stoned over at some stranger's place one night and never found again, telling of the divers, who would come, not now but soon, and descend into the Flood and bring back up for us "whatever has been taken," the voice promised, "whatever has been lost. . . ."

With no transition her eyes came wide open and there was DL stripping off the mask and shaking out her hair, DL's face in the interior sky, slowly connecting with her name and memory, lost in the flare-ridden night after Weed died.

"Howdy," DL smiling, "you awake? 'Cause we have this sort of time problem. You have shoes someplace, a pair of pants?"

Frenesi groped around. "He's not here," she kept mumbling. "He left here hours ago."

"Too bad, I was hoping for the pleasure at last, another time perhaps — you ready?"

"Are you sure this is —"

"I'll get you out, don't worry."

"No, I mean. . . ." DL had her by the arm and out of the room by then, and after she reactivated the marshal they all proceeded up and then out to the motor-pool area, where DL selected a stock jeep with a two-way radio and got them out in the wind. When the lights of the compound were only a heavenly blur above some ridgeline, she stopped and took the marshal off his limbic sub-routine. He sat weaving in the dark, white showing all around his irises, trying to readjust, figure out what was going on. . . .

"Say, Officer," clapping her hands in his face, "talk to us. Shit, I thought I set it on low."

He croaked and swallowed for a while before saying, "Listen, would you like to go out sometime, maybe, for drinks? I mean I'm like a white-wine person myself, but, you know, whatever."

"Hrrumph" — DL, rolling her eyes, rattled open a map, snapped on a penlight — "this road here, coming out the north end of the reservation, near the creek?"

All sheep's eyes, he directed them onto a turnoff that connected with the road out. Radio traffic stayed routine, and soon they'd passed the unmanned gate and were back in public mapspace again. DL put on the brakes and nodded at the door. " 'Fraid you'll have to hike back into Dodge, Marshal."

"Don't suppose there's any chance you could show me, uh —"

DL allowed him a quick but genuine sympathy shrug. "Takes years to learn, and by the time you do, it's no fun anymore."

They left him beside the road, gazing after. "Thought of this sooner," DL muttered, "we could've turned the Pentagon into a dove ranch." No response. Frenesi was in tears, twisted around in her seat, trying not so much to see the marshal as just to look back the way they'd come. DL might've been expecting more of a welcome, but decided she'd wait till later to comment. Just as well.

After the rendezvous with Howie and Sledge she hightailed it over to I-5, blasting on southward to I-80, dropping off the boys at the University Avenue exit, ending up with a monosyllabic and distant Frenesi at last in the not-yet-trendy Mexican fishing village of Quilbasazos, on the Pacific coast, down a brief but challenging few miles of dirt road from the coastal highway. By then they'd switched to a Camaro of uncertain age and color, mainstreaming their ID's, scarves over their heads, driving a little under the limit, a holiday plunge into old Mexico. They woke up at sunset in a dilapidated hotel at the edge of town, hearing marimba music from the cantina across the street, smelling heated garlic, roasting meat, baking cornmeal, suddenly — Frenesi in a brief dimly smiling return — both hungry. Emerging from a courtyard full of hanging flowers and caged birds just at the hour when the lights came on, and ghosts came out, they saw their fun-house shadows taken by the village surfaces drenched in sunset, as sage, apricot, adobe and wine colors were infiltrated with night, and up and down the wandering streets they followed their noses at last to the waterfront, lampglow smeared about each municipal bulb up on the green-painted iron posts, music coming all directions, from radios, accordions, singers unaccompanied, jukeboxes, guitars. Newsvendors with the late editions from the capital ran in and out of bars and cafés repeating the word "*Noticias*" at intervals regular as birdcalls, while the surf kept splashing in at a different rhythm. DL and Frenesi found wood chairs and a table outside a small restaurant where the day's special was a seafood stew heavy on garlic, cumin, and oregano, hot with chiles, crowded with an oceanic anthology of scraps from the fishing that day, a joy to look at not to mention eat, which they did in a hurry, much of it with their hands or using tortillas. As the young women went pigging out, bottles of beer, rice and beans, mangoes, and pineapple slices with powdered cinnamon also showed up, until, just about the time Frenesi was going "Whoo-wee!" and reaching in her bag for a pack of Kools, the owner came out and started putting plastic sheets over the other tables. "*A llover*," he advised, indicating the sky. They moved inside just as the evening rainstorm came on, sat back in a corner and drank coffee, the first time in neither could remember how long they'd had a chance to relax and talk without interruption from timetables, Red Squads, doorstep fugitives, or movie shots — most of all those framable pieces of the time, which had demanded, when the bookkeeping was done, damn near everything.

Carefully they exchanged updates on their broken collectivity, Krishna stepping away out of the red-orange light from a disabled VW with its battery failing into an unreconnoitered darkness, toward a voice she thought was calling her name . . . Mirage shocked into silence, gone back to Arkansas after giving away all her ephemerides, reference books, worksheets, even her black-light zodiac posters . . . Zipi and Ditzah off boisterously to a bomb-making commune up in central Oregon, calling, "Goodbye to the land of make-believe," and hollering, "Reality Time!" and "Powder to the People!"

Carefully also, Frenesi raised her eyes to those of her friend. "Looks like those Pisks were right," her voice so sad that DL couldn't answer. "Feel like we were running around like little kids with toy weapons, like the camera really was some kind of gun, gave us that kind of power. Shit. How could we lose track like that, about what was real? All that time we made ourselves stay on the natch? might as well have been dropping Purple Owsley for all the good it did." She shook her head, looked down at her knees. "And it wasn't only Weed who got offed, story going around the camp is there were others, and the FBI covered it up? So what difference did we make? Who'd we save? The minute the guns came out, all that art-of-the-cinema handjob was over."

"News on the street in Berkeley is that Rex has split the country."

But Frenesi had heard something in her voice. "What else?"

"You won't like it." The anguished scrap of sound borne in to her by this Pacific storm was Inoshiro Sensei, all the way back in Japan, once again screaming, "No, no, idiot, didn't you learn anything?" But she went on. "Rumor you set him up? I got into a couple of encounters over that, matter o' fact."

"Yeah. They were right. I could have kept it from happening." Sounding guilty, all right, but a little too readily. DL's phony-baloney sensors went on full alert. Her mouth, alas, should only have been as finely tuned.

She said, "The Prosecutor's name also came up."

Frenesi put her coffee cup back down. "Alleging some kind of a conspiracy, I'll bet."

"Well what *is* the story, Frenesi?"

"What do you care?" From there on it got louder. As they talked their hands kept flying out across the table, nearly touching, then drawing back, again and again. Frenesi chain-smoked and

DL tried not to feel too hurt or short of breath as each new detail, another blow unanswered, brought them that much closer to a decision that much less in doubt. Soon it had grown too loud for where they remembered they were, so they took it back through the last of the rain, back up the lampless streaming lanes, guided by the smudge of neon on the roof of their hotel. They stayed up the rest of the night, crying separately and together, demanding, pleading, exchanging insults, repeating formulas, getting things wrong on purpose, and more and more wrong as it went on falling to pieces.

"I'm not some pure creature," Frenesi wanted to cry, "the Film Queen, some no-emotion piece of machinery, everything for the shot, come on, DL . . . please . . . you know what happens when my pussy's runnin' the show, you saw me do stuff he'll *never* see," and DL, not as angry by then, might've answered, "I *made* you do stuff, bitch," and Frenesi would have felt a bodylong twinge of clear desire for her already ex-partner, a preview of delicious trouble . . . for DL's body, whose rangy sweetness she loved, now was just as likely to try and hurt, even cripple her, and who knew but what she deserved it . . . worse would be knowing she'd pushed DL into losing it — that fine clean self-command they'd all taken for granted — DL the steady-beating heart of the collective, who could never have made the deal with Brock that Frenesi had — and feeling at the same time mean satisfaction in provoking her out of that saintlike control, yep one more rap she'd have to take. . . . But at last it was mercy she'd have to plead for, reduced to playing helpless, blaming external drug molecules for each of her failures, complicities, and surrenders — as indeed national governments were even then learning to do, with an already devastating impact on any humans who happened to be in their way. "He took me behind the Thorazine curtain, man," Frenesi with a nasalized little-girl croak then reciting her adventures in the world beyond the temporal veil of a drug well known for its antagonism to memory. They'd started her on 5mg Stelazine plus 50 of Thorazine, injected in ever-increasing doses till they thought she was calmed down enough to take it orally. She learned to spit it out slowly, a sly dribbling. "They hid it in my food, I made myself throw up, so they went back to shots and suppositories. They classified me as a Persistent Drug Evader, but I was just teasing. What happened was . . . I got to like it. Only took a couple of days. I started looking forward to it — I wanted them to come and hold me down, stick needles in me, push things up my ass. Wanted that ritual . . . like they had to keep the two drugs out of the light till the last minute, then they'd mix them together, real quick, and give it to me. Shrinks never figured it out, but the orderlies, the workin' stiffs who actually had to do it all, handle me, hold me still, pull apart the cheeks of my ass, they knew all right, 'cause they were digging it just as much as I was. . . ." She waited, guttering with a small meek defiance, standing at the window and trembling, moonlight from a high angle pouring over her naked back, casting on it shadows of her shoulder blades, like healed stumps of wings ritually amputated once long ago, for some transgression of the Angels' Code.

"It took another day and night," as DL remembered it, "but it was all just sad human shittiness. We came back over the border at Nogales and I let her off at an exit called Las Suegras, and that was the last time I ever saw her."

"Well according to my dad," said Prairie, "that's where they met, was in Las Suegras, the Corvairs had a two-week gig at Phil's Cottonwood Oasis, and it was love at first sight."

"It usually was," DL more wistful than snide.

They were in Ditzah's kitchen, eating microwaved frozen Danish and drinking coffee, when the phone rang, and Ditzah went to answer. Prairie, reentering nonmovie space, felt like the basketball after a Lakers game — alive, resilient, still pressurized with spirit yet with a distinct memory of having been, for a few hours, expertly bounced. Her mom, in front of her own eyes, had stood with a 1,000-watt Mickey-Mole spot on the dead body of a man who had loved her, and the man who'd just killed him, and the gun she'd brought him to do it with. Stood there like the Statue of Liberty, bringer of light, as if it were part of some contract to illuminate, instead of conceal, the deed. With all the footage of Frenesi she'd seen, all the other shots that had come by way of her eye and body, this hard frightening light, this white outpouring, had shown the girl most accurately, least mercifully, her mother's real face.

DL waited for eye contact, but they hadn't managed it by the time Ditzah came back in, looking serious.

"Uh, where's the bathroom?" Prairie heading out of earshot.

"No, maybe you'd better hear this. That was my sister Zipi, back on Long Island." Where, Prairie calculated, it was well after midnight. Last week, the last time the sisters had talked, Zipi had mentioned Mirage, who kept in touch from Fort Smith, which she had never left after moving back there. Determined to deny all she had learned by way of the stars, to turn back to Earth, to resubmerge in the simple meat suffocation of a family whose driving emotion had always been resentment more than love — she had once actually heard her mother curse the sky for not matching the color of her dress — Mirage had learned instead it was the stars that had chosen her, and her fate after all would be to read them to others. This summer something secret and momentous was turning beneath the visible everyday . . . Pluto, which had been retrograde, was making a station, appearing to pause before going direct again. For most planets this would be a change for the better, but for the ruler of the Land of Death, retrograde was the best it ever got — then, people with power, instead of using it for short-term and sooner or later harmful ends, had a chance, at least, while Pluto soared backward against the ground of stars, to learn mercy and wisdom in applying it. Megalomaniacs suddenly reached out to strangers, asking if they were OK, road dogs rolled belly-up and smiled at mail deliverers, developers gave up plans to rape pieces of countryside, kids who had sprayed CHOOSE DEATH on bridge abutments now were seen, often in matching outfits, assisting at religious services. But this summer all that, according to Mirage, was ending. Pluto was about to get back to its ancient underworld and nihilistic ways, also known as Business As Usual.

"Meaning Reagan gets reelected," Zipi had suggested.

"Meaning we all have to be extra paranoid," a pale woodwind voice she'd picked up over the years, "because it's squaring each of us in a different way." Ever since she'd computerized and built a data base, it had been no problem, nostalgically now and then, to progress the charts of everyone in the old 24fps gang, see how their lives were going and, if it was really critical, to try and get in touch. She had first contacted Zipi, in fact, three years before, in the very worst part of a divorce with the sound track, though not the amiability, of a teen slash-'em-up at the drive-in. Mirage had cast Sheldon's chart immediately and found out he was seeing a Virgo somehow connected with his business life, and what do you know, sure enough. "It's a miracle!" screamed the impressed Zipi. "It's the Venus aspect to his midheaven, actually," Mirage replied. But ever since, she had been Zipi's oracle, even passing along tips on the races at Aqueduct that always earned at least walking-around money, and now here she was with this curious Pluto alert. After two and a half centuries of wandering — though not exile — out in the zodiac, the grim overlord was about to return to Scorpio, its home territory, the sign it ruled jointly with Mars and which, as DL was quick to point out, also happened to be Brock Vond's birth sign. Since early 1980, as if repeatedly running into trouble at the frontier, negotiating with caretaker governments that scarcely recognized him, Pluto had been shifting, direct to retrograde and back again, stuck within a few degrees of the cusp, trying to get out of Libra, creating a heavy intensification, according to Mirage, of his effects, which were hardly benign to begin with.

But Zipi had not called at this hour just to pass along information available at any newsstand. Mirage also reported that Howie, having been afflicted in his Fifth House of fun, had just been popped for cocaine, a substance he'd never used. Trying to phone all the 24fps people she could, Mirage had found that two, possibly three more had dropped out of sight abruptly, leaving no explanation. She was getting scared, and now so was Zipi, and neither knew what they should do.

"What'd you tell her, Ditzah?"

"Said I'd talk to you. Mind you, this is all in a strange personal code, kind of idiolalia you find in twins, so I don't know if anybody bugging us heard much."

"First thing, we ought to sweep," it seemed to DL. "You got a li'l FM radio handy someplace?"

"Here you go. I unscrewed the phone, couldn't find anything, but I assume they've put a Title III intercept."

DL had the pocket-size radio on and was doing a slow t'ai chi walk through the house, tuning back and forth on the dial, a procedure that would weed out only cheaper, less professional-type bugs, which tended to use the same band of frequencies. But the minute she hit the workroom in back there came a horrendous squeal, obliterating a Madonna single that Prairie had been getting into. They found the unit, clunky even by 1984 standards, definitely low-end, wires showing and so forth — "Almost insulting, isn't it?" Ditzah remarked.

"Typical Brock Vond, f' sure — pure contempt. But this was still too easy to find. They've been using more up around 457, 467 megahertz. So either we were meant to find this or, I don't even like to say it, they've suddenly started deploying so many bugs they ran out of 'em, had to start using the cheap stuff."

"We're probably just being paranoid," Ditzah a shade too brightly. "It only begins to assume some nationwide pattern here, right? Tell me I've been watching too much old footage tonight. Tell me this isn't what it looks like." Prairie saw how they were both breathing, the deliberate way you were told to do when otherwise you might want to panic.

"In the olden days we called it the last roundup," DL explained. "Liked to scare each other with it, though it was always real enough. The day they'd come and break into your house and put everybody in prison camps. Not fun or sitcom prison camps, more like feedlots where we'd all become official, nonhuman livestock."

"You've seen camps like this?" At once there seeped into the cheery space a silence like a stain in the light. Ditzah, at her editing table trembling, seemed to turn her body from what DL would say, to present less of a target, but DL only answered evenly.

"Yep, I've seen 'em, your mom was in one, you'll recall, but better than us reminiscing and boring you, go to the library sometime and read about it. Nixon had machinery for mass detention all in place and set to go. Reagan's got it for when he invades Nicaragua. Look it up, check it out."

Prairie offered, "I didt'n mean, you know —"

"DL," said Ditzah, quickly gathering what she'd need, "what do we do?"

"Stay out of the way till we figure out what's going on. You got someplace secure for tonight?"

"You'll pull off the road, I'll make a phone call. What about all this film, not to mention my own work?"

"Takeshi could get it tomorrow with the truck."

Ditzah took her pack and they were out of there, in the Trans-Am of Darkness. "Thought we were all through with this shit." She sounded plaintive.

"Seems otherwise."

"Why would he come after us? Is he trying to roll back time? What is it that's so hard for him to live with?"

"Turn on his past like 'at, don't know, Ditzah, sounds too weird even for Brock."

"Then again, it's the whole Reagan program, isn't it — dismantle the New Deal, reverse the effects of World War II, restore fascism at home and around the world, flee into the past, can't you feel it, all the dangerous childish stupidity — 'I don't like the way it came out, I want it to be my way.' If the President can act like that, why not Brock?"

"You always did look at things more historically. What I just figure is is he's a mean mother fucker, that's a technical term, and a lot of these MMF's as we call 'em tend to be spoilers which if there's somethin' they can't have, or they know they've already lost, why, they'll just go try and destroy as much as they can anyway, till it's over."

"But what if it keeps going?" inquired Prairie, "what if he hasn't 'lost'?"

"Oh, Prairie, you must've thought I was talking about your mom. . . . I'll admit, this is a lovelorn cop, OK, the worst kind of adversary 'cause there's no rules, no codes of behavior, all bets are off, gentleman goes on abusing his power and believin' it's all in the name of love, deputy sheriff with a longneck in front of him listenin' to Willie Nelson and struggling to hold in 'em tears, I understand that, but this is something else between men, it's about whoever's runnin' Brock thinking, What can I get him to do for me, what are his limits, and Brock thinking, I did this deed for him, it wasn't so bad, but what'll he ask me to do next? Maybe your mom's only in there to make it look normal and human so the boys can go on discreetly porkin' each other."

"DL," Ditzah announced, "have you picked up an attitude."

"Yeah, I had it figured a little more romantic than that myself, actually," Prairie said.

"Don't believe me, ask Takeshi — according to him, unless you can call on troops in regimental strength, and the hardware that goes with 'em, best not even think about messing with Brock. Ain't just that he's a monomaniac and a killer, but there's *nothing holding him back*. He's allowed to do anything you can imagine, and worse. Somehow it don't strike me as no Fred and Ginger. I think he's after Frenesi 'cause he's lookin' to use her for some task. Just like he used her to set Weed up, long ago. This is the lowest of the five classes of kunoichi — Yu Jen, or the Fool. Always surprised when she finds out who she's been working for."

"You think she'd be that surprised?" Prairie disconsolate.

"I never believed your mom ever sat down and deliberately chose anything. Same time, I always believed in her conscience. There were days when my personal ass was depending on that conscience. You don't just put that on Pause and walk away, sooner or later, when you don't expect it, it comes back on, hollerin' and blarin' at you."

"I'm not saying some people might not've found him cute back then," Prairie said, "but knowing what was at stake for all you guys, how could she?"

Ditzah cackled. "Cute!"

"I had enough trouble just accepting that she did it, I never figured out why. Just as well, it could've ate up my life. Maybe it did." So the bad Ninjamobile swept along on the great Ventura, among Olympic visitors from everywhere who teemed all over the freeway system in midday densities till far into the night, shined-up, screaming black motorcades that could have carried any of several office seekers, cruisers heading for treed and more gently roaring boulevards, huge double and triple trailer rigs that loved to find Volkswagens laboring up grades and go sashaying around them gracefully and at gnat's-ass tolerances, plus flirters, deserters, wimps and pimps, speeding like bullets, grinning like chimps, above the heads of TV watchers, lovers under the overpasses, movies at malls letting out, bright gas-station oases in pure fluorescent spill, canopied beneath the palm trees, soon wrapped, down the corridors of the surface streets, in nocturnal smog, the adobe air, the smell of distant fireworks, the spilled, the broken world.

WHEN had Brock ever possessed her? There might have been about a minute and a half, just after the events at College of the Surf, the death of Weed Atman, and the fall of PR³, though he was no longer sure. He remembered a morning drizzle, at first light, at the camp up north, pulling in in a motor-pool Mercedes with his partner, Roscoe, at the wheel, cruising past the cloudbeaten rows of barracks, stopping out on the asphalt, waiting in the cyan glare of the security lights. Officially he was up to have a look at the physical plant and inspect the population of his Political Re-Education Program, or PREP, Brock's own baby, his gamble on a career coup, his thin-ice special, just about to be put in as a rider to what would be the Crime Control Act of 1970 by a not-so-neo fascist congressman from Trasero County, a friend of friends in returning whose several kindnesses this solon had more than once found himself creeping within squinting range of the chain-link perimeters of Allenwood, Pa. But then again — Brock could get excited just thinking about it — suppose the gamble paid off. The law, *his* law, would provide that detainees in civil disturbances could be taken to certain Justice Department reserves and there examined for snitch potential. Those found suitable might then be offered a choice between federal prosecution and federal employment, as independent contractors working undercover for, but not out of, the DOJ's Political Intelligence Office. After undergoing a full training curriculum that included the use of various weapons, they could be transferred — the contracts essentially sold — to the FBI and under that control be infiltrated, often again and again, into college campuses, radical organizations, and other foci of domestic unrest. So that in addition to immunity from the law, another selling point for hiring on would turn out to be this casual granting of the wish implied in the classical postcollegiate Dream of Autumn Return, to one more semester, one more course credit required, another chance to be back in school again — yes, as long as it was paid for in services useful enough to them, the FBI could even put you on the time machine if that's what you wanted, is how heavy those coppers were even back in those days. Brock Vond's genius was to have seen in the activities of the sixties left not threats to order but unacknowledged desires for it. While the Tube was proclaiming youth revolution against parents of all kinds and most viewers were accepting this story, Brock saw the deep — if he'd allowed himself to feel it, the sometimes touching — need only to stay children forever, safe inside some extended national Family. The hunch he was betting on was that these kid rebels, being halfway there already, would be easy to turn and cheap to develop. They'd only been listening to the wrong music, breathing the wrong smoke, admiring the wrong personalities. They needed some reconditioning.

This morning at PREP, there would be no breakfast call — the mess hall wasn't yet up to speed, so only staff ate regularly, leaving the "guests," in endless negotiation, to eat as they could . . . as they did. Brock had not come to see that. He'd come for Morning Assembly, Morning Reports. Whether they would wake hungry, however they had slept, warm enough or not against these North Pacific fronts, the reveille on the PA would bring them outside . . . then he would see. What even he knew he'd really come for was the sight of Frenesi *among them,* the long-haired bodies, men who had grown feminine, women who had become small children, flurries of long naked limbs, little girls naked under boyfriends' fringe jackets, eyes turned down, away, never meeting those of their questioners, boys with hair over their shoulders, hair that kept getting in their eyes . . . the sort of mild herd creatures who belonged, who'd feel, let's face it, much more comfortable, behind fences. Children longing for discipline. Frenesi might not — short of torture, anyway — believe that he could ever imprison her. He knew she would try to keep guarded what she thought to be some inner freedom, go on imagining herself secure, still whole . . . but there he'd be, her inescapable witness, watching her in a context she couldn't deny — the rest of them, all she had for human company, as they were. Cold comfort for Brock Vond —

though back in the deep leather upholstery, with one eye on the "Today" show and an ear to the tactical frequencies patched to front and rear speakers, breathing the steam of his decaffeinated coffee, he wasn't all that surprised to find himself with a hardon.

Roscoe knew that this A.M. visit was confidential. So far, officially, with the enabling and money bills still making their way through Congress, this place didn't even exist. He could tell how nervous Brock was — the rearview mirror was full of furtive gestures. Here they were, him and the Hotshot, in DOJ transportation, on DOJ time, playing out one more of young Vond's confusing power-and-sex games, which he would have denied if Roscoe'd been fool enough to bring it up. Roscoe sure 's heck wouldn't be here himself if his time were his own, which it hadn't been since that fateful four in the morning the Internals had shown up all Kevlar and Plexiglas, and blacked gunmetal at the ready. "Fellas!" he tried to protest thickly through the last mouthful of free L.A. cheeseburger deluxe he would know for a while. "Jeez I know I'm bad but —" He wanted to quote the Shangri-Las and point out, "But I'm not evil," but had inhaled a piece of burger roll and started to cough instead.

Since he'd been with Brock, Roscoe had come to see himself not as sidekick so much as Cagey Old Pro, passing on all kinds of useful lore if the pup would ever bother to listen. These birds in this facility here, for instance — "Don't know," he'd muttered, "you've been out there on the line, seen these kids close up — some of 'em's in it for real, all right, and they're tough cookies, long hair and all. Never turn 'em — never trust 'em if you did."

"They'll get remanded someplace else — we always knew what to do with them. I'm counting on that other 90%, amateurs, consumers, short attention spans, out there for the thrills, pick up a chick, score some dope, nothing political. Out in the mainstream, Roscoe, that's where we fish."

No point in pursuing it when Brock could always shut him up by finding a way to remind Roscoe how much he would forever owe, but also because he'd let himself believe that young Vond was profound enough to interpret his silences, some of them eloquent as lectures. Brock, for his part, valued Roscoe's silences, all right, and the more of them the better. They were part of his conception of the perfect underling, whom he imagined as a sort of less voluble Tonto. And to the extent that he tried not to bother the Prosecutor with details of how, often semimiraculously, he got things done, it may also have been how Roscoe imagined it. Who, after all, besides teaching him every Indian piece of know-how, had saved the Lone Ranger's life?

Yet not even that ultimate favor had wiped out his debt to Brock, who once, exactly when it had swung the most weight, had intervened for him. The payback was to be in units of unconditional loyalty, including but not limited to lifesaving, one shift after another till retirement, with the question of his pension still up in the air, and with lawyers on both sides looking into it. Not only had he literally saved Brock's life, but more than once this job he knew he was lucky to have as well, making this unhappy phase of his own career out of covering the backside of Vond's. In that memorable dope-field shoot-out, Brock had followed Roscoe dumb and terrified as a recruit obeying his sergeant, through the dense resin smell, as a great nation pursued its war on a botanical species, rounds whinging and burring hotly by through shade leaves, breaking stems, knocking seeds out of *colas*, Brock following every move of Roscoe's stuck like a shadow, till they made it to the chopper and rose so swiftly, like a prayer to God, like a pigeon to the sky — "Roscoe," Brock Vond was babbling, "I owe you, oh boy do I, the very biggest one, the Big L itself, and maybe I don't always know when I do, but this time I swear —" Roscoe still breathing too hard to ask him to put it in writing. When he did speak, wheezing, it was to holler over the beat of the blades, "Feel like we been in a Movie of the Week!"

In the clarity of that crisis, at least, the Prosecutor had nailed it. He really didn't know always how much, or even when, he owed anybody. In their first days together Roscoe, mighty annoyed, had taken it for such snot-nosed ingratitude that he nearly decided to hell with it, he'd put in his papers and go find some security-consultant hustle, far from our nation's capital — who needed this? Only after more scrutiny did he find out how dirt-ignorant his boss actually remained, on quite a number of occasions, of real-world steps being taken on his behalf. It wasn't that Vond was following any moral code of his own, though he might have wanted it to look that way — but Roscoe recognized it as simple, massively protective insulation. Some things in life had just never touched this customer, he would never have to think about them — which could only give the kid an edge, but maybe not begin to account for Brock's supernatural luck, the aura that everybody, winners and losers, picked up, which Roscoe swore under oath he'd observed during that pot-plantation run-in as a pure white light surrounding Brock entirely, which Roscoe believed would keep him, then and after, immune to gunfire. Who had been sticking close to whom, that fragrant morning long ago?

Iron speakers up on stripped fir poles crashed alive with the national anthem. Brock got out of the car and stood, not at attention but leaning one elbow on the car roof, watching as one by one the detainees began to appear out on the assembly ground. They only came as close as they had to to make sure Brock wasn't bringing something to eat — then they withdrew into small clusters at the margins of the asphalt, speaking together, at this distance inaudible.

Brock scanned face after face, registering stigmata, a parade of receding foreheads, theromorphic ears, and alarmingly sloped Frankfurt Horizontals. He was a devotee of the thinking of pioneer criminologist Cesare Lombroso (1836–1909), who'd believed that the brains of criminals were short on lobes that controlled civilized values like morality and respect for the law, tending indeed to resemble animal more than human brains, and thus caused the crania that housed them to develop differently, which included the way their faces would turn out looking. Abnormally large eye sockets, prognathism, frontal submicrocephaly, Darwinian Tipped Ear, you name it, Lombroso had a list that went on, and skull data to back him up. By Brock's time the theory had lapsed into a quaint, undeniably racist spinoff from nineteenth-century phrenology, crude in method and long superseded, although it seemed reasonable to Brock. What really got his attention was the Lombrosian concept of "misoneism." Radicals, militants, revolutionaries, however they styled themselves, all sinned against this deep organic human principle, which Lombroso had named after the Greek for "hatred of anything new." It operated as a feedback device to keep societies coming along safely, coherently. Any sudden attempt to change things would be answered by an immediate misoneistic backlash, not only from the State but from the people themselves — Nixon's election in '68 seeming to Brock a perfect example of this.

Lombroso had divided all revolutionists into five groups, geniuses, enthusiasts, fools, rogues, and followers, which in Brock's experience about covered it, except for the unforeseen sixth, the one without a label Brock was waiting for, who at last came striding toward him now through the drizzle, a few pounds thinner, her hair full of snarls, barelegged, her camera taken away, no weapon of witness but her eyes. She stopped a few feet from him, he stared at the glistening of her thighs, as he moved closer she shivered, tried to cross her arms, hug herself into an invisible shawl or the memory of one she used to wear . . . but he was too close. He reached with one finger to lift her chin, force her to look at him. They faced each other in light from which all red was missing. She looked in his eyes, then at his penis — yep erect all right, creating pleats in the front of the pale federal trousers.

"Been thinking about you too," her voice ragged from a pack and a half of jailhouse smokes a day.

Smart mouth. One day he would order her down on her knees in front of all these cryptically staring children, put a pistol to her head, and give her something to do with her smart mouth. Each time he daydreamed about this, the pistol would reappear, as an essential term. But now, as his heartbeat picked up a little, he gave career advice instead. "How do you like our campus?" He waved around going mine-all-mine. "Full athletic program, chaplain's office with a minister, a priest, *and* a rabbi, maybe even a few rock concerts."

She started to laugh, coughed a while instead. "Your taste in music? It's outlawed by the Geneva convention. Not a selling point, Cap'n."

"Did you think we were negotiating?"

"I thought we were flirting, Brock. Guess it's one more disappointment I'll have to live with." She caught herself watching his cock again, then saw he was grinning at her, amorously, he must've thought. "The commandant here has my number. Don't delay, operators are standing by." He brought away his finger with a flip that sent her chin a half inch higher.

She breathed through her nose and glared at him. The politically correct answer would have been "When your mother stops giving head to stray dogs." Later she would think of others she might have used. But just then, when it could have still made a difference, she said nothing at all, only stood, head up, watching the old heartbreaker's ass till he'd taken it back inside the Germanic sedan. She had a vivid, half-second hallucination of Brock in the Oklahoma stormlight, the hard blued body, the unforgiving shore against which, on breaking waves whose power she felt but would never understand she had ridden, would ride, again and again. . . .

Roscoe started up the car. Watching the bedraggled girl in the stained miniskirt, he hit the gas pedal to make the engine sing in a rising, suggestive phrase. "Don't blow my effect here," Brock Vond leaning forward from the back, more than a little annoyed, "OK? All I need right now is one of your old-time comedy routines, to undo all the work I just did out there. Trying to destabilize the subject, not serenade her."

"Only to let 'em know we've been here's all," muttered Roscoe, hooking a U and peeling away, halfway to the gate getting into a skid, leaving behind a set of big S's that remained awhile on the wet blacktop.

A provincial whiz kid called early, brass choirs on the sound track, to power in the white mother city, where he would become, as he had dreamed, the careful product of older men, Brock, of medium height, slender and fair-haired, carried with him a watchful, never quite trustworthy companion personality, feminine, underdeveloped, against whom his male version, supposedly running the unit, had to be equally vigilant. In dreams he could not control, in which lucid intervention was impossible, dreams that couldn't be denatured by drugs or alcohol, he was visited by his uneasy anima in a number of guises, notably as the Madwoman in the Attic. Brock would be moving through rooms of a large, splendid house belonging to people so rich and powerful he'd never even seen them. But while they allowed him to stay there, it was his job to make sure that all doors and windows, dozens of them everywhere, were secure, and that no one, nothing, had penetrated. This had to be done every day, and finished with before nightfall. Every closet and corner, every back staircase and distant storeroom, had to be checked, till at last there was only the attic left to do. The day would have grown, by then, quite late, the light almost gone. It was that phase of twilight, full of anxiety, when mercy in this world and the others is apt to be least available. Energies were on the loose, masses could materialize. He climbed the attic stairs in the dusk, paused in front of the door. He could hear her breathing, waiting for him — helplessly he opened, entered, as she advanced on him, blurry, underlit, except for the glittering eyes, the relentless animal smile, and accelerating leapt at him, on him, and underneath her assault he died, rising to wake into his own rooms, the counterpane white and neatly folded as butcher's paper around a purchase of meat — face up, rigid, sweating, shaken by each heartbeat.

Out in the waking world, of course, he was an entirely different fellow, so thoroughly personable, in fact, that maintaining even dislike for the Prosecutor was always a chore, even for the criminal degenerates he helped put away. He projected a charm that appeared to transcend politics, and was known both inside the Beltway and out in the field as a sought-after raconteur and bon vivant who appreciated fine distinctions in food, wine, music. Women found him intensely appealing for reasons they later could or would not specify. Colorful little third-world grandmothers tending flower stalls on forlorn city street corners would rush to embrace him and present, curtsying, bunches of violets to Brock's invariably impressed dates, usually beautiful high-fashion packages to the memory of whose merest peripheral appearance in the street that day any number of men would already have rushed back into some kind of privacy to masturbate as quickly as possible, without asking too many questions.

Well, what a life, you'd ordinarily say. But Brock coveted more.

He'd caught a fatal glimpse of that level where everybody knew everybody else, where however political fortunes below might bloom and die, the same people, the Real Ones, remained year in and year out, keeping what was desirable flowing their way. Prosecutor Vond wanted a life there, only slowly coming to understand that for someone of his background there would be no route to this but self-abasement, fawning, gofering, scrambling for tips and offering other such hints of his eagerness to be brevetted on life's battlefield to a rank higher than he would ever, by the terms of his enlistment, have deserved. Though his defects of character were many, none was quite as annoying as this naked itch to be a gentleman, kept inflamed by a stubborn denial of what everyone else knew — that no matter how much money he made, how many political offices or course credits from charm school might come his way, no one of those among whom he wished to belong would ever regard him as other than a thug whose services had been hired.

But Brock didn't feel like any thug or, more important, look like one either. Whenever he shaved, the humming small life solid in his hand, what he saw was Lombrosian evidence of a career plausibly honest enough to sell his ideas, his beliefs, to anybody, at any level. And the same went for his body image, Brock in those days being known as something of a recreational-area Don Juan, for whom sport and sex were naturally connected. Over time he had learned to extend his Lombrosian analysis from faces to bodies, and discovered that there were such things as criminal bodies. He would see them often in his line of work and would also, less consciously, look for signs of transgressor status in women he met and even desired, the guilty droop of head, the bestial turn of an ass-cheek, the spine furtively overflexed. Some of these women turned out to be "great fucks," as Brock later described them, mainly for the sake of his reputation, because secretly, though he enjoyed and even got obsessed about sex, he was also — imagine — scared to death of it. In nightmares he was forced to procreate with women who approached never from floor or ground level but from steep overhead angles, as if from someplace not on the surface of Earth, feeling nothing erotic but only, each time it was done, a terrible sadness, violation . . . something taken away. He understood, in some way impossible to face, that each child he thus produced, each birth, would be only another death for him. When news of Frenesi's escape from PREP reached him back in the great marble plexus, Brock went right around the bend — flew back to L.A., came storming into the fortress at Westwood with this out-of-control mind-hardon, and for a brief time acted like a terrorist holding the place hostage. Nobody knew anything. At that point they were all running around trying to manage the public-relations overtime arising from his "success" at College of the Surf. All the files on the 24fps film collective, including Frenesi's, seemed to be temporarily out of the building. The case was no longer Brock's, and he couldn't find out whose it was. By the time he might have, he'd driven himself past exhaustion, adrift in the unsleeping clockless iterations of some hotel near the airport, where men in wrinkled suits, jet-lagged and aimless, populated the corridors and the uproar in the sky never took a break. He cried, he beat himself with his fists on head and body, did all that old stuff, feeling like a skier on an unfamiliar black-diamond slope, seized by gravity, in control, out of control . . . this descent took him all night and wore him at last into unconsciousness. On the plane back to Washington, the little girl he sat down next to got one look at his face and started screaming. "He's gonna molest me, Mom! We're all gonna die!" Brock, croaking something about being a U.S. Attorney, went fumbling for his ID, though some onlookers thought it was for a weapon and began wailing and crossing themselves. The plane wasn't even moving yet. Too depressed to believe he had anything to lose, Brock doggedly proceeded to bully flight attendants and crew into ejecting the little girl and her mother from the airplane. "Snotty bitch," he whispered as, trembling, the child arose and had to slide the backs of her thighs past his knees.

In Washington again, scrambling to explain his behavior and protect his back, Brock really might have had no time to track Frenesi down, as he told it later, but it didn't stop him having fantasies about her. Pretty soon he was jerking off every night to images he remembered of her, lying in bed, sitting on the toilet, walking down the street, on top and bottom, dressed and naked, Brock lying all alone in the air-conditioning on a rented psyche-delic-print sofa in his new apartment out on Wisconsin, in the sullen Tubeflicker, straining into his past, feeling the pressure of tears he was confident would never come. It wasn't that things weren't fine on the job, the compartments in his brain were all Frenesi-tight as far as work went, though now and then lust's drowsy watchman left a latch open, usually around the full moon, when he'd find himself heading down to Dupont Circle and other gathering spots of the young and uncritical, trying to mingle with the hippies, blacks, and drug abusers, to put up as sportingly as he could with their music and closeness, looking for strong slender legs, a fine rain of hair, with luck, fatally, those eyes of Pacific blue, hoping in light cooperative enough to find a girl to project Frenesi's ghost onto, someone who'd hand him a flower, offer a joint — groovy! — agree to be led back here, to this come-stained couch, and be taken, and —

Brock, Brock, get a grip on yourself! But some other adviser lay coiled in ancient shadow, whispering *Kick loose*. Brock knew how much he wanted to, feared what would happen if he couldn't contain the impulse. Once, not too many years ago, sober, wide awake, he'd begun to laugh at something on the Tube. Instead of reaching a peak and then tapering off, the laughter got more intense each time he breathed, diverging toward some brain state he couldn't imagine, filling and flooding him, his head taken and propelled by a supernatural lightness, on some course unaccounted for by the usual three dimensions. He was terrified. He glimpsed his brain about to turn inside out like a sock but not what would happen after that. At some point he threw up, broke some cycle, and that, as he came to see it, was what "saved" him — some component of his personality in charge of nausea. Brock welcomed it as a major discovery about himself — an unsuspected control he could trust now to keep him safe from whatever his laughter had nearly overflowed him into. He was careful from then on not to start laughing so easily. All around him in those days he was watching people his age surrendering to dangerous gusts of amusement, even deciding never to return to regular jobs and lives. Colleagues grew their hair long and ran off with adolescents of the same sex to work on psychedelic-mushroom ranches on far-away coasts. Stalls in the glass-block and travertine toilets of the Justice Department itself boomed and echoed with Pink Floyd and Jimi Hendrix. Everywhere Brock looked he saw defects of control — while others, in their turn, were not so sure about Brock.

Internal review boards within Justice had had him under surveillance at least since his early gypsy jury days, when he was spreading around the smart-assed charisma on local TV news, call-in radio shows, and speaking engagements before "private" groups in the banquet rooms of suburban eateries known for forms of red meat. When Frenesi came into the picture, interest perked up. Here was entertainment — a federal prosecutor carrying the torch for some third-generation lefty who'd likely've bombed the Statue of Liberty if she could. Weeks' salaries were wagered and lost over how long Brock could hold on to his job, with the over-under line usually reckoning his longevity in days. Brought in, at length, for the Basic Little Chat, he was exactly as forthcoming as he knew he needed to be to quiet the Board, but not a word beyond. If inside a certain radius all lay camouflaged and deeply fortified, nonetheless he did deny her, joked about her with his interrogators, about her tits, her pussy, refusing to react, to seem to defend her. "Next time, Brock, just come on in, let us know, we can punch you up anything you want, you like radical snatch, hey, no problem, bro." He got crazy enough once in a while to take them up on it. They offered a wide choice of sizes, colors, and ages, not to mention neo-Lombrosian face and body types. But he chose women most likely from their files to have crossed paths with Frenesi, living for the off chance of finding her name tucked casually into small talk over drinks. With a patience and gentleness that cost him, Brock tried to steer the dialogue always toward that one dim star.

Still, eyes were upon him, and if he'd actively initiated any search after the Gates woman's whereabouts, most easily through her mother in L.A., a longtime Person of Interest, Brock's overseers would have known about it immediately, and what the memos

referred to as a fecoventilatory collision might very well have en-
sued. It was the old, unhappy tale, Brock would insist, of romance
versus career. He didn't want to choose and so he temporized,
pursuing his PREP master plan, clearing the brush and leveling
the lots. By the time things were solidly enough in place and he
could finally get back to California for an extended season of
mischief, the ache was no worse than a Beltway sinus, the lunar
prowls among the hippies had all but ceased, and sometimes a
week would go by in which he only took hold of his penis for
pissing.

In the year that had elapsed, Frenesi had met and married Zoyd
and given birth to Prairie, none of which Brock had known about,
none of which she volunteered when at last they were face-to-face
again. The year before in Las Suegras, standing at the edge of a
gas-station apron watching DL in the Camaro ascend to the freeway and vanish, rolling blind into her own future, Frenesi had
considered calling Brock, going back into PREP. There was no
way back to 24fps, or to the person she'd been — beyond any way
to clear it she had set up Weed's murder and was in the federal
law-enforcement files now and forever, shared with every last amateur cop groupie in the land, listed as a species her parents had
taught her to despise — a Cooperative Person.

"It's what you want, isn't it?" the dark apparition of Brock
Vond questioned her from continental distance. " 'Forever,' isn't
that supposed to be as romantic as it gets? Well, we can provide
you with Forever, no sweat. What DOJ promises, we deliver." Did
he know what she wanted? Even have any right to say he did?
Just because she didn't? As night fell, she'd wandered down to
Phil's Cottonwood Oasis, which was a tavern with a motel in
back, beside a darkening green piece of creek-bank crowded with
Fremont cottonwoods, with a dance deck built out over the creek.
She sat in front of a beer bottle and a glass and couldn't focus on
anything, while twilight drinkers technically on the way home
came drifting in, and motel occupants looking for supper, some
famished, some quarreling, and then the Corvairs, billing themselves here as the Surfadelics.

As standard practice, just to get it over with, the band started off the set with "Louie Louie" and "Wooly Bully," whether or not anybody wanted to hear these traditional favorites. By then Zoyd, in those days a generic longhair with a Zappa mustache and wire-rimmed yellow shooting glasses, casing the room, had spotted Frenesi, called one of his own compositions, taken the mike and the vocal.

> Whoo! is this the start of a
> Cheap ro-mance,
> Nothin' much to do with
> High fi-nance,
> Is it th' start of,
> Another cheap ro-mance?

(Here Scott Oof, as he had for thousands of identical renditions, filled with a phrase stolen from Mickey Baker on "Love Is Strange" [1956].)

> This hot tomato's lookin'
> Mighty sweet,
> Uh just th' thing to git me,
> Off my feet,
> Oboy, the start of,
> Another cheap ro-ho-mance!
>
> Yep — looks like the start of
> Another cheap ro-ho-
> Ma-a-a-ance . . .
> Gits ya thinkin', is it
> Me, or is it mah
> Pa-a-a-hants?
>
> Well cheap romance is my
> Kind of thing,
> Uh just in case you were
> Wondering,
> "Is it the start of,
> Another cheap ro-wo-mance?"

"*That's* what made her fall in love at first sight?" Prairie inquired, years later, when Zoyd told her.

"Well, that and my good looks," said Zoyd. But when

everything was coming apart he'd also screamed at Frenesi, "It could've been anybody, Scott, the two junkie saxophone players, all's you was lookin' for was some quick cover."

The baby slept on silently in the other room. Frenesi had been watching Zoyd for weeks as he clumsily pieced the story together. She could have helped but was hoping, by then naively, that he'd take a false turn, come out with a version where she'd look a little better, caring less about his opinion, finally, than about her mother's. Zoyd, anyway, didn't oblige — just kept stumbling and bullying, missing details but getting it basically, mercilessly right, Brock, Weed, Brock's return, all of it, allowing her no pathways to safety.

Though to the romantically inclined observer it might seem like Brock had come looking for her, at least had included finding her on his list of chores during his West Coast visit, Frenesi had been making it as easy for him as she could, spending more time than she normally would have over at Sasha's on the assumption that the same surveillance she remembered growing up with, the creepy twitching highlights off camera lenses, the threatening forms and sounds at night, all was again in place, and that she would be seen, and seen by him. And that sooner or later he would come and get her.

She moved into the house at Gordita Beach as "Zoyd's chick," then "Zoyd's old lady." Pregnant with Prairie, she sat with a few other young women in the band's social orbit out on the screened deck of the house, facing the sea, spending sometimes whole days together, drinking from earthen mugs infusions of herbs thought to promote higher mind/body states, listening to KHJ and KFWB, ice plant in bloom spilling down to the white beach, sea breezes swirling in through the screens. The line of girls' eyes gazing in a locus of attention fixed at the horizon . . . in her second trimester she fell into UFO reveries, saw them clearly any number of times, though she got teased, popping in and out of the sky-blue Rayleigh scattering as if through a perfectly elastic sheet, advance units for some other force, some pitiless advent. Meanwhile, landward, back up the long built-over dunes, across the coastal highway, the great Basin, intoxicated, traffic-infested, shadow-obsessed, extravagantly watered and irradiated, drew Zoyd away from the beaches

he was musically supposed to be representing, out on restless com-
mutes as long as working hours into thickest billowings of smog
soup, roof and gutter work during the day, Corvairs gigs at night,
in smaller clubs and bars from Laguna to La Puente. It happened
to be the ripe, or baroque, phase of L.A.'s relations with rock and
roll, which had swept in on what to Zoyd, with his surfer's eye,
judged to be a twenty-year cycle — movies back in the twenties,
radio in the forties, now records in the sixties. For one demented
season the town lost its ear, and talent was signed that in other
times would have kept on wandering in the desert, and in what
oases they found, playing toilets. On the assumption that Youth
understood its own market, entry-level folks who only yesterday
had been content to deal lids down in the mail room were suddenly
being elevated to executive rank, given stupendous budgets, and
let loose, as it turned out, to sign just about anybody who could
carry a tune and figure out how to walk in the door. Stunned by
the great childward surge, critical abilities lapsed. Who knew the
worth of any product, or could live with having failed to sign the
next superstar? Crazed, heedless, the business was running on pure
nerve, with million-dollar deals struck on the basis of dreams,
vibes, or, in the Corvairs' case, minor hallucination. Scott Oof had
somehow hustled the band a species of recording contract with
Indolent Records, an up-and-coming though bafflingly eclectic
Hollywood label, and the day they came in to sign the papers, the
head of A & R, not yet out of high school, having just made the
mental acquaintance of some purple acid with a bat shape em-
bossed on it, greeted them with unusual warmth, believing them,
as it developed, to be visitors from another dimension who, after
observing him for years, had decided to materialize as a rock and
roll band and make him rich and famous. By the time they left,
the Corvairs were believing it too, although they had to take the
standard contract of the day just the same, further clauses being
impossible to get, written as they would have had to be in some
human language, a medium for the moment inaccessible to the by
now audibly vibrating department head ("Department *head!*" he
screamed, "everybody around here's a department . . . *head!* Ha!
Ha! Ha!").

As the weeks rolled along like less than perfect waves and the weekly tear-off options went crumpling one by one with no album commitment from Indolent, not exactly gloom, but a sort of dimmed calm, took over. After all, the Corvairs were working pretty steadily, getting a reputation as a bar band if not as a "Surfadelic" one. Dutifully, they did keep setting aside time to drop acid together at inspiring day and night locales around the Southland, but nothing much ever happened for them, nothing coordinated anyway, Van Meter's reliving of an earlier life as a buffalo roaming the plains in a herd the size of a Western state seeming to have little in common with Scott's delight in the omnicolored streams of cartoon figures that liked to issue from his fingertips. Lefty the drummer had nightmare sessions full of snakes, decomposing flesh, and easy-listening music tracks, the sax players, both fond of heroin, often dematerialized someplace, perhaps to inject their drug of choice, though perhaps not, while Zoyd kept going through endless tangled scenarios with a luminously remote Frenesi, Frenesi his life sentence, she who could make him forget even the eye-catching production values of LSD.

And who meanwhile waited, watched the aliens' steel horizon, or borrowed people's cars to drive in and visit with Sasha, out in the little patio in back, drinking diet sodas and picking at salads. From the beginning Frenesi tried to get her mother asking the questions it would hurt most to answer. DL's name came up right away. Frenesi said, "She's gone. I don't know. . . ." Sasha sent her a look and, "You two were so close . . . ," but soon they were back to the unavoidable subject of the baby on her way.

"You can always stay here, you know, there's nothing but room." The first time this happened, Frenesi semideclined, "Oh, Zoyd might not go for that." To which Sasha nodded, "Great. I wasn't asking him." Later adding, "Time marches along, and I hope you don't intend to have the baby at the beach."

"I wanted her to hear the surf."

"If it's positive vibrations you want, how about your old bedroom? A little continuity. Not to mention comfort."

Frenesi hated to admit that her mother had a point. When she brought it up with Zoyd, he nodded, bleakly. "Your mom hates me."

"No, c'mon Zoyd, she doesn't really *hate* you. . . ."

"She said 'hippie psychopath,' didn't she?"

"Sure, that night you were trying to run us over, but —"

"I was tryin' to get the fuckin' thing in Park, darlin', it jumped into Drive by itself, 't's what the recall was all about, 'member I showed you in the paper —"

"But, your screaming and stuff, she must have thought it was on purpose. And she could've called you worse than that."

Zoyd sulked. "Yeah? How come she don't even walk us out to the car anymore?" But though a few seconds might remain on the clock here, Zoyd knew the game was over and the women would prevail, the only question being, would they allow him in Sasha's house to see his own kid get born?

Of course they would and so it came to pass, one sweet May evening, with mockingbirds singing up and down the street, that Prairie's slick head came squeezing into this world, Sasha holding tight to her daughter's hands, Leonard the midwife easing the rest of the baby on through, and Zoyd, who at the last minute had dropped just a quarter of a tab of acid on the chance of glimpsing something cosmic that might tell him he wouldn't die, gazing mind-blown at the newborn Prairie, one of her eyes plastered shut and the other rolling around wild, which he took to be a deliberate wink, the lambent faces of the women, the paisley patterns on Leonard's Nehru shirt, the colors of the afterbirth, the baby with both eyes open now looking right at him with a vast, an unmistakable, recognition. Later people told him it wasn't personal, and newborns don't see much, but at the moment, oh God, God, she knew him, *from someplace else.* And these acid adventures, they came in those days and they went, some we gave away and forgot, others sad to say turned out to be fugitive or false — but with luck one or two would get saved to go back to at certain later moments in life. This look from brand-new Prairie — oh, you, huh? — would be there for Zoyd more than once in years to come, to help him through those times when the Klingons are closing, and the helm won't answer, and the warp engine's out of control.

What no one acknowledged — certainly not Zoyd in his cheery haze of paternity, less certainly Sasha — was how deeply, for an unbearable day and then the weekend, Frenesi was depressed. No amnesia, no kind leaching bath of time would ever take from her memories of descent to cold regions of hatred for the tiny life, raw, parasitic, using her body through the wearying months and now still looking to control her . . . there were no talk shows back in those days, no self-help networks or toll-free numbers to learn anything from or ask for help. She didn't, so surrendered to her dark fall, even know she needed help. The baby went along on its own program, robbing her of milk and sleep, acknowledging her only as a host. Where was the clean new soul, the true love, her own promised leap into grown-up reality? She felt betrayed, emptied out, watching herself, this beaten animal, only just hanging on, waiting for everything to end. One 3:00 A.M., in front of the Lobster Trick Movie, Sasha rocking the baby, Frenesi in a slow tuned throb, breasts in torment, bathing in Tubelight, whispered, "You'd better keep her out of my way, Mom. . . ."

"Frenesi?"

"I mean it —" oh fuck, why bother? lurching toward the bathroom, taken over by a rising hoarse groan that broke into such terrible spasms of crying that Sasha was unable to move, could only remain holding the sleeping Prairie while her daughter wrenched out tile-echoed sobs painfully into the world one by one . . . was the baby getting this primally unhappy message by ESP link, and how, Sasha wondered, did you throw yourself between them, absorb the assault? She cried, "Oh, Punkin . . . please, no, it'll get better, you'll see . . . ," waiting for Frenesi to answer, answer anything. She thought of what was available in the bathroom, and all the ways Frenesi could do herself harm in there. About the time she put down the baby and started in, Frenesi came back, took her mother by one wrist and in a voice Sasha had never heard, ordered, "Just — get her the fuck out of here." Her blue eyes, with this precise placement of room lamps, gathering most of the light, eyes so long loved, glaring now, savage with a foreglimpse of some rush into fate, something shadowless and ultimate.

It was in those hours of hallucinating and defeat that Frenesi had felt Brock closer to her, more necessary, than ever. With his own private horrors further unfolded into an ideology of the mortal and uncontinued self, Brock came to visit, and strangely to comfort, in the half-lit hallways of the night, leaning darkly in above her like any of the sleek raptors that decorate fascist architecture. Whispering, "This is just how they want you, an animal, a bitch with swollen udders lying in the dirt, blank-faced, surrendered, reduced to this meat, these smells. . . ." Taken down, she understood, from all the silver and light she'd known and been, brought back to the world like silver recalled grain by grain from the Invisible to form images of what then went on to grow old, go away, get broken or contaminated. She had been privileged to live outside of Time, to enter and leave at will, looting and manipulating, weightless, invisible. Now Time had claimed her again, put her under house arrest, taken her passport away. Only an animal with a full set of pain receptors after all.

An awkward time for any more men to be showing up, but not long before breakfast, who of all people should arrive in a taxi lit up like a canteen truck but Hubbell Gates, who'd received word of his new grandchild over the phone from Zoyd, at the opening of a discount furniture store outside Sacramento, just as he was cracking apart the first white-flame carbons of the evening into sky-drilling beams of pure arc light. The band hired for the occasion struck up the Gershwins' "Of Thee I Sing (Baby)," and that was how Hub entered grandfatherhood, among the twinkling spinners and national bunting, the upbeat music, with Sno-Cone and hot-dog stands and kids bouncing on the king-size waterbeds out in the lot, and his own fleet of photon projectors aimed at the purple sky, calling out across the miles of great valley to wage-earning families snug at the table and restless cruisers out on old 99 alike, here we are, forget the night falling and come on over, have a look, TV, stereo and appliances too, no cosigners or credit references, just your own honest face . . . one of those evenings when everything felt in harmony, at ease, and how long'd it been since that had happened? So Hub decided, "Heck with it, history can go on Pause for a little while," and, leaving the spotlights and trailer rigs to his crew, Dmitri and Ace, hopped a complicated system of buses local and intercity, ending up long after midnight at a phone booth way out in Hacienda Heights, where he was obliged to go through a legal-history check before the taxi would consent to charge him an arm and a leg to get here, hence the late, or did he mean early, hour. . . .

Instead of "Just what I need" or "Oh, you," Sasha greeted him with an uncustomary embrace, sighing, clumsy. "Hi there, Hubbell, we've got trouble."

"Huh? Not the baby —"

"Frenesi." Sasha told him what she'd seen. "All I could do was keep her company, but I've got to get some sleep."

"Where's 'at Zoyd at?"

"He clocked out as soon as the kid was born, probably off on one of the lesser-known planets by now."

"Don't know if I'm any Dr. Spock." He gave her a gentlemanly wink and, following close, a pat on the ass as she crept in on aching feet to collect the baby and keep her from Frenesi.

"Mind if I have a look at this kid?" The minute Hub was in range he got a bleary half a smile. "Oh, come on," he whispered, "I know better 'n that. That's no smile. No. That's no smile."

Frenesi was curled in her old bed, curtains drawn against the night street. "Hi, Pop." Well, Jesus, she did look awful . . . almost a different person. . . . Hub's idea of therapy, which he kept trying out on others, was just to sit down and start complaining about his own life. Though he had never known his daughter this defenseless, hurt, grimly he began with a pretty generic tale of woe, not expecting much, but as he went on, sure enough, he could feel her start to calm down. He tried to drone steadily, not cause any reactions plus or minus. It became a monologue he had already recited more than once since the first separation, to seatmates on the bus, to dogs in the yard, to himself in front of the Tube at night. "What it was, 's your mother lost her respect for me. She'd be too honorable to say it, but that was it. She'd think these things all the way through, politically, but I'd only be trying to get out of the day in one piece. I was never the brave Wobbly her father was. Jess stood up, and he was struck down for it, and there was all of American History 101 for her, right there. How the hell was I gonna measure up? I thought I was doing what was necessary for my wife and my baby, freedom didn't come into it the way it did for Sasha, your grandpa understood that taking 'free' as far as you can usually leads to 'dead,' but he was never afraid of that, and I was, 'cause they can drop a Brute 450 on you just as easy as a tree. . . ." Not that he hadn't taken a hit or two, beginning the first day he reported to the Warner studio and found out there was a strike on and his "job" was to be one of a thousand IATSE goons hired to break it. Turned out they were looking for a larger, meaner type of individual anyway, but Hub just stood there for a while, bewildered, shaking his head — he'd thought he was fight-ing World War II to keep just this from happening to the world. Fuck it, he concluded, and went around the corner and across the street and asked if he could join the pickets, even if he wasn't working there, and before he knew it he'd been hit literally with a bolt from the sky, a lag bolt about the size and weight of the bar a steel guitar player uses, which Hub in his time had also been a target of, thrown by one of the IA gents deployed up on the roofs of the sound stages. It knocked him silly but also informed him that he'd made the right choice, though it was Sasha who was to become entangled in the fine details of the politics in the town at the time. The struggle between the IATSE, a creature of orga-nized crime in collusion with the studios, and Herb Sorrell's Con-ference of Studio Unions, unapologetically liberal, progressive, New Deal, socialist, and thus, in the toxic political situation, "Communist," had been going on all through the war but now broke into the open in a series of violent strike actions against the studios. All the newspapers pretended it was an organizing dispute between two unions. In fact it was the dark recrudescence of that hard-cased antiunion tradition which had brought the movie busi-ness to California in the first place, where it had gone on to enjoy till only recently its free ride on the backs of cheap labor. The minute this was threatened, in came the studio-created scab locals of IATSE and their soldiers, often in battalion strength. And the outcome was foredoomed, because of the blacklist. In one of Amer-ican misoneism's most notable hours, a complex system of accu-sation, judgment, and disposition, administered by figures like Roy Brewer of IATSE and Ronald Reagan of the Screen Actors Guild, controlled the working lives of everyone in the industry who'd

ever taken a step leftward of registering to vote as a Democrat.
For technical people, rehabilitation was straightforward — join
the IA, renounce the CSU. But Hub, stubborn, not yet grown out
of his wartime patriotism, stuck with the losers till the end —
without analysis, but less forgivably naive, he assumed everybody
else saw the world as clearly as he did, and so was apt to make
remarks out loud that others would either take issue with or else
keep silent at, pretending not to differ but later entering a transcript
into a dossier someplace. Each time a call wasn't answered or a
story got back to him about how somebody had named him to
yet another kangaroo jury board, a small hurt look came on his
face, suddenly a kid's again, thinking, No, it isn't supposed to be
this way. . . .

And they'd started off such happy-go-lucky kids, driving down
to Hollywood, Sasha at the wheel, Hub with a uke from Hawaii
singing "Down Among the Sheltering Palms" to Frenesi the baby
between them, wearing one of the crateful of Hawaiian shirts he'd
brought back from Pearl, sleeves just the right length for a colorful
baby outfit, and easy to wash and hang-dry too. The Hollywood
Freeway was brand-new, some evenings they'd go out just for a
spin, city lights flowing and checking along chrome stripes and
wax jobs, passing back and forth a Benzedrine inhaler nose to
nose and singing bop tunes like "Crazeology" and "Klacto-
veedsedsteen" to each other, switching off sax and trumpet parts.
They were living in Wade and Dotty's garage — the L.A. housing
shortage had people out in trailers and tents, and on the beach
too — spending nights at the Finale Club on South San Pedro in
what had been Little Tokyo before the residents were all shipped
off to detention camps, and listening to Bird, Miles, Dizzy, and
everybody else then on the Coast, under the low metal ceiling
among all the boppers, reefers, goatees, and porkpie hats. The
world was being born again. The war had decided that, hadn't it?
Even Sasha found herself looking at Hub a little gaga for what it
seemed he'd done, gone out day after day to fire hoses and tear
gas, saps, chains, and pieces of cable, hit, arrested, Sasha up all
night bailing him out, working when he could, still trying to apprentice as a gaffer, repairing table lamps and toasters on the side,

finding jobs at the margin, beyond the official reach of the anti-communist machine, giving and taking kindnesses, off the books, studying under ancient electricians, masters whose hands, especially about the thumbs, had been blitzed and scarred solid from the years of testing line current and ignoring wattage ratings, who'd saved his life many times over by teaching him how to work with one hand in his pocket so he wouldn't ground himself. "But that was just my problem, according to your mother, I'd always, in some political way that was a bit deep for me, had one hand in my pocket and not out there doing the world's work, implying o' course that if I wasn't greedily counting my spare change over and over, why then I was selfishly enjoying a quiet round of pocket pool, ask your husband what that means, it's sorta technical . . . it wasn't her fault she wanted me purer than I was. And then the other life was happening, the work itself . . . it was just when the Brute was first coming in. Jesus, all those amps. All that light. Nobody told me about the scale of it. After a while I couldn't see that much else. I needed to work with that light. Maybe it was some form of insanity, except that lets me off too easy. Then there was Wade, my ol' canasta partner and picket-line buddy, fighting shoulder to shoulder all those years, one day he went over, and we stayed friends, and finally you saw what'd it matter who'd be taking those dues off the paycheck, Al Speede's people, th' IATSE, whatever. It'd been over for a long time anyway, though we'd had to pretend otherwise, and what was it for, all those sets we lit, those exotic nightclub sets, the hotel rooms with the neon outside, the passenger coaches with the rain against the windows, all of it just shadows, even if it's on safety stock in some air-conditioned vault that's still all it is, I let the world slip away, made my shameful peace, joined the IA, retired soon's I could, sold off my only real fortune — my precious anger — for a lot of got-damn shadows."

He gazed at the young woman lying face up now, her eyes shut, at first glance a simple fine-featured long-haired beauty, though a closer look would reveal, not so much in the eyes as around her mouth and jaw, a darkness of expression, a held secret Hub knew he wouldn't be asked to share. "Hey there, Young Gaffer?" he whispered, to see if she was asleep. No answer. "Well I'd've called you my Best Girl," he went on, "but that was always your mother."

Frenesi's tears would slow and dry, her postpartum lust for death would cool, she would on a day not far off actually find herself liking this infant with the offbeat sense of humor, and she and Sasha would take up, not as before, but maybe no worse than before. But there were still the secrets, Trasero County and Oklahoma secrets. More than any man she had ever wanted for anything, more than a full pardon from some unnamed agency for what she'd done, more than DL in her arms, the State in final rubble, guns silent, tanks and bombs all melted down, more than anything she'd ever wished for over a lifelong childhood of praying to a variety of Santas, Frenesi wanted, would have given up all the rest for, a chance to go back to when she and Sasha had talked hours, nights, with no restraints, everything from penis folklore to Mom, where do we go when we die? Of all her turnings, this turn against Sasha her once-connected self would remain a puzzle she would never quite solve, a mystery beyond any analysis she could bring to it. If her luck held, she'd never have to know. The baby was perfect cover, it made her something else, a mom, that was all, just another mom in the nation of moms, and all she'd ever have to do to be safe was stay inside that particular fate, bring up the kid, grow into some version of Sasha, deal with Zoyd and his footloose band and all the drawbacks there, forget Brock, the siege, Weed Atman's blood, 24fps and the old sweet community, forget whoever she'd been, shoot inoffensive little home movies now and then, speak the right lines, stay within budget, wrap each day, one by one, before she lost the light. Prairie could be her guaranteed salvation, pretending to be Prairie's mom the worst lie, the basest betrayal. By the time she began to see that she might, nonetheless, have gone through with it, Brock Vond had reentered the picture, at the head of a small motorcade of unmarked Buicks, forcing her over near Pico and Fairfax, ordering her up against her car, kicking apart her legs and frisking her himself, and before she knew it there they were in another motel room, after a while her visits to Sasha dropped off and when she made them she came in reeking with Vond sweat, Vond semen — couldn't Sasha *smell* what was going on? — and his erect penis had become the joystick with which, hurtling into the future, she would keep trying to steer among the hazards and obstacles, the swooping monsters and alien projectiles of each game she would come, year by year, to stand before, once again out long after curfew, calls home forgotten, supply of coins dwindling, leaning over the bright display among the back aisles of a forbidden arcade, rows of other players silent, unnoticed, closing time never announced, playing for nothing but the score itself, the row of numbers, a chance of entering her initials among those of other strangers for a brief time, no longer the time the world observed but game time, underground time, time that could take her nowhere outside its own tight and falsely deathless perimeter.

BUT when he found out about Prairie — though he never named her, only smirked "So you've reproduced" at Frenesi — something else, something from his nightmares of forced procreation, must have taken over, because later, in what could only be crippled judgment, Brock was to turn and go after the baby and, noticing Zoyd in the way, arrange for his removal too. One mild overcast Saturday nearly a year after Frenesi had moved out, Zoyd and Prairie, returning from a midday stroll down the alley to the Gordita Pier and back, found inside their house who but Hector, posed dramatically in the front room next to the biggest block of pressed marijuana Zoyd had ever seen in his life, too big to have fit through any door yet towering there, mysteriously, a shaggy monolithic slab reaching almost to the ceiling. " 'Scuse me just a second." Finger to his lips, Zoyd went and put his daughter, who'd nodded out in the salt breezes, down on the bed in the other room, and her bottle and her duck nearby, and came back in eyeballing the oversize brick, getting nervous.

"Let me guess — *2001: A Space Odyssey* [1968]."

"Try *20,000 Years in Sing Sing* [1933]."

Zoyd lounged against the giant slab, needing the support. "Wa'n't even your idea, was it?"

"Somebody over in Westwood really hates your ass, pardner."

Zoyd rolled his eyes slowly toward the room where Prairie slept, waited a beat, then rolled them back. "Know this dude from Justice name of Brock Vond?"

Shrugging, "Maybe seen the name on some DEA 6?"

"I know about him and my ex-old lady, Hector, so don't be embarrassed."

"None of my business, and my policy is, is that I have never went into areas like that, ever, with a subject, Zoyd."

"Admire that, for sure, always have, but where is this li'l gentleman, and why'd he send you out to do the shitwork, huh? Plant the evidence, pop the subject, confiscate the baby, like you're working for the two o' them now, or what?"

"Whoa, *trucha, ése,* I don't snatch no babies, what's wrong with you?"

"Come on — this isn't just some jive excuse to take away my kid?"

"Hey, man, this ain't even my ticket, all's I'm doín, is a favor, for a friend." And he gave that injured cadence a peculiar emphasis, as if leaving open the meaning of *friend.*

"Uh-huh, just following orders from above."

"Don't know if you've been keepín up, but with Nixon and shit there's been a couple years of reorganization where I work, lot of old FBN doorkickers done got the blade, colleagues of mine, and I'm lucky I still have any job, OK, even runnín estupidass marriage-counselor errands like this."

"Li'l . . . piece of foam there on your lip, Hector . . . nah, it's OK, I — I know what you're goin' through, Keemosobby."

"Knew you'd understand." He pulled out a chrome referee's whistle and blew on it. "OK, fellas!"

"Hey, the baby." In came stomping half a dozen individuals in black visor caps and windbreakers labeled BNDD, with tape recorders, field investigation kits, two-way radios, a range of sidearms both custom and off the shelf, not to mention cameras, still and movie, with which they took pictures of each other standing beneath the herbaceous polyhedron before starting to wrap it in some dark plastic sheeting.

"Oh Captain, can I at least, please, call up my mother-in-law to help me with the baby?"

"That is called a favor." Grotesquely kittenish. "Favors have to be paid back."

"Inform on my friends. Sure would put me in a squeeze."

"Your child's well-beín against your own virginity as a snitch, oh yes, quite a close decision indeed, I should say." And about then who but Sasha should come bouncing in the door, setting Hector's eyes atwinkle with what a stranger in town might've called innocent mischief.

"Why, you scamp — you called her, didt'n you?"

"Zoyd what have you got yourself into now — oh, my," as she registered the looming block of cannabis, "God? with the little *baby* in the house, are you sick?"

On cue, Prairie woke up into all the commotion and started to yell, more out of inquiry than distress, and Zoyd and Sasha, both heading for the door at the same time, collided classically and staggered back screaming, "Stupid pothead," and "Meddling bitch," respectively. They then glared at each other till Zoyd finally offered, "Look — you're a old Hollywood babe, been up and down the boulevard a couple times," reaching a cloth diaper out of a cupboard in the bathroom, which by now they'd been jammed together into closer than either would have liked by the increasingly mysterious activities necessary to get Hector's colossal dopechunk out of the house again, "can't you even see this is a setup?" proceeding to the bedroom, followed attentively by Sasha. "They're tryin' to get her away from me. Hi there, Slick, 'member your grandma?" While Sasha talked and played, Zoyd took off Prairie's diaper, got rid of the shit and rinsed off the diaper in the toilet, threw it in with the others along with some Borax in a plastic garbage can that was just about heavy enough to pack up the hill to the laundromat, came back in with a warm cloth and a tube of Desitin, made sure his ex-mother-in-law noticed he was wiping in the right direction, and only about the time he was pinning the new diaper on remembering that he should have paid more attention, cared more for these small and at times even devotional routines he'd been taking for granted, now, with the posse in the parlor, too late, grown so suddenly precious. . . .

Sasha was at the window, sunlight coming through, holding her, Prairie with her arm out pointing in perfect baby articulation of wrist, hand, and fingers toward the thumping and crashing from the other room, making a puzzled face.

"Didn't mean to holler," Sasha muttered.

"Me neither. Hope this won't be a hassle."

"I'd love to take her, it's been a while anyway, so at least that part works out."

" 'Cept for me goin' in the slam, o' course," Zoyd breaking into an episode of surprise cackling, which Prairie enjoyed, beginning to rock in Sasha's arms, stretching her mouth to accommodate a smile she could not yet feel the limits of, making high squeals now and then. "Oh, ya like that, do ya. Yer Da-da's gittin' popped!" He put his finger in his mouth against the inside of his cheek, sucked, and popped it out at her. She gazed, smiling, tongue out. "Uh-huh, well, you'll be seeing a lot of this lady right here, you know her as Grandma —"

"Gah ma!"

"And maybe not so much of me." Following the wisdom of the time, Zoyd, bobbing around among the flotsam of his sunken marriage, had been giving in to the impulse to cry, anytime it came on him, alone or in public, Getting In Touch With His Feelings at top volume, regardless of how it affected onlookers, their own problems, their attitude toward life, their lunch. After hearing enough remarks like "No wonder she left you," "Blow your nose and act like a man," and "Cut your hair while you're at it," he'd come to think of crying as another form of pissing, just as likely at the wrong time and place to get him in trouble, and he learned after a while how to hold it all in till later, till he could safely be taken by the high salt wave, often while some door was still closing, some emergency brake just notched up tight. This time he really had to wait for the rest of the day, grim and clenched, till he'd been handcuffed, led out through an audience of neighbors mostly staring in wonder, or in forms of mental distress such as fear, at the tall prism, now miraculously outside again, secured on a flatbed trailer, ready to be hauled back to whatever spacious Museum of Drug Abuse it had been borrowed from, while Zoyd was put into the back of a taupe Caprice with government plates and taken away up the hill out of Gordita Beach, angling by surface streets southward and eastward, on into less developed neighborhoods full of oil wells and nodding pumps, green fields, horses, power lines, and railroad trestles, pulling in at last to a collection of low sand-colored structures that could have been some junior high school campus, with yellow tile walls and a lot of U.S. Marshals inside, on through strip search, fingerprinting, picture taking, and form typing, the early line for supper — miscellaneous pork pieces, instant mashed potatoes, and red Jell-O — then into the domicile area and a cell of his own, where he waited the noisy cold-lit Tubeless hours till lights out, when he could finally let go, surrender to the flood, mourn the comical small face already turned as he was taken away . . . would she miss him, tottering and peering tomorrow around Sasha's house, with her puzzled frown, going, "Dah Dee?" Zoyd ya fuckin' fool, he addressed himself between spasms, what are you doing, crying yourself to sleep? Likely so. Next thing he knew the overhead cell light was on again and a natty little dude in a sky-blue double-knit safari suit was poised on a folding metal chair, calling, "Wheeler," over and over, like a Doberman at night somewhere the other side of a creek. By the time Zoyd's eyes adjusted to the glare and his pulse to the mid-watch awakening, he had figured out that this was Brock Vond.

"So," Brock nodding in false sociability, looking at Zoyd's face, it seemed to Zoyd, in some prolonged detail as he kept nodding. "So. Would you mind turning your head — no, the other way? Give me a profile. Ah. Hah. Yes now if you could look up at that corner of the ceiling? thanks, and maybe pull back your upper lip?"

"What is this?"

"Want to get an idea of your gnathic index, and that mustache is in the way."

"Oh, w'll hell, why'n't you say so," Zoyd peeling back his lip for Brock. "Want me to cross my eyes, drool, anything like 'at?"

"You're in a sprightly mood for someone looking at the rest of his life in prison. I had hoped for a level of serious and adult conversation, but maybe I was wrong, maybe you've spent too much time in the infant world, hm? gotten more comfortable there, maybe this will have to be simplified for you."

"This has anythin' to do with my former wife, Cap'n, it sure ain't about to be simple."

Brock Vond's nostrils went wide, a vein began to beat next to one eye. "She's not your business anymore. I know how to take care of Frenesi, asshole, understand that?"

Zoyd looked back, eyes swollen, mouth shut, sweating, his hair, not to mention the brain beneath, all matted down. As an average doper of the sixties, the narc's natural prey, he expected from any variety of cop at least the reflexes of a predator, but this went beyond — it was personal, malevolent, too scarily righteous. Why? This was the first time Zoyd had even seen ol' Loverboy here, the great unknown she had come in to Zoyd out of, for a little while, and to which, her choice, he guessed, she'd now returned. Taking care not to provoke the Prosecutor, Zoyd waited on the edge of his rack, holding his head, while Brock got up, metal creaking, and began to pace the room, as if lost in thought. According to Frenesi, Brock had been born under the sign of the Scorpion, the only critter in nature that could sting itself to death with its own tail, reminding Zoyd of self-destructive maniacs he'd ridden with back in his car-club days, beer outlaws speeding well above the limit, dreaming away with these romantic death fantasies, which usually gave them hardons they then joked about all night, bright-eyed, don't-fuck-with-me-sincere country boys with tattoos reading ME 'N' DEATH inside hearts dripping blood, who feared nothing unless it was taking apart a transmission, who might have ended up cops and coaches and selling insurance, soft-spoken as could be, Mister Professional, good grip on the world, but underneath all the time there'd been the onrushing night road, the yellow lines and dashes, the terrible about-to-burst latency just ahead, the hardon, and this Brock here looked like a big-city edition of that same dreamy fatality.

Brock suddenly whipped out some pack of whiteguy smokes, lit up, seemed to recall a subclause of the Gentleman's Code, and held the pack out to Zoyd, though still a little more abruptly than in the true gentleman's perfect mimicry of compassion. Zoyd took a cigarette and a light anyhow.

"Baby's all right? Hm?"

Here at last came those rectal spasms of fear, crashing in on Zoyd one by one. Yes this crazy motherfucker was after his child, what else could it be?

"Going to jail means many things," Brock Vond was pointing out. "You lose your custody. Maybe once in a very great while, because the Bureau of Prisons is not unmerciful, she'll be allowed to visit. Maybe if you're good we'll let you out, under guard, to go to her wedding, hm? Even a sip of champagne at the reception, although that technically would be drug use." He let Zoyd throb a beat or two more and sighed theatrically. "But I have to take a chance, gamble on your character."

"You guys want to adopt Prairie," Zoyd hazarded, "why do this to me, just find a judge."

Brock exhaled smoke impatiently. "How am I even supposed to talk to you people? Maybe you could relate to — like, another planet? Hm? Where not everyone's fate is to produce and bring up children. But some rebel against that, try to run away, hm? get locked into a domestic arrangement as fast as they can — a woman, say, trying to be an average, invisible tract-house mom, anchoring herself to the planet with some innocent hubby, then a baby, to keep from flying away back to who she really is, her responsibilities, hm? Who struggles against her fate."

"So she finds a spaceship," Zoyd continued, "and escapes to our own planet Earth, where folks are allowed to behave the way they want, even have a baby with a lowlife bum who can't afford to buy a house, if that happens to be their trip, without no cops always putting in."

Not the Earth Brock was acquainted with. "But the police of her planet," unperturbed, "who are sworn to protect all their people, cannot allow her to escape what everyone else must accept, hm? So they follow her to Earth. And they bring her back. And she never sees the baby again."

"Yeah, or the father."

"Who makes sure of it."

They'd been smoking up a storm and could see each other only dimly through the nicotine weather, despite the strong light from overhead. Somewhere down the road from this federal facility, carried by the midnight wind from a bikers' bar called Knucklehead Jack's, came live, loud rock and roll, ever-breaking waves of notes in squealing screaming guitar solos that defied any number of rules, that also lifted the blood and reassured the soul of locked-up Zoyd, who now had to reassess the nature of the threat and could still not believe Brock was telling him the terms of an actual deal. Were they plea bargaining? Did Brock really *not* want Prairie?

"I don't worry about Sasha, because she'll never let Frenesi near the baby, not anymore . . . but let me share what worries me about you. Say I were to let you resume your dubious parenting of this child — squalid surroundings, drug abuse, irregular work hours, and undesirable companions, hm? all on the assumption that we understood each other, and then — who knows? she calls up one night, the moon happens to be full, you start talking more and more softly, singing those golden oldies together, hm? next thing you know, there's the three of you, out at the all-night Burger King, dribbling food, having all that fun, the basic triangle, the holy family, all together, heartwarming, hm? they make a commercial, you're all in it, you get famous, and finally that's when it comes to my attention, you see? The point is, somehow I would always find out."

"But if I took my daughter and just —"

Brock shrugged. "Disappeared. We might not find you for a while. Quite a while. You could get married again, have a life?"

"Is this what Frenesi wants?"

"It's what I tell you. I have her power of attorney, she gave me that even before she gave me her body, so don't waste my time here, question pending is do you want to go inside forever, because there's a bed open on the top tier in cellblock D, waiting just for you, your cellmate's name is Leroy, he is a convicted murderer, and next to eating watermelon, his favorite pastime is attempting to insert his oversized member into the anus of the nearest white male, in this case, you. Are you getting any clearer sense of your options here?"

Zoyd wouldn't look him in the face. The son of a bitch wanted an answer out loud. "OK."

"Believe me," Brock with the salesman's instinct for congratulating the customer on his purchase, "she'd have done the same to you."

"Helps a lot, thanks."

"So . . . I'll just get the paperwork started on this. But we'll have to do something about your tone of voice." Brock went to the door and hollered, "Ron?" Bootsteps approached, and Ron, a large athletic U.S. Marshal, unlocked. "Ron, are you cleared for nonjudicial motivation?"

"Sure am, Mr. Vond."

"Hit him," Brock ordered on his way out the door.

"Yes, sir. How many —"

"Oh, once will be plenty," a fading steel echo.

Ron wasted no time, chasing Zoyd to the corner of the cell and hitting him with a blinding solar-plexus punch that sent him down into paralysis and pain, and unable to breathe. Ron stood awhile, as if evaluating the job — Zoyd could presently make out in a blur his motionless boots and, still too desolate even to cry out, waited for a kick. But Ron turned and left, locking up, and shortly after that the lights went off. And Zoyd curled in anguish and looked for his breath, and didn't drift under till just before the count at 5:30 A.M.

Hector showed up right after breakfast, beaming at him over a mustache the maintenance of whose microstructure back then was costing him twenty minutes a day of precious time. "Political office decides they don't need you after all. But even if we call you the mule, you're still lookín at a zip six indeterminate for that half a metric ton in your house, and somebody figured I could be of help. . . . You look like shit, by the way."

"Get yourself bounced by Wyatt Earp out there, see how you feel." Zoyd exhaled loudly through his nose, red-eyed, accusative. "Really a fuckin' late hit, man . . . all these years I thought you respected me enough not to force me to snitch. Now, what's so fuckin' important, to make you do this?"

A strange trick of the light, no doubt, or else Zoyd was inopportunely hallucinating, but the highlights on each of Hector's eyeballs had vanished, the shine faded to matte surfaces that were now absorbing all light that fell on them. "You know what, I got to start thinkín about lunch. Do we have to keep playín fuck-fuck with this? Órale, get you the right judge, dig it! a nice minimum joint, a farm, you can grow vegetables? flowers, you people like flowers, right? All's I need, really Zoyd, is to know the story on this gentleman, a mutual contact I am sure, name of . . . Shorty?"

"Christ, Hector," croaking, shaking his head, "only Shorty I ever knew lives out in Hemet now and since his Vietnam days is takin' zero chances, won't even fly on the airplane no more, not too promising for you, outside of a little Darvon he cops off his ol' lady, he ain't even good for a Class III beef far 's I know."

"That's him!" cried Hector, "that's the fucker all right, down in EPT they know him as Shorty the Bad, and it took supersnitch potential like yours to just break this case wi-i-i-ide open! *Muy de aquellos,* wait'll I tell my boss — you got a future in this business, *ése!*"

It occurred to Zoyd more belatedly than usual that Hector could all along have been running some exercise in narc humor for his own entertainment. He risked, "Why this thing about popping my cherry, Hector, can't you see I have a kid to look after now, no choice, I had to turn into a straight citizen and go on the natch anymore, no time for these hardened criminal drug dealers I used to hang out with, I'm totally reformed, man."

"Yeah, some natch, chain-smokín pot, acid on weekends, when you gonna cut your hair? Quit playín that shit music, learn a couple nice Agustín Lara tunes? Li'l *conjunto?* And really start thinkín about gettín married again too, Zoyd. Debbi and me was both each other's second time around, and we could not be happier, *palabra.*"

"Now you tell me about your sister-in-law, the one you always try to fix up with everybody, even those you arrest."

"Naw, she's livín in Oxnard now, married one of *los vatos de Chiques.* Debbi says it's in their blood, all the women in her family, they can't resist a suave, romantic Latino."

"Sure hope you're keepin' her away from anybody like that."

"*Ay muere,* give me a break," shaking his head, flinging wide the door of Zoyd's cell, "go on, get out of here."

So that evening around sunset he was at Sasha's, in a fragrant street lined with older palm trees, with a light desert wind blowing in the sounds of late-rush-hour traffic from the choke point miles up Wilshire and suppertime blooming in side windows up and down the long blocks. Prairie was all gussied up in some kind of brand-new toddler outfit, including shoes and hat, that her grandmother had bought for her, in Beverly Hills no doubt, and when she saw Zoyd she hollered, though not exactly in welcome. "Dah Dee no!"

"Say Slick," down on one knee, holding his arms open.

Prairie scooted around behind Sasha and regarded him with her lower jaw pushed forward and her eyes bright. "No!"

"Aw, Prairie."

" 'Ippie *bum!*"

"*You* taught her that, I knew it, got your meathooks on her for one day —" But after Brock Vond and his colleagues, this was not the humiliation it might've been in times of peace.

"Zoyd, what happened, you look terrible."

"Oh . . . ," creaking up on his feet, "that fuckin' Brock Vond, man. Your daughter can sure pick 'em." He didn't know if he'd share the final routine Brock had put him through. Before he was to be cut quite loose, Zoyd had had to stand between two marshals, one of them his assailant, Ron, unobserved in the afternoon shade, while Brock led out into the parking lot a steadfastly smiling Frenesi — who'd been somewhere inside all along, in Brock's custody — sun in her hair and face, those bare legs so poised and smooth . . . obliged to watch her go down, the smile held every step of the way, dapper pastel Brock in his custom shades opening the rear door of the car for her, to watch him then seize her hair, how Zoyd had loved that hair, to guide her head below the roofline and into the padded shadows, though not exactly to notice the way her neck was bent, the anticipation, the long erotic baring of nape, as if willingly, for some high-fashion leather collar. . . .

"I just defrosted a pizza, come on in."

Prairie finally came to kiss him hello after all, and then later good night. When she was asleep in the spare room, Zoyd told Sasha about the deal he thought he'd made.

"But you can't really disappear," Sasha said.

Right — which is where the mental-disability arrangement came in. "Just a way for us to know where you are," Hector had explained, "long as you're pickín up those checks, nobody'll bother you — but if you stop for even one time, the alarm goes off and we know you're tryín to skip."

Zoyd looked miserable enough about it for Sasha to lean, sock him in a precise, friendly way on the shoulder, and say, "All that fascist prick wants is to keep Frenesi from seeing her child again. Usual thing, men making arrangements with men about the fates of women. Would you really help keep them apart?"

"I don't think I could. How about you? Brock says you're no problem, you'll never let her near Prairie."

" 'Cause I'm an old push-button lefty, ideology before family, well let him think so, gives us that much more room to breathe. Listen, what about this?" And she told him about Vineland, how they all used to visit in the summers when Frenesi was little and how she'd loved to explore, must have followed every creek on that whole piece of coast as far up into Vineland each time as she could get, disappearing for days on end with a canteen of Kool-Aid and a backpack full of peanut-butter-and-marshmallow sandwiches.

"Seems a lot of folks heading that way lately," Zoyd nodded.

"Well, once a year we still all get together up there, cook out, play poker, carry on, all the Traverses and Beckers, my parents and their relatives. It used to be the high point of Frenesi's year, but she stopped coming after high school. You know, there'd be worse places for you and the ol' bundle to live, have a home, beautiful country, only a short spin up or down 101 from everything, from the Two Street honky-tonks to the eateries of Arcata to the surfing at Shelter Cove, and you'd have a social life, 'cause lately this mass migration of freaks you spoke of, nothing personal, from L.A. north is spilling over into Vineland, so you'd have free baby-sitting too, dope connections, an inexhaustible guitar-player pool?"

"Sounds groovy for sure, but the only jobs are fishing and lumbering, right, and I'm a piano player."

"You might have to live by your wits, then."

"How's the hiding?"

"Half the interior hasn't even been surveyed — plenty of redwoods left to get lost in, ghost towns old and new blocked up behind slides that are generations old and no Corps of Engineers'll ever clear, a whole web of logging roads, fire roads, Indian trails for you to learn. You can hide, all right. So could she, then and now. Which is why, any year now, say even around Becker-

Traverse reunion time, who knows, she might show up. Lover-boy's charm has to wear off sometime."

"Didn't notice much of that."

"About the only thing'll get a fascist through's his charm. The newsfolks love it."

"And you think she'll come to Vineland. And Prairie and me'll just happen to be there. . . ." Sure, well where'd he ever have been without fantasies like that to help bridge him across the bad moments when they came? That night on Sasha's phone he talked to Van Meter, who, himself demoralized by Zoyd's arrest, was joining the trek northward, happy to take along Zoyd's car, stereo, albums, and so forth. They agreed to connect soon at one of the phone numbers Van Meter gave him.

With Prairie hanging off him like a monkey in a tree, he waved goodbye to Sasha at the nearest Santa Monica Freeway exit and immediately got picked up by a VW bus painted all over with flowers, ringed planets, R. Crumb-style faces and feet, and less recognizable forms, all headed for the Sacramento Delta country, where flourished a commune, deep in, beyond the shallowest of boat drafts, sanctuary for folks on the run from court orders, process servers and skip tracers, not to mention higher and more dangerous levels of enforcement. This refuge from government happened to be lodged in the heart of a regionwide network of military installations that included nuclear-weapons depots and waste dumps, mothball fleets, submarine bases, ordnance factories, and airfields for all branches of the service, from SAC down to the Marines, whose flying stock, none of it equipped with noise suppressors, roared overhead without letup day and night.

They decided to stay a night or two, though the baby was not crazy about all the racket in the sky. For a while she hollered back but finally went looking for shelter inside Zoyd's perimeter, by then running on the tight side. People came to their door at unexpected hours looking for parties that could easily have been fantasies of the mind. A population of dogs and cats carried on their own often far from domestic dramas likewise without apparent reference to clock time. Sulfurous fogs came and stayed all day, everything smelled like diesel and chemicals, now and then

Zoyd'd have to take his shirt off, wring it out, and put it back on again. When the ducks made highball and comeback quacks in intervals between airplane sorties, Prairie at their voices might begin to perk up, but then in over the patchwork rooftops, too loud and sudden, would come throbbing another chorus of national security, and she'd start to cry again, which eventually, more than the mindshattering roar, got Zoyd wondering just how desperate he was. Mosquitoes whined, sweat ran, Prairie kept waking up every couple hours, all the way back to her old baby ways, partygoers bellowed and shrieked, distant muffled explosions ripped the night, the worst stations on the dial played background music, dogs contended in the beaten mud shadows for thirdhand remnants of road kills. In the morning, gonging with insomniac beer and tobacco headache, Zoyd stumbled to the residence of the Commune Elder and gave notice. "How's that?" cupping an ear as an F-4 Phantom came screaming, invisible in the swamp haze.

"Said that we're gonna be —" the rest swallowed in a fugue of B-52's.

"F-4 Phantom, I think!" screaming through megaphone hands.

"Well thanks, got to be going," Zoyd mouthed without wasting his voice, smiled, waved, tipped his hat and was off hitchhiking with the baby and their effects inside the quarter hour. Prairie, glad to be moving anywhere, fell asleep as soon as they got a ride. They proceeded toward San Francisco, coming to rest at the posh Telegraph Hill town house of Wendell ("Mucho") Maas, a music-business biggie whom Zoyd knew by way of Indolent Records, entering black iron gates to a long Spanish courtyard of flowered tiles, plants with giant leaves, and working fountains, whose splash woke Prairie with that puzzled look on her face. Exotic trees bloomed in the dark and smelled like someplace far away. They both looked around, Prairie bright-eyed. "OK Slick, he must still be payin' the rent." The courtyard led to an entry full of house-plants under a skylight, where up to them came skipping this pure specimen of young Californian womanhood of the period, ironed hair down to the small of her back, perfectly bikini-tanned, forever eighteen, sweetly stoned and surrounded by a patchouli haze with which she'd announced herself by a minute or two. "Hi, I'm

Trillium," she whispered, head to one side, "Mucho's friend. Oh, what a cute baby, a little Taurus, yes, isn't she?"

"Um," Zoyd too astonished to recall the date, "how'd you know that?"

"Mucho's Rolodex, I'm supposed to check out everybody." She had taken Prairie, who already had two delighted fistfuls of that long hair. "Mucho's on retreat for the weekend up in Marin? But the place is oll yerz tonight, 'cz I'll be at the Paranoids concert at the Fillmore." She was leading him into one of those high-sixties record-business interiors, to which Prairie reacted with a prolonged, approving sort of "Gaaahhh. . . ." Next week, next year it could all be gone, open to wind, salt fogs, and walk-in visitors, phones unringing on the bare floors, echoes of absquatulation in the air, careers being that volatile in those days, as revolution went blending into commerce. But here was period rock and roll, over audio equipment that likewise expressed, that long-ago year, the highest state of the analog arts all too soon to be eclipsed by digital technology, Trillium dancing to it, and in her arms the baby jumping and jiving. Zoyd put on dark glasses, shook back his hair, snapped his fingers, did a few amiable time steps, looking around the place. Things blinked, swirled, transformed, came and went everywhere. Distraction. Pinball machines, television sets of many makes and sizes that never got turned off, showing all channels then known, stereo piped to every room and space, incense burning, black-light effects throwing deep purple spills, in the main room a giant tent, peaking twenty feet overhead in a pavilion of fabrics in zany colors including invisible except when they stirred or glittered. Views from here out over the City and Bay, especially at night, were psychedelic even if you happened to be on the natch, as Trillium reminded them, heading out the door presently with a busload of costumed young folks who'd all met and enjoyed the baby. "Groovy baby!" "Rilly!"

Prairie slumped singing in her father's arms, a sort of voiced dribbling, contented, soon to nod. They found the kitchen, he put her up on a table, raided the oversize fridge, fed her some boysenberry yogurt, a lot of it ending up on his shirt, filled bottles with juice and milk, and retired to a guest room across the patio from the kitchen, searched all over the place for any evidence of a guest stash, had to roll and light one of his own before putting Prairie down to sleep with an original and infallible lullaby called

LAWRENCE OF ARABIA

Oh — Lawrence,
Of Arabia, with his
Wig, wag, woggledy doo!
In-surance,
In Arabia,
Don't co-ver what, he do. . . .
No! He's out there with his camel,
In the day or night,
Cruisin' in the desert, just
Lookin' for a fight — he don't care 'cause he's
Lawrence,
Of Arabia, with that
Wig, wag, woggledy doo!

With the volume all the way down, Zoyd settled in in front of the Tube, Woody Allen in *Young Kissinger,* and slowly relaxed, though the absence of marijuana in the place was mystifying. Psychedelicized far ahead of his time, Mucho Maas, originally a disk jockey, had decided around 1967, after a divorce remarkable even in that more innocent time for its geniality, to go into record producing. The business was growing unpredictable, and his takeoff was abrupt — soon, styling himself Count Drugula, Mucho was showing up at Indolent, down in the back-street Hollywood flats south of Sunset and east of Vine, in a chauffeured Bentley, wearing joke-store fangs and a black velvet cape from Z & Z, scattering hits of high-quality acid among the fans young and old who gathered daily for his arrival. "Count, Count! Lay some dope on us!" they'd cry. Indolent Records had rapidly become known for its unusual choices of artists and repertoires. Mucho was one of the very first to audition, but not, he was later to add hastily, to call back, fledgling musician Charles Manson. He almost signed Wild Man Fischer, and Tiny Tim too, but others got to them first.

By the standards of those high-riding days of eternal youth, Count Drugula, or Mucho the Munificent, as he also came to be known, figured as a responsible, even sober-sided user of psychedelics, but cocaine was another story. It hit him out of nowhere, an unforeseen passion he would in his later unhappiness compare to a clandestine affair with a woman — furtive meetings between his nose and the illicit crystals, sudden ecstatic peaks, surprising negative cash flow, amazing sexual occurrences. Just as he arrived at that crisis point between wild infatuation and long-term commitment, his nose went out on him — blood, snot, something unarguably green — a nasal breakdown. He did not go into rehab, the resources in those days not yet having achieved the ubiquity they did in later years of national drug hysteria, but instead sought the help of Dr. Hugo Splanchnick, a dedicated and moralistic rhinologist working out of a suite of dust-free upper rooms in Sherman Oaks. "You'll do me a small favor? I have to take some blood —"

"Huh?"

" — only enough for you to dip this pen into here, and sign your name to this short letter of agreement —"

"Says no coke for as long as I live? What if I —"

"That'll be back with the penalty clauses, basically the traditional range of sanctions — fines, imprisonment, death."

"Death? What? For snorting coke?"

"You're trying to kill yourself anyway, what would it matter?"

A throb of pain went through Mucho's nose. "Can I at least get some Novocaine?" pronouncing it "Dovocaide."

"Soon as you sign."

"Doc! This is worse than a producer's loan-out agreement."

An annoyed sigh. "Regretfully, then," flinging open another door leading deeper into the suite, "we must proceed to the next phase, the 'Room of the Bottled Specimens.'" Lurid pink light, from the cheaply acquired meat displays of a failed supermarket, poured forth.

This didn't look promising. "Um, say, maybe I'll sign after all, add thed you'll gimb be the Dovocaide, right?"

"Ah, much much too late, I'm afraid, as I think you've already glimpsed here in Jar Number One, the —" pretending to read the label, " 'Cross Section Through Jazz Musician's Skull'? eh? revealing the structure of this very interesting abscess, come, have a look, I promise," chuckling, "you won't have to eat it."

To the drug-ruffled nap of Mucho's brain it did not seem at all unlikely that some form of life, somewhere, would find the Bottled Specimens not only edible but appetizing as well, and so he refrained from sharing the snoot croaker's merriment.

"Fine, fine — now for the Necrotic Sinus." On it went, Mucho stumbling, eyes oscillating and nose throbbing, through the Wax Museum, the Emergency Room Footage, the Examples in the Freezer, till at length pain, exhaustion, and the beginning of a new head cold drove him to ink, or rather blood, this nose medic's dubious pact. At last he could beam at the paper over a nose hypodermically iced out. What interesting reading material. Ha, ha, ha! What idiot did they think would ever sign this?

But as he would describe it later, often to people who didn't even know him, and at some length, it proved to be a turning point in his life. Reeling out onto Ventura Boulevard, he was nearly run down by a stop-me-search-me VW bus, brightly repainted and full of long-haired young desperados out cruising, who recognized him and began clamoring for acid. But Mucho, with a spaced and born-again look to him, only announced in a robotized oracular voice, "Why brothers, the new trip, the only true trip, is The Natch, and being on it."

"Aw," said the dopers, the speech balloon emerging from their tailpipe as they rolled away.

Though Mucho had relocated since then to the Acid Rock Capital, his dedication to The Natch had only deepened, and he'd begun to be known in some parts of town as a source of rectal discomfort on the subject, not even sparing his old rock and roll buddy Zoyd his thoughts on the evils of drug abuse. Eat at the mission, sit still for the sermon. But Zoyd was ready with a lecture of his own.

"Mucho, what happened, you were the Head of Heads, and not that long ago. This can't be you talking, it must be the fuckin' government, which this is all their trip anyway, 'cause they need to put people in the joint, if they can't do that, what are they? ain't shit, might as well be another show on the Tube. They didn't even start goin' after dope till Prohibition was repealed, suddenly here's all these federal cops lookin' at unemployment, they got to come up with somethin' quick, so Harry J. Anslinger invents the Marijuana Menace, single-handed. Don't believe me ask ol' Hector, remember him? He'll tell you some shit."

Mucho shivered. "Uh-uh, that dude. Thought he'd be off your case by now." Back down south at the Indolent studios, Hector had made a strong impression. Just when it had seemed the Corvairs' luck was turning, and they were actually beginning to cut one or two masters, with Mucho himself producing, suddenly heavily hanging out, faithful as a groupie, was the drug agent, silent and glittering at first but all too soon putting in, as if unable not to, not only negotiating lyrics, which was certainly bad enough, but also arguing about notes, which was crazy — "Hey, those are soul licks! surfers ain' spoze to be playín like that, spoze to play Anglo, like do-re-mi, man, Julie Andrews? up in those Alps? with all those white kids?" so forth, causing Scott Oof to start glowering. "Here he is again, your buddy the rock reviewer, pickier 'n ever. How does he like the beat? Is the string track OK?"

"Strings," Hector narrowing his eyes, ominously on defense, "I didt'n hear no strings."

"Now come on cats, let's all be cool," Mucho in his Count Drugula gear trying to emcee, "I'm happy you enjoyin' your backstage look at the world of rock and roll, mah man in the reverse-chic shoes, but the latest in from the beach is, not even the Surfaris are playing white anymore."

"First the shoes," Hector swiveling to inform him, "are my old Stacey Adamses, *me entiendes como te digo?*"

"Oops. . . ." Mucho was aware of the mystique, all right, and quick to beg forgiveness.

"Aw, it's OK," Hector putting on his face a goofy and dangerous look, as of some old-time pachuco flying high on reefer, a preferred intimidation technique that extended to his suit, which he'd had semi-retailored to suggest a zoot of the 1940s, "but let me tell you, 'causs sometimes I hear records on your label when I'm out, you know, cruisín, so I really want to tell *you*, man, about my car radio?" He moved closer to Mucho, who'd already read and filed Hector's story by now, and would presently begin to edge away. "Which is kin' of unique 'causs it only gits this one station? KQAS! Kick-Ass 460 on th' AM dial! I got their decal on my car window, you can look at it later if you want. I got their T-shirt too, but I'm not wearín it today. 'S too bad, 's got a good picture on it. 'S what it is, it's this close-up, of a foot, an' a ass? you know? like a freeze-frame, right where the foot is . . . ju-u-uust makín that firs' contact with th' ass, right?"

"We're running late," Mucho said. "Zoyd, fellas, you're in competent hands, and nice meeting you, whatever your badge number was."

"Tell the ol' neckbiter here how much I'm enjoyín myself," darkly advised the sensitive federale.

"Yes, check the drape of his suit," Zoyd had counseled then, "and exercise caution."

"These federal guys," Mucho, back in real time, was telling Zoyd, "if they're anything like nasal therapists, they're in your life forever. I didn't think you were dealing anymore."

"Me neither. So last week, what happens? He finally tries to set me up." He told Mucho of his brief but educational time in federal custody.

Mucho blinked sympathetically, a little sadly. "I guess it's over. We're on into a new world now, it's the Nixon Years, then it'll be the Reagan Years —"

"Ol' Raygun? No way he'll ever make president."

"Just please go careful, Zoyd. 'Cause soon they're gonna be coming after everything, not just drugs, but beer, cigarettes, sugar, salt, fat, you name it, anything that could remotely please any of your senses, because they need to control all that. And they will."

"Fat Police?"

"Perfume Police. Tube Police. Music Police. Good Healthy Shit Police. Best to renounce everything now, get a head start."

"Well I still wish it was back then, when you were the Count. Remember how the acid was? Remember that windowpane, down in Laguna that time? God, I knew then, I knew. . . ."

They had a look. "Uh-huh, me too. That you were never going to die. Ha! No wonder the State panicked. How are they supposed to control a population that knows it'll never die? When that was always their last big chip, when they thought they had the power of life and death. But acid gave us the X-ray vision to see through that one, so of course they had to take it away from us."

"Yeah, but they can't take what happened, what we found out."

"Easy. They just let us forget. Give us too much to process, fill up every minute, keep us distracted, it's what the Tube is for, and though it kills me to say it, it's what rock and roll is becoming — just another way to claim our attention, so that beautiful certainty we had starts to fade, and after a while they have us convinced all over again that we really are going to die. And they've got us again." It was the way people used to talk.

"I'm not gonna forget," Zoyd vowed, "fuck 'em. While we had it, we really had some fun."

"And they never forgave us." Mucho went to the stereo and put on *The Best of Sam Cooke*, volumes 1 and 2, and then they sat together and listened, both of them this time, to the sermon, one they knew and felt their hearts comforted by, though outside spread the lampless wastes, the unseen paybacks, the heartless power of the scabland garrison state the green free America of their childhoods even then was turning into.

Downtown, in the Greyhound station, Zoyd put Prairie on top of a pinball machine with a psychedelic motif, called Hip Trip, and was able to keep winning free games till the Vineland bus got in from L.A. This baby was a great fan of the game, liked to lie face down on the glass, kick her feet, and squeal at the full sensuous effect, especially when bumpers got into prolonged cycling or when her father got manic with the flippers, plus the gongs and lights and colors always going off. "Enjoy it while you can," he muttered at his innocent child, "while you're light enough for that glass to hold you."

Crossing the Golden Gate Bridge represents a transition, in the metaphysics of the region, there to be felt even by travelers unwary as Zoyd. When the busful of northbound hippies first caught sight of it, just at sundown as the fog was pouring in, the towers and cables ascending into pale gold otherworldly billows, you heard a lot of "Wow," and "Beautiful," though Zoyd only found it beautiful the way a firearm is, because of the bad dream unreleased inside it, in this case the brute simplicity of height, the finality of what swept below relentlessly out to sea. They rose into the strange gold smothering, visibility down to half a car length, Prairie standing up on the seat gazing out the window. "Headin' for nothin' but trees, fish, and fog, Slick, from here on in," sniffling, *till your mama comes home,* he wanted to say, but didn't. She looked around at him with a wide smile. "Fiss!"

"Yeah — fog!"

Trees. Zoyd must have dozed off. He woke to rain coming down in sheets, the smell of redwood trees in the rain through the open bus windows, tunnels of unbelievably tall straight red trees whose tops could not be seen pressing in to either side. Prairie had been watching them all the time and in a very quiet voice talking to them as they passed one by one. It seemed now and then as if she were responding to something she was hearing, and in rather a matter-of-fact tone of voice for a baby, too, as if this were a return for her to a world behind the world she had known all along. The storm lashed the night, dead trees on slow log trucks reared up in the high-beams shaggy and glistening, the highway was interrupted by flooding creeks and minor slides that often obliged the bus to creep around inches from the edge of Totality. Aislemates struck up conversations, joints appeared and were lit, guitars came down from overhead racks and harmonicas out of fringe bags, and soon there was a concert that went on all night, a retrospective of the times they'd come through more or less as a generation, the singing of rock and roll, folk, Motown, fifties oldies, and at last, for about an hour just before the watery green sunrise, one guitar and one harmonica, playing the blues.

Zoyd caught up with Van Meter in Eureka, at the corner of 4th and H, as, suddenly disoriented, he observed his '64 Dodge Dart, unmistakably his own short, with the LSD paint job, Day-Glo hubcaps with the eyes on them, nude-with-streamlined-tits hood ornament, and at the wheel a standard-issue Hippie Freak who looked *just like him.* Woo-oo! An unreal moment for everybody, with the driver staring twice as weirdly *right back at Zoyd!* Van

Meter meantime was wondering why Zoyd didn't wave hello, taking Zoyd's mental confusion for anger, and decided to just keep going, though by that time Zoyd had recovered and begun to chase Van Meter through the lunch-hour traffic, waving and hollering, only adding to the bass player's anxiety. Zoyd caught up with his car at a red light and got in on the rider's side.

"Don't be pissed!" in a high nervous voice. "It's running great, I just sprang for a whole tank of gas —"

"Thought I was having a out-of-body experience for a second. What's the matter, you look kind of, uh. . . ."

"Hey, I'm cool. Where's that Prairie?"

Zoyd had left her with friends here, had been house hunting all week with no luck, was just about to go pick her up and head back to Vineland.

"Well soon as I can find your keys, I'll give you your ride and you can run me back up there."

"In the ignition, I think."

"Oh. . . ."

They collected Prairie, from a day-care co-op of friends of friends from down south. She was in blue corduroy overalls and greeted Van Meter, her godfather, with squeals and smiles, high-fiving him with two grubby hands. She'd settled right in up here, didn't seem to miss the beach at all, already knew a couple of kids she fought and played with regularly. Soon as they were out on 101 again, she climbed in the back seat and went to sleep.

"A Harbor of Refuge," as the 1851 survey map called it, "to Vessels that may have suffered on their way North from the strong headwinds that prevail along this coast from May to October," Vineland Bay, at the mouth of Seventh River, was protected from the sea and its many unsolved mysteries by two spits, Thumb and Old Thumb, and an island out in the bay, called False Thumb. The spits were joined by a bridge, as was the inner of the two, Old Thumb, with the city of Vineland, which curved the length of the harbor's shoreline, both spans being graceful examples of the concrete Art Deco bridges built all over the Northwest by the WPA during the Great Depression. Zoyd, who was driving, came at last up a long forest-lined grade and cresting saw the trees fold

away, as there below, swung dizzily into view, came Vineland, all
the geometry of the bay neutrally filtered under pre-storm clouds,
the crystalline openwork arcs of the pale bridges, a tall power-
plant stack whose plume blew straight north, meaning rain on the
way, a jet in the sky ascending from Vineland International south
of town, the Corps of Engineers marina, with salmon boats, power
cruisers, and day sailers all docked together, and spilling uphill
from the shoreline a couple of square miles crowded with wood
Victorian houses, Quonset sheds, postwar prefab ranch and split-
level units, little trailer parks, lumber-baron floridity, New Deal
earnestness. And the federal building, jaggedly faceted, obsidian
black, standing apart, inside a vast parking lot whose fences were
topped with concertina wire. "Don't know, it just landed one
night," Van Meter said, "sitting there in the morning when everybody woke up, folks seem to be gettin' used to it. . . ."

Someday this would be all part of a Eureka–Crescent City–
Vineland megalopolis, but for now the primary sea coast, forest,
riverbanks and bay were still not much different from what early
visitors in Spanish and Russian ships had seen. Along with noting
the size and fierceness of the salmon, the fogbound treachery of
the coasts, the fishing villages of the Yurok and Tolowa people,
log keepers not known for their psychic gifts had remembered to
write down, more than once, the sense they had of some invisible
boundary, met when approaching from the sea, past the capes of
somber evergreen, the stands of redwood with their perfect trunks
and cloudy foliage, too high, too red to be literal trees — carrying
therefore another intention, which the Indians might have known
about but did not share. They could be seen in photographs beginning at about the turn of the century, villagers watching the
photographer at work, often posed in native gear before silvery
blurred vistas, black tips of seamounts emerging from gray sea
fringed in brute-innocent white breakings, basalt cliffs like castle
ruins, the massed and breathing redwoods, alive forever, while the
light in these pictures could be seen even today in the light of
Vineland, the rainy indifference with which it fell on surfaces, the
call to attend to territories of the spirit . . . for what else could the
antique emulsions have been revealing?

Money had never been found in Sacramento or Washington to bypass 101 around Vineland, so that once into town, the freeway narrowed to two lanes and made a couple of doglegs on and off South Spooner, following unsynchronized traffic lights that drove Van Meter crazy but gave Zoyd a good look at downtown, the Lost Nugget, Country Cantonese, Bodhi Dharma Pizza, the Steam Donkey, before they were back on North Spooner, heading uphill to the bus station, where Zoyd and Prairie were living out of a locker. Van Meter offered to shoehorn them in where he was staying, a commune out past Intemperate Hill. Zoyd figured that with lines waiting on every locker space in the station, he might as well let somebody else move into his. The great northerly migration had caught Vineland flatfooted. The bus station, which took up a whole city block, was acting as a temporary dormitory for those who had nowhere to stay — and there were plenty of these Southland transplants milling everywhere. Zoyd left Prairie with some folks they'd come up with on the bus who'd all got into the habit of looking after each other's kids, and with Van Meter walking slack made a zigzag for the indigo ambience of the Fast Lane Lounge, known for the "harmless liquid" swabbed routinely onto the rims of the bar glasses, making them glow in the ultraviolet frequencies abroad in this room. Some of it was sure to come off on a drinker's mouth. Men usually wiped it away, women either allowed it to diffuse through their lipstick, for which the substance had a strange affinity, until the entire lip area was aglow, or else avoided all contact by drinking through straws, content to admire the glass-rim effect as one might admire an angelless halo. They sat in front of cold longnecks and Zoyd brought Van Meter up to date.

"Well," beaming vacantly, " 'ere's worse places for a desperado to hide out. You understand, every guy up here looks just like we do. You're dern near invisible already. Hey! Where'd you go?" groping around the vicinity of Zoyd's head.

"And it turns out, old Slick's got family up here, don't know 'f I should look 'em up or not."

"On the one hand, you don't want this turning into your mother-in-law's trip, on the other hand, they might know about someplace to crash, if so don't forget your old pal, a garage, a woodshed, a outhouse, don't matter, 's just me and Chloe."

"Chloe your dog? Oh yeah, you brought her up?"

"Think she's pregnant. Don't know if it happened here or down south." But they all turned out to look like their mother, and each then went on to begin a dynasty in Vineland, from among one of whose litters, picked out for the gleam in his eye, was to come Zoyd and Prairie's dog, Desmond. By that time Zoyd had found a piece of land with a drilled well up off Vegetable Road, bought a trailer from a couple headed back to L.A., and was starting to put together a full day's work, piece by piece. Out in the perpetual rains on that coast back then, with a borrowed ladder and rolls of aluminum foil, he cruised middle-class neighborhoods for clogged or leaking gutters, doing quick fixes on the spot, then coming back between storms to make the jobs more permanent. He sold vanloads of plastic raincoats from Taiwan along with car wax and pirated Osmonds tapes at the weekend swap meets at the Bigfoot Drive-In, spent Februaries along with everybody else he knew going around in hip waders in the Humboldt daffodil fields, cutting them green, picking up poison rashes, and then, when the cable television companies showed up in the county, got into skirmishes that included exchanges of gunfire between gangs of rival cable riggers, eager to claim souls for their distant principals, fighting it out house by house, with the Board of Supervisors compelled eventually to partition the county into Cable Zones, which in time became political units in their own right as the Tubal entrepreneurs went extending their webs even where there weren't enough residents per linear mile to pay the rigging cost, they could make that up in town, and besides, they had faith in the future of California real estate. Idealistic flower children looking to live in harmony with the Earth were not the only folks with their eyes on Vineland. Developers in and out of state had also discovered this shoreline in the way of the wind, with its concealed tranquillities and false passages, this surprise fish-trap in the everyday coast. All born to be suburbs, in their opinion, and the sooner the better. It meant work, but too much of it nonunion and bought shamefully cheap. Zoyd's relations with the Traverses he did get in touch with were complicated by his scab activities, though Zoyd would've preferred "independent contractor." These were old, proud, and strong union people, surviving in one of the world's worst antiunion environments — spool tenders, zooglers, water bucks, and bull punchers, some had fought in the Everett mill wars, others from the Becker side had personally known Joe Hill, and not mourned, and organized, and if they were allowing in over their doorsills from time to time nonunion odd-jobbing Zoyd, it was only out of sympathy for his hair and life-style, which they blamed on his mental disability, and love for their distant relative Prairie, who as a true Traverse would piss on through despite her father's shortcomings just fine. Zoyd didn't get points either for the divorce, though if he had custody and nobody'd seen Frenesi for years, it didn't make her look much better. Sasha's cousin Claire, credited in the family with paranormal abilities, quickly enough read Zoyd, noted the unguttering flame on the torch he carried, and started having him over for supper and to look at old family snapshots, telling what she remembered of young Frenesi the explorer and the reports she'd come back with about rivers that weren't supposed to be where she found them, and of the lights on the far banks, and the many voices, hundreds it seemed, not exactly partying, nor exactly belligerent either. Boulders too heavy for anyone but Bigfoot to lift come thudding all around her in the middle of the night, torrents of summer-run steelhead the size of dogs, glowing more than glittering, abandoned logging sites, boilers and stacks and flange gears looming up out of the blackberries . . . and the strange "lost" town of Shade Creek, supposedly evacuated in a flood of long ago, now unaccountably repopulated with villagers who never seemed to sleep.

"It was those Thanatoids, of course," said Claire, "they were just beginning to move into the county then, and if it scared her at all, being up there amid so much human unhappiness, why, she never mentioned it." Since the end of the war in Vietnam, the Thanatoid population had been growing steeply, so there was always day work out at Thanatoid Village, a shopping and residential complex a few miles further into the hills above Shade

Creek. Shape-ups were held in the predawn down by the Vineland courthouse, shadowy brown buses idling in the dark, work and wages posted silently in the windows — some mornings Zoyd had gone down, climbed on, ridden out with other newcomers, all cherry to the labor market up here, former artists or spiritual pilgrims now becoming choker setters, waiters and waitresses, baggers and checkout clerks, tree workers, truckdrivers, and framers, or taking temporary swamping jobs like this, all in the service of others, the ones who did the building, selling, buying and speculating. First thing new hires all found out was that their hair kept getting in the way of work. Some cut it short, some tied it back or slicked it behind their ears in a kind of question-mark shape. Their once-ethereal girlfriends were busing dishes or cocktail-waitressing or attending the muscles of weary loggers over at the Shangri-La Sauna, Vineland County's finest. Some chose to take the noon southbound back home, others kept plugging on, at night school or Vineland Community College or Humboldt State, or going to work for the various federal, state, county, church, and private charitable agencies that were the biggest employers up here next to the timber companies. Many would be the former tripping partners and old flames who came over the years to deal with each other this way across desktops or through computer terminals, as if chosen in secret and sorted into opposing teams. . . .

After a while Zoyd was allowed into the Traverse-Becker annual reunions, as long as he brought Prairie, who at about the age of three or four got sick one Vineland winter, and looked up at him with dull hot eyes, snot crusted on her face, hair in a snarl, and croaked, "Dad? Am I ever gonna get bett-or?" pronouncing it like Mr. Spock, and he had his belated moment of welcome to the planet Earth, in which he knew, dismayingly, that he would, would have to, do anything to keep this dear small life from harm, up to and including Brock Vond, a possibility he wasn't too happy with. But as he watched her then, year by year, among these reunion faces her own was growing more and more to look like, continuing to feel no least premonitory sign of governmental interest from over the horizon beyond the mental-disability checks that arrived faithfully as the moon, he at last began, even out

THE pasture, just before dawn, saw the first impatient kids already out barefoot in the dew, field dogs thinking about rabbits, house dogs more with running on their minds, cats in off of their night shifts edging, arching and flattening to fit inside the shadows they found. The woodland creatures, predators and prey, while not exactly gazing Bambilike at the intrusions, did remain as aware as they would have to be, moment to moment, that there were sure a lot of Traverses and Beckers in the close neighborhood.

Some had chosen to sleep inside their recreational vehicles, others lay out on mattresses in the beds of pickup trucks, a few had packed on further into the woods, and many had pitched tents in the meadows. Presently, as the light came up and birds started in, clock-radio alarms began to kick on in a thickening radio fugue of rock and roll till dawn, Bible interpretation, telephone voices still complaining about yesterday's news. Behind the mountains that climbed from here inland, morning-glory-blue light grew in the sky. Soon toasters and toaster ovens, wood fires, RV kitchen microwaves, gong-size skillets over propane flames, all working on bacon, links, eggs, flapjacks, waffles, hash browns, French toast, and hush puppies, were sending out branching invisible fractals of smell, reaching all over the place, fat smoke, charring spices, toasted bread, just-made coffee. People who'd slept overnight in the woods began to wander in. Blue jays appeared on foraging patrols, shrieking, bullying, scavenging, seagulls of the redwoods. Radio weather reports called for a real scorcher, even down in Vineland after the fog burned off. Younger cousins looked at the sky and into one another's backpacks. Fishermen set off along the creek bed to see what might be up and feeding, and golfers tried to scheme ways to slip off for a quick eighteen holes down at Las Sombras, a genuine links beside the fog-hung coast of Vineland. The marathon crazy eights game in a battered but shined-up Becker

Airstream proceeded ageless as generation begetting generation, like a pot-au-feu of nickels, dimes, chips, greenbacks, and nuggets that might have been simmering continuously here since the times of the Little Gold Rush. Elsewhere in camp there were other games, poker, pinochle, dominoes, dice — but it was the Octomaniacs, as they thought of themselves, who as a crowd carried a more coherent look, as if they ought to be wearing matching T-shirts, while among the assortment of semi-strangers in and out of the other games, talent and judgment might vary by orders of magnitude, causing delays, astonishment, and episodes of consanguineous discombobulation.

Some were waking up hungry, bottomless-pit, how-come-it's-not-on-the-table-yet style, while others had only to think of a frying egg to feel nauseated till noon. Some needed to take in columns of print from morning papers that weren't there, others coffee from any container that didn't leak, at least not too fast. Many who woke with eye more than stomach hunger stayed as long as they could in sleeping bags or back in camper shells with portable TV sets bootlegged onto the cable out on the highway by ingenious pole-climbing teenagers. Somewhere beyond earshot was the wash of morning traffic down along the freeway they'd come in on, as the workweek began to roll to another finale, though everybody here had taken off early, sometimes weeks early. While some of the bigger kids were dollying in different-sized refrigerators and running electric lines back to the nearest outlets, luckier ones got drafted to ride on up into Thanatoid Village to help pack in last-minute supplies as well as have a look at what there might be in the way of mall thrills among this community of the insomniac unavenged.

In fact, out of a long memory of strange dawns, this morning in the Shade Creek–Thanatoid Village area would stand forth as an exception. Not only had the entire population actually slept the night before, but they were also now wakening, in reply to a piping, chiming music, synchronized, coming out of wristwatches, timers, and personal computers, engraved long ago, as if for this moment, on sound chips dumped once in an obscure skirmish of the silicon market wars, expedited in fact by Takeshi Fumimota, as part of a settlement with the ever-questionable trading company of Tokkata & Fuji, all playing together now, and in four-part harmony, the opening of J. S. Bach's "Wachet Auf." And not the usual electronic stuff — this had soul, a quantity these troubled folks could recognize. They blinked, they began to turn, their eyes, often for the first time, sought contact with the eyes of other Thanatoids. This was unprecedented. This was like a class-action lawsuit suddenly resolved after generations in the courts. Who remembered? Say, who didn't? What was a Thanatoid, at the end of the long dread day, but memory? So, to one of the best tunes ever to come out of Europe, even with its timing adapted to the rigors of a disco percussion track able to make the bluest Thanatoid believe, however briefly, in resurrection, they woke, the Thanatoids woke.

This time what went rolling out, whistling in the dark valleys, chasing the squall lines, impinging upon the sensors of more than one kind of life in the countryside below, wasn't just the usual "Call of the Thanatoids" — this was long, desolate howling, repeated over and over, impossible for Takeshi and DL, even in their high-tech aerie down south, to ignore. They found Radio Thanatoid on the peculiar band between 6200 and 7000 kilohertz and tuned it in for Prairie, who after a while shook her head sadly. "What are you gonna do about this?"

"We have to respond," DL said. "Question is, do you want to come with us."

Well, Prairie wasn't having much luck here in L.A., though she had managed to hook up again with her old friend Ché, whose grandfolks Dotty and Wade went back into ancient Hollywood history with her own grandparents. But Sasha was out of town, had been since Prairie'd started calling, and according to her message on the answering machine, there was most likely a wiretap on the line too.

Among the first mall rats into Fox Hills, aboriginal as well to the Sherman Oaks Galleria, Prairie and Ché had been known to hitchhike for days to get to malls that often turned out to be only folkloric, false cities of gold. But that was cool, because they got to be together. This time they'd arranged to meet in lower

Hollywood at the new Noir Center, loosely based on crime movies from around World War II and after, designed to suggest the famous ironwork of the Bradbury Building downtown, where a few of them had been shot. This was yuppification run to some pitch so desperate that Prairie at least had to hope the whole process was reaching the end of its cycle. She happened to like those old weird-necktie movies in black and white, her grandfolks had worked on some of them, and she personally resented this increasingly dumb attempt to cash in on the pseudoromantic mystique of those particular olden days in this town, having heard enough stories from Hub and Sasha, and Dotty and Wade, to know better than most how corrupted everything had really been from top to bottom, as if the town had been a toxic dump for everything those handsome pictures had left out. Noir Center here had an upscale mineral-water boutique called Bubble Indemnity, plus The Lounge Good Buy patio furniture outlet, The Mall Tease Flacon, which sold perfume and cosmetics, and a New York-style deli, The Lady 'n' the Lox. Security police wore brown shiny uniform suits with pointed lapels and snap-brim fedoras and did everything by video camera and computer, a far cry from the malls Prairie'd grown up with, when security was not so mean and lean and went in more for normal polyester Safariland uniforms, where the fountains were real and the plants nonplastic and you could always find somebody your age working in the food courts and willing to swap a cheeseburger for a pair of earrings, and there even used to be ice rinks, back when insurance was affordable, she could remember days with Ché, in those older malls, where all they did for hours was watch kids skate. Weird music on the speakers, an echo off the ice. Most of these skaters were girls, some of them wearing incredibly expensive outfits and skates. They swooped, turned, leapt to the beat of canned TV-theme arrangements, booming in the chill, the ice glimmering, the light above the ice green and gray, with white standing columns of condensation. Ché nodding toward one of them once, "Check this out." She was about their age, pale, slender and serious, her hair tied back with a ribbon, wearing a short white satin number and white kid skates. "Is that white *kid,*" Ché wondered, "or *white* kid?" All eyes and legs, like a fawn, she had for a while been flirting, skating up to Prairie and Ché, then turning, flipping her tiny skirt up over her ass and gliding away, elegant little nose in the air.

"Yep," Prairie muttered, "perfect, ain't she?"

"Makes you kinda want to mess her up a little, don't it?"

"Ché, you're rilly evil?" It didn't help that inside, Prairie liked to imagine herself as just such a figure of luck and grace, no matter what hair, zit, or weight problems might be accumulating in the nonfantasy world. On the Tube she saw them all the time, these junior-high gymnasts in leotards, teenagers in sitcoms, girls in commercials learning from their moms about how to cook and dress and deal with their dads, all these remote and well-off little cookies going "Mm! this rilly *is* good!" or the ever-reliable "Thanks, Mom," Prairie feeling each time this mixture of annoyance and familiarity, knowing like exiled royalty that that's who she was supposed to be, could even turn herself into through some piece of negligible magic she must've known once but in the difficult years marooned down on this out-of-the-way planet had come to have trouble remembering anymore. When she told Ché about it, as she told her everything, her friend's eyebrows went up in concern.

"Best forget it, Prair. All looks better 'n it is. Ain't one of these li'l spoiled brats'd even make it through one night at Juvenile Hall."

"Just it," Prairie had pointed out, "nobody'll ever send her to no Juvenile Hall, she's gonna live her whole life on the outside."

"A girl can have fantasies, can't she?"

"Ooo-wee! No-o-o mercy!" This was their star-and-sidekick routine, going back to when they were little, playing Bionic, Police, or Wonder Woman. A teacher had told Prairie's class once to write a paragraph on what sports figure they wished they could be. Most girls said something like Chris Evert. Prairie said Brent Musberger. Each time they got together, it suited her to be the one to frame and comment on Ché's roughhouse engagements with the world, though more than once she'd been called on for muscle, notably during the Great South Coast Plaza Eyeshadow Raid, still being talked about in tones of wounded bewilderment at security seminars nationwide, in which two dozen girls, in black T-shirts and jeans, carrying empty backpacks and riding on roller skates, perfectly acquainted with every inch of the terrain, had come precision whirring and ticking into the giant Plaza just before closing time and departed only moments later with the packs stuffed full of eyeshadows, mascaras, lipsticks, earrings, barrettes, bracelets, pantyhose, and fashion shades, all of which they had turned immediately for cash from an older person named Otis, with a panel truck headed for a swap meet far away. In the lucid high density of action, Prairie saw her friend about to be cornered, between a mall cop and a kid in a plastic smock, hardly older than they were, bought into it young, hollering as if it were his own stuff — with the cop, clear as a movie close-up, unsnapping his holster, oo-oo, look out — "Ché!" Kicking up as much speed as she could, she went zooming in, screaming herself semidemented, paralyzing the pursuit long enough to sail alongside Ché, take her by the wrist, twirl her till they were aimed the right direction, and get rolling with her the hell on out of there. It felt like being bionically speeded up, like Jaime Sommers, barreling through a field of slo-mo opposition, while all through this the background shopping music continued, perky and up-tempo, originally rock and roll but here reformatted into unthreatening wimped-out effluent, tranquilizing onlookers into thinking the juvenile snatch-and-grab mission couldn't have been what it looked like, so it must be all right to return to closing time, what a relief. The tune coming out of the speakers as the girls all dispersed into the evening happened to be a sprightly oboe-and-string rendition of Chuck Berry's "Maybellene."

Whenever Ché and Prairie met, it was by way of zigzag and trick routes, almost like they were having an affair, slipping away from PO's or caseworkers, or only steps ahead of the bright attentions of Child Protective Services, not to mention, these days, the FBI. Ché arrived at Noir Center all out of breath, dressed in leather, denim, metal, and calico, with a bazooka rocket bag slung over one wide precise shoulder and her hair today Tenaxed up into this amazing feathery crest, in a blond shade soured to citric.

"You're all gussied up, girl."

"All for you, my little Prairie Flower."

Prairie went shivering in with her hands under her friend's arm, while around them, in the uniform commercial twilight, plastic flowed, ones and zeros seethed, legends of agoramania continued. They stopped at a House of Cones, where they eyeballed each other, politely but without mercy, for changes in fat distribution while sucking, with more and less metaphoric attention, on the ice cream in their cones. Back when they were girls, all it ever took was eye contact to topple them into laughter that might go on all day. But Ché's much-valued smiles today were only tight quick Polaroids of themselves.

It was her mom's boyfriend again. "At least you have the whole set, you're not a semiperson," Prairie used to mumble.

"A mom who watches MTV all day and her boyfriend who transforms into Asshole of the Universe anytime he gets to see a inch of teen skin, family of the year for sure, you want it, I can fix you up with Lucky, no prob, just remember to wear somethin' short." And that was back when he was only harassing her, before they'd started fucking. Which when her mom found out about it she never brought up to Lucky's face, turning on Ché instead and blaming her for everything. "Callin' me all this shit, sayin' she wished she never had me . . . ," keenly watching to see how it went over, but Prairie was all sympathy and calming touch. For years they'd had this ongoing seminar on the topic of Moms, a category to which Ché's mother, Dwayna, was not much credit. The tension in the house would rise to an explosive level, with Ché coming on to Lucky, whom she couldn't stand, right in front of her mom just to piss her off, then the uproar would go on all night, with Ché stomping out each time swearing that was it, staying on the loose for weeks, turning for money to more and more desperate shit and the company of some odd young gentlemen, some with runny noses, some with money in their hand, some fresh from the school-yard and some that played in a band, often in situations hazardous to her health, till the only choice left her was to get popped so Dwayna would come down again and get her out, which she didn't have to but always did. Hugs and tears at the sergeant's desk, cries of "My baby" and "I love you, Mom," Ché would go home, Lucky would leer hello, and the whole cycle would start over, her rap sheet each time picking up new pages.

"Sure is a good thing you're beautiful," Prairie, the adoring sidekick, mooned.

"Remember that time over at my grandma Dotty's, we must've been six or something . . . one of those rainy Sundays with a major Monday comin' up . . . I remember I looked over at you during a commercial, thinking — I've known her forever."

"Six? Took you that long to figure it out."

They sauntered along companionably as New Age mindbarf came dribbling out of the PA system. "Moms are a mixed blessing," Ché announced.

"Rilly. But try having that part of your life missing."

"You'd love it in the joint, Prair, 'cz that's exactly what the girls are into, 's that hookin' up together in threes, one's the Mommy, one's the Daddy, and one's the little child — hard, soft, and helpless. I figure, what's the difference, bein' in a family out here, or being in the joint? Is why I've got this need to escape all the time, especially now. . . . You remember Lucky's collection of Elvis decanters, 'member his favorite, with the sour mash in it, that he only brought out for Super Bowl and his birthday? sort of full-color metalflake glaze on it?"

"Don't tell me —"

"Put it this way — that old Patsy Cline song 'I Fall to Pieces'? Well, the King just covered it."

"You told me he used to take it to bed with him, like a stuffed toy."

"It was a close call, you could see he was torn between coming after me and tryin' to save that bourbon — last I saw as I was running out he was down tryin' to suck what he could up off of the floor, had to keep spittin' out little slivers of Elvis's head — but he looked up at me, and his face was just full of murder, you know that look?"

Prairie realized she didn't . . . and then, with a stab of sadness, that Ché did. "So what the fuck," Ché asked softly, "am I supposed to do? I keep getting these business offers from gentlemen in mega-stretch limos, and some of 'm I think seriously about."

The girls had moved along to Macy's, where Ché, smooth and

sweatless, was working through the lingerie department with fingers spider-light while Prairie fronted, blocking her from what store cameras they'd managed to locate, keeping up a dizzy teen monologue, boys, recording stars, girlfriends, girl enemies, grabbing items at random, holding them up going "What do you think?" getting salespeople involved in long exchanges about discontinued styles as Ché blithely went on filching and stashing everything in her size that was black or red or both, so invisibly that not even Prairie after all these years could ever see the exact instant of the crime. Meantime, with a special tool swiped from another store, Ché was deftly unclipping the little plastic alarm devices on the garments and hiding them deep in the other merchandise — all at a fairly easy what Brent Musberger might've called level of play, a routine long perfected and usually just for getting warmed up with. But today, instead, they felt already nostalgic, shivery with autumnal chances for separate ways, so that each came to be performing for the other, as a kind of farewell gift, two grizzled pros, one last caper for old times' sake before moving on. . . .

Soon as she was old enough to see out the windshield, Ché had learned to drive, didn't give a shit really about ever being street-legal, not even if she lived to be that old, which it was part of her bad young image to doubt. Times she liked to flirt, times she was out to hurt, it depended. On the freeway she liked to cruise at around 80, weaving and tailgating to maintain her speed. "We are children of the freeway," she sang, fingertips on the wheel, boot on the gas,

> We are daughters of the road,
> And we've got some miles to cover,
> 'Fore we've finally shot our load —
> If you see us in your mirror,
> Better clear a couple lanes,
> 'Cause we're daughters of the freeway,
> And speedin's in our veins. . . .

None of the cars she drove were hers, but usually hustled off boys she knew, or sometimes borrowed via slim jim and hot-wire from strangers. When she couldn't get her hands on a car, she'd hitch a ride and try to talk the driver into letting her take the wheel. She could get anywhere in Southern California as fast as wheels could move. Sasha called her the Red Car, after the old interurban trolley system.

When they got someplace secure — which turned out to be the apartment of Ché's friend Fleur, east of La Brea and down in the flats — Ché shook from the rocket bag and from under her shirt this amazing fluffed volume of underwear.

"What, no aqua?" Prairie said.

"Aqua's what they give their wives, honey," Ché told her. "Black and red," twirling from a short-nailed finger a pair of lace bikinis in that combination, "is what they like to see on a bad girl."

"Night and blood," amplified Fleur, who'd recently begun working as a professional out of her apartment and was trying to talk Ché into joining the string she was on, "it's like they 's programmed for it or somethin' — oh, hey, nice, Ché, do you mind?"

" 'Course not," Ché in the middle of sliding into a short see-through number herself.

Prairie watched them playing centerfold and thought, strangely, of Zoyd, her dad, and how much he would have enjoyed the display. "Not exactly a innocent teen fashion message here," she commented.

"It never has worked on Ché," said Fleur. "Put her in anything pink or white," fingerslash across her throat, "her street plausibility's all shot to hell."

"While on the other hand you, my dear," Ché flinging at Prairie something almost weightless in those colors, "belong inside this item, stolen expressly for you." Which turned out to be an intricate silk teddy full of lace, ribbons, ruffles, bows, which it took awhile for Prairie, blushing and protesting, to be persuaded to try on. Whenever Ché got this way with her, courtly, using her eyelashes, it put her into this weird warm daze for minutes at a time. This one lasted till she'd resumed her street uniform, sweatshirt, jeans, and running shoes, and was standing outside on the steps, gazing up at Ché framed in the doorway, twilight coming down in a great blurred stain, and hard lemon light in the room behind her . . . Prairie felt like it was steps of a boat landing and that one of them was setting off on a dangerous cruise across darkened seas, and that it could be a long time, this time, till they saw each other again.

"Hope you find your mom," pretending it was coke that was making her sniffle. "Do somethin' about your hair."

Prairie got back to Takeshi's office and found the place in upheaval. They'd just got back from what was left of Ditzah Pisk's house. Ditzah's anxiety about the safety of the 24fps archives had turned out to be prophetic after all. Both DL and Takeshi had sensed exits away that something was up, when they came upon a loose formation of midsize, neutral-colored, dingless and clean Chevs, each with exactly four Anglo males of like description inside, and little octagoned E's, for "Exempt," on their license plates. Ascending into Ditzah's neighborhood, they began to hear hill-warped traffic on the scanner, up around Justice Department frequencies. Before long there was a police roadblock, so Takeshi parked farther downhill while DL switched herself on *Inpo* mode and disappeared into the landscape. Inside the perimeter she met, coming the other way, a Youth Authority bus with bars on the windows, the kind that usually carried brushcutting crews or fire-camp swampers, jammed with restless, sweating Juvenile Hall bad-asses all whooping and hollering like a school team bus after a victory. She smelled something like burning plastic but not quite, stronger, more bitter as she drew close, and smoke from burning gasoline.

It could have been handled with far fewer personnel, but some-body — DL could guess who — had determined to give the neigh-bors a show. In front of Ditzah's garage, on the cement, conical black heaps smoked, glowed, flared here and there into visible fire. Metal reels and plastic cores were scattered all over, and besides all the unspooled film burning there was a lot of paper, typed pages mostly, any scraps that temporarily escaped, spinning in eddies from the updraft, sent back into the flames by a sweeping crew. None of those observing the fire seemed to be civilians — the neigh-bors must have all been scared indoors. She noticed that the windows of the house had all been broken, the car trashed, trees in the yard taken down with chain saws and youthful muscle — she assumed it was the juvies in the buses who'd done all the physical work.

"How about Ditzah?"

"Still with her friends, hiding out. She's OK, but she's scared."

Well so was Prairie. She had no choice but to stick with these two, and was only marginally reassured by the $135,000 manufacturer's suggested retail price of the ride they took to Vineland, the ultimate four-wheeling rig, a Lamborghini LM002, with a V-12 engine that put out 450 horsepower, custom armed, wired and dialed to the hubcaps. It was like being taken off in a UFO. "Sometimes," she'd told Ché, "when I get very weird, I go into this alternate-universe idea, and wonder if there isn't a parallel world where she decided to have the abortion, get rid of me, and what's really happening is is that I'm looking for her so I can haunt her like a ghost." The closer they got to Shade Creek, the more intense this feeling grew. The speakers were all one cross-spectrum massive chord of discontent and longing by the time they reached the WPA bridge and began to thread the complex obstacle course into town.

Takeshi and DL had long been set up in a restored Vicky dating from Little Gold Rush days, when it had been an inn and brothel. They found a crowd of Thanatoids on the porch when they got there, and an atmosphere of civic crisis. CAMP search-and-destroy missions by now were coming over on a daily schedule. Brock Vond and his army, bivouacked down by the Vineland airport, had begun sending long-range patrols up Seventh River and out into some of the creek valleys, including Shade Creek. And now there was a full-size movie crew up here, based out of Vineland but apt to show up just about anyplace, prominent among whom, and already generating notable Thanatoid distress, was this clearly insane Mexican DEA guy, not only dropping but also picking up, dribbling, and scoring three-pointers with the name of Frenesi Gates.

"See?" DL nudged Prairie, whose mouth was ajar and abdomen tingling with fear, "what'd we tell you?"

They'd only missed Hector by about twenty minutes — he was

headed for the Vineland nightlife, looking to see who else he could inveigle into his project, driving a muscular '62 Bonneville he'd borrowed, or, OK, commandeered, from his brother-in-law Felipe in South Pasadena. In the back seat, on loud and bright, was a portable Tube, which Hector had angled the rearview mirror at so he could see, for the highway was a lonely place, and a man needed company. He'd stolen the set the last time he'd broken out of the Tubaldetox, this time, he swore, for good. Scientists. What did any of them know? The theory, when Hector was first admitted, had been homeopathic — put him on a retinal diet of scientifically calculated short video clips of what in full dosage would, according to theory, have destroyed his sanity, thus summoning and rallying his mind's own natural defenses. But because of his dangerous demeanor, which the doctors only found out later was his everyday personality, they rushed him into therapy without the full set of workups, and misjudged his dosage. Who could have foreseen that Hector would have such an abnormally sensitive mentality that scarcely an hour of low-toxicity programming a day would be more than enough to jolt it into a desperate craving for more? He crept out of his ward at night to lurk anywhere Tubes might be glowing, to bathe in rays, lap and suck at the flow of image, more out of control than ever before in his life, arranging clandestine meets in the shadows of secluded gazebos and window reveals with dishonest Tubaldetox attendants who would produce from beneath their browns tiny illicit LCD units smuggled from the outside, which they charged exorbitant rent for and came at dawn to take back. After lights out, all the detoxees who could afford to would settle down beneath their blankets with primetime through-the-air programming, all networks plus the four L.A. independents. By the time Hector ran out of money, the homeopaths were in disgrace and young Doc Deeply, at the head of his phalanx of New Agers all armored in the invincible smugness of their own persuasion, had beamed into power, proclaiming a new policy of letting everybody watch as much as they wanted of whatever they felt like seeing, the aim being Transcendence Through Saturation. For a few weeks, it was like a mob storming a palace. Schedules were abolished, the cafeteria stayed open around the

Yoo Hoo! The
Tube. . . .
It knows, your ev'ry thought,
Hey, Boob, you thought you would-
T'n get caught —
While you were sittin' there, starin' at "The
Brady Bunch,"
Big fat computer jus'
Had you for lunch, now Th'
Tube —
It's plugged right in, to you!

All he had for hope — how he fingered it, obsessively, like a
Miraculous Medal — was a typed copy, signed by Hector, Ernie
Triggerman, and his partner, Sid Liftoff, of an agreement on this
movie deal, or, as Ernie liked to say, film project, now stained
with coffee and burger grease and withered from handling. Despite
his personal savagery, which no one at the 'Tox chose to acknowl-
edge, let alone touch, Hector in these show-biz matters registered
as fatally innocent, just a guy from the wrong side of the box
office, offering Ernie and Sid and their friends a million cues he
wasn't even aware of, terms used wrong, references uncaught,
details of haircut or necktie that condemned him irrevocably to
viewer, that is, brain-defective, status. Could he, with all the Tube
he did, even help himself? Sitting in those breezy, easygoing offices
up in Laurel Canyon with the hanging plants and palm-filtered
light, everybody smiling, long-legged little *bizcochos* in leather
miniskirts coming in and out with coffee and beers and joints
that they lit for you, and coke that they held the *spoon* for you
and shit? was he supposed to sit there like some Florsheim-shoed
street narc, taking names down in a daybook? Why not join in
the fun?
     The deal was that Sid Liftoff in his vintage T-Bird had been
stopped one recent night on Sunset out west of Doheny, where
the cops lurk up the canyon roads waiting to swoop down on
targets selected from all the promising machinery exceeding the
posted limits below, only to be found, aha! with a lizard-skin etui
stuffed with nasal goods under the seat on the passenger side,

which to this day he swore had been planted there, probably by an agent of one of his ex-wives. Lawyers arranged for Sid to work off the beef with community service, namely by using his great talents and influence to make an antidrug movie, preferably full-length and for theatrical release. Hector, then attached to the Regional Intelligence Unit of the DEA office in Los Angeles, was assigned as liaison, though RIU work was understood to be punishment for 1811's with dappled histories, and this Hollywood posting, Hector was required to appreciate, was a favor, to be returned one of these nights and in a manner unspecified.

But soon enough, Hector's thoughts grew vertiginous, and he began to believe he'd been duked in to some deal, less and less willing to say when, or whether, he acted at the behest of DEA and when not, and neither Ernie nor Sid could quite decide how to ask. "The fucker," Sid told Ernie, at poolside, in confidence, "wants to be the Popeye Doyle of the eighties. Not just the movie, but *Hector II,* then the network series."

"Who, Hector? Nah, just a kid at the video arcade." They discussed the degree of Hector's purity, as then defined in the business, and ended up making a small wager, dinner at Ma Maison. Ernie lost. Sid started with the duck-liver pâté.

What Hector thought was his edge came about courtesy of an old colleague in the arts of foot-assisted entry, Roy Ibble, now a GS-16 with a yen for regional directorship, who called in from Las Vegas with word that Frenesi and Flash had shown up in town. Without even thinking about it Hector obtained a confiscated Toronado and went ripping all night across the Mojave toward the heavenly city, denial of desert, realm of excess. In the movie it would be a Ferrari, and Hector would be wearing a carefully distressed Nino Cerruti suit and some hyper-cherry A.T.M. Stacey Adams *zapos.* Liftoff and Triggerman would see to that. Yeah, those guys would get him just about anything these days. He cackled out loud. These days it was Hector who wasn't answering no phone calls, *ése.*

For according to a rumor sweeping the film community, a federal grand jury was convening to inquire into drug abuse in the picture business. A sudden monster surge of toilet flushing threatened water pressure in the city mains, and a great bloom of cold air spread over Hollywood as others ran to open their refrigerator doors more or less all at once, producing this gigantic fog bank in which traffic feared even to creep and pedestrians went walking into the sides of various buildings. Hector assumed parallels were being drawn to back in '51, when HUAC came to town, and the years of blacklist and the long games of spiritual Monopoly that had followed. Did he give a shit? Communists then, dopers now, tomorrow, who knew, maybe the faggots, so what, it was all the same beef, wasn't it? Anybody looking like a normal American but living a secret life was always good for a pop if times got slow — easy and cost-effective, that was simple Law Enforcement 101. But why right now? What did it have to do with Brock Vond running around Vineland like he was? and all these other weird vibrations in the air lately, like even some non-born-agains showing up at work with these little crosses, these red Christer pins, in their lapels, and long lines of civilians at the gun shops too, and the pawnshops, and all the military traffic on the freeways, more than Hector could ever remember, headlights on in the daytime, troops in full battle gear, and that queer moment the other night around 3:00 or 4:00 A.M., right in the middle of watching Sean Connery in *The G. Gordon Liddy Story,* when he saw the screen go blank, bright and prickly, and then heard voices hard, flat, echoing.

"But we don't actually have the orders yet," somebody said.

"It's only a detail," the other voice with a familiar weary edge, a service voice, "just like getting a search warrant." Onto the screen came some Anglo in fatigues, about Hector's age, sitting at a desk against a pale green wall under fluorescent light. He kept looking over to the side, off-camera.

"My name is — what should I say, just name and rank?"

"No names," the other advised.

The man was handed two pieces of paper clipped together, and he read it to the camera. "As commanding officer of state defense forces in this sector, pursuant to the President's NSDD #52 of 6 April 1984 as amended, I am authorized — what?" He started up, sat back down, went in some agitation for the desk drawer, which stuck, or had been locked. Which is when the movie came back on, and continued with no further military interruptions.

There was a weirdness here that Hector recognized, like right before a big drug bust, yes, but even more like the weeks running up to the Bay of Pigs in '61. Was Reagan about to invade Nicaragua at last, getting the home front all nailed down, ready to process folks by the tens of thousands into detention, arm local "Defense Forces," fire everybody in the Army and then deputize them in order to get around the Posse Comitatus Act? Copies of these contingency plans had been circulating all summer, it wasn't much of a secret. Hector knew the classic chill, the extra receptors up and humming, gathering in the signs, channels suddenly shutting down, traffic scrambled and jammed, phone trouble, faces in lobbies warning you that you don't know them. Could it be that some silly-ass national-emergency exercise was finally coming true? As if the Tube were suddenly to stop showing pictures and instead announce, "From now on, I'm watching you."

He deliberately dragged his feet on it but at last did Ernie and Sid the favor of taking a meeting. He found the mood in Holmby Hills a little more depressed than the last time he'd been up, the play areas empty of starlets now, the pool gathering leaves and algae, an autumnal string quartet on the audio instead of the usual K-tel party albums, and the only recreational drug inside the property line a case of Bud Light, which was disappearing fast, often without Ernie or Sid even waiting for it to get cold in the tiny patio fridge. Both men were nervous wrecks, covered with a sweat-like film of desperation to ingratiate themselves with the antidrug-hysteria leadership, suddenly perceived as the cutting edge of hip. Sid Liftoff, having owed much of his matey and vivacious public image to chemical intervention, often on an hourly basis, now, absent a host of illicit molecules in his blood, was changing, like Larry Talbot, into the wild animal at the base of his character, solitary, misanthropic, more than ready to lift his throat in desolate, transpersonal cry. Ernie, meanwhile, sat in a glazed silence that would have suggested his return, in this time of crisis, to his childhood religion, Soto Zen, except for the way he was unable to keep from handling his nose, with agitated fussing movements, as if trying to primp it into shape like a hairdo.

The pair, trembling and tense, had been exchanging remarks as Hector approached, calling, "Hi, guys," his shoes flashing in the sun. Sid took a very professional beat and a half before leaping up violently, knocking over his custom deck chair, running to Hector, falling on his knees, and crying, "Fifty percent of producer's net! That's out of our own profits, isn't that right, Ernie?"

"Uh-huh," Ernie on some dreamy internal delay, through which Sid continued, " 'Course you appreciate that won't happen till we get to the break-even point —"

"Do me a favor," Hector struggling to get loose of the importunate Sid, dragging him a step at a time toward the pool, "and please, *mis cortinas,* man — take that producer's net, use it to chase butterflies, around the grounds, of whatever institution deals with people who think I'm about to settle, for anythín short of gross participation here, *me entiendes como te digo?*"

Sid went flat on his face and burst into tears, kicking his feet up and down. "Hector! Amigo!" — further blowing it by most injudiciously reaching for Hector's shoes, whose finish the world knew, or ought to know, that Hector had long entertained homicide among his options in defending. But now he skipped backward, reminding himself the man was distraught, mumbling courteously, "Sid, you might want to, ahm, you know, check yourself out. . . ."

Sid fell silent and presently got to his feet, wiping his nose on his forearm, rearranging his hair and neck vertebrae. "You're right of course, frightfully immature of me Hector, I do apologize — for my outburst and also for my shortcomings as a host . . . please, here, a Bud Light? Not exactly *bien fría,* but the warmer temperature brings out more of the flavor, don't you think."

Graciously nodding, taking a beer, "Is that I would rather not hear no more about some 'break-even,' please, save that for Saturday morning, with the Smurfs and the Care Bears and them, OK?"

The two movie guys cried in unison, "Maybe a rolling gross?"

"La, la, la-lalla la," Hector pointedly singing the Smurf theme at them, "La, la-lalla laahh. . . ."

"Just tell us then," Sid pleaded. "Anything!"

How he had dreamed of this moment. He knew his mustache

was perfect, he could feel where every hair was. "OK, a million in front, plus half of the gross receipts after gross equals 2.71828 times the negative cost."

Sid's tan faded to a kind of fragile bisque. "Strange multiple," he choked.

"Sounds real natural to me," Ernie twisting his nose back and forth. They screamed and yelled for the rest of the day till they had a document they could all live with, though Hector much more comfortably than the others, even imposing upon the project his own idea of a zippy working title, "Drugs — Sacrament of the Sixties, Evil of the Eighties." The story hit the trades just about the time the grand-jury scare was cresting, so it got banner treatment and even a ten-second mention on "Entertainment Tonight" — no doubt about it, Ernie and Sid, first out of the chute into the antidrug arena, were making the town look good. Day after day skywriters billowed BLESS YOU ERNIE AND SID and DRUG FREE AMERICA in red, white, and blue over Sherman Oaks, though soon guerrilla elements were launching skyrockets charged to explode in the shape of a letter s and aimed at the space right after the word DRUG, changing the message some. Ernie and Sid found themselves allowed back into places like the Polo Lounge, where right after Sid's bust he'd been if not 86'd, then at least, say, 43'd. And then Reagan's people got wind of it and the two started hearing their names in campaign speeches. "Well . . . all I can say iss . . . ," with the practiced shy head-toss of an eternal colt, "if theere'd been moore Sid Liftoffs and Ernie Triggermans in Hollywood, when I worked theere . . . we might not've had . . . soo minny cahmmunists in the unionss . . . and my jahb might've been a lot eassier . . . ," twinkle. Die-hard industry lefties wrote in to publications to denounce Sid and Ernie as finks, Nazi collaborators, and neo-McCarthyite stooges, all of which was true but wouldn't deflect them an inch from making the picture, which they must have thought, dope-clouded fools, would purchase them immunity from the long era of darkness they saw lying just ahead. The town attended, now wistful, now cruelly amused, depending how hysterical the news was that day, to the boys out running point for the rest of them. Go, fellas, go.

Above-the-line checks started clearing the bank, motel rooms were booked, weather maps consulted, and crews assembled, and nobody had the least idea of what the movie, in fact, was supposed to be. Sid and Ernie, by now both deeply afraid of Hector, dared not ask, stuck with only vague assurances that the star element would be Frenesi Gates. Frenesi, working in Las Vegas one on and one off at a minor establishment on the wrong side of the Interstate, Chuck's Superslab of Love Motor Inn and Casino, cocktailwaitressing, had no inkling of the madness developing in her name till Hector showed up in town. Just before he called, she saw from the corner of her eye the snarled telephone lead, all by itself, like a snake in its sleep, give a slow loose shiver.

By the time they got there neither could remember why they'd picked the Club La Habañera, deep within a thousand-room resort-casino much too close to the airport, designed after the legendary gambler's paradise of pre-Castro Havana, where the smoke of genuine Vuelta Abajo filler and the fumes of Santiago rum, smuggled past the long embargo, mingled with a couple dozen brands of perfume, the band wore arm ruffles, and the sequined vocalist sang,

> Mention . . . [rattle of bongos] to me, [picking up slow
>   tropical beat]
> "Es posible,"
> And I won't need a replay,
> My evening, is yours. . . .
>
> Yes that's all, it takes,
> Incre-íble,
> Would it be so . . . ter-reeb-lay,
> To dare hope for more?
>
> ¿Es posible?
> Could you at last be, the one?
> Increíble,
> Out of so many mil-lyun,
> What fun,
>
> If you [bongo rattle, as above] would say,
> "Es po-ho-seeb-lay,"

While that old *Mar Carib'* lay
'Neath the moonlight above,
Es posible,
Increíble,
It's love . . . [fill phrase such as B–C–E–C–B flat]
It's love . . . [etc., board-fading]

Deeply tanned customers in dimly white tropical suits, with straw hats on the back of their heads, danced lewdly with hot-eyed packages in spike heels and tight bright flowered dresses, while beyond the seething blur of flame and parrot colors, sinister creatures, wrapped objects of unusual shape passing among them, bargained in the shadows. They were all yuppies on a theme tour, from places like Torrance and Reseda.

She recognized Hector right away, even after all the years, but the sight didn't raise her spirits. He looked like shit — run-down, congested in every system of circulation, appearing to her as at the edge of a circle of light, out of the frozen dark of years in service, of making deals and breaking them, betrayed himself, tortured, torturing back . . . long-term ravages . . . He ought to've broken by now — what kept him going? Somebody he loved, some drug habit, simple stubborn denial? She breathed his tobacco aura, withstood his crooked jovial born-to-lose laugh. So this was who he'd become — who, at least through her lack of surprise or any but reflex sorrow, she, down at her own modest level, must have become as well.

Just to get it done, she asked, "Is this official? Do you have any backup from DEA or Justice on any of this, or are you working some private angle?"

Hector began to pop and roll his eyes, as if working up to a full-scale freakout. Back at the Tubaldetox he'd had women talking to him like this all the time, another reason to escape, obliged never to scream back at them, as this earned him demerits that would even further postpone his release date. How he would have preferred violent body contact, shock, the recoil of a weapon, some scream of aggro, some chance just to drum his heels on something, but his options these days didn't even include teethgrinding. Once suave and master of himself, the fed was now having some trouble "trying," as Marty Robbins once put it in a different context, "to stay in the saddle."

Frenesi felt a little anxious for him. "Hector, you ever just think about beaming up, getting yourself out of this?"

"Not till I've got you and Brock Vond in a two-shot, smiling."

"Oh dear. No — Hector, it isn't 'This Is Your Life' here, in fact it could turn out the opposite. . . . Don't you know anymore what Brock is? Those quacks at the Tubaldetox have got you so Tubed out you can't even think straight."

"Listen to me!" screaming through his lower teeth like a lounge comic doing Kirk Douglas. She foresaw his attempt to grab her by the lapels and slipped in ahead of his, yes definitely looser reflexes, on her feet, turned and planted, telling herself *I'm ready*. Here she was with a homicidal narc having a midlife breakdown, without, fool, having remembered to bring anything tonight more threatening than a purse-size can of hair spray. But Hector, exhausted, folded back into the rattan chair, squeaking and creaking.

"You're an honest soldier, Frenesi, and we been out on so many of the same type calls over the years. . . ." Here came some sentimental pitch, delivered deadpan — cop solidarity, his problems with racism in the Agency, her 59¢ on the male dollar, maybe a little "Hill Street Blues" thrown in, plus who knew what other licks from all that Tube, though she thought she recognized Raymond Burr's "Robert Ironside" character and a little of "The Captain" from "Mod Squad." It was disheartening to see how much he depended on these Tubal fantasies about his profession, relentlessly pushing their propaganda message of cops-are-only-human-got-to-do-their-job, turning agents of government repression into sympathetic heroes. Nobody thought it was peculiar anymore, no more than the routine violations of constitutional rights these characters performed week after week, now absorbed into the vernacular of American expectations. Cop shows were in a genre right-wing weekly *TV Guide* called Crime Drama, and numbered among their zealous fans working cops like Hector who should have known better. And now he was asking her to direct, maybe write, basically yet another one? Her life "underground," with a heavy antidrug spiel. Wonderful.

"Your story could be an example to others," Hector was purring, trying for a Latin Heartthrob effect, "an inspiration."

"Get them off drugs, right? Hector, Hector. I grew up hearing too much of this all the time, one movie pitch after another, my mother was a reader, then a story editor, even a writer, at first I thought they were all real, all I had to do was wait a little and I'd get to see every one of them on a screen someday." Sasha had finally wised her up, likening it to one sperm cell out of millions reaching and fertilizing an egg, a comparison by then that Frenesi could relate to, though she felt the same shock and depression as when she'd found out that babies come not from Heaven but from Earth. Things now, for a moment, went likewise a little hollow. She'd brought to this rendezvous some wispy 2 or 3 percent hope that Hector might not be crazy. Though he and Brock both nominally worked for the Meese Police, just handicapping personalities, playing percentages, she'd have been willing to bet on some support from the DEA man — but now, outside again after all these years, back with the rest of the American Vulnerability, she could see, desolate, how anytime soon, in the cold presence of trouble already on the tracks, better she keep her change in her mitten than molest herself calling Hector for any help. He reminded her of herself when she was in 24fps, inside some wraparound fantasy that she was offering her sacrifice at the altar of Art, and worse, believing that Art gave a shit — here was Hector with so many of the same delusions, just as hopelessly insulated, giving up what seemed already too much for something just as cheesy and worthless.

He was nodding his head now, with a faraway look, as the Local 369 folks played "A Salute to Ricky Ricardo," a medley of tunes actually sung by Desi Arnaz on the "I Love Lucy" show, including "Babalu," "Acapulco," "Cuba," and "We're Having a Baby (My Baby and Me)," from the episode in which first mention is made of what turns out to be Little Ricky, a character in whom Hector took unusual interest. "Yes and a hell of a li'l percussionist, on top of everythín else. Just like his dad."

Frenesi peered. Something was up. His eyes had this moist gleam, growing brighter by the moment. Then she tumbled. "*Oh no.* We all settled that years ago, don't be doin' this to me now."

"Come on, open up them world-class ears, don't be tell' me you're not itchín to hear certain pieces of news."

"Warnin' you Hector, don't get me pissed."

But he had advanced across the tabletop, like a tile in a game, a Polaroid, mostly green and blue, North Coast colors, of a girl wearing jeans and a Pendleton shirt in a Black Watch plaid, sitting on a weathered wood porch beside a large dog with its tongue out. There was no sun, but both were squinting. "You fucker," said Frenesi.

"Zoyd took this one. You can tell from the weird angle. See the dog? name's Desmond — Brock chased him away. The house there? took Zoyd years to build, Brock came took that away under civil RICO, and they're probably never gonna live there again. The deal we all thought we had, the deal we honored all these years, is now all blown to shit because of Mad Dog Vond, you listenín to me?"

"No, asshole, I'm tryin' to look at my daughter's face. That all right?" She glared at him. "If you're so worried about the breakdown of your private little boys-only arrangement, bring it up with Reagan next time you see him, he's the one took the money away."

"Correct. But did you know he took it away from Brock too? Imagine how pissed off he must feel! Yeah, PREP, the camp, everythín, they did a study, found out since about '81 kids were comín in all on their own askín about careers, no need for no separate facility anymore, so Brock's budget lines all went to the big Intimus shredder in the sky, those ol' barracks are fillín up now with Vietnamese, Salvadorans, all kinds of refugees, hard to say how they even found the place. . . ."

"Hector —" shaking her head, unable to stop looking at the Polaroid.

He beamed her a tight teary smile. "She wants to see you."

She took a breath and enunciated carefully. "Look, I've seen some no-class behavior go on trying to get a picture made, and considering your life history, usin' somebody's kid on them ain't even a misdemeanor, but remember to put in your report that subject took deep exception to Agent Zuñiga's spiritual molestation of her child."

Hector frowned, trying to figure that out. "This ain't on the books — that what you think? Naw — families belong together, is all. Just 'cause I couldn't save my own marriage don't mean I can't try to help, does it?" Under the influence of, by then, quarts of a house specialty known as Battista's Revenge, Hector went off mooning about his ex-wife Debbi, who during the divorce proceedings, on the advice of some drug-taking longhair crank attorney, had named the television set, a 19-inch French Provincial floor model, as corespondent, arguing that the Tube was a member of the household, enjoying its own space, fed out of the house budget with all the electricity it needed, addressed and indeed chatted with at length by other family members, certainly as able to steal affection as any cheap floozy Hector might have met on the job. As long as she'd happened, moreover, to've destroyed this particular set with a frozen pot roast right in the middle of a "Green Acres" rerun that Hector had especially looked forward to viewing, possibly thereby rendering moot her suit, he decided in the heat of his own emotions to make a citizen's arrest, charging Debbi with Tubal homicide, since she'd already admitted it was human. In the movie of his life story, with Marie Osmond as Debbi and no one but Ricardo Montalban as Hector, it would be one of those epic courtroom battles over deep philosophical issues. Is the Tube human? Semihuman? Well, uh, how human's that, so forth. Are TV sets brought alive by broadcast signals, like the clay bodies of men and women animated by the spirit of God's love? There'd be this parade of expert witnesses, professors, rabbis, scientists, with Eddie Albert in an Emmy-nominated cameo as the Pope. . . . All just dreams of what might have been — in non-Tubal "reality," both actions were thrown out as frivolous, and they got a simple no-fault divorce, on the condition that Hector immediately enter a Tubal Detoxification program.

"As kindly as I can," since no one else was telling him, "between the television set and those New Age psychobabblers back at your Detox, I fear that very little, beyond the minimum needed for basic tasks, remains of your brain."

"OK. Swell. You don't care about your kid, or the War on Drugs, I can even buy that, but I can't believe you'd just walk away from a chance to get back into film again."

"Oh, 'film,' well, 'film,' I thought you said Triggerman and Liftoff, I hope you aren't mistaking what they do for 'film,' or even a class act."

"Look, with or without you, this will, git made. The money is committed, the papers are signed, all except for the director's agreement, and that's you . . . if you want. Shootín starts next week, soon as I leave here that's where I'm headed."

He wanted her to ask where. "Where?"

"Vineland."

"Hector, it's probably old news to you, but since I went under I've been all across the USA, Waco, Fort Smith, Muskogee too, rode up and down every Interstate in the land, some don't even have numbers, sweated my ass off in Corpus Christi, froze it in Rock Springs and fucking Butte, honored my side of it, always went where I got sent, and not once, that was the deal, never did I have to go anywhere near Vineland. It suited Brock's control-freak desires to keep me away from my child, and bein' a hard case and cold bitch, why, it suited me too."

They were both just about crying, Hector more with frustration than anything. "Is what I been tryín to tell you," in his forced, whispered grunt, "is that there is no deal anymore. OK? Brock has taken over the airport in Vineland with a whole fuckín army unit, and he seems to be waitín for somethín. Now what do you suppose that could be? Some think it's the dope crops, 'cause he is coordinating with CAMP and their vigilantes. Some think it's more romantic than that."

"This the way it is in your movie script, Hector?"

"Frenesi, there's no more reason for you to stay away any-more — see your kid again if you want, the game was called off. Come on back to Vineland, think how long it's been, all your mom's side of the family, gonna be up at those campgrounds on Seventh River —"

She drilled him with the double blues. "Who the fuck are you, trackin' the comings and goings of my family?"

He shrugged, with a look that if they'd been talking about virginity she would have called a leer. "Is it Brock? Are you afraid of him?"

"You're not?"

"You know Clara Peller, the lady in the burger commercial goín 'Where's the-beef? Where's the-beef?' well that's exactly my problem with you and Brock. How bad could it be? How personal? His dick was too short?"

She guffawed quietly. "Inquisitive tonight. Are you saying — you really think Brock and I should find a qualified third party, sit down, talk things out, share our feelings?"

"There you go!"

" 'Mad Dog Vond'?"

Hector allowed his face to flush and widen in a smile, angled his hand at the band. "¡Caramba! don't this stuff just get my blood throbbín to that beat! How about yourself, Mrs. Fletcher?"

"What?"

"Do me the honor?" It was a subset of northernized Perez Prado charts, mambos, cha-chas, steps she hadn't done since she was a girl. Despite his attempt to convey seedy decrepitude, she discovered grace, muscles, and that rhythm in his shoes. Hector was interested to find himself with a hardon, not for Frenesi who was here, but for Debbi who wasn't, that girl in the Mormon makeup who'd always held the pink slip to his heart, and the memory of the last time they'd danced together, to the radio, in the kitchen, with the lights off, and the night of love and sex strangely as always intermingled. . . . In other embedded rooms the croupiers called, the winners shrieked and the drunks cackled, plastic foliage the size and weight of motel curtains rippled slowly, just below the human threshold for seeing it, arching high against the room lights, throwing lobed and sawtoothed shadows, while a thousand strangers were taken on into a continuing education in the ways of the House, and in general what would be expected of them, along with the usual statistics and psych courses, and Frenesi and Hector had somehow danced out into all the deep pile and sparkle of it, like a ritzy parable of the world, leaving the picture of Prairie face up on the table, she and Desmond, both squinting upward at nothing, at high risk for hostile magic against the image, the two most likely means in here being fire and ice, but there the Polaroid lay, safe, till it was rescued by a Las Vegas showgirl with a hard glaze but a liquid center whom Prairie reminded of a younger sister, and who returned it to Frenesi when she came around the next day, her heart pounding, her skin aching for it still to be there, to find it again and claim it.

Just before they left for the airport, step-lively time once again, Justin took her aside. "Is something after us, Mom?" According to his dreams, a nightly news service, the thing pursuing was big and invisible. Would she even let on that she knew about it? "Don't worry," she told him, "it doesn't eat kids," but didn't sound that sure. They had both been acting weirder than Justin had ever seen them, flaring up at each other and at him, drinking and smoking too much, appearing and disappearing on no schedule he knew of. The smartest kid Justin ever met, back in kindergarten, had told him to pretend his parents were characters in a television sitcom. "Pretend there's a frame around 'em like the Tube, pretend they're a show you're watching. You can go into it if you want, or you can just watch, and *not* go into it." The advice came especially in handy when they got to McCarran International and found some service workers out on strike, and a picket line. "Uh-oh," said Frenesi. Uh-oh, went Justin to himself. His mom didn't cross picket lines — she told him someday he'd understand.

"Darlin'," Flash advised her, "these folks don't *fly* the airplane, all's they take care of's the maintenance in the terminal, so just don't use the toilet or nothin', OK?"

"Can't use the *toilet?*" Justin said.

"Fletcher, we can get on the bus, take the plane from someplace else?"

"Sweetheart — they took the bags already."

"No — you go in and get 'em back."

His head and neck suddenly forward at an angle she'd learned to connect with meanness on down, "Telling me to do what, now?" his tone and volume enough to bring some pickets out of the line to have a listen, along with a few passengers from the waiting area who were forsaking the daytime dramas on their coin-operated TV sets for this free episode. "You know what it is, it's your fuckin' family, tryin' to keep 'at old union-kid cherry for your daddy."

"Don't you bring Hub into this, motherfucker, not that she would have noticed if you did —"

"Nothing," Flash bellowed, "about her, all right? Bitch?"

Frenesi smiled, inhaling through her nose. "Tell you what," in a strenuously perky voice, "*I'll* cross *your* picket line if *you'll* go and get fucked up your *ass*, OK? 'N' *then* we can talk about busted cherries — unless o' course there's something you haven't told me. . . ."

Finally a picket coordinator came over. "We took a vote," she told Frenesi. "Just this once, it's OK, you can go on through."

"Was it close?"

"Unanimous. You a good child. Enjoy your flight."

Justin made a point of sitting between them. He already had the bowl haircut, and it had been a short step for him to learn to get in there and push them apart like Moe separating Larry and Curly, going, "Spread out, spread out!" But by the time they'd reached cruising altitude, the quarrel seemed to've been left below. Instead, too late, they'd begun to wonder why, with Brock's people bivouacked at Vineland International, they were flying in, beyond the fact that Hector had sprung for the tickets, having left them at the Regional Office with Roy Ibble, one of Flash's old handlers. "Only message was he'd see you all in Vineland," Roy said, passing Flash a funny look along with the envelope.

"That's it, Roy? Nothin' you might want to tell me, just as a human being? Nothin' for that brave little guy who once gave you the most important telephone number of your life, maybe turned your whole career around?"

"I'm as nostalgic as the next fella, Flash, I could go moanin' over those Nixon Years forever, but most of you old-timers, I hate to say it, you've been bumped off the computer to make way for the next generation, all 'em deeply personal li'l ones and zeros got changed to somebody else's, less electricity than you think, put it across your dick on a good night chances are you wouldn't even feel it."

Flash understood that Roy's career had included duties such as this, and even still might, but true to his motto, "Whine or Lose," he started in, in an all but unendurable singsong, "Well, Special Agent Ibble, maybe you've been off the street too long, maybe you never knew what it is to have your woman and your little boy out there at the mercy of any numb-nose Class IV offender with a buck knife from a swap meet who thinks his story's sad enough, after all these years walkin' point for you, so you could git home on weekends, so you could drive 'at fuckin' BMDubya, so's your wife, Mrs. Ibble, could keep fartin' on silk — 'at's right, Roy m'man, don't you give me that irate-husband look, I can read the married-man blues right on your face, so save it, 'cause I'm the victim here, while your happy household continyas to waller in bliss, mine's as helpless as worms out on the hardpan, waitin' for that first chicken 'th enough dumb luck to find its way home to roost, and *damn* 'at irritates the hell outa me, Roy?"

Roy, in some strange paralysis of will, had slowly been rolling away in his office chair and was now cowering against his credenza, chin trembling. "Please, no more! I'll tell you what I know. . . ." He even showed Flash the teletype of the burn notice out on him and Frenesi. Nobody, Roy confessed, knew what Brock Vond was up to, beyond some connection with Reagan's so-called readiness exercise, code-named REX 84 — or maybe it was just the election year getting to everybody. "For the moment," said Special Agent Ibble, "let's say you never came in here, and furthermore," impulsively rolling back to punch some phone buttons, "Hello Irma my darling, can you give me the spot figure on the imprest money right now? . . . Couple K, old twenties? OK, tens . . . mm, me too . . . bye."

"Roy, I'm overcome, you shouldn't't've."

"After a certain basketball game tonight, I may wish I hadn't."

"What, you — you guys gamble, w-with federal funds? Holy cow, maybe there *is* a budget squeeze around here!"

"We're nobody's protégé this administration, State Department hates our ass, NSC thinks we're scum, if Customs don't steal it out from under us, Justice and FBI try to either run it or fuck it up, and frankly," lowering his voice, "notice how cheap coke has been since '81? However in the world do you account for that?"

"Roy! Is you're sayin' the President himself is duked into some deal? Quit foolin'! Next you'll be tellin' me George Bush."

Roy kept a prop Bible on his desk, useful when he needed to get along with the born-agains in the Agency. He opened it and pretended to read. "Harken unto me, read thou my lips, for verily I say that wheresoever the CIA putteth in its meathooks upon the world, there also are to be found those substances which God may have created but the U.S. Code hath decided to control. Get me? Now old Bush used to be head of CIA, so you figure it out."

Irma showed up with the money, which Flash pretended to count. "And now what was this for again?"

"For staying so cute all these years," Irma blowing a kiss as she departed.

"She said that, I didn't," Roy added.

"What happens when we get in to VLX?" Frenesi wanted to know. Flash was curious himself. From the first he'd had his ideas about why Brock was out like this, just as he'd always known, since the days at PREP when he'd worshipped her from afar as Brock Vond's Woman, unattainable, that if it ever came to saving her, finally winning her love, it would have to mean facing Brock and taking her away from him. This long progress of postings into what she called Midol America because it always felt like her period, the air-conditioner throbbing, the rare moments of breeze in over the wrecking yards and oil-well pumps, cottonwoods in hazy distance, backyards facing the Santa Fe tracks, had never taken her outside Brock's long-distance possession — marriage and Justin and the years had brought her no closer to Flash. They had both been content to leave it that way, to go along in a government-defined history without consequences, never imagining it could end, turn out to be only another Reaganite dream on the cheap, some snoozy fantasy about kindly character actors in FBI suits staked out all night long watching over every poor scraggly sheep in the herd it was their job to run, the destined losers whose only redemption would have to come through their usefulness to the State law-enforcement apparatus, which was calling itself "America," although somebody must have known better.

VLX stood south of town in a broad valley just inland from the Seventh River floodplain. Wild hares lived in the grass between the runways, and cows browsed and seagulls scavenged at the far edges. The approach brought the plane lapsing in industrious wheeze across 101, but something about the light, as angles flattened out and the atmosphere thickened, wasn't right — glare, location, something. Rumors filtered back from the cabin that the air controllers down there sounded like they used to in Vietnam, none of the usual civilians were on the job, and there was heavy traffic on all the military frequencies. They crossed the little harbor and a first evening sprinkling of lights, the steeples, antennas, and power lines, across the freeway and darkening marsh to merge unfelt with solid ground again, and that was how Flash first came, and Frenesi returned, to Vineland.

The airport had been turned into a staging area, with military vehicles everywhere. Each deplaning passenger was being stopped, briefly questioned while an operator at the keyboard entered names and numbers, and then either waved on through or sent to a bullpen area to wait.

"Think that fuckin' Hector set us up?" it had occurred to Flash.

"Maybe not. Check this out." There he was, and a full film crew too, lights, a Panaflex, and some hand-held Arris. He sauntered on up to Flash, Frenesi, and Justin and escorted them out of line and through the terminal, ignoring stenciled directions taped to doors and columns, waving his badge and a newly acquired business smile at any security they met, and soon had them all checked in at the Vineland Palace, courtesy of Triglyph Productions, Inc., for the duration of the shoot. Frenesi just kept shaking her head. "That Hector. He's like me when I was twenty, maybe even more of an ingenue than that, he really believes he's immune. That Panaflex is his shield. He's bought in. He's another Sid Liftoff already." It wasn't till room service showed up with the cheeseburgers and fries and hot fudge sundaes and carafes of Hefty Burgundy that she began to admit maybe Hector hadn't been bullshitting and maybe there really was a picture. "Don't worry about him, Mom," Justin told her, "he's the real thing, all right."

"How do you know that?"

"Can tell by the way he watches television." The two of them had gone off to watch Twi-Nite Theatre, which tonight featured John Ritter in *The Bryant Gumbel Story*, and soon they were deep into a discussion of Tubal nuances that could have gone on all night, but Hector had to run up to the Cucumber Lounge to catch Billy Barf and the Vomitones, who might, if they'd work cheap enough, do some of the music for the movie. He didn't get to the Cuke quite in time to miss Ralph Wayvone, Jr., in a glossy green suit accented with sequins, who was cracking jokes into the mike to warm this crowd, who in Ralph's opinion needed it, up.

Things work out funny sometimes. His father had sent him up here to Vineland as punishment for a string of venial business errors. But he'd never wanted the Wayvone empire, he wanted to be a comedian, and it turned out that the Cucumber Lounge provided him with just what he'd always dreamed of, a workshop for getting his stand-up routines together. "So the other day I'm eating my wife's pussy, she says —" he waited for a reaction but heard only the air-conditioning and some glassware. "Eating pussy, wow, you know? It's just like the Mafia. . . . Yeah — one slip of the tongue, you're in deep shit!" A couple of teenage boys barked nervously, and Van Meter, tending bar, tried to help out. Nothing worked. Ralph Jr. grew desperate, driven at length to self-inflicted anti-Italian jokes. Finally, having squeezed the crowd for as much rejection as he thought he could handle, he used the unspeakably derogatory "How to Get an Italian Woman Pregnant" for his big punch line, smiled, sweating, and blew kisses as if he'd received an ovation. "Thank you all, thank you, a-a-a-nd now" — a drum-roll from Isaiah Two Four — "those maestros of the metallic, direct from a gig at a nudist golf course, where they *barely* escaped with their *balls,* yes let's hear a big Cucumber Lounge welcome, for Billy Barf! . . . and the Vomitones!"

Having learned its audience by now, the band started right off with Billy's own "I'm a Cop," a three-note blues —

> Fuck you, mister,
> Fuck your sister,
> Fuck your brother,
> Fuck your mother,
> Fuck your pop —
> Hey! I'm a cop!
>
> Yeah, fuck you, yuppie,
> Fuck your puppy,

Fuck your baby,
Fuck your lady,
Yes I can,
Hey! I'm the Man!

The crowd, reacting to this as if it were gospel singing, hollered
back, clapping and footstomping, "How true!" and "I can relate
to that, rilly!"

Zoyd, beard gone and hair shorter, lurking around the back of
the room disguised as the Marquis de Sod's idea of an ordinary
Joe, including the loan of a necktie from the Marquis's own un-
failingly hideous collection, was a little sensitive at the moment
on the subject of police, so all he did was nod along with the bass
line. Under terms of a new Comprehensive Forfeiture Act that
Reagan was about to sign into law any minute now, the government had filed an action in civil court against Zoyd's house and
land. He'd been up there a few times just to have a look, getting
close enough to hear the sound of his own television set from
inside his house. Federal Dobermans, shortly after whose meal-
times Zoyd had soon learned to arrive, lay behind new chain-link
boundaries, blood dreams for the moment less urgent. According
to the latest rumor, Zoyd's own dog, Desmond, who'd taken off
at the first signs of invasion, had been spotted out by Shade Creek,
having lately joined up with a pack of dispossessed pot-planters'
dogs from Trinity County who were haunting the local pastures
and not above ganging innocent cows at their grazing, an offense
that could carry a penalty of death by deer rifle. More for Zoyd
to be anxious about.

Leaving only a couple of marshals to guard the house, most of
Brock's troops had departed after terrorizing the neighborhood
for weeks, running up and down the dirt lanes in formation chanting "War-on-drugs! War-on-drugs!" strip-searching folks in public, killing dogs, rabbits, cats, and chickens, pouring herbicide
down wells that couldn't remotely be used to irrigate dope crops,
and acting, indeed, as several neighbors observed, as if they had
invaded some helpless land far away, instead of a short plane ride
from San Francisco.

Starting with a small used trailer shaped like a canned ham and a drilled well that he'd had to find a pump for, working by himself or with friends, using lumber found washed up on the beaches, scavenged off the docks, brought home from old barns he helped take down, Zoyd had kept adding on over the years — a room for Prairie, a kitchen, a bathroom, a tree house built among four redwoods that grew down the hill, set level with the loft in the house and connected to it by a rope bridge. A lot of it was nowhere near up to code, especially the plumbing, a sure cause of indigestion, running to many different sizes of pipe, including the prehistoric ⅝-inch, and requiring transition fittings and adapter pieces that could take whole days at swap meets or even at the great Crescent City Dump to find. While he lived in the house, he'd thought of it, when he did, as a set of problems waiting to get serious enough to claim his time. But now — it was like a living thing he loved, whose safety he feared for. He'd begun to have terrifying dreams in which he would come around a curve in the road and find the place in flames, too late to save, the smell of more than wood destroyed and sent forever to ash, to the blackness behind the flames. . . .

When the set ended, Zoyd headed outdoors with Isaiah Two Four, Van Meter ducking out from under the bar to join them. They went out in back to Van Meter's place and stood on the porch smoking, with the usual full-scale kvetchathon proceeding spiritedly inside. "Briefly," Zoyd addressed the high-rise drummer, "Van Meter has some folks lined up, now what we need is something they can express themselves with, preferably with a full-automatic option."

"There's this bunch of little Finnish knockoffs of a AK that shoot .22's I know I can get a price on, but somebody'll have to do the kit conversions besides going down to Contra Costa and pickin' 'm up. . . ."

"The Sisters have their headquarters in Walnut Creek," Van Meter twinkled, "so no prob." He referred to the Harleyite Order, a male motorcycle club who for tax purposes had been reconstituted as a group of nuns. Van Meter had run across them in the course of his quest after the transcendent, and been immediately surprised and impressed by the spirituality they all seemed to radiate. Taking as their text the well-known graffito "If they won't let Harleys into Heaven, we'll ride them straight to Hell," the Sisters pursued lives of exceptional, though antinomian, purity. They went on as before with all the drug and alcohol abuse, violence symbolic and real, sexual practices upon which Mrs. Grundy has been known to frown, and an unqualified hatred of authority at all levels, but with every act now transfigured, the vital difference being Jesus, the First Biker, according to Sister Vince, the Order's theologian.

"You might say, no bikes back then," wimple askew, passing Van Meter a bottle of supermarket tequila he'd been using to chase some barbiturate capsules, "but hey — how'd he get around out in the desert? Why do you think they call it Moto*cross*, dude?" and so forth, till drowsiness overtook his thoughts. Van Meter still kept in touch, was happy to fix them up with Zoyd and his scheme, though doubts lingered.

"Sure this is the best way, now, to go about it, Z Dub? All's they have to do's kill you to solve *their* problem, and this could be makin' it easier."

"Why I thought I'd bring some backup . . . you saying they might not want to do it now?"

"The Sisters? they don't give a shit. Their club tattoo says 'Full of Grace.' They believe whatever they do, it's cool with Jesus, including armed insurrection against the government, which, I'm no lawyer, but I think is the technical name for this."

"I'll ask Elmhurst." Zoyd's lawyer, who'd inherited his father's practice and role as North Coast attorney for the damned, had taken Zoyd's case without asking for a fee, prophetically fearing that this civil RICO weapon would be the prosecutorial wave of the future and figuring that he might as well get educated now. It had still been an effort for Zoyd to go in and see him. According to Vato Gomez, one of the heavy-dutiest of Mexican curses goes, "May your life be full of lawyers." Zoyd had come to consider the "legal system" a swamp, where a man had to be high-flotation indeed not to be sucked down forever into its snake-infested stench. Elmhurst cheerfully admitted that this was the case. "Am I complaining? Do plumbers complain about shit?" Not only did he look like something shoplifted from a toy department, but his tone of voice likewise suggested Saturday morning more than prime time. Zoyd observed the furry hand emerging from the lawyer's tweed sleeve, resting on a shaggy winter-cowhide briefcase covered with straps and buckles, bought years ago on layaway at some Berkeley leather store. Even the twinkle in this small-sized and potentially crazy attorney's *eye* was furry.

"You, uh, look eager," Zoyd remarked. "Done many of these?"

"The law's brand-new, the intentions behind it are as old as power. I specialize in abuses of power, I'm good, I'm fast, I enjoy it."

"My dentist talks like that. This will be fun." Resisting the impulse to stroke Elmhurst's head, Zoyd tried to smile.

The burden of proof, Elmhurst explained, would be reversed here — to get his property back, Zoyd would first have to prove his innocence.

"What about 'innocent till proven guilty'?"

"That was another planet, think they used to call it America, long time ago, before the gutting of the Fourth Amendment. You were automatically guilty the minute they found that marijuana growing on your land."

"Wait — I wasn't growin' nothin'."

"They say you were. Duly sworn officers of the law, wearing uniforms, packing guns, bound to uphold the Constitution, you think men like that would lie?"

"Glad you're not charging any money for this. How can we win?"

"Get lucky with the right judge."

"Sounds like Vegas."

The lawyer shrugged. "That's because life is Vegas."

"Oboy," Zoyd groaned, "I've got worse trouble here than I've ever had, and I'm hearing 'Life is Vegas'?"

Elmhurst's eyes moistened, and his lips began to tremble. "Y-You mean . . . life *isn't* Vegas?"

Making his way back into the Cuke, Zoyd ran smack into Hector, who ID'd him immediately, so much for disguises, and was so eager to announce "I just saw yer ol' lady, man!" that he missed his mouth with the cigar he was holding, nearly singeing the beard of a logger next to him, which could easily have meant a major detour off his freeway of life. "A-And accordín to my Thanatoid sources, your kid otta be in Shade Creek about now." "All I need's my mother-in-law," Zoyd bantering, still not absorbing the facts he was hearing.

"Now you mention it —" To the great delight of Sid Liftoff, who'd known her since their days as regulars at Musso and Frank's, and a senior gaffer who'd worked with Hub, Sasha had come wheeling into the valet parking at the Vineland Palace in a Cadillac the size of a Winnebago and painted some vivid fingernail-polish color, alighting and sweeping into the lobby a step and a half ahead of her companion, Derek, considerably younger and paler, with a buzz cut that nearly matched the car, an English accent, and a guitar case he was never seen to open, picked up on the highway between here and the Grand Canyon, where she'd parted from her current romantic interest, Tex Wiener, after an epic screaming exchange right at the edge, and on impulse decided to attend that year's Traverse-Becker get-together up in Vineland, leaving Tex on foot among the still-bouncing echoes of their encounter, which had brought tourist helicopters nudging in for a closer look, distracted ordinarily surefooted mules on the trail below into quick shuffle-ball-changes along the rim of Eternity, proceeded through a sunset that was the closest we get to seeing God's own jaundiced and bloodshot eyeball, looking back at us without much enthusiasm, then on into the night arena of a parking lot so dangerously tilted that even with your hand brake set and your wheels chocked, your short could still end up a mile straight down, its trade-in value seriously diminished. She'd been fooled, once again, by the uniform, a bright silver custom jumpsuit with racing stripes, flames, and a shoulder patch discreetly reading "Tex Wiener Ecole de Pilotage."

And perhaps about to be by Derek, a terminal sobriety case who favored leather, metal, Nazoid regalia, and the attitude that went with them, whose longest sentence was "Weww — it's oow rubbish, i'n' i'?" The perversity of the attraction made Sasha stretch and shiver, so she had little else on her mind as they went wandering into the Vineland Palace's Bigfoot Room, where she and

her daughter, Frenesi, as guests at the same hotel often do, came
face-to-face.

Though Ernie and Sid had done their best in advance to cushion
the shock, it was still an instant off the scale, from which neither
woman would return to the world she had left. Sasha looked
younger than either could remember, and Frenesi glowed like a
cheap woodstove. They sat in a Naugahyde booth beside a wall
covered in red-and-gold-flocked wallpaper, so unwilling to break
eye contact, as if one of them might disappear, that Derek, made
weird by such intensity, withdrew to the solitude of the men's
toilet and was never heard from again. "Did they scream?" Hector
tried to debrief Sid, "cry, hug? C'mon, Sid."

Sid grinned with movie avuncularity. "They danced."

"Yeah, they jitterbugged," said Ernie.

"The piano player knew a lot of old swing tunes. 'Polka Dots
and Moonbeams,' 'In the Mood,' 'Moonlight Serenade.' . . ."

"Huh," said Hector, "Too bad we can't use it. But screamín,
and confrontations, is much better, actresses love that shit."

"You're right, Hector," Sid and Ernie replied, in harmony.

Early in the morning Sasha dreamed that Frenesi, perhaps under
a sorcerer's spell, was living in a melon patch, as a melon, a smooth
golden ellipsoid, on which images of her eyes, dimly, could just
be made out. At a certain time each month, just at the full moon,
she would be able, by the terms of the spell, to open her eyes and
see the moon, the light, the world . . . but each time, in some
unexplained despair, would only cast her gaze down and to the
side, away, and close her eyes again, and for another cycle she
could not be rescued. Her only hope was for Sasha to find her at
the exact moment she opened her eyes, and kiss her, and so, after
a wait in the fragrant moonlight, it came about, a long, passionate
kiss of freedom, a grandmother on her knees in a melon patch,
kissing a young pale melon, under a golden pregnant lollapalooza
of a moon.

Prairie, meanwhile, was wandering around gaga. The easiest
way for her to see her mother at last would be to show up at the
Traverse-Becker reunion. Just be there. "But I don't know if I want
to anymore," she told DL.

"Know the feeling," DL confessed. They were all sitting in the booth at the Zero Inn that had been DL and Takeshi's Amen Corner ever since the early days of their practice here. There had been redecorating since, and outside talent was getting booked in with some regularity these days, tonight's being a band up from the East Bay called Holocaust Pixels, on a return visit, actually, being chartbusters around Shade Creek with their recent "Like a Meat Loaf." As if doing a mike check, the bass player leaned in and sang,

Like a meat loaf. . . .

The accordion player joined him —

Like a meat loaf. . . .

Then the electric violinist, making it three-part harmony,

Like a meat loaf for, your, lunch. . . .

As they hovered on the about-to-be-resolved seventh, the place erupted in cheers and tabletop-beerglass percussion, and then the accordionist took the vocal.

Like a meat loaf in, a lunch-box,
Like monkeys in, a grave,
We went among the Vietnamese,
Some souls for to save. . . .
Them souls did some scufflin',
Uh them uh monkeys, did too,
'Twas your bleedin' feedin' time, at the zoo.

Clapping and stomping, these Thanatoids tonight were acting rowdier than DL or Takeshi had ever seen them. Were changes in the wind, or was it only a measure of their long corruption by the down-country world, by way of television? The melody was rooted in Appalachia, in a tradition of hymn and testimony, and the beat was almost — well, lively.

So we took in, the Mar-ble Moun-tain,
And the Perfume River too,
Sometimes, we found, a bunch of them,

Sometimes, we missed a few,
And most times, the things, we seen, we didt-
'N want to see much more than once,
Like the graveyard full of meat loaf,
And monkeys for your lunch. . . .

Like a meat loaf,
Like a meat loaf,
Like a meat loaf for, your, lunch. . . .

Well we followed our dicks [applause] just a couple o'
    clicks,
Down the trail, by the bor-derline,
Somebody said, it was 'sixty-eight,
Others said 'sixty-nine [cheering],
But sometimes it felt like neither one, and other
Times it felt like both,
With a grave-box for your lunch meat,
Full of good ol' monkey loaf.

Ortho Bob stopped by with Weed Atman, both of them acting chirpy for the first time DL could remember. Prairie felt embarrassed, like she ought to be apologizing for her mom or something.

"Well I was almost you," Weed informed her.

"Oh, I'm sure." But Weed explained about the after-death state, the Bardo, with its time limits for finding a new body to be born into — seeking out men and women in the act of sex, looking for a just-fertilized egg, slipping to and fro with needful dim others in a space like a bleak smoke-tarnished district of sex shows and porno theaters, looking for the magical exact film frame through which the dispossessed soul might reenter the world.

"Made the basic error," Weed confessed, "too much still on my mind, couldn't find 'em, time ran out. So I'm here instead."

"You knew about me?"

"Thought this might be her strange idea of making it right. A life for a life, zero out the account."

"So if I'm not you, who am I?"

"Makes you think," Takeshi nodded, "doesn't it?"

"What are you gonna do to my mom?" Prairie wanted to know.

Here he was, after all, even in the peculiar formal getup, bordering on the semigross, that he was wearing, still a cell of memory, of refusal to forgive, sailing like a conscious virus through the population, seeking her out.

But Weed only shrugged. "The condition I'm in? not much. As a Thanatoid one's reduced to hanging around monitoring the situation, trying to nudge if you don't think it's moving along fast enough but basically helpless and, if you give in to it, depressed, too."

"But if I am the payback? If your account *is* zeroed out at last?"

"It'd depend a lot on who you've turned out to be, and the karmic chits *you've* been accumulating."

"Little complicated."

"Easier since Takeshi computerized. Still a danger of collapsing into a single issue, turning into your case, obsessed with those who've wronged you, with their continuing exemption from punishment. . . . Sometimes I lose it, sure, go out in the night, malevolent, mean, and I find your mom and mess with her. She cries, she gets into fights with her husband. So what, I figure, it isn't even the interest on what she owes me. But lately I've just been letting her be . . . figuring, maybe forget, but never forgive.

"I dream — Thanatoids dream, though not always when we think we do — I'm inside a moving train that exists someplace whether I dream it or not, because I keep going back to it, joining it on its journey. . . . I'm conscious, laid out horizontal on some bed of ice, attended by two companions who keep trying, one stop after another, to find a local coroner willing to perform an autopsy on me and reveal to the world at last my murder, my murderers. . . . I can never make out the faces of these other two, though they come in to sit with me now and then. It's always cold, always night, if there is a daytime maybe I sleep through it, I don't know. Out riding on steel too many years, every jurisdiction we come rolling into well notified in advance, each time men in hats, carrying weapons, standing on the platform, waving us on, who only want to swear they never saw us. In the face of this, the devotion of my two remembrancers, town to town, year after year, is extraordinary. They live on club-car coffee, cigarettes, and snack food, play a lot of bid whist, and argue like theologians over Brock's motives in wanting me, you'd have to say, iced. 'It was all for love,' says one, and 'Bullshit,' the other replies, 'it was political.' . . . 'A rebel cop, with his own deeply personal agenda.' 'Only following the orders of a repressive regime based on death.' So forth . . . I hear them late in the rhythmic dark hours, the last of my honor guard, faithful to the last depot, the last turndown."

Well, "Sounds like DL and Takeshi," to Prairie.

"Sometimes I think it could be my parents . . . still there, you know, looking out for me, kept going by this belief they always had in some 'higher justice,' they called it. Their pockets are empty by now, the wind whistles through, their own night rolls on, but they're both as sure as a fixed address, someplace safe and free, that this'll all come out right someday."

"That case, shouldn't somebody be goin' after that Rex guy, the one who did it?"

"Rex, why? He's only the ceremonial trigger-finger, just a stooge, same as Frenesi. Used to think I was climbing, step by step, right? toward a resolution — first Rex, above him your mother, then Brock Vond, then — but that's when it begins to go dark, and that door at the top I thought I saw isn't there anymore, because the light behind it just went off too."

He looked so forlorn that by reflex she took his hand. He flinched at her touch, and she was surprised not at the coldness of the hand but at how light it was, nearly weightless. "Would you mind if I . . . came and visited, now and then, you know, at night?"

"I'll keep an eye out for you." In fact they were soon to become an item around Shade Creek, out to all hours among the milling sleepless of the town, along the smoky indoor promenades lit by shadow-patched fluorescent bulbs, across covered bridges lined with shops and stalls, beneath the many clockfaces beaming from overhead, past Thanatoid dogs lounging in groups, who had learned how to give up wagging their tails and now gestured meaningfully with them instead. Weed would stuff himself with bucket after bucket of popcorn, Prairie would show him secrets of pachinko, seldom if ever would either talk about Frenesi, whom

Prairie had managed at last to meet. Unable after all to stay away from the Traverse-Becker wingding, in the course of saying hello again to faces she hadn't seen for a year, she got roped into the traditional nonstop crazy eights game, whose stakes were as low as the atmosphere was meanspirited. Distantly related sleazoids and the occasional megacreep drew from the bottom of the stock, stole from the kitty, signaled confederates in belching and farting codes, and tried to mark decks with nosepickings, their own and others'. So far the two big winners were Prairie and her uncle Pinky, looking sinister in a shapeless Ban-Lon leisure suit that might once long ago have been a brighter shade of pea-green. When Sasha came around to put her head in the Airstream, he was out of diamonds and Prairie was playing them, forcing him to draw. In some doubt as well were the whereabouts of the Mother of Doom, as the spade queen was known in the Octomaniac community. Uncle Pinky thought it was in the stock, but Prairie thought her cousin Jade had it.

"Dimple check!" her grandmother called. Prairie had to ask her to wait until the Mother situation had been resolved, finally risking an eight and calling spades, whereupon at last She emerged, looking mean as ever and obliging Uncle P. to draw five more cards, which, valiantly though he played on, proved to be one card too many.

Outside the trailer with Sasha was a woman about forty, who had been a girl in a movie, and behind its cameras and lights, heavier than Prairie expected, sun damage in her face here and there, hair much shorter and to the cognizant eye drastically in need of styling mousse, though how Prairie could bring the subject up wasn't clear to her.

Sasha, still giddy with her own daughter's return, tried to clown them through it. "Commere lemme check those dimples, yes *there*, they *are*, and *let* yer *grand*, -ma *check*, for *lint*, she's *just*, the *cute*, -est *lit*- tle *thing!*" — returning her relentlessly to babyhood, squeezing her cheeks together and her mouth up into a circle, pushing one way then the other.

"Hnof ikh, Angh-ah!"

"My *own* ado*rable grand*child," slinging the girl's head gently away at last. "I want you to sing the 'Gilligan's Island' theme for your mother," she commanded.

"Grandma!"

"First time she ever noticed the Tube, remember, Frenesi? A tiny thing, less than four months old — 'Gilligan's Island' was on, Prairie, and your eyes may've been a little unfocused yet, but you sat there, so serious, and watched the whole thing —"

"*Stop*, I-don't-want-to-hear-this —"

"— after that, whenever the show came on, you'd smile and gurgle and rock back and forth, so cute, like you wanted to climb inside the television set, and right onto that *Island* —"

"Please —" She looked to Frenesi for help, but her mother looked as bewildered as she felt.

"You could sing the lyrics before you were three, *all of 'em!* in this little babbling voice, with little gestures, the lightning bolt — 'Boom!' you'd go — 'If not for the courage of the fearless crew . . . ,' swinging those chubby fists back and forth, modulating each time around, just like a little lounge vocalist."

"All right all right!" cried Prairie. "I'll sing it." She looked around. "Does it have to be out in public like this?"

"It's OK," said Frenesi, "I think it's her way of trying to help." She grabbed Sasha, pretending to shake her back to sanity.

"Rilly. Sorry, Grandma." The girl followed them to a beer and soda cooler beneath an oak tree, where they would sit and hang out for hours, spinning and catching strands of memory, perilously reconnecting — as all around them the profusion of aunts, uncles, cousins, and cousins' kids and so on, themselves each with a story weirder than the last, creatively improved over the years, came and went, waving corncobs in the air, dribbling soda on their shirts, swaying or dancing to the music of Billy Barf and the Vomitones, while the fragrance of barbecue smoke came drifting down from the pits where Traverse and Becker men stood in a line, a dozen of them, in matching white chef's hats, behind fires smoking with dripped fat, tending great cuts of beef executed by assault rifle and chain-sawed on the spot in some raid off a steep pasture between here and Montana, beside some moonless dirt road, dressed out, wrapped, ready for the fire. A squad of kids stood by with squirt bottles full of secret marinades and sauces, which they shot from time to time as the meat went turning, and the magical coatings clung, flowed, fell, smoked, rose, seared. Soon Traverses and Beckers were filling up the benches at the long redwood tables, as the potato salad and bean casseroles and fried chicken started to appear, along with pasta dishes and grilled tofu contributed by younger elements, and the eating, which would continue into the night, got under way with some earnestness. It was the heart of this gathering meant to honor the bond between Eula Becker and Jess Traverse, that lay beneath, defined, and made sense of them all, distributed from Marin to Seattle, Coos Bay to downtown Butte, choker setters and choppers, dynamiters of fish, shingle weavers and street-corner spellbinders, old and beaten at, young and brand-new, they all kept an eye on the head of the table, where Jess and Eula sat together, each year smaller and more transparent, waiting for Jess's annual reading of a passage from Emerson he'd found and memorized years ago, quoted in a jailhouse copy of *The Varieties of Religious Experience,* by William James. Frail as the fog of Vineland, in his carrying, pure voice, Jess reminded them, " 'Secret retributions are always restoring the level, when disturbed, of the divine justice. It is impossible to tilt the beam. All the tyrants and proprietors and monopolists of the world in vain set their shoulders to heave the bar. Settles forever more the ponderous equator to its line, and man and mote, and star and sun, must range to it, or be pulverized by the recoil.' " He had a way of delivering it that always got them going, and Eula wouldn't take her eyes off him. "And if you don't believe Ralph Waldo Emerson," added Jess, "ask Crocker 'Bud' Scantling," the head of the Lumber Association whose life of impunity for arranging to drop the tree on Jess had ended abruptly down on 101 not far from here when he'd driven his week-old BMW into an oncoming chip truck at a combined speed of about 150. It'd been a few years now, but Jess still found it entertaining.

As night fell, Hub Gates, who'd brought all his arc lights up here with him along with his old partners Ace and Dmitri, lit up a couple for the kids. He was between jobs but had a gig up in Beaverton, Oregon, in a week. Somehow he'd managed to keep his little business, Lux Unlimited, profitable enough that he ate every day, though where he slept wasn't always up to code. Enough people still responded to the mystery of a powerful beam of light, miles in the distance. He showed his newly met grandson, Justin, how to rock the carbons to get the best beam, and how to keep them trimmed, till Frenesi came by and Justin remembered it was almost prime time.

"Hey there, Young Gaffer."

"Hi, Pop." She had dreamed about him the night before, rolling, clanking away from her down a straight old macadam road, out in the country, fields and hills in metallic cloudlight toward the end of the day, aware of exactly how many hours and minutes to dark, how many foot-candles left in the sky, bringing behind him like ducklings a line of lamps, generators, and beam projectors each on its little trailer rig, heading for his next job, the next carnival or auto lot, still wanting nothing but the deadly amps transmogrified to light, the great white-hot death-cold spill and flood and thrust, wherever he had to go, on whatever terms he had to take, to get to keep doing it. She called after him, but he wouldn't turn, only went on at the same laden crawl, answering but denying her his face, "Take care, Young Gaffer. Take care of your dead, or they'll take care of you."

Hurt, furious, she yelled back, "Yeah, or maybe they're just too busy being dead." And though she couldn't see it, she could feel the emptiness that came into his face then, and that was when she woke. . . .

Justin found his father and Zoyd in the back of a pickup, watching "Say, Jim," a half-hour sitcom based on "Star Trek," in which all the actors were black except for the Communications Officer, a freckled white redhead named Lieutenant O'Hara. Whenever Spock came on the bridge, everybody made Vulcan hand salutes and went around high-threeing. About the time the show ended, Prairie came by, Zoyd and Flash went off looking for beer, and she and Justin settled down, semi-brother and sister, in front of the Eight O'Clock Movie, Pee-wee Herman in *The Robert Musil Story*. It was mostly Pee-wee talking in a foreign accent, or sitting around in front of some pieces of paper with some weird-looking

marker pen, and the kids' attention kept wandering to each other.
"There's the Movie at Nine," Justin said, looking in the listings,
"*Magnificent Disaster*, TV movie about the '83–'84 NBA play-
offs — wasn't that just back in the summer? Pretty quick movie."
"They've been getting quicker over the years, from what I re-
member," Prairie said.

"Hey, Prairie, would you like to baby-sit me sometime?"

She gave him a look. "Some baby. Maybe I'll have to kid-sit
you."

"What's that?"

"Involves some tickling," Prairie already headed for her new
brother's armpits and flanks, and Justin squirming even before
they touched.

Out under yellow bulbs at a long weathered table, Zoyd found
himself trying to help Flash with the shock of meeting so many
in-laws in one place, both men from time to time looking around
fearfully, like unarmed visitors in a jungle clearing, as out beyond
this particular patch of light Traverses and Beckers went practicing
on scales, working on engines, debating, talking back to the Tube,
sending up gusts of laughter like ritual smoke cast to an unap-
peasable wind. A Traverse grandmother somewhere was warning
children against the October blackberries of this coast, "They belong to the Devil, any that you eat are his property, and he don't
like blackberry thieves — he'll come *after ya*." Even skeptical adolescents weaved in her voice's spell. "When you see those unhappy
souls out by the roadside, back up the lanes, in the ruins of the
old farms, wherever the briars grow thick, harvesting berries out
in the clouds and rain of October, why just drive by, and don't
look back, because you'll know where they've come from, and
who their labor belongs to, and where they'll have to go back to
at the close of day." And other grandfolks could be heard arguing
the perennial question of whether the United States still lingered
in a prefascist twilight, or whether that darkness had fallen long
stupefied years ago, and the light they thought they saw was coming only from millions of Tubes all showing the same bright-
colored shadows. One by one, as other voices joined in, the names
began — some shouted, some accompanied by spit, the old reliable

names good for hours of contention, stomach distress, and insomnia — Hitler, Roosevelt, Kennedy, Nixon, Hoover, Mafia, CIA, Reagan, Kissinger, that collection of names and their tragic interweaving that stood not constellated above in any nightwide remotenesses of light, but below, diminished to the last unfaceable American secret, to be pressed, each time deeper, again and again beneath the meanest of random soles, one blackly fermenting leaf on the forest floor that nobody wanted to turn over, because of all that lived, virulent, waiting, just beneath.

"Political family," Zoyd remarked, "for sure."

Flash, listening with his face held against changes of expression, nodded, hazarded, "Yep — sounds just like her, don't it?"

They were learning already how to talk about Sasha, and Brock Vond, and even Hector, but neither had any idea how or even if they should be talking, much less blurting anything, about Frenesi. It didn't help that Zoyd saw Flash as a charming psychopath pretending to be sane but given away by nuances — the length and placement of sideburns on the maul-shaped head, a black country Latino accent straight from the joint, a tattoo on his arm of a crossed M16 and AK-47 with the legend "Brothers In Death." But Flash also had the sound of a man with Frenesi on the brain — crazy to hold long beery seminars on the subject, once begun maybe impossible to stop . . . for some curious short pause, it seemed like they'd exchanged lives, and it was Flash who'd lost her long ago but couldn't forget her, and Zoyd who'd been soldiering along the decade and more, maybe by her side, both would be quick to complain, but never really with her. Zoyd, seeing the need behind the desperado lamps, knew he'd have to be the comforter in this, with the years of her absence to insulate and protect him after all, whereas this unfortunate 'sucker was right down helpless in the middle of it. So, "I was only a opening act," he reminded Flash, "don't go thinkin' like we ever got to know each other or nothin'."

"Just so you're not avoiding her on account of me, 's all," Flash earnestly cranking up the baby blues.

"Oh. Well. Now, see, 's a matter of fact —"

But Isaiah Two Four came by with the latest update on his assault-rifle deal, unrecoverably in the act of falling through, and probably just as well, given the attitude prevailing among the Harleyites since their appearance last week on the Donahue show. Suddenly, with development deals for movies and miniseries, plus T-shirts, collector dolls, lunch boxes, and so forth, the membership had to a nun all been finding themselves too big and busy for anything as small-time as helping Zoyd get his place back anymore.

"Whole problem 'th you folks's generation," Isaiah opined, "nothing personal, is you believed in your Revolution, put your lives right out there for it — but you sure didn't understand much about the Tube. Minute the Tube got hold of you folks that was it, that whole alternative America, el deado meato, just like th' Indians, sold it all to your real enemies, and even in 1970 dollars — it was way too cheap. . . ."

"Well I hope you're wrong," Zoyd breezed on, " 'cause plan B was to try and get my case on '60 Minutes,' or one of them."

"Soon as they find out about Holytail," Isaiah said, "you start even looking like a drug figure, there goes your case in court."

"Sounds like my lawyer." Elmhurst had strongly urged Zoyd to stay out of Holytail for the duration of this season's CAMP raids against the harvests. Each day now saw new columns of fragrant smoke ascending somewhere above the green Vineland hills to smudge the sky, and on each News at Six Sheriff Willis Chunko gleefully slashing into yet another patch of mature plants with his celebrated gold-handled chain saw, vowing to extinguish the feared herb from the soil of Vineland, as Skip Tromblay and the news team squirmed and cooed. No time for Zoyd to be anywhere near Holytail, much less helping truck out lawn and leaf bags full of newly picked sinsemilla buds or plants hastily pulled up whole, often in midnight games of hide-and-seek with deputies in ruggedized Dodge cruisers propelled by monster Mopars dialed and eager for the chase, rumbling in wet roostertails of dirt and stone chips up and down the old logging roads and over the wood and cable bridges between Holytail and the freeway — but it had been his job for the past couple of weeks nonetheless, trying, like everybody else, to get as much of the crop as possible out before Willis's big barbecue, too little time remaining on the clock, but wordlessly all agreeing fuck the clock, fuck it, play to the end.

Out on those runs, speeding after moonset through the smell of
the redwoods, with all the lights out, trying to sense among the
different patches of darkness where the curves were, and what gear
to be in for grades that were nearly impossible to see, bouncing
along in a vintage Power Wagon, Zoyd from among somebody's
collection of beat-up old 8-tracks usually found himself listening
to the Eagles' *Greatest Hits,* in particular "Take It to the Limit,"
basically his whole story these days, singing mournfully along,
though obliged from time to time to interrupt himself as some new
set of headlights appeared — "OK Zoyd, back on defense —" half
hoping for a run-in with Brock, knowing by now it was never
going to happen in any frontal way, attempting to get back his
own small piece of Vineland, but out here at the periphery, in
motion, out on one of the roads that had taken him away from
his home, and that must lead back. . . .

But every other night lately he was visited by the dream of the
burning house. Each time it became clearer to him that his house,
after twelve years together from scratch, was asking him to torch
it, as the only way left to release it from its captivity. Having glided
out to visit between trunks of the trees, the dogs sensing him,
getting up to prowl anxiously below, Zoyd would soundlessly enter
and haunt, finding nothing inside anymore of himself or Prairie,
only stripped and vacuumed spaces, public or hired security shift
after shift, and the dogs who came and scratched at the sills just
around sunrise.

"You know," Flash suggested, "easiest thing might just be to
go find the son of a bitch and cancel his series for him, ever think
about that?"

An intriguing suggestion that they were just about to get into
when Prairie came by from hustling Justin into his sleeping bag,
carrying her own, on the way out to the woods to be alone for a
while. "Feeling totally familied out," she told Zoyd, "nothin' personal, o' course." She had a long look at him, and after having
just spent hours with Frenesi's face, found it easier now to make
out, past the quaquaversal beard and smudged eyeglass lenses, as
clearly as she ever would in Zoyd her own not-yet-come-to-terms-
with face. A day would come when she'd ask, "Didn't you ever

worry that you might not be my father? That maybe it was Weed, or Brock?" This time, in his arms.

"Nope. What I was more afraid of was, 's 'at I might belong to Brock."

Now all he dared was, "How's your mother?"

"Well, I think I make her nervous," Prairie said. "She's lookin' for anger, but she's not gettin' it from me."

"She makin' *you* nervous?"

"Oh . . . it's like meeting a celebrity. I'm OK, rilly. And I can see why you guys married her."

"Why?" asked Zoyd and Flash, quickly and together.

"You're adults, you're supposed to know."

"Give us a hint?" Zoyd pleaded. But she was already on her way, on into the trees till she reached a piece of the woods that she'd never seen, a small clearing inside a grove of Sitka spruce and alder, where she spread her bag and, enjoying the solitude, must've drifted off to sleep. The beat of helicopter blades directly overhead woke her. As she stared, down out of it, hooked by harness and cable to the mother ship above, came Brock Vond, who looked just like he had on film. For about a week Brock, whom his colleagues were calling "Death From Slightly Above," had been out traveling in a tight formation of three dead-black Huey slicks, up and down the terrain of Vineland nap-of-the-earth style, liable to pop up suddenly over a peaceful ridgeline or come screaming down the road after an innocent motorist, inside one meter of the exhaust pipe, Brock, in flak jacket and Vietnam boots, posing in the gun door with a flamethrower on his hip, as steep hillsides, thick with redwoods, the somber evergreen punctuated with bright flares of autumn yellow, went wheeling by just below, as the rotor blades tore ragged the tall columns of fog that rose from the valleys.

But at the moment here, Brock was linked by remote control to the motor of the Huey's hoist, able to lower himself to within centimeters of the girl's terrified body, where she could stare into the dim face, backlit by the helicopter lights. The original plan, as he'd recapped for Roscoe, who'd frankly had more recaps on this than Mark C. Bloome, had been to go in, cross-plot the subject, come down vertical, grab her, and winch back up and out — "The key is rapture. Into the sky, and the world knows her no more." Roscoe in his time had done a heckuva lot worse than abduct kids. He imagined himself grown oversize, beastlike, scuffling along beside a more human-faced Brock Vond. "Her tits, Master —"

"Nice firm adolescent tits, Roscoe, tits like juicy apples."

She lay paralyzed in her childhood sleeping bag with the duck decoys on the lining and saw that even in the shadows his skin glowed unusually white. For a second it seemed he might hold her in some serpent hypnosis. But she came fully awake and yelled in his face, "Get the fuck out of here!"

"Hello, Prairie. You know who I am, don't you?"

She pretended to find something in the bag. "This is a buck knife. If you don't —"

"But Prairie, I'm your father. Not Wheeler — me. Your real Dad."

Nothing that hadn't occurred to her before — still, for half a second, she began to go hollow, before remembering who she was. "But you can't be my father, Mr. Vond," she objected, "my blood is type A. Yours is Preparation H."

By the time Brock figured out the complex insult, he was also feeling mixed signals through the cable that held him. Suddenly, some white male far away must have wakened from a dream, and just like that, the clambake was over. The message had just been relayed by radio from field headquarters down at the Vineland airport. Reagan had officially ended the "exercise" known as REX 84, and what had lain silent, undocumented, forever deniable, embedded inside. The convoys were to pack up and return to their motor pools, the mobile prosecution teams to disband, all the TDY's in the task forces to return to their regular commands, including Brock, his authorizations withdrawn, now being winched back up, protesting all the way, bearings and brake pads loudly shrieking, trying to use his remote but overridden by Roscoe at the main controls.

They fought about it through the flight back down to VLX, Roscoe, the career counselor, pointing out the virtues of obedience and patience, and Brock screaming, "Asshole, they're all together, one surgical strike, we can't just let them get away. . . ." He seemed to calm down after landing, but hung around his command helicopter awhile, suddenly produced a service revolver, got in the pilot's seat, and prepared to ascend.

"OK, have it your way, Brock," Roscoe hollered as the Huey started to rise, too loud for Brock to hear anymore, "but I can't guarantee you Ed Meese is gonna like it!" but by then he was gone, following his penis — what else could it be? — into the night clouds over Vineland.

As, meanwhile, gently, the trees around her, the spruces tall and massive, the alders slenderer, quicker, began, in a stirring of breeze, to dance together, a sight she'd grown up with out her old bedroom window, these particular partners, Prairie was joined in the clearing by a young man so blond and by the standards of her generation foxy-looking that at first she suspected UFO involvement. He had heard the bladebeats and her shouting, and was carrying by its neck an old acoustic guitar with Cyrillic stenciling on it, as if he'd been prepared to use it as a weapon. His name was Alexei, and he was on liberty from a Russian fishing boat that had had to put into Vineland for some emergency repairs to its generator. "You're defecting?" Prairie asked.

He laughed. "Looking for American rock and roll. You know Billy Barf and Vomitones?" Did she. "Very famous in Soviet Union. You know '83 Garage Tapes?"

"Yeah, they put 'em in a big peanut-butter jar, sealed and waterproofed it, dropped it off the Old Thumb jetty into the ocean, you mean —"

"Got much airplay in Vladivostok. I learn all solos of Billy, Meathook too. *Bolshoi metallisti.* Can you take me where they are? I would like to sit in."

The Movie at Nine, more than the usual basketball epic, was a story of transcendent courage on the part of the gallant but doomed L.A. Lakers, as they struggled under hellish and subhuman conditions at Boston Garden against an unscrupulous foe, hostile referees, and fans whose behavior might have shamed their mothers had their mothers not been right there, screaming epithets, ruining Laker free throws, sloshing beer on their children in moments of high emotion, already. To be fair, the producers had tried their best to make the Celtics look good. Besides Sidney Poitier as K. C. Jones, there was Paul McCartney, in his first acting role, as Kevin McHale, with Sean Penn as Larry Bird. On the Laker side were Lou Gossett, Jr., as Kareem Abdul-Jabbar, Michael Douglas as Pat Riley, and Jack Nicholson as himself. Vato and Blood, who were watching this down at the garage in Vineland, being both passionate Laker fans, had to find something else to bicker about. "Say Blood," Blood remarked, aggressively, "some righteous-looking shades Jack's wearing tonight."

Vato snorted. "You wear them for workín on mufflers, Vato, lookit 'em, they ain' even big enough to cover his eyeballs."

"What's that you're wearing on your own face, Blood? What do you use them for, messin' with Contras? — Whoo!" both of them distracted for a minute as Lou Gossett, Jr., appeared to execute a perfect skyhook.

It was a slow night, no calls all through the picture, by the harrowing conclusion of which Vato and Blood had used up a box of Man-Size Kleenexes between them. Close to midnight they got a phone call. Vato took it and hung up blinking and shaking his head. "You know who it was, don't you."

"If it's more heartbreak, Blood, don't tell me."

"It's Brock Vond, man. In person. His Huey's on the hillside, his ride is in the creek."

"Time to lock and load, Blood."

"Let's hit it, Vato."

Brock had been vague over the phone about how he'd started off in a helicopter and ended up in a car. He hadn't been aware of any transition. But it had been an unusual sort of car, almost without compression, unable to get over any but the easiest grades until at last it slowed to a halt and would start no more. And there was the telephone beside the road, and the lighted sign said DO IT, so he had picked up, and there was Vato at the other end. He felt in some way detached, unable to focus or, oddly, to remember much before he found himself at the wheel of the failing, unfamiliar car, whose battery now finally went dead as the headlamps dimmed weakly into darkness.

At last he saw the lights in the distance, like running lights of a ship out on the sea . . . there was nothing else in the landscape by now — Brock could scarcely see the road. The F350, *El Mil Amores*, came nearer and louder, and finally stopped for him.

"Hop in, Blood."

"What about the car?"

"What car?"

Brock looked around but couldn't see the car anywhere. He climbed in next to Blood and they started off along the nearly lightless road. Soon the surface changed to dirt, and trees began to press in on either side. As he drove, Vato told an old Yurok story about a man from Turip, about five miles up the Klamath from the sea, who lost the young woman he loved and pursued her into the country of death. When he found the boat of Illa'a, the one who ferried the dead across the last river, he pulled it out of the water and smashed out the bottom with a stone. And for ten years no one in the world died, because there was no boat to take them across.

"Did he get her back?" Brock wanted to know. No, uh-uh. But he returned to his life in Turip, where everyone thought he'd died, and became famous, and told his story many times. He was always careful to warn against the Ghosts' Trail leading to Tsorrek, the land of death, traveled by so many that it was already chest-deep. Once down under the earth, there would be no way to return. As he stared out the window, Brock realized that around them all this time had been rising a wall of earth each side of the narrowing road, in which tree roots twisted overhead now, and mud, once glistening, had grown darker, till only its smell was present. And soon, ahead, came the sound of the river, echoing, harsh, ceaseless, and beyond it the drumming, the voices, not chanting together but remembering, speculating, arguing, telling tales, uttering curses, singing songs, all the things voices do, but without ever allowing the briefest breath of silence. All these voices, forever.

Across the river Brock could see lights, layer after layer, crookedly ascending, thickly crowded dwellings, heaped one on the other. In the smoking torch- and firelight he saw people dancing. An old woman and an old man approached. The man carried objects in his hands that Brock couldn't make out clearly. Then he began to notice, all around in the gloom, bones, human bones, skulls and skeletons. "What is it?" he asked. "Please."

"They'll take out your bones," Vato explained. "The bones have to stay on this side. The rest of you goes over. You look a lot different, and you move funny for a while, but they say you'll adjust. Give these third-worlders a chance, you know, they can be a lotta fun."

"So long, Brock," said Blood.

The word was out immediately on the Thanatoid grapevine, causing Takeshi and DL to be summoned back from a midnight raid on a local egg ranch, where Takeshi had been planning to steal a sackful of chicken feed for the high-productivity amphetamines it contained, since, with his intake a little higher than usual this week, he'd run out of *shabu* once again — suddenly his pager went off and two thousand chickens started to squawk and carry on, bell and siren alarms kicked in, and the two culprits had to run for it. Back at the Zero Inn, they found a party going on, a lot of gloating, Weed drinking mango daiquiris and trying on different kinds of hats, Ortho Bob sitting in with the band and also singing, though nothing slower tonight than "Your Cheatin' Heart."

Takeshi and DL, crankless, took a turn around the dance floor. "The kid — you miss her, I bet!"

"Readin' my mind, T'kesh."

"Why don't you — go on up there and visit! Ten-minute drive!"

"Yeah — try fifteen years."

"No more Brock, *ne?* Good opportunity!"

Had it only been, as she'd begun to fear, that many years of what the Buddha calls "passion, enmity, folly"? Suppose that she'd been meant, all the time, to be paying attention to something else entirely? Two or three years ago, in Trans-Am mode, out following an intricate Thanatoid trail from one oilpatch bank account to another, on impulse they'd made a loop through East Texas and into Houston to visit her mother, Norleen, who took DL aside first chance they got and, pretending to help load the dishwasher, started raving about Takeshi, his looks, charm, and sophistication. "It's that glamour job you always wanted," so unironic that DL was surprised to feel a little wave of tenderness.

"But Mama," gently, "there is a good chance he's crazy. I know he's got all kinds of people after him, and some others he won't even tell me about. For years now, I've been his accomplice in . . . I don't know what you'd call it, a life of international crime? . . ."

"The Lord gives us these difficulties to be overcome, Darryl Louise, it's just called gettin' on with your life. Why, anyone at all can see how he needs you, and adores you, and my gracious — he looks just like a Jap Robert Redford! I think the one that's crazy's you."

DL couldn't quite bring herself, then or later, to tell her mother, who did keep asking, any of the details of how they'd met — no Japanese whorehouses or Vibrating Palms — nor of his resurrection by Puncutron Machine, nor their yearly visits back to the Retreat of the Kunoichi Attentives to be checked out and to roll over the partnership agreement — none of that. She understood that if she ever started to tell the tale, why sooner or later the matter of the no-sex clause would emerge and Norleen's kindly dreaming be perhaps fatally contradicted, only earning DL her mother's contempt. Why get into it? But that turned out to be the year she and Takeshi finally renegotiated the no-sex clause, and DL found out what she'd been missing those other years. "Whooee!" is how she expressed it.

"Oriental love magic!" Takeshi wiggling his eyeglasses, which he had not removed, at her languidly, "right?"

Hmm, not exactly, but intense enough to make her curious. "Takeshi, I didn't know you felt like this. . . . I didn't know I felt like this. What's going on?" Even after the clause change, it had taken them days' travel, back on I-40 again, to get around to this, and if she hadn't been so off-balance she probably wouldn't be asking. They were in a penthouse suite high over Amarillo, up in the eternal wind, with the sun just set into otherworld transparencies of yellow and ultraviolet, and other neon-sign colors coming on below across the boundless twilit high plain, and she was watching him now with newly cleansed attention, her light-bearing hair, against the simplicity out the window, a fractal halo of complications that might go on forever . . . one of those moments men are always being urged to respond to with care and sensitivity.

But Takeshi was cackling, "You — should have been there the

first time, Toots — you wouldn't have to ask!" Far from ever being offended, Takeshi continued to find it amusing that she'd been so focused on murdering Brock that night in Tokyo that she'd completely missed the sex part. And according to Sister Rochelle, that Brock obsession, appearing like a cop cruiser in the dark sooner or later down every roadway her life took, had also been afflicting DL's spirit, acting as a major obstacle, this time around, to fulfilling her true karmic project.

"Which is?" DL had had the boldness to inquire.

"Oh, the usual journey from point A to point B. But what if this disagreeable little gent was never any destination at all, only the means of transport, maybe only some ticket, one the conductor even forgot to punch?" Another koan to drive DL crazier, just what she needed.

As for Takeshi, the Head Ninjette had managed to corner him while he was on the Puncutron Machine, all hooked up with no escape, and while an inkjet printer moved along the meridians of his naked skin, laying down trigger-point labels in different colors, adding reference numbers and Chinese ideograms, and a Senior Ninjette Puncutech stood by with an ivory fescue, noting and commenting to a small bevy of teen novices, all in white *gi* with trainee armbands, Sister Rochelle, as so often in the past, now socked Takeshi with another of her allegories, this time about Hell. "When the Earth was still a paradise, long long ago, two great empires, Hell and Heaven, battled for its possession. Hell won, and Heaven withdrew to an appropriate distance. Soon citizens of the Lower Realm were flocking up to visit Occupied Earth on group excursion fares, swarming in their asbestos touring cars and RV's all over the landscape, looking for cheap-labor bargains in the shops, taking pictures of each other in a blue and green ambience that didn't register on any film you could buy down in Hell — till the novelty wore off, and the visitors began to realize that Earth was just like home, same traffic conditions, unpleasant food, deteriorating environment, and so forth. Why leave home only to find a second-rate version of what they were trying to escape? So the tourist business began to dwindle, and then the Empire was calling back first its administrators and soon even its troops, as if drawing inward, closer to its own chthonian fires. After a while, the tunnel entrances began to grow over, blur, and disappear behind poison oak and berry bushes, get covered by landslides, silted up in floods, till only a few lone individuals — children, neighborhood idiots — now and then would stumble on one, out in a deserted place, but dare inside only as far as the first turnings and loss of outdoor light. And then all the gateways to Hell were finally lost to sight, surviving only in local tales handed down the generations, sad recitals that asked why the visitors never came anymore, and if they would again, stories as congested and dark as UFO stories are ethereal and luminous. And always shame-faced, with an air not of UFO elation but of guilt, at having somehow not been good enough for them, the folks who lived in Hell. So, over time, Hell became a storied place of sin and penitence, and we forgot that its original promise was never punishment but reunion, with the true, long-forgotten metropolis of Earth Unredeemed."

That was the story, and nearly all she'd cared to send them back out with at the end of that visit — the year the no-sex clause didn't get rolled over, the first year, as black conifers rose behind them into the cloud cover and gone, that it *didn't* feel like a descent — not really a blessing, though you could tell that the Head Ninjette was interested at least in a scientific way in whether the Baby Eros, that tricky little pud-puller, would give or take away an edge regarding the unrelenting forces that leaned ever after the partners into Time's wind, impassive in pursuit, usually gaining, the faceless predators who'd once boarded Takeshi's airplane in the sky, the ones who'd had the Chipco lab stomped on, who despite every Karmic Adjustment resource brought to bear so far had simply persisted, stone-humorless, beyond cause and effect, rejecting all attempts to bargain or accommodate, following through pools of night where nothing else moved wrongs forgotten by all but the direly possessed, continuing as a body to refuse to be bought off for any but the full price, which they had never named. But at least on the night Brock Vond was taken across the river, the night of no white diamonds or even chicken crank, the foreign magician and his blond tomato assistant, out stealing a

couple of innocent hours away from the harsh demands of their
Act, with its imitations of defiance, nightly and matinees, of gravity
and death, only found themselves slowed to a paranoid dancers'
embrace at the unquiet center of the roadhouse party crowd, with
scarcely a 'Toid here in fact even noticing them, so many kept
pouring in, so much was going on. Radio Thanatoid arrived with
a remote crew to beam and bounce the proceedings out to the
other pockets of Thanatoia here and there in the country of the
living, "Direct, though not necessarily live," as the announcer put
it. A tour bus, perhaps only lost in the night, swept in with a wake
of diesel exhaust and waited idling for its passengers, some of
whom would discover that they were already Thanatoids without
knowing it, and decide not to reboard after all. There were free
though small-sized eats for everyone, such as mini-enchiladas and
shrimp teriyaki, and well drinks at happy-hour prices. And the
band, Holocaust Pixels, found a groove, or attractor, that would've
been good for the entire trans-night crossing and beyond, even if
Billy Barf and the Vomitones hadn't shown up later to sit in,
bringing with them Alexei, who turned out to be a Russian Johnny
B. Goode, able even unamplified to outwail both bands at once.

Prairie would hear about this the next day, having seen Alexei
only as far as the Vomitone van, when she'd regretfully peeled
away to return, terrified but obliged, to the clearing where she'd
had her visit from Brock Vond. He had left too suddenly. There
should have been more. She lay in her sleeping bag, trembling,
face up, with the alder and the Sitka spruce still dancing in the
wind, and the stars thickening overhead. "You can come back,"
she whispered, waves of cold sweeping over her, trying to gaze
steadily into a night that now at any turn could prove unfaceable.
"It's OK, rilly. Come on, come in. I don't care. Take me anyplace
you want." But suspecting already that he was no longer available,
that the midnight summoning would go safely unanswered, even
if she couldn't let go. The small meadow shimmered in the starlight,
and her promises grew more extravagant as she drifted into the
lucid thin layer of waking dreaming, her flirting more obvious —
then she'd wake, alert to some step in the woods, some brief bloom
of light in the sky, back and forth for a while between Brock

fantasies and the silent darkened silver images all around her, before settling down into sleep, sleeping then unvisited till around dawn, with fog still in the hollows, deer and cows grazing together in the meadow, sun blinding in the cobwebs on the wet grass, a redtail hawk in an updraft soaring above the ridgeline, Sunday morning about to unfold, when Prairie woke to a warm and persistent tongue all over her face. It was Desmond, none other, the spit and image of his grandmother Chloe, roughened by the miles, face full of blue-jay feathers, smiling out of his eyes, wagging his tail, thinking he must be home.